16

A PLACE AT OUR TABLE

This Large Print Book carries the
Seal of Approval of N.A.V.H.

A Place at Our Table

Amy Clipston

THORNDIKE PRESS
A part of Gale, a Cengage Company

Farmington Hills, Mich • San Francisco • New York • Waterville, Maine
Meriden, Conn • Mason, Ohio • Chicago

GALE
A Cengage Company

LIBRARY OF CONGRESS CIP DATA ON FILE.
CATALOGUING IN PUBLICATION FOR THIS BOOK
IS AVAILABLE FROM THE LIBRARY OF CONGRESS

ISBN-13: 978-1-4328-4626-8 (hardcover)
ISBN-10: 1-4328-4626-4 (hardcover)

Published in 2018 by arrangement with The Zondervan Corporation LLC, a subsidiary of HarperCollins Christian Publishing, Inc.

Printed in Mexico
5 6 7 8 9 22 21 20 19 18

*For all the brave men and women
who are serving or have served
as firefighters and emergency
medical technicians*

GLOSSARY

ach: oh
appeditlich: delicious
bedauerlich: sad
boppli: baby
bruder: brother
bruderskind: niece/nephew
bu, buwe: boy, boys
daed: dad
danki: thank you
dat: dad
Dietsch: Pennsylvania Dutch, the Amish
  language (a German dialect)
dochder, dochdern: daughter, daughters
Dummle!: Hurry!
English, Englisher: non-Amish, a non-
  Amish person
fraa: wife
freind, freinden: friend, friends
froh: happy
gegisch: silly
gern gschehne: you're welcome

Gude mariye: Good morning
gut: good
Gut nacht: Good night
haus: house
Ich liebe dich: I love you
kaffi: coffee
kapp: prayer covering or cap
kichlin: cookies
kind, kinner: child, children
kuche: cake
kumm: come
liewe: love, a term of endearment
maed, maedel: young women, young woman
mamm: mom
mei: my
mutter: mother
naerfich: nervous
narrisch: crazy
schee: pretty
schweschder, schweschdere: sister, sisters
sohn: son
Was iss letz?: What's wrong?
Wie geht's: How do you do? or Good day!
wunderbaar: wonderful
ya: yes

AMISH HOMESTEAD SERIES FAMILY TREES

Marilyn m. Willie Dienner
|
Simeon (deceased)
Kayla
Nathan
Eva m. Simeon (deceased) Dienner
|
Simeon Jr. ("Junior")
Savilla m. Allen Lambert
Dorothy m. Vernon Riehl
|
James ("Jamie")
Mark (Laura's twin)
Laura (Mark's twin)
Cindy
Elsie m. Noah Zook
|
Christian

NOTE TO THE READER

While this novel is set against the real backdrop of Lancaster County, Pennsylvania, the characters are fictional. There is no intended resemblance between the characters in this book and any real members of the Amish and Mennonite communities. As with any work of fiction, I've taken license in some areas of research as a means of creating the necessary circumstances for my characters. My research was thorough; however, it would be impossible to be completely accurate in details and description, since each community differs. Therefore, any inaccuracies in the Amish and Mennonite lifestyles portrayed in this book are completely due to fictional license.

ONE

A long, shrill tone screamed through the loud speaker, jarring Jamie Riehl from sleep. He sat up with a gasp and rubbed his eyes. At the same time, the fluorescent lights in the small room automatically flipped on, forcing him to focus.

"All available units respond to a barn fire, 816 Irishtown Road in Ronks," the bodiless voice over the radio blared. "Repeat. All available units respond to a barn fire, 816 Irishtown Road in Ronks."

Adrenaline pumped through Jamie's veins and he was instantly wide awake. That address was only a few miles away, making theirs the closest fire unit. He jumped up from his bed, pulled on uniform pants, and slipped on his boots.

"Let's go," Jamie told Leon King, still lying in the bed next to his. "Barn fire in Ronks." He stretched his arms into a button-up, collared shirt boasting his fire

13

station's number: Station 5.

"I just fell asleep." Leon moaned, shielding his eyes with his forearm. "Wasn't one call enough tonight?"

"That's not how it works, and you know that." Jamie kicked his colleague's bedframe with one booted foot as he finished buttoning his shirt. "Get up, Leon."

"Fine, fine." Leon yawned as he pushed himself to a sitting position. Still fully clothed from the last call, he put on his boots and followed Jamie into the hallway. "Where do you find your energy?"

"I don't know." Jamie shrugged. "I live for this. It's in our blood."

"*Ya,* I know." Leon yawned again as they pushed through double doors into the large apparatus area that housed their trucks and equipment. "I just hope this is the last call of the night. That car accident about did me in." He glanced toward the large clock on the wall above them as they entered their locker room. "We barely got an hour of sleep. It's not even two thirty."

"We've had worse nights with no sleep at all." Jamie and Leon pulled on their turnout gear, including trousers and jackets. Brody Morgan appeared in the doorway. Their chief was already wearing his gear. Not for the first time, Jamie noted that at forty-five,

14

Morgan still carried his six-foot-two, muscular frame well.

"Let's go." Brody motioned toward the engine.

Jamie climbed into the passenger seat, Leon sank into the back, and Brody slipped into the driver's seat and steered the truck out of the large bay. The siren wailed.

Jamie peered down at the computer screen to read the location of the fire. "Do either of you know anyone who lives on Irishtown Road?" he asked as their truck roared through an intersection.

Brody glanced at Leon in his rearview mirror. "Isn't the Dienner farm on that road?"

"*Ya,* I think so." Leon yawned yet again.

Jamie twisted around and glared at him. "You need to wake up. You can't be half asleep while we're fighting a fire."

"I realize that." Leon's eyes narrowed to slits as he nearly spat the words. "You don't need to keep lecturing me. You're not *mei daed.*"

Jamie bit back the bitter response that threatened to leap from his lips. Leon and Jamie met nine years earlier when they both began training to be volunteer firefighters. They were sixteen and became fast friends. But then they were assigned to different

15

volunteer stations. They'd reconnected a month ago when Jamie was reassigned to Station 5. Leon's whining was irritating, but Jamie considered him a good firefighter and a loyal friend.

"All right, you two," Brody yelled over the blare of the siren. "It's time to get your heads in the game. This is a barn fire, and thanks to the dry summer we're having, it's going to be brutal if it spreads. Quit your bickering and concentrate on safety."

"Yes, chief," Leon grumbled.

"I hope Noah meets us there." Jamie's thoughts turned to his best friend since first grade. "His farm isn't far from Irishtown Road, and we're going to need his help."

"I imagine Noah is already on his way if he heard the call on his radio. You're right. We're going to need all the help we can get." Brody steered the engine onto Irishtown Road.

Jamie momentarily thought back to a conversation he'd had with his sister, Cindy, just a few days earlier. She was reflecting on recently seeing Jamie, Noah, and Leon together.

"You know, you three all look a lot alike. You're not only similar in height and have dark-brown hair, but Noah's clean-shaven too." The bishop in their district had made

16

an exception to the rule about married men wearing beards — a requirement because of the custom-fit facemasks the firemen wore. "If you didn't have blue eyes to their brown eyes," she'd said, "you'd practically look like triplets! You're even all twenty-five."

Jamie had laughed at that. But now the scent of burning wood filled the cab of the truck, bringing him back to the present. Brody pulled into a rock driveway and stopped alongside a two-story farmhouse, pointing the fire engine's headlights toward a large red barn where dark, gray smoke billowed.

So far fire licked up the walls on only the right side of the structure. Good. They might still have time to rescue any animals in there before the entire barn was engulfed in angry flames.

Jamie leaped from the engine. The hot, humid June air clung to the back of his neck as acrid smoke threatened his lungs. A light mist of much-needed rain fell as thunder rumbled above him.

Jamie glanced toward the house's back porch and spotted a man with a lantern. Two women dressed in robes and with scarves on their heads stood with him. He grabbed his respirator and helmet and sprinted toward them. He could hear Leon right behind him.

As he and Leon closed in on the porch, Jamie could tell the family was Amish. The man looked to be in his mid-fifties, and the woman on his right seemed about the same age. She was most likely his wife.

"Do we need to save any animals?" Jamie skipped the pleasantries as he called to them.

"*Ya.*" The man pointed toward the barn. "Two horses."

"Willie. Marilyn. Eva." As Leon nodded to each one, they nodded in return. Jamie blinked. How did Leon know this family? Maybe they were the Dienners Brody and Leon thought they remembered living on this road.

"Where are the horse stalls located?" Jamie asked.

"On the far left side of the barn. There's a separate door there."

"*Gut.* We still have time to get them."

"Where is Nathan?" Jamie heard a thread of worry in the older woman's voice. Leon had called her Marilyn.

"You said Nathan went to the phone shanty," the younger woman named Eva responded. Jamie followed her eyes as she turned toward the shed at the top of the driveway. "He saw the lightning hit the barn

18

and ran to call for help. Didn't Kayla follow him?"

"But where are they both now?" Marilyn's voice rose, and she turned to Willie. "Do you think Nathan would go into the barn to save the horses?" Then to Jamie and Leon, she said, "Would you please see if our *sohn* is in there? He's only fourteen."

"*Ya.*" Jamie turned to Leon. "Let's go. *Dummle!*"

"Jamie!"

Jamie blew out a sigh of relief as Noah Zook loped over, clad in his turnout gear and holding his helmet and respirator as well.

"I got here as quickly as I could," Noah managed between deep breaths. "Brody is doing the scene size-up and making sure more companies are coming to help us keep this fire under control."

Brody moved past them as he talked into his radio and Jamie brought Noah up to speed as the three younger men hastened toward the barn. "They have two horses, and they think their fourteen-year-old son may have gone in to try to save them."

"*Ach,* no," Noah said.

"Nathan!" a voice screamed.

Jamie was surprised they hadn't seen the young woman standing near the open barn

19

door as soon as they arrived. But the fire had already advanced across the roof line, further illuminating everything on that side of the barn.

This has to be Kayla. Her thick golden-blonde hair wasn't covered. Instead it hung down the back of her blue robe to her waist, shimmering in the bright firelight.

"Nathan!" she screamed again. "Get out of there before you get yourself killed! Leave the horses! Help is already here."

Jamie's pulse spiked. He broke into a run ahead of his partners, and as he approached Kayla, she turned and collided with him. She grabbed the front of his coat, gasping. "My little brother is in the barn! You have to get him."

"How long has he been in there?" Jamie shucked his turnout jacket.

"I don't know." She shook her head as Jamie yanked his shirt over his head. "A few minutes. I thought I heard him scream. I was going to go after him, but the smoke . . . and I don't have any shoes . . ." Her voice cracked as her eyes searched his. Jamie noticed they were sky-blue. "Please get him out. Please don't let him die!"

"I won't let him die." Jamie swiveled toward the other men as he pulled his turnout jacket back on and stuffed the shirt

20

into his pocket. "Leon, stay with her. Noah, let's go in. Take off your shirt. We'll need to shield the horses' eyes so we can lead them out. We don't have much time!"

Kayla squeezed Jamie's arm. "His name is Nathan."

"I'll get him." Jamie glanced at Noah. "You ready?"

Noah quickly nodded as he pulled off his collared shirt. "Always."

As Noah pulled his jacket back on, the sirens that had been blaring in the distance suddenly stopped, announcing the arrival of another fire company and an ambulance. Jamie hesitated just long enough to see members of the other fire department begin to pull out hoses. They'd have to use water from the tanker. No fire hydrants were anywhere near the barn.

"Jamie! Noah!" Brody hollered from somewhere in the distance. "Give me your status!"

"They're going in for a teenager and two horses," Leon called back. "Tell the paramedics to be ready in case the boy is injured."

Jamie and Noah put on their helmets, facemasks, and respirators and rushed inside the barn. Jamie's vision was immediately blurred by smoke. A hard smack

21

on his arm drew his attention to Noah, who pointed to the stall beside them. The boy was sprawled on the ground with a large wooden beam resting on his legs, and he was coughing.

"We found Nathan," Jamie said over the radio. "He's on the floor, trapped by a fallen beam. He seems to be injured. I'll bring him out. Have the paramedics ready to treat him."

"Ten-four," Brody responded. "We're ready."

Jamie squatted beside Nathan and touched his arm.

"Nathan," he said, and the boy looked up. "We're going to help you."

Jamie nodded at Noah, and together they lifted the heavy beam from Nathan and dropped it beside him.

Jamie leaned in close to Nathan. "Can you stand?" He motioned up.

Nathan shook his head and pointed to his legs. Another coughing fit overcame him, and he covered his mouth with his arm.

Jamie lifted the boy and hefted him over his shoulder. He carried him out the barn door where Brody, Leon, Kayla and two paramedics waited. Jamie deposited him on his feet, and the boy stumbled. His sister and one of the EMTs rushed forward and grabbed him, lowering him to the ground.

"Nathan!" Willie called. He and the two other women ran toward them.

Kayla looked up at Jamie. Her eyes sparkled with unshed tears as she whispered something that looked like *"Danki."*

"Let's get you over to the ambulance and the rest of us back from this smoke," one of the EMTs said to Nathan as she tapped a gurney. "Can you climb up on here?"

Jamie raced back into the barn and found Noah already leading one horse toward the door. Noah's shirt was tied around its head, and he pulled on one sleeve to guide the horse. Jamie moved past him and made his way to the second horse stall. He quickly tied his own shirt around that horse's head and pulled him forward.

Jamie stumbled and stopped, suddenly disoriented. The smoke had become a thick fog, diminishing his sense of direction. The horse nodded its head and whinnied in protest, and the hair stood up on the back of Jamie's neck. Where was Noah? It was against station policy to be in a burning structure alone. Yes, Noah went for the horses when Jamie carried Nathan outside, but only because he knew he'd be back for the horses in seconds. Yet now he appeared to be on his own. Noah must have thought he was right behind him as left the barn.

Jamie took a deep breath as his training kicked in.

"This is Riehl. I'm lost," he hollered into the radio. "I was in the stall with the remaining horse. I think it's five feet from the barn entrance." He glanced down at the illuminated oxygen gauge on his shoulder. "I have a quarter of a bottle left."

"I'm on my way!" Noah called back. "Heading into the barn to find you."

The smoke was worse. He had no choice but to temporarily let go of the horse. He dropped to his knees and crawled toward where he thought the wall was. His thoughts spun. He had to find the exit and get himself and the horse out in time.

Jamie's fingers brushed the wall, and he crawled toward where he believed the exit was.

"I'm here," he heard Noah say. "I see you. The horse is right behind you."

A hand grabbed Jamie's shoulder and yanked his arm.

"This way." Noah's voice crackled over the radio as he pointed behind him. "Let's get the horse and get out."

Danki." Jamie breathed a sigh of relief before grabbing the shirt tied to the horse and following Noah out of the barn. Harsh

24

beams came from several sets of headlights. More crews had arrived. Once they were well away from the burning barn, he removed his helmet and facemask as a crowd gathered around. Leon was holding on to the first horse Noah had brought out.

"Does anyone know where they want the horses?" Jamie asked.

"We'll take them," a teenage boy said as he sidled up to them. "Our barn is just down the street, and we have plenty of room. And if Willie wants us to, we can call a vet."

"We brought reins," a second boy said. "We'll guide them over."

"*Danki.*" Jamie slid his forearm over his brow.

"*Gern gschehne.*" The first boy pulled the shirts off the horses' heads, handed the shirts to Jamie, and began attaching the reins.

Jamie shoved his shirt into the pocket of his jacket. He surveyed the scene, taking in the two additional fire companies spraying the barn with water. The structure was now almost entirely engulfed in flames. If Noah hadn't . . .

Jamie shoved away the thought, cleared his throat, and turned toward his best friend. "*Danki* for coming back for me."

Noah's eyebrows lifted. "Are you joking? I turned around and you weren't there. Why wouldn't I have come back for you?"

Jamie rubbed his chin as he glanced toward the ambulance, where Kayla stood beside her mother. They were both looking inside, speaking animatedly, their arms waving wildly. Jamie hoped Nathan wasn't badly hurt. He hadn't seemed to be.

"Let's go see if the boy is okay."

Noah lifted his chin toward their fire engine, where Brody was talking with Willie. "I'm going to check in with Brody and see if he needs any help. I'll see you in a minute."

A mist of rain drifted over his cheeks as Jamie made his way toward the ambulance, nodding greetings as he wove past firefighters he knew from nearby companies. He stepped onto the rock driveway just as Marilyn started for the house. He watched as she climbed the porch steps and disappeared inside.

Inside the ambulance, Nathan was seated on a gurney with a blanket draped around his shoulders. He held an oxygen mask over his mouth and nose. His trousers were ripped, revealing large gauze pads covering his legs where the beam must have cut them. His right foot was covered with an ace bandage, and an ice pack adorned his ankle.

Jamie divided a gaze between Nathan and his older sister. He saw a distinct family resemblance between the two. The boy's hair was light brown compared to Kayla's golden blonde, but they shared the same heart-shaped face and brilliant blue eyes. He guessed Kayla was in her early to mid-twenties.

He took in her striking features — high cheekbones, rosy lips, and a long, thin nose. She was attractive. Not that he was interested. His only purpose for being here was to do what he could to save lives and property.

Kayla narrowed her eyes at her brother. "What you did was *narrisch,*" she berated him, apparently oblivious to Jamie's presence. "No, it wasn't *narrisch.* It was dangerous. You could have been killed!"

Nathan removed the oxygen mask and glared back at her. "You're being overly dramatic."

"No, I'm not!" She waggled a finger at him. "We could have lost you, just like we lost . . ." She suddenly turned, her expression softening as her gaze collided with Jamie's. She stood erect and pushed her hair over her slight shoulder. "I didn't see you

27

standing there."

"I'm sorry." Jamie shifted his weight from one foot to the other and held up his hands as if surrendering. "I didn't mean to intrude."

"You're not intruding." She folded her arms at her waist, and Jamie noted she was only slightly shorter than his nearly six feet. "*Danki* for saving *mei bruder*. I mean, thank you."

"*Gern gschehne.*" He leaned his leg against the bumper and looked up at Nathan, who grinned.

"You're Amish," Nathan pointed out.

Jamie nodded. "That's right."

"I'm Nathan Dienner."

So they are the Dienners.

Nathan nodded toward his sister. "This is *mei schweschder,* Kayla. She acts like she's *mei mamm,* though."

Kayla pursed her lips, and Jamie bit back a chuckle.

Jamie lowered himself onto the corner of the truck's bumper. "It's nice to meet you. I'm James Riehl." He looked up at Nathan. "How are you feeling?"

Nathan shrugged. "I'm fine." He nodded toward his legs. "I had a tetanus shot last year and the EMT thinks my cuts will heal fine. I'm sure I only sprained my ankle, but

28

she wants me to go to the hospital for an X-ray. *Mei mamm* says it isn't necessary. She's going to treat it at home, and she'll take me to a doctor if it doesn't get better in a couple of days."

"That's probably a *gut* idea," Jamie said, agreeing with that plan. "You don't want to walk around on it if it's broken. It could cause more problems later if it doesn't heal right." He rested his arms on his lap. "I heard you were the one who called nine-one-one."

Nathan sat up a little straighter and dropped the blanket onto the gurney beside him. "That's right. I was restless, and I saw lightning out my bedroom window. When I heard the thunder I had a feeling the lightning was close." He pointed toward the upper floor of their home. "I got up and looked out the hallway window. Smoke was already coming up from the barn roof. That was when I woke up *mei dat* and *mamm* and ran out to the phone shanty to call nine-one-one."

"And as soon as I realized what was happening, I ran out behind him," Kayla chimed in, hands on hips. "I had a feeling he might do something *narrisch*. And by the time I got outside, he was already on his way to the barn. Unfortunately, I couldn't

29

catch up with him in time to stop him."

Jamie raised his eyebrows as he glanced up at Nathan, who'd lowered his head to stare down at the gurney. "Did you fall when you ran inside?"

"*Ya,* I did." Nathan sighed and raised his head. "I think I tripped over a pitchfork. The pain in my ankle was bad, and I knew I had to get out of there because smoke started pouring into that part of the barn. I felt like I was choking. I was going to crawl to the door, but when I went to get up, that beam collapsed on me. I tried to move it, but it was too heavy to lift by myself."

Kayla took a step toward Jamie. "Tell Nathan he shouldn't have run into the barn on his own. Explain to him how serious this could have been."

Jamie paused, sizing up Nathan. He looked to be a healthy young man. He was definitely brave too. "You're fourteen, right?"

Nathan nodded. "*Ya.* My birthday was last month."

"If you're really interested in learning to fight fires, then you can go to training. You're old enough." Jamie folded his arms over his chest.

Nathan's expression brightened. "I am?"

Kayla gasped. "Don't tell him that!"

Jamie looked at her and felt his brow furrow. "I'm telling him the truth. I was sixteen when I started training, but we take volunteers as young as fourteen."

"Nathan doesn't need to train to be a firefighter." Kayla's stare was intense and her jaw tightened. "He's too young, and it's too dangerous."

"That's why we train." Jamie was careful to keep his words measured. "We take every safety precaution."

"I'm certain you do, but accidents still happen." Something more than frustration flickered in her eyes. Fear? "He's not interested in becoming a firefighter."

"*Ya,* I am interested, and I don't need you to speak for me." Nathan lifted his chin.

Kayla's expression hardened. "It's not up for discussion. You're not doing it."

"You're not *Mamm* or *Dat,*" he groused.

"You need to drop it. I won't allow it," she spat back.

Kayla swiped at a wet tendril of hair that had fallen against her cheek. Even in the shadows, her hair reminded Jamie of sunshine. He pushed the thought away and forced himself to focus on the subject at hand. Why was she so against her brother becoming a firefighter?

"Kayla!" Their mother appeared dressed

31

in a blue dress and black apron. She handed Kayla a purple scarf and pair of blue Croc shoes. "You're getting soaked out here."

"Danki," Kayla muttered as she tied on the scarf and slipped on the shoes. For a split second, Jamie was disappointed to see her hair covered, but he shook off the thought. What was wrong with him?

Marilyn turned to Jamie and he stood. "You're the firefighter who saved my Nathan and our horses. Thank you so much." She held her hand out to Jamie, and he shook it. "I'm Marilyn Dienner."

"Gern gschehne, and I'm James Riehl."

He glanced toward the Station 5 fire truck. Brody, Leon, and Noah were there with members of other companies, watching the firefighters who continued to spray the barn with four different hoses. They were ready to relieve them if necessary.

"I should get back to work."

"Wait, James," Nathan said. "You said I'm old enough to start firefighter training. What do I have to do to get into the classes?"

"Well . . ." Jamie hesitated. He had a feeling Kayla's still-irritated expression was focused on him, and he had no idea how their mother would feel about this idea. "You need your parents' permission, first of all."

"Can I do it, *Mamm*?" Nathan's eyes widened as he held his hands together, as if praying.

Marilyn gave him a gentle smile. "We'll talk about it later."

"There's nothing to talk about," Kayla insisted. "The answer is no. He doesn't need to become a firefighter."

"Kayla." Marilyn's voice held a hint of warning. "I said we will discuss it later."

Jamie cleared his throat as unease stole over him. He needed to remove himself from this private family conversation. "I'm going to go talk to my chief. Let me know if you need anything."

"Danki," Nathan said. "I'm glad you arrived when you did."

"I am too." Jamie shook Nathan's hand, nodded at Marilyn and Kayla, and left to join his company.

TWO

Anger surged through Kayla as she watched James Riehl walk away. Who did he think he was, encouraging her brother to become a firefighter? He didn't know Nathan, nor, apparently, did he know what their family had endured the past year. Unless he just didn't care.

He needed to go back to his firehouse and mind his own business.

But James saved Nathan's life.

The thought caught her off guard. Yes, he had saved Nathan's life. Embarrassment heated Kayla's cheeks as she remembered how she'd grabbed onto James's jacket and begged him to save her brother. She'd never before been so forward with a man, but the thought of losing Nathan had rocked her. Her family couldn't possibly endure another loss.

When Kayla first saw James, he had seemed larger than life. He was taller than her father and Simeon, her older brother. She guessed he had to be close to six feet. His astute ice-blue eyes were a stark and intriguing contrast to his dark hair. He had a strong, dimpled jaw, which seemed a fitting complement to the confidence that radiated from him.

The man hadn't hesitated when she'd pleaded for help. Instead, he'd taken charge of the situation. James Riehl was her family's hero — until he encouraged Nathan to sign up for firefighter training. He put that dangerous and horrible idea into her impressionable brother's head.

James had overstepped his bounds.

Her eyes narrowed as she watched him approach Brody Morgan, who was addressing one of the firefighters manning a hose. James said something to Brody, and Brody patted James on his shoulder. Leon was there too. Kayla's stomach twisted as memories of the last time she'd seen Brody and Leon assaulted her senses. It was the day of Simeon's funeral, during the worst time of her life. It seemed like only yesterday, not almost a year ago.

"Mrs. Dienner, are you certain you don't want us to take Nathan to the hospital for an X-ray?" The young EMT named Kristi wrenched Kayla from her mental tirade. She had kind eyes.

"*Ya,* I'm sure. I can take care of his ankle just fine. We've had quite a few sprained ankles on our farm. But thank you for the offer." *Mamm* smiled, but Kayla could almost feel her mother's stress. Surely this ordeal brought back the horrible memories of Simeon's death for her as well.

Kristi climbed into the back of the ambulance and touched Nathan's shoulder. "How are you doing?"

"Okay. I can breathe fine." Nathan shifted on the gurney. "My legs and ankle are sore, but I think I can get up now."

"Let me check your lungs first." Kristi pulled out her stethoscope and placed it on Nathan's chest and then his back as she listened. "You sound great. I can let you go now." She glanced over at *Mamm.* "I have some paperwork for you to sign."

"Oh, of course," *Mamm* said. Kristi grabbed a clipboard stuffed with paperwork and jumped down from the ambulance.

"I'll help Nathan to the *haus,*" Kayla offered. She held out her arm. "Let me help you down from there."

"I'm not a *boppli,*" Nathan snapped with a glare.

Kayla swallowed a frustrated sigh. "I know that, but you said your ankle and legs hurt.

36

Stop being so proud and let me help you."

Nathan's expression softened, and he reached for her arm. Once he was down, Kayla thanked Kristi and she and Nathan started toward the back porch.

The steady mist had dissipated, and the sky was clear and full of twinkling stars — which seemed an ironic contrast to the barn now reduced to a smoky pile of ashes. The smell of burning wood filled the air and squeezed at Kayla's lungs.

When they reached the back porch, Nathan winced as he held on to the banister and pulled himself up each of the six steps. A few lanterns lined the edge of the porch, illuminating the back of the house.

"I don't know how you're going to get up to your bedroom," Kayla said. "You might have to sleep on the sofa downstairs."

Nathan stopped dead in his tracks, his body rigid. "I'm not ready to go inside. I'd rather sit out here."

Kayla rubbed the bridge of her nose. *Not this again.* "You need to rest and elevate your foot."

"I can elevate it on this glider. I'm not going inside."

She blew out a frustrated sigh. "Fine." She pointed to the glider. "Sit."

His glare was back in full force. "I'm not

a dog, Kay." He gingerly sank into one corner of the glider and stretched out his right leg.

Regret soaked through Kayla as she watched her brother rub his swollen ankle.

"I'm sorry." She sat down on the rocker beside him. "I didn't mean to be so hard on you. I was just really worried earlier." She took a deep breath as tears stung her eyes. "You scared me. I thought we were going to lose you."

Kayla turned to look at Nathan, and his expression was clouded. "I know. I'm sorry."

Kayla sniffed and swiped her cheeks with both hands. "When you ran into that barn, I was afraid it was the last time I was ever going to see you." She swallowed against a threatening lump in her throat. "All I could think about was Simeon and how much it would hurt to lose you too."

"Hey." Nathan reached over and touched her arm. "I'm okay, thanks to James."

"I know." Kayla cleared her throat as she looked toward the Station 5 fire engine, lit by the headlights of other vehicles. James still stood with Brody and the other fire-fighters, and as if he sensed her gaze, he turned toward the porch and lifted his hand. She returned the gesture with a half-hearted wave.

"Why are you so against the idea of me becoming a firefighter?"

Kayla angled her body toward him. "I can't believe you're even asking me that."

"I'll be careful." He held out his hands as if to keep her calm. "I'll take the training seriously — really seriously. I'll listen to my chief and only do what he says." He pointed toward the fire engine where James stood. "James seems like a great guy. I'll see if he'll be my mentor and take me under his wing. I could learn a lot from him."

She shook her head. If only life were as predictable as Nathan believed. "It's not that simple. Things happen. Accidents happen when we least expect them."

He leaned forward and lowered his voice. "I'm not going to die like Simeon did."

"How could you know that?" Her voice wobbled. "Do you think Eva expected to be raising Junior alone?"

"Eva isn't raising him alone. She has us."

"*Ya*, she does, but she doesn't have a husband, and Junior doesn't have a *daed*. In fact, Junior will never know his *daed*. He'll never know firsthand what he looks like or hear his voice. Simeon will be someone he knows only through stories. He won't be a real person to Junior."

Nathan looked out toward the smoky ruin

that was once their barn, and Kayla could sense his whirling thoughts.

After several moments, Nathan turned toward her, his lips pressed into a hard line. "Just because Simeon died in an accident doesn't mean I will." He nodded again toward the fire engine. "Look at James. He said he's been a firefighter since he was sixteen. Why don't we ask him if he's ever been in danger?"

"He's in danger every time he runs into a burning building. He was in danger earlier when he saved you and then went back in for the horses."

Nathan rolled his eyes. "That's not what I meant."

"I know what you meant, but you're not listening to what *I'm* saying. *Mamm* and *Dat* don't need to lose another *sohn*." She pointed to her chest. "*I* don't need to lose my only remaining *bruder*."

"*Dat* will understand when I talk to him," he grumbled under his breath. "He'll let me train."

I hope not. Kayla settled back in the rocker and took in the scene in front of her. *Dat* stood with Brody and some of the other firefighters, gesturing toward the rubble. *Mamm* had moved from the ambulance to stand beside *Dat*. Four fire hoses were still

40

spraying the pile of burned timbers. It was as if she were dreaming. It somehow didn't seem real that her father's barn, built long before she was born, had been reduced to nothing but kindling in less than an hour.

Kayla's eyes lingered on James as he leaned back against the fire engine and crossed his arms over his chest. Her mind swirled with questions about him. Where did he live? Had Simeon known him?

Several minutes passed as she and Nathan sat in silence. Then *Mamm* and *Dat* crossed the driveway hand in hand and walked up the steps. *Mamm* held a handful of documents Kayla assumed were from the paramedic.

Dat sat down on the bench beside Nathan's glider. "How are you?"

"I'm fine." Nathan winced as he lifted his leg and set it on the floor of the porch. "I want to talk to you about something."

Mamm sat down on the glider beside Nathan and rubbed his arm.

"What is it?" *Dat* asked.

"Did you meet James, the firefighter who saved me?" Nathan asked. *Dat* nodded. "He said he started volunteering when he was sixteen. He said I could become a volunteer, too, because they allow people to start training at fourteen. How old was Simeon when

41

he started volunteering?"

Kayla braced herself, silently praying that *Dat* would tell Nathan to stop entertaining the idea of following in their older brother's footsteps.

Dat rubbed his beard, a sign that he was debating his response. "I think he was about sixteen."

Nathan's eyes lit up. "I didn't realize he was that young."

"Nathan," *Mamm* began slowly, "I don't think this is the time to discuss this."

Kayla blew out the breath she hadn't realized she'd been holding.

Nathan's shoulders wilted. "But I thought it was the best time to talk about it since Brody is here. You have to give him permission before I can even sign up for training."

Dat shook his head and frowned. "Your *mamm* is right. There's too much going on right now. We've lost everything in the barn, and I'm not in the right frame of mind to consider this. Let's talk about it some other time."

Kayla's lips formed a frown. *Dat* didn't say yes, but he also didn't say no. Perhaps sometime after the issues with the barn were settled she could get him alone and convince him not to allow Nathan to train.

Dat's frown deepened. "I thanked James

for getting you out of there so quickly. I never thought you'd try to save the horses."

Nathan shrugged. "I figured that's what Simeon would've done."

"But Simeon wouldn't have run in without turnout gear," Kayla chimed in.

"Kayla," Nathan snapped. "I got your point the first ten times you said that. You can drop it now."

"Please." *Mamm*'s voice was weary. "Stop bickering. All that matters now is that Nathan is okay."

"You're right, *Mamm.*" Kayla looked down at her lap. "I'm sorry."

Dat stared toward the smoke still rising. "I'm grateful James and the other firefighters were able to save the horses, but I have to make a list of everything else we've lost. And I'll have to see how soon we can get people to come for a barn raising."

"It will be okay, Willie," *Mamm* said softly, her voice shaking. "We'll get through this. We have each other."

"*Ya, ya,* you're right." But *Dat* didn't sound convinced.

"The Lord will provide for us," *Mamm* insisted, her voice still a bit thin and wobbly. "He always has. You know that."

Dat nodded before resting his elbow on his thigh and setting his chin on his palm. A

43

wave of sadness washed over Kayla as she took in the grief in her father's eyes. She gripped the arms of her rocking chair and bit her lower lip. She hadn't seen her father look this distraught since Simeon's death and the days following his funeral.

The screen door opened and Eva appeared wearing a green dress and black apron. Her hair was covered with a prayer *kapp.* She stepped onto the porch and sat down on a rocking chair beside Kayla.

"How is Junior?" *Mamm* asked.

"I finally got him back to sleep." Eva cupped her hand to her mouth to stifle a yawn. "I was beginning to think he would never go down, but I just kept rocking him and singing until he finally gave up." She looked out toward the remains of the barn.

"I didn't realize he'd woken up," Kayla said.

"*Ya,* I went to check on him earlier, and he was crying. I guess all the sirens woke him." Eva turned toward Nathan. "Are you all right?"

"I'm fine." Nathan shrugged. "My ankle and legs are sore, but I'll be okay."

"I'm *froh* to hear it. You gave us a scare."

Simeon had confided to Kayla that he'd fallen head over heels in love with this beauty with light-brown hair and warm hazel eyes the moment he met her at a youth gathering. They were both nineteen and inseparable from that day on. Now she was twenty-five and a widow.

Kayla often wondered if she'd ever find the kind of love her brother and Eva had shared. She thought she found true love in Abram Blank, but less than two months after Simeon died Abram broke up with her. His rejection made a deep cut in her soul, and she wasn't sure if she'd ever be ready to trust another man with her heart.

Eva rocked back in her chair. Her eyes focused intensely on the firefighters standing by their trucks. She seemed to be contemplating something.

Kayla touched her arm, and Eva jumped with a start. "You should go to bed. Junior will have you up early tomorrow morning. I mean, later *this* morning."

Eva shook her head, her eyes still trained on the firefighters. "I was thinking about giving the firefighters a snack. They've been working so hard for nearly an hour."

"I'll do it." Kayla stood, relieved to have something to focus on other than her brother's obsession with joining the volunteer fire department. "I have some fresh lemonade, and we have those cookies from the restaurant. You and *Mamm* can go to bed and get

45

some sleep. We still have to open the restaurant on time for the breakfast rush."

"Don't be *gegisch*. We'll help you." *Mamm* stood and touched Kayla's back. "We should thank the firefighters for keeping our family safe. Not only did they save Nathan and our horses, but they kept the fire contained to the barn. We could have lost our home."

"All right," Kayla said, giving in. "Why don't we just invite the firefighters and EMTs to come up here for *kichlin* and lemonade? We can bring everything outside and put it on the porch tables."

"That's a *gut* idea," Eva said.

"I'll invite them. You two get everything ready." *Mamm* started down the porch steps toward the fire engines and *Dat* followed her.

Inside Kayla ran up to her room and quickly dressed in a rose-colored dress with a black apron before covering her hair with a matching scarf. Then she rushed back to the kitchen and found the pitcher of lemonade and some plastic cups.

Eva held up a tray filled with large chocolate chip, macadamia nut, and peanut butter cookies. "What do you think? They're our best sellers at the restaurant, so I'm glad your *mamm* baked extra for us."

"Perfect." Kayla nodded toward the mud-

46

room. "Let's take this all outside and then you can go to bed."

Back on the porch, her gaze landed on James as her parents talked to him and some of the firefighters and EMTs. Frustration sizzled anew in her veins. He wasn't the influence Nathan needed right now, and she hoped this would be the last time she'd ever see James Riehl.

THREE

"We really appreciate all you've done for our family today," Marilyn said to Jamie, Leon, and Noah. "May we offer you a little snack before you head back to the fire station?" She pointed to the back porch. "My daughter and daughter-in-law have cookies and lemonade for you."

"That's really kind of you," Leon said, hedging. He looked between Jamie and Noah.

"We'd love to." Jamie waved a hand to include them all, sure Brody would approve. *"Danki."*

"Great." Marilyn clapped her hands together as if their acceptance meant the world to her. "Willie and I will ask the other fire companies to join us as well."

The three firefighters started walking across the rock driveway toward the house. Jamie decided he'd ask Leon how he and Brody knew this family later.

"I'm so tired I can hardly move." Leon pushed his hand through his hair. "We still need to load up the truck. It's around three thirty now, isn't it?"

"Let's just have a quick snack and then head back." Jamie's boots clomped up the wooden steps to the long porch that spanned the back of the large, white, two-level farmhouse. He noticed a one-level addition jutting out from the right side. He'd been too high on adrenaline to notice when they arrived.

That must be where either the parents or the son and daughter-in-law lived. But where is the older son?

When he reached the top of the steps, Jamie leaned back against the porch railing and folded his arms over his chest. He swiped the back of his hand across his forehead and blew out a deep sigh. He was still hot and sweaty from the combination of the fire and the humid June night. He longed to get back to the fire station to enjoy a cool shower, followed by some sleep.

"Would you like some *kichlin*?"

The question yanked Jamie from his thoughts. He glanced down at the brunette who'd just come from inside. He'd briefly talked to her on the porch when they first arrived at the scene. *This must be the daughter-in-law.*

"Ya. Danki." He reached for a cookie and hesitated.

She balanced the tray on one hand and pointed to each selection. "We have chocolate chip, macadamia nut, and peanut butter."

"Peanut butter is a favorite." He lifted one of the large cookies and nodded. *"Danki."*

"Gern gschehne." She held out her hand, and he shook it. "I'm Eva."

"It's nice to meet you. I'm James."

"Danki for all you did tonight for my brother-in-law." Her smile faded, and her lower lip trembled almost imperceptibly. "We were really scared when we realized he'd run into the barn."

"I'm just glad we were here in time to help him." Jamie bit into the cookie and savored the sweet taste.

"How are you doing, Eva?" Leon asked as she stepped over toward him.

Jamie's eyebrows lifted. Renewed curiosity filled him as he again wondered how Leon knew the Dienner family.

"I'm okay. I have *gut* days and bad days." Eva nodded toward the tray. "Would you like some *kichlin?*"

"Are you kidding? The Dienner women make the best *kichlin.* Of course I want some." Leon took one of each variety. *"Danki."*

Jamie studied Leon. Brody seemed to know the family too. How did they know them so well?

Noah introduced himself to Eva and took two cookies before he leaned back against the railing, next to Jamie.

"How is Elsie doing?" Jamie asked before taking another bite.

"She's *gut*." Noah grinned. "Christian is keeping her hopping. He's walking all over the place. She turned her back for a second yesterday and realized he was gone. She found him in the linen closet, yanking out all the bath towels. Last week he pulled out all the pots and pans from the bottom of the cabinet and started drumming on them."

Jamie and Leon laughed.

"How old is he now?" Leon asked.

"Eighteen months." Noah shook his head as his smile deepened. "I can't believe how big he's grown."

"Would you like lemonade?"

Jamie turned to see Kayla standing in front of him as she held up a tray with a pitcher and plastic cups. He studied her sky-blue eyes, trying to determine what the intensity there meant. Was she still upset with him or just upset about the fire? He recalled finding the same fierceness in her expression earlier when he suggested firefighter training for Nathan. She seemed as if she wanted to say something, but she was hesitating.

The tray teetered, and he reached for the pitcher. "Let me help you with that."

She quickly pulled it away. "*Danki*, but I've got it." She raised her eyebrows. "It's fresh. I made it earlier today."

"*Ya*, please," he said.

She turned toward Leon and Noah to offer them each a cup, and they nodded as well.

Kayla set the tray on a small table behind her and filled three cups. She handed one to Jamie first, and he thanked her.

"It's *gut* to see you, Leon," Kayla said as she gave him his cup.

"How are you doing?" Leon looked concerned. Why?

"We're okay." She shrugged. "We're making it, but it's tough."

"I'm sure it is." Leon shook his head. "I think of your family often."

"*Danki.*" She lifted her tray. "Let me know if you need a refill."

Jamie fought the sudden wave of envy nipping at him. What did Leon know about

Kayla that he didn't? And why did it bother Jamie so much?

"Excuse me," Kayla said softly as she started to move past him toward another group of firefighters.

"Kayla, wait," Jamie blurted without forethought.

She stopped and looked up at him, her blonde eyebrows knitted together. "What?"

"Could I speak with you privately?"

She hesitated, but then gave him a curt nod. *"Ya."* She pointed to the far corner of the porch. "We can go over there."

He followed her. She rested the tray on the corner of the railing and then turned to face him. He took another sip of lemonade and then set his cup on the railing.

"What is it?" She folded her hands over her middle.

"I want to apologize." He rubbed the back of his neck. "I'm sorry for butting into your business earlier. I didn't mean to upset you by suggesting your *bruder* start training to become a firefighter."

Kayla looked across the porch to where Nathan and Willie stood talking to Brody. Then she swiveled toward Jamie, and her eyes narrowed to a steely gaze. "You have no idea what you did by putting those ideas into Nathan's head. Now he's trying to convince *mei daed* to allow him to sign up."

He blinked. *Where is this hostility coming from?* "I realize it's none of my business, but I honestly don't understand why you're so upset. Are you really that worried about his safety? We don't take risks with our youngest volunteers. He won't actually enter a burning building until he's older. It's very safe."

"I can tell you it's not always safe." She took a step toward him. "I'd prefer you not discuss firefighting with *mei bruder* again. In fact, I think it would be best if you stayed away from Nathan."

He held up his hands in an attempt to stave off whatever this animosity was. "I didn't mean to offend you. I only thought that —" Before he could finish his sentence, she was gone, stalking toward the opposite side of the porch with the tray in her hands. She stopped in front of two firefighters, smiling sweetly. Her hands shook slightly, though. What had he said to affect her so deeply? What had he done wrong?

Noah appeared at Jamie's side. "What did you say to her?"

"You sure do have a way with *maed.*" Leon snickered. "I see now why you're still single."

"Do I have to remind you that you're also

single, Leon?" Noah retorted as he lifted his cup to his lips.

"That's by choice," Leon quipped.

Jamie did his best to ignore their banter as he gazed at Kayla. Tension and confusion swirled in his gut as he mentally replayed their conversation. He couldn't fathom what he'd done to warrant such a rejection.

"What did you say to her?" Noah's repeated question wrenched Jamie from his thoughts. He explained his conversation with Nathan and Kayla while Nathan was being treated at the ambulance and then his conversation a few moments earlier before she'd stormed off.

"I don't understand why she's so upset with me." Jamie turned up his palms. "I was just being honest with Nathan and her. I thought it would be safer for him to take the training than to run into burning buildings without any firefighting knowledge at all."

Leon's smile faded, and his expression grew serious. "You don't know who these people are, do you?"

"What do you mean?" Jamie turned to Noah, who shrugged.

"Do you remember Simeon Dienner?" Leon lowered his voice. "He was the fire-fighter killed last year. Kayla is his *schwesch-*

55

der, and Eva is his *fraa.*" He nodded toward where Kayla now stood with Eva.

Jamie gasped. Simeon Dienner and his company at Station 5 were saving a family whose farmhouse had caught on fire. Simeon was the last one to head for an exit, but he never made it. The floor in the mudroom gave way, and he fell into the basement. As soon as he hit the basement floor, the house collapsed on him. Simeon was crushed and died at the scene.

Jamie's breath came out in a whoosh as a chill ran up his spine. Simeon was the older son missing from this family. Jamie and Noah were both assigned to a different fire station then, but Jamie had met Simeon a few times when the two fire companies responded to the same incident. Simeon had been friendly and a good firefighter. Jamie heard about the accident on that tragic day. "No. I didn't make the connection with this Dienner family."

"I should have told you." Leon leaned back against the railing. "I'm sorry, but I thought you knew Brody was Simeon's chief. Brody moved to Station 5 just before that happened. It was horrible."

"I can't even imagine." Noah clicked his tongue. "I met Simeon a few times on calls, but I didn't know this was his family. And I wasn't assigned to this station until after he passed away, just like Jamie."

"Yeah. It wasn't common knowledge, but some of the crew asked for reassignment after Simeon died, and Brody understood how they felt. That's why you two ended up reassigned to Station 5." Leon lifted his cup. "Simeon was a great guy. He was funny, but he was also serious when he needed to be. He loved his family."

Regret and guilt rained down on Jamie as he studied Kayla. "Now I understand why she's so upset with me. I don't blame her for not wanting Nathan to train."

"You didn't know," Leon said.

Jamie cupped his hand to his forehead. *How could I be so stupid?* "I need to apologize to her."

"I don't know if that's a good idea." Noah frowned. "She seemed pretty determined to avoid you."

"No, I need to tell her I was wrong and explain I had no idea Simeon was her *bruder.*" Jamie started toward Kayla, determined to make things right.

"Would you like more?" Kayla held up the pitcher as she stepped over to where Brody was talking to *Dat* and Nathan.

"Yes, thank you." Brody smiled as she

57

refilled his cup, emptying the pitcher. "We really didn't expect you to feed us. Then again, my Amish friends are always so welcoming."

"We wanted to do something nice for you since you all worked so hard for us." *Dat* patted Brody on the shoulder. "I appreciate what you and your company did, especially for Nathan and our horses."

Brody took a sip of his lemonade. "I'm sorry we couldn't do more. Barns just go up so quickly, not only because they're wood, but because of the hay. All we can do is spray the fire until it fizzles out."

"My family and I are grateful." *Dat* glanced toward the barn. "You stopped the fire from spreading."

"Will we have a barn raising to rebuild?" Nathan asked.

"Ya." Dat rested his arm on Nathan's shoulder. "I'll see if I can get someone here right away to clear the land. Then we'll rebuild."

"We can cater it for all the volunteers," Kayla said.

"That's a great idea," Eva said. "We'll have to think about a menu."

Kayla nodded in the direction of the back door. "I'm going to get more lemonade. I'll be back."

When she turned around, she slammed into James. The tray slipped from her hands and everything on it fell to the floor with a loud clatter. She could feel an embarrassing blush crawling up her neck and heating her cheeks.

"I'm so sorry," James muttered. "I didn't mean to startle you."

"It's okay." Her face flaming, Kayla immediately bent down to retrieve the plastic tray, pitcher, and cups. But James did as well, and their heads collided with a *clunk!* She straightened and moaned in pain as she cupped her hand to her head.

"Oh, I'm so sorry," James repeated as he rubbed a red spot forming on his forehead.

He grinned, and to her surprise, a soft laugh escaped her lips. James had a nice smile that lit up his entire face and made his blue eyes sparkle. She shoved the thought away as quickly as it popped into her mind.

He swiped his hand down his clean-shaven jaw as he turned his gaze to the porch floor. "I really made a mess of things."

"It's fine." She looked down. Thank goodness everything was plastic. Relief flooded her as conversations once more resumed around them. She couldn't stand the thought of everyone staring at her.

"Let me get it." He gathered up the cups and pitcher and balanced them on the tray. "Were you taking these into the *haus*?"

"*Ya. Danki.*"

She reached for the tray, but he held onto it as his smile faded. "I came over to apologize for upsetting you again."

"There's no need to —"

"*Ya,* there is," he said, interrupting her. He looked serious. "Leon just told me you're Simeon's *schweschder.*" He nodded over his shoulder toward Leon and Noah, who looked on with interest. "I met Simeon a few times, and he was a really *gut* man. It would be devastating if I lost one of my siblings, and I'm so sorry you went through that. If I had known Simeon was your *bruder,* I never would have talked to Nathan about volunteering. Please forgive me."

"Of course I forgive you. It's our way." She yanked the tray out of his hands and took a step back. "Excuse me. I need to make more lemonade."

As Kayla stepped into the house, she felt James's gaze follow her, and she tried to ignore the wild thumping of her heart.

FOUR

"Thank you." Jamie handed Blake Morris some money and then pushed open the passenger side door of the driver's pickup truck. "I hope you have a great day."

"You too." Blake waved. "Call if you need me."

"I will." Jamie climbed out of the truck, swung his duffel bag onto his shoulder, and started up the rock driveway toward the large two-story farmhouse where he and his three siblings had been born and raised. The white clapboard structure was a sight for sore eyes. His sore legs felt like two blocks of cement, and his whole body ached. He swallowed a yawn as he approached the large dairy barn. His father and younger brother, Mark, stood in the doorway.

"Jamie!" *Dat* called. "How was your shift?" *Dat*'s graying light-brown hair and matching beard betrayed his age — double Jamie's — but his blue eyes still sparkled with youthful energy.

"It was busy." Jamie shook his head. "I think I got maybe two hours of sleep before my alarm went off this morning."

"What kind of calls did you have?" Mark asked.

"Yesterday was quiet. We spent the day washing the trucks. But then things heated up late last night." Jamie set his bag on the ground. "We had a car accident around eleven, and we were there a little over an hour. As soon as Leon and I got back to sleep, we were called to a barn fire."

"Yikes." Mark grimaced and picked up Jamie's bag. "You must be exhausted. You should take a nap."

"No, I'll help you clean out the barn."

Dat clapped Jamie on the shoulder. "You need your sleep, *sohn.*"

"I can sleep tonight."

Dat grinned. "Why don't we argue after breakfast?"

"That sounds *gut.*" Jamie turned to Mark. "*Danki,* but I can carry my own bag."

"You look like you're going to fall over. I've got it." Mark made a sweeping gesture toward the back porch. "Go on."

"All right." Jamie followed his father up their back-porch stairs and into the mudroom, where Mark dropped the bag. The

62

aroma of eggs, bacon, freshly baked bread, home fries, and coffee caused his stomach to growl. He hadn't realized how hungry he was until he stepped into the house.

In the kitchen his two sisters and mother were finishing preparations for their breakfast.

"Hey, Jamie's home." Laura set some plates on the table as she smiled at him, her blue eyes dancing. Jamie always got a kick out of her coloring matching his but not Mark's, despite those two being twins. Mark's hair was a much lighter brown, like *Dat*'s. "How was your shift?"

"Busy toward the end." Jamie moved to the sink and greeted his mother as he washed his hands. "Breakfast smells *appeditlich*."

"*Danki*." *Mamm* smiled. "I assumed you'd be hungry when you got home."

"*Mamm* always thinks of her *kinner*, right?" *Dat* sidled up next to *Mamm* and rubbed her shoulder. "*Danki* for another *wunderbaar* meal."

"*Gern gschehne*." *Mamm* gazed up at *Dat* with the light-blue eyes she'd passed on to Jamie and Laura. Jamie noted that, only a few years younger than *Dat*, she could boast that her dark hair still had little gray in it.

Dat kissed her cheek and moved to the

sink to wash his hands. "I checked the voice mail messages, and you had one from Ruthie Glick. She asked you to call her back."

"Oh *ya*?" *Mamm* smiled. "I'll call her back later. I saw her at the market the other day and she told me she and Seth are going to Pinecraft in October. They're going to rent a van and a few couples are going to join them. She invited us too. I imagine Florida in October is so *schee*. We haven't been able to go with them in the past. What do you think, Vernon?"

Dat frowned. "I don't think so. We have so much to do around here in the fall."

Mamm's smile faded. "Oh."

"Mark and I can manage." Jamie leaned his back against the counter as he dried his hands with a paper towel. "Right, Mark?"

"Of course."

Dat shook his head.

"Really. We can handle it all," Jamie insisted.

Dat looked at Jamie and then Mark. "Not by yourselves. You'd have to feed all one hundred animals twice a day, including the calves that have to be bottle-fed. You'd have to haul the manure, milk our sixty cows, care for the animals that get sick, and harvest and bale the hay. That's not even mentioning how often we have to clean the milkers and the barns. Then there's upkeep on the buildings and fencing."

He sighed as though the burden was almost too much for three men. "It takes all three of us to keep this dairy farm going, and you know how important that is to our family. And you're so busy with the fire department too, Jamie."

Jamie opened his mouth to protest but then closed it.

Dat turned back to *Mamm*. "I'm sorry, Dorothy, but I don't think it's a *gut* idea for us to leave the farm."

"I understand." *Mamm* cleared her throat and turned toward Cindy. "Do you need any help?"

"No, *danki*. I've got it." Cindy set a platter of home fries on the table and then turned to Jamie. "I thought of you last night when I heard sirens. Did you have a call nearby? Was anyone hurt?"

At seventeen, the youngest Riehl, Cindy, was usually the first member of the family to ask Jamie about the people he served. He loved that about her.

"*Ya.* We were called to a car accident out here on Route 340 around eleven." Jamie pointed in the direction of the main road that ran through their town of Bird-in-

Hand, Pennsylvania.

"What happened?" Cindy's own light-blue eyes widened. Her light-brown hair turned a golden hue in the summer sun, reminding Jamie for a moment of Kayla Dienner. But he pushed that thought aside, noting Cindy had recently grown taller than both their mother and Laura.

"A woman rear-ended a truck." Jamie tossed the paper towel into the trash can.

"Was it bad?" Laura began filling each mug on the table with coffee from the percolator.

"*Ya.*" Jamie stepped over to his usual seat beside Mark and across from Cindy. "The front end of the woman's car was smashed. We had a tough time getting her out, but I think she'll be okay."

"That sounds terrible." Cindy put a platter of scrambled eggs and a basket of bread in the center of the table.

"And then he had a barn fire," Mark chimed in while washing his hands.

"Where was the fire?" *Mamm* asked.

"In Ronks."

Once the food was served, the family sat down, and after the silent prayer they loaded their plates.

As Jamie buttered a warm roll, his thoughts turned again to Kayla. He hoped

66

she'd been able to get some rest last night. He'd wanted to talk to her again before he and his company headed back to the fire station, but when she returned to the porch with a full pitcher of lemonade, he could have sworn she turned her back to him to start a conversation with someone else before he could speak.

Despite her forgiveness when he apologized, it was apparent Kayla had meant it when she told Jamie to stay away from her brother. And that meant staying away from her.

Why did her rejection bother him so much?

"Hello? Jamie? Are you awake?"

Jamie's head snapped up and he found his brother grinning at him.

"What?"

"I asked you what family lost the barn." Mark spooned eggs into his mouth.

"Oh, it was Willie and Marilyn Dienner." Jamie broke the bread in half and took a bite, savoring the warm sweetness.

"Willie and Marilyn." *Dat* turned to *Mamm*. "Do we know them, Dorothy?"

"The names sound familiar." *Mamm* tapped her chin. "Do they have any *kinner*?"

"*Ya.*" Jamie scooped some home fries from his plate. "Their oldest *sohn,* Simeon, was a firefighter. He died in that fire last year when the *haus* collapsed."

As if on cue, the three women all gasped.

"That's so *bedauerlich*." Cindy was already wiping her eyes. "How terrible."

"Do they have other *kinner*?" Laura asked.

"*Ya.* Kayla, who I would guess is about my age, and then Nathan, who's fourteen. Simeon's *fraa* and *sohn* live there too." Jamie considered sharing how Nathan wanted to be a firefighter, but he'd rather keep his embarrassing conversations with Kayla to himself.

"Were you able to save the barn?" Cindy placed a few pieces of bacon onto her plate and then handed the platter to Jamie.

"*Danki,*" Jamie said before dropping a handful of pieces onto his own plate. "No. Barns just go up too quickly."

"Oh. Right." Cindy's cheeks flushed bright pink. "That was a dumb question."

"No, it wasn't." Jamie smiled at her. "You wouldn't have known."

Cindy shrugged and trained her eyes on her plate.

"I wonder if they'll have a barn raising. If they do, we should go help." Mark bit into a piece of bacon.

"That's a great idea," *Dat* chimed in.

"Maybe you can go by their farm and ask, Jamie."

Laura tapped her fork on her plate. "Maybe we'll bake a couple of apple pies for it. What do you think, *Mamm*?"

"*Ya*, we can do that," *Mamm* agreed before lifting her mug of coffee. "I'll have to go shopping to get the ingredients. We're running low on some supplies."

Jamie cupped his hand to his mouth to shield a yawn.

"You should take a nap." *Mamm* pointed her fork at Jamie. "You look wiped out."

"I'm fine." Jamie scooped a forkful of egg into his mouth.

"I said the same thing to him, but he insists he'll sleep tonight," Mark quipped. "You know how stubborn he is."

"We all know that," Laura retorted.

"I have things to do. I don't have time to sleep until tonight." Jamie lifted his mug as the twins shared a knowing look. They often enjoyed ganging up on him and Cindy. At times they acted as though they were their own separate family unit inside the Riehl family.

"Mark, I do have a favor to ask you before you go out to work in the barn." *Mamm* poured more coffee into her mug.

"*Ya, Mamm.* What is it?"

69

"The banister on the basement steps is loose again. Would you take a look at it?"

Jamie set his fork beside his half-clean plate. "We should replace it. We've tried to fix it more than once. I think it's time to just put up a new banister."

"That's a *gut* idea." Mark buttered a roll.

"So what's on the agenda for today, *Dat*?" Jamie asked.

"We need to finish planting the corn this morning. And we need to make a supply run this afternoon." He pointed to the counter. "I have a list for the hardware store over there."

Jamie looked at Mark. "You and I can go. We can take my buggy. Maybe we can have lunch in town."

"Okay." Mark set his knife on his empty plate. "Are you ready to get our chores done before we start planting?"

"*Ya,*" Jamie said. "I'll get changed and then we can get to work."

Kayla covered her mouth against a yawn as she stepped out of the kitchen. The dining room in her family's restaurant was already half full with lunch customers, and as if they hadn't had a barn fire hours earlier, their day had so far been typically busy. While her parents cooked, Kayla waitressed with

Eva. Nathan bussed tables and washed dishes. Unencumbered by responsibility, Junior was currently asleep in the portable crib they'd installed in the office.

Glancing at the clock on the wall, Kayla stifled a moan. It was only one o'clock, which meant she had six more hours before the restaurant closed and she could go home and relax. How was she going to make it through the rest of this day with only two hours of sleep?

The front door opened and closed, the bell attached to it announcing new customers. Kayla hurried to the hostess podium, and without really looking at the two men standing there, she bent down to reach two menus from the shelf underneath.

"Welcome to Dienner's Family Restaurant. Will there be two of you dining today?" When she looked up, she came face-to-face with James Riehl. She felt her eyes widen, unable to stop them. "James?"

"Kayla." James's eyebrows careened toward his hairline. "Hi." He wore a blue shirt that complemented his soulful blue eyes. And with his black trousers, suspenders, and a straw hat, today he looked Amish. The look suited him.

He jammed his thumb toward the front glass etched with the restaurant name. "I didn't realize your family owned this restaurant. I've never been here before."

"*Ya,* my parents opened it when they were first married almost thirty years ago." She reflexively touched her prayer covering to make sure it was straight. Why was she suddenly worried about how she looked?

When she glanced at the man standing next to James, she found he wore an amused expression. "Are you going to introduce me to your *freind*?"

"Kayla, this is *mei bruder,* Mark." James gestured to each of them. "Mark, this is Kayla Dienner."

"Hi." Mark continued to grin as he shook Kayla's hand. "Nice to meet you."

"You too." Kayla hugged the menus to her chest as she studied the two brothers. They bore a family resemblance with a similar shape to their faces, but James's jaw was dimpled. She guessed he was a year or two older than Mark. Kayla shook herself from her thoughts and cleared her throat.

"Well, you two came here to eat and not chat with me," she said. "Why don't I seat you?"

"That sounds great." Mark rubbed his hands together. "I heard the meat loaf here is the best."

"*Ya, mei mamm* has a great recipe. It's one

of our most popular dishes." She started walking to the far end of the dining room. "Please follow me."

Self-consciousness pushed Kayla faster as she led the men to a table. Last night she'd done her best to avoid James after retreating into the kitchen and taking her time mixing up more lemonade. Then when she emerged back outside, she deliberately spoke to other firefighters until Jamie's crew packed up their truck and headed back to their station. She'd been sure that would be the last time she'd see James Riehl.

Wait a minute. She hadn't put it together last night, but his fire truck had Station 5 painted on it. That had been Simeon's station. That's where Brody and James were both volunteering? The station just down the street? Why had she never seen either of them in here before?

Now questions about James's family swirled through her mind. Last night he'd mentioned he would be devastated if he lost one of his siblings. How many siblings did he have? And why did she care to know more about him?

She pushed the questions out of her head as she set the menus on their table and stood to one side. "Will this table work for you?" She fished her notepad and pencil from her apron pocket.

"This is perfect." Mark grinned at her as they slid into their seats, and then he turned his attention to the menu.

She opened her mouth to tell them the day's specials, but James cut her off.

"How are you?"

The concern in his expression stole her words for a moment.

"I'm fine, *danki.*" She poised her pencil on her notepad. "May I get you something to drink?"

"Did you get any sleep before you had to come to work?"

She looked at him for a moment. Why did he care if she got any sleep last night? "I slept for about two hours." She shrugged. "I'm fine."

Mark looked up from the menu, a confused look on his face. "Sounds like you both are going to pass out tonight. I don't know how you're standing up. I'm a mess if I don't get my required seven hours of sleep."

"Oh." She needed to change the subject to something less personal. "The lunch special today is a pork barbecue sandwich with French fries. What would you like to drink? I can give you a few minutes to decide what to order if you want."

"I'll take a Coke." Mark perused the menu once more. "And I'd like the meat loaf platter with a side of buttered noodles."

She wrote quickly and then took his menu. "Okay."

Then she looked at James, who flipped through the menu before looking up at her.

"I'll have the same." He handed her the menu.

"You want a Coke too?" she asked.

"*Ya,* please." He smiled, and her heart thumped.

"I'll bring your drinks right out," she muttered before rushing off to the kitchen.

Why is this man I hardly know having such a strong effect on me? I must be losing my mind.

FIVE

"You've been holding out on me." Mark leaned toward Jamie and raised his eyebrows. "Who is Kayla, why haven't you told me about her, and why did you want to know how she slept last night?"

"I haven't been holding out on you." Jamie watched Kayla disappear through one side of two swinging doors. "I just met her last night at the fire."

Mark snapped his fingers. "Oh, right. Dienner. So her *bruder* is the one who died in the fire last year."

"Right." Jamie kept his focus on the doors, awaiting her return. She looked pretty in her blue dress and black apron, with her golden hair peeking out from under a prayer covering. When he noticed the dark circles under her eyes, he felt compelled to ask her how she was feeling, and she seemed surprised by the question. He longed to be her friend, but that was impossible given her feelings toward him.

"You should ask her out."

"What?" Jamie's attention snapped to his brother.

"I said you should ask her out." Mark chuckled. "Why are you looking at me like I'm *narrisch*?"

"Because you *are* crazy." Jamie pulled a paper napkin from the metal holder in the center of the table and began to fold it. "She doesn't like me."

"Then she fooled me." Mark gestured in the direction of the kitchen. "Didn't you see her face when she recognized you? I thought her eyes were going to fall out of her head."

"She was just surprised to see me." Jamie shrugged and stared at the napkin as he folded it over and over again.

"You like her."

Jamie sighed. "No, I don't like her. I don't even know her."

"You could get to know her." Mark leaned back and folded his arms over his chest. "Listen. I know how *maed* work. They want you to pursue them. You just have to show interest. Ask her out."

"Trust me." Jamie shook his head. "She won't go out with me."

"Why are you so sure?" Mark lifted an

eyebrow.

"She made it clear last night when she told me to stay away from her younger *bruder.*"

"What did you do?"

Jamie told him. "So I don't think she'd go out with me."

"You won't know until you ask her." Mark tapped the table. "Trust me. I know. The *maed* love me because I give them attention. You just need to talk to her. Tell her how *schee* she is, and she'll want to go out with you."

Jamie set the napkin next to the holder. His brother definitely knew what he was talking about when it came to women. It always amazed Jamie to watch the young women flock to him when he went to youth gatherings. All he had to do was smile and say hello and they followed him in droves. He had a gift when it came to attracting women, a gift Jamie had never possessed. Not that Jamie wanted to attract so many women. He'd always thought he'd find that one woman meant for him . . . someday.

"It doesn't matter." Jamie glanced down at the folded napkin. "I don't have time to date anyway."

"What are you saying?"

"You know how busy my life is." Jamie

looked up at his brother's shocked expression. "Between keeping up with the chores on the farm and volunteering at the station, I don't have time for a *maedel* right now."

Mark frowned. "You need to make time. You're almost thirty. Don't you want to get married and have a family? That's what we're called to do."

"Stop being dramatic." Jamie threw the folded napkin at Mark, who caught it with lightning-fast reflexes. "I'm only twenty-five."

"James!"

Jamie turned to see Nathan rushing over to their table. "Oh, hi, Nathan."

"I didn't realize you were here." Nathan rested a large plastic tub full of dirty dishes and utensils on the edge of their table and turned to Mark. "Hi." He shook Mark's hand.

Jamie introduced them. "This is *mei bruder,* Mark. Mark, this is Kayla's *bruder,* Nathan."

"It's great to meet you." Mark grinned. "I've heard a lot about you."

Jamie resisted the urge to kick Mark under the table. The last thing he wanted was to encourage Nathan.

"Are you a firefighter too?" Nathan asked.

Jamie inwardly groaned.

"No, I'm not." Mark gestured at Jamie. "*Mei bruder* is the only firefighter in our family. He joined with a group of his *freinden* when they were teenagers. *Mei freinden* are more into camping."

"Oh." Nathan turned to Jamie. "I've never seen you here before."

"No, although I'm now stationed down the street when I'm on duty, this is my first time. I just don't get out for lunch too often. Mark and I are in town today to get some supplies for our dairy farm, and he wanted to try it here."

"Great. So you were saying I could start training. I talked to *mei daed* about it, and he said we could discuss it. Do you know when the classes start?"

Jamie rubbed his chin as he mentally debated his response. "I'm not so sure it's a *gut* idea for us to talk about this."

Nathan's forehead furrowed. "Why not?"

"Because your *schweschder* said I should stay away from you."

"Why would she say that?"

"She doesn't want me to discuss firefighting with you, and I don't want to upset her." Jamie looked toward the kitchen doors in search of Kayla. Relief flooded him when he didn't see her. "It's probably best if we don't talk."

"That's ridiculous." Nathan scowled. "She thinks I'm going to get hurt because our *bruder,* Simeon, was a firefighter and died during a rescue." He pointed at Jamie. "But you've been volunteering since you were sixteen. Not every firefighter gets hurts."

Jamie grimaced. "No, not everyone gets hurt, but I can understand her fear."

"She can't stop me if *Dat* says it's okay. She's not my boss, even though she thinks she is." Nathan glanced back toward the kitchen and then looked at Jamie. "Besides, it doesn't matter if she gets angry. She can't control what I discuss with *mei freinden.* We are *freinden,* right?"

"*Ya,* sure we are." Jamie stole a glance at Mark, who raised his eyebrows and grinned.

Nathan leaned on the edge of the table. "What was your most memorable call?"

Jamie blew out a deep sigh as his years of volunteering swept through his mind. He settled back in his chair and crossed his arms over his chest as he considered his answer.

After giving her parents James's and Mark's orders, Kayla filled two plastic cups with chopped ice and added Coke. She was setting the cups on a tray when Eva walked up behind her.

"Are you okay?" Eva asked.

"I'm fine. Why?" Kayla lifted the tray.

"You seem — I don't know — stressed." Eva studied her. "Is something wrong?" She pointed toward the doors that led to the dining area. "Is a customer hassling you like the guy who came in last week and said his steak was too pink?"

"No, no, it's not that."

"So what is it?" Eva rested one hand on her hip. "Kayla, I've known you for six years. I can tell when you're keeping the truth from me. Go ahead and tell me. You'll feel better when you get it off your chest."

Kayla blew out a deep breath. She and Eva weren't related by blood, but Eva was like the older sister she'd always wanted.

"Fine. One of the firefighters from last night is here. He's having lunch with his *bruder*."

"Really?" Eva's eyes brightened. "Was he one of Simeon's *freinden*?"

"No." Kayla paused. How could she explain who James was without going into their whole conversation about Nathan's dream of volunteering? "He was the one who saved Nathan."

"Really?" Now Eva's whole face lit up. "We need to tell *Dat*. We should comp his meal." She started toward the main cooking

82

area. "*Mamm! Dat!* You'll never guess who came in for lunch."

Kayla took that opportunity to head back out to the dining area. She didn't want to tell Eva about her conversation with James. Eva would probably insist it was rude of her to say James should stay away from Nathan after his heroics.

Her feet slowed when she spotted Nathan leaning on James's table, listening intently as James spoke. She bit her lower lip. Surely James wasn't encouraging Nathan again.

"I bet that was scary," Nathan was saying as she approached them.

"*Ya,* it was, but I followed the hose back and found my way out of the building. That's the best way to —" James glanced up at Kayla. "You're back."

Kayla handed James and Mark their drinks, and Nathan stood up straight and faced her.

"Did you clean those tables over in the corner?"

"I was on my way over there." Nathan lifted the plastic container. "I wanted to say hi to James first."

"You need to clean them before more customers come in. It's going to get busy." She pointed toward the dirty tables. "Go on."

83

Nathan glared at her and then turned toward James and Mark. "I'll try to come see you before you leave."

As Nathan walked away with a slight limp, Kayla moved her attention to James. "I hope you weren't encouraging him to pursue volunteering."

"No, I wasn't." James held up his hands in defense, and it only made her anger boil. "Nathan asked me about my most memorable calls, and I told him. I didn't encourage him at all." He looked at his brother as if for support. "Did I?"

"Nope, he didn't." Mark took a long drink.

Kayla had the suspicion Mark was shielding a smile. Why would he find this humorous? This was a serious subject.

"I don't want you to encourage *mei bruder,*" she reminded James as she rested the tray under her arm. "He looked up to Simeon even before he died, and now I think he's searching to find someone to take Simeon's place in his life. I don't think firefighting is the right path for him."

"I know. You made that abundantly clear last night." James's expression was serious as he nodded. "Like I said, I didn't encourage him. In fact, Mark can attest to the fact that I told Nathan we shouldn't discuss it at

84

all. Nathan started asking me questions about the calls I've had. He brought the subject up, not me."

She pursed her lips. "Fine. I put in your orders. They should be out soon."

"*Danki,*" James said.

"I can't wait to taste the meat loaf," Mark added.

She hurried back to the kitchen.

"Eva told me James Riehl is here," *Dat* said as he stood by the large stove.

"*Ya,* he is." She placed two meals ready to serve on her tray. "He and his *bruder* came for lunch."

"I'll walk out with you when we have their food ready," he said. "I'd like to say hello to him and meet his *bruder.*"

"I agree with Eva that we should give them their lunch for free." *Mamm* poured salad dressing into small containers as she spoke. "I'm so grateful to him."

"*Ya,* I am too." Kayla hurried out of the kitchen to deliver the meals. Then she sat a couple who had just walked into the restaurant, took their drink order, and placed their food order in the kitchen. As she stepped back into the dining area, Eva approached her holding a tray stacked with empty cups.

Eva nodded toward James's table. "I stopped by to say hello while I was delivering food, and he introduced me to Mark. They're very friendly."

"Ya." Kayla's back stiffened as she glanced toward James, who seemed deep in conversation with his brother.

Eva smiled at Kayla. "James is handsome. Mark is, too, but there's something about James." She balanced the tray in one hand and tapped her lip. "I can't put my finger on what it is."

Kayla took in James's bright blue eyes and dark hair. He was ruggedly handsome, but she wasn't interested in a relationship. She'd already had her heart broken by Abram. When they first met, everything seemed perfect, and she quickly fell in love with his handsome smile and sense of humor. Yet as the relationship wore on, she began to notice how he repeatedly took her for granted.

She'd loved Abram with all her heart, putting him before her friends, but her love wasn't reciprocated. She'd wait on the porch for him to visit and he would never arrive. Later he'd tell her he'd been busy with his friends. Soon she realized he almost always chose their company over hers. Her frustration with his neglect grew, especially when he made excuses for his behavior.

But then when her brother died, she

forgot all that. She needed him and expected him to be there for her. But Abram was mostly absent as her family grieved. He attended the wake and funeral, but while other members of the community sat with her family for several hours, he left as soon as possible.

She planned to confront him, but he ended their relationship before she had the chance. He said he wasn't ready for a serious relationship. Abram had broken her trust, and she vowed to never allow another man to take her for granted. She wasn't ready to risk her heart again, especially with a firefighter.

"James is okay." Kayla shrugged, and Eva laughed.

"He's okay?" Her sister-in-law eyed her with suspicion. "What aren't you telling me?"

"Nothing. I have to deliver these drinks." She took a step and Eva pulled her back. "What?"

"Are you afraid of getting hurt again?" Eva's smile faded. "Kayla, Abram was immature. He wasn't ready for a serious relationship, but that was his problem, not yours. Don't let his mistakes affect the rest of your life. God will find you the perfect match. Just have faith and keep your heart open to the possibility of true love."

"I will." Kayla forced a smile. "We'll talk later, okay?"

Eva nodded and disappeared into the kitchen.

Kayla delivered the drinks and took the couple's order. Then she busied herself with checking on her other customers and refilling drinks. When she stepped back into the kitchen, James's and Mark's orders were ready.

Dat handed her one of the meat loaf platters. "I'll carry one, and you carry the other."

"Okay." Kayla followed her father to James and Mark's table.

"It's so *gut* to see you." *Dat* set the plate in front of James. "I'm glad you came by today."

"*Ya,* it's *gut* to see you too." James shook *Dat*'s hand. "I didn't realize this was your restaurant. Willie, this is *mei bruder,* Mark."

"It's great to meet you." Mark shook *Dat*'s hand. "*Danki,*" he said as Kayla lowered his plate to the table.

"*Gern gschehne,*" she muttered as she folded her hands in front of her apron.

"Your lunch is on us today." *Dat* pointed to their food. "Let us know if you'd like any dessert too."

"Oh, no." James shook his head. "I can't accept —"

"Of course you can." *Dat* patted James's broad shoulder. "You earned it earlier today. I'm glad I can give you something as a thank-you. Please enjoy your lunch. It's our pleasure, right, Kayla?" *Dat* turned to her the same time James and Mark did.

Kayla nodded and felt her cheeks heat.

"I'm really excited to try your meat loaf," Mark told *Dat.* "A few of *mei freinden* have eaten here and raved about it."

Dat grinned. "I'm *froh* to hear that. Again, enjoy."

"Mark and I were wondering if you're going to plan a barn raising."

"*Ya,* we'd love to come and help you," Mark said.

"That's so generous of you." *Dat* rested his hands on the edge of the table.

Kayla bit back a glower. Now James wanted to help with their barn raising? So much for her plan to keep him away from Nathan.

"I'm hoping we can do it next week," *Dat* continued. "I made some calls earlier today, and I found a company that can clear the lot either tomorrow or Friday. If that works out, then I can order the supplies and have the barn raising early next week. Maybe

Tuesday."

"That would be great." James glanced at Mark, who nodded. "Our *mamm* and *schweschdere* said they'd like to bake for it too."

So James has more than one sister. Not that she really cared.

"Oh, that's very kind, but it's not necessary. We would close the restaurant and cater it. We don't expect volunteers to bring food too."

Kayla glanced toward the front of the restaurant, where two men stood waiting to be seated. She hadn't even heard the bell. She rushed over, led them to their table, and took their drink orders. As she walked past James's table, her father was still there.

A feeling of foreboding took hold of her as she moved past the three men. James was worming his way into her life, and she was going to have a difficult time convincing him to stay away from her family.

Still, he had saved her brother, and she determined to be as nice as she dared.

SIX

"Don't tell *Mamm,* but that was the best meat loaf I've ever had." Mark leaned back in his seat and rested his hands on his flat abdomen.

Jamie swallowed the last of his Coke. "It was *gut.* Are you ready to go?"

"Would either of you like dessert?" Kayla was back.

"No, *danki.*" Mark shook his head. "I don't have any more room."

"Are you sure?" She turned to Jamie. "I can pack something up for you to take with you. *Mei mamm*'s strawberry cupcakes are very popular with our regular customers."

"No, *danki.*" Jamie patted his own middle. "I have to be careful or my turnout gear won't fit." He wanted to take back the words as soon as he said them, but to his surprise, she smiled. And her smile was electric, lighting up her entire face and making her eyes sparkle. She was beautiful, and

91

he suddenly wanted to know her better.

"All right." She stacked their plates on her tray. "*Danki* for coming in to see us today."

"We'll see you next week at the barn raising." Mark lifted his cup and took the last draw of Coke before setting it back on the table.

"Oh. *Gut.*" She glanced from one to the other as she lifted the tray onto her shoulder. "It was nice meeting you, Mark. Have a *gut* afternoon."

"You too," Jamie called after her as he pulled his wallet from his pocket. He took out a few bills and set them on the table.

"What are you doing?" Mark asked. "Lunch was free."

"I know, but I'm still leaving her a tip." Jamie stood and shoved his wallet into his back pocket. "Are you ready to go?"

"*Ya.*" Mark stood. "I still say you should ask her out."

"Please just drop it." Jamie pushed in his chair. "It's not going to happen, so let it go."

"Listen to me. She would go out with you if you asked. I really think she likes you."

"She doesn't like me. She's just being nice today." Jamie followed Mark toward the exit. He waved at Nathan as they passed a table he was wiping down, and Nathan

92

waved back.

Mark glanced over his shoulder. "Look at her over there, Jamie. She's really *schee.* Any guy in his right mind would snatch her up if he had the chance."

Jamie craned his neck. Kayla was laughing with some customers. Mark was right. She was stunning, and he was certain the right man would snatch her up. "She probably already has a boyfriend."

"I doubt it after the way I saw her looking at you." Mark pushed open the front door.

"You just want me to ask any *maedel* out. That's why you're always pressuring me to go to your youth group gathering, even though I'm way too old for your group."

"You talk like you're eighty," Mark deadpanned.

"Well, you already called me old when you said I was almost thirty." Jamie glanced back at Kayla once more and found her looking at him. When their gazes met, she quickly turned her head. He faced his brother. "We'd better get going. We have a lot to do at the farm."

They started down the sidewalk toward his buggy. As Jamie climbed inside, one question filled his mind. *Does Kayla have a boyfriend?*

■ ■ ■ ■

When they arrived home, Jamie and Mark unloaded their supplies and stored them in the barn.

"I'm going to put my work clothes back on before we muck out the stalls." Jamie started toward the house.

"Wait for me." Mark caught up with him.

Laura waved as she walked back from the henhouses. She was holding a basket full of eggs. "The prodigal *sohns* have finally returned from their trip to town. I was beginning to wonder if you two had run away."

"We would've been home sooner, but we ran into Jamie's girlfriend when we stopped for lunch." Mark elbowed Jamie in the ribs as he snickered.

"Knock it off," Jamie grumbled as he climbed the porch steps.

"Jamie has a girlfriend?" Laura gasped as she picked up speed. "What's her name?"

"It's Kayla Dienner. Jamie met her last night at her family's barn fire, but he failed to tell us about her." Mark faced his twin. "Her family owns Dienner's Family Restaurant down the street from his fire station and she's really *schee*. I just have to convince him to ask her out."

"Oh, that's *wunderbaar*!" She grinned at Jamie. "Maybe we'll have a wedding in the fall. It's about time you met someone and settled down. You're almost thirty."

"You sound just like your twin." Jamie rolled his eyes as he stood by the back door.

"Your whole problem is you need to be more outgoing and try harder." Mark climbed the porch steps and leaned against the railing. "If you would just put yourself out there and let the *maed* know you're interested, they'll respond to you." He gestured widely. "You're too quiet and *maed* find that intimidating."

"Don't take advice from the man who leads *maed* on and never asks them out." Laura rested a hand on her hip as she scowled at Mark.

"What's that supposed to mean?" He gave her a feigned look of annoyance.

She shook a finger at him. "You enjoy having a group of *maed* following you around, but you refuse to commit to any one of them."

Mark shrugged. "I'm just choosy, that's all."

Jamie wrenched open the back door. "I don't have time for this. I have chores waiting for me in the barn."

"Wait a minute, Jamie. We're just trying to encourage you," Mark countered. "Kayla seems like the perfect *maedel* for you. She's outgoing and not afraid to speak her mind."

"What do you mean?" Laura asked.

"Apparently Kayla is upset that Jamie was telling her little *bruder* about firefighter training."

Jamie went into the house, closing the screen door behind him and leaving their conversation on the back porch.

"Oh, you're back." *Mamm* met him at the door leading from the mudroom to the kitchen. She paused, tilting her head. *"Was iss letz?"*

"Your twins are trying to marry me off." He kicked off his boots and set them under a bench.

She chuckled. "What do you mean?"

"Every time one of them sees a *schee maedel* talking to me, Mark and Laura start pressuring me about getting married. It gets old." He rested his forearm on the doorframe.

"Don't worry about those two. It will happen for you when the right *maedel* comes along. God has the perfect plan for all of us."

"Right." He started toward the stairs. "I'm going to get changed."

"If you see Cindy, would you please ask her to come down and help me with some baking?"

"*Ya,* of course."

Upstairs, he headed down the hallway, past Mark's room, and stopped in the doorway to the sewing room. It was next to the bedroom his sisters shared. Jamie stuck his head in the doorway. The room was crammed with two sewing machines, a desk, and a mountain of material. Cindy sat at the older sewing machine, working on a quilt.

She glanced up and gasped, placing her hand on her chest.

"I'm sorry." He leaned his right shoulder against the doorframe. "I didn't mean to startle you. What are you working on?"

"It's a quilt one of *Mamm*'s customers ordered. A lone star." She held it up and he took in the pattern of a multicolored star in the center of the large quilt.

"That's fantastic. You're so talented."

She shrugged and looked down. "It's pretty basic."

"You don't give yourself enough credit."

"How was your trip to town?"

"*Gut.* Mark and I had lunch at Dienner's Family Restaurant."

"Oh, I heard that place is great." She

97

leaned toward the sewing machine. "We'll have to go there sometime."

"*Ya*. That's a *gut* idea. *Mamm* asked me to tell you she needs your help with some baking."

"Oh." She jumped up. "I hadn't realized I'd been up here so long. She must be upset I haven't come back down to help her."

"She wasn't upset." He tapped the door-frame. "I'm going to get changed so I can get started on chores. I'll see you in a bit."

"Okay."

He continued down the hallway to his bedroom, the largest room on the second floor. As for all the walls in the house, his walls were plain white. His double bed was adorned with the blue-and-gray log cabin quilt Cindy made for him for Christmas last year. Shelves filled with his favorite books and mementos from his childhood and two dressers furnished the rest of the space.

As he opened his closet and pulled out his work clothes, Jamie's thoughts returned to Kayla and her stern words about his discussions with Nathan. While it was clear she didn't want him to influence her brother, he had an inexplicable longing to see her again. He needed to wipe her from his mind, but her pretty face and gorgeous eyes kept creeping into his subconscious. Did that mean he liked her? And wasn't she a bit more friendly when she offered them dessert?

No, Jamie needed to concentrate on his responsibilities and forget about Kayla Dienner — even if that did seem an impossible task.

Since the restaurant didn't close until seven, Dienner family dinners at home were late — unless they ate in shifts at the restaurant before closing.

Eva fed spoonsful of baby food to Junior as the rest of the family ate. His baby seat was propped up in his high chair.

"James told me an interesting story today when I stopped by his table at lunchtime," Nathan began when there was a break in the conversation. "He said he once got lost in a fire at a large warehouse where they sell furniture. The smoke was so bad he got disoriented. He had to follow the hose back to the door."

Kayla stopped chewing her chicken potpie and stared across the large kitchen table at her brother.

"He said it was one of the times he was really scared." Nathan grinned. "I guess that means even if you've been serving for years, you're still reminded of how vulnerable you are in a burning building."

Kayla glanced at her mother, and in the light shining from the nearby propane lamp she could see her blue eyes glimmering with unshed tears.

"Nathan, I think we should change the subject." Kayla forced a smile and turned toward her father, sitting in his usual spot at the head of the table. "The restaurant was busy today. I heard a lot of compliments on the strawberry cupcakes. I think they were a hit."

"Stop trying to change the subject on me," Nathan growled. "You never let me talk about firefighting. You're not *mei mamm*."

"Nathan," *Dat* warned. "Don't talk to your *schweschder* that way."

"I'm tired of her telling me I can't talk about firefighter training." He dropped his fork onto his placemat. "It's not her decision if I start training. It's up to you and *Mamm*. It's not Kayla's place to tell me I can't do something I want to do."

Kayla opened her mouth to respond but stopped when she felt a hand on her shoulder. She turned toward Eva, who shook her head as if to tell her to be quiet. Kayla closed her mouth as Eva pulled her arm back and returned to eating.

"I really want to start training." Nathan

looked at each of their parents. "I'm fourteen now, and I'm old enough to help our community. It would mean a lot to me if you'd let me do it."

Kayla's shoulders stiffened as she prayed *Dat* would say no.

"What do you think, Marilyn?" *Dat* glanced over at *Mamm,* who sniffed as she wiped a napkin over her eyes.

"No." *Mamm* shook her head as she crumpled the napkin in the palm of her hand. "I'm not comfortable with the idea of Nathan training to become a volunteer. We need him at the restaurant."

Kayla nearly wilted with relief. *Oh, thank goodness!*

"It's settled then." *Dat* turned back to Nathan, who glowered. "This is not a *gut* time for you to train. Let's drop the subject for now."

Nathan ground his teeth together. *"Ya, Dat."*

Silence fell over their conversation like a dense fog. Only the sound of utensils scraping dishes and Junior's gurgling while eating his food filled the large room.

"How are the plans going for the barn raising?" Eva's question broke through the silence.

"They're coming together," *Dat* said.

"The contractor is coming on Friday to clear the lot, so we can move forward with the barn raising next week. I've already ordered the supplies. The new barn is going to be a little smaller since we don't need as much space. I think we'll have plenty of help. I've asked people to put the word out to different church districts. I'm hoping for Tuesday."

"That's *wunderbaar.*" *Mamm* smiled. "We can start talking about a menu for lunch and dinner."

"*Ya,* I was thinking that. I've also ordered a new buggy. I've made a list of everything lost in the barn, and I'll start replacing what else I need the most right away."

As *Dat* spoke on about his plans, Kayla looked at Nathan. He was staring at his plate as he moved the remnants of his meal around with his fork. She felt a niggling of guilt mixed with triumph as her brother sulked. She dismissed her guilt. She was right to protect her younger brother, the only sibling she had left. But if she was right, then why did she feel so bad about it?

After supper, Kayla carried dishes to the counter.

"Nathan and I are going to take care of the animals." *Dat* gave *Mamm* a quick kiss on her cheek before he and Nathan started

102

for the mudroom.

"Would it be all right if I gave Junior his bath?" *Mamm* unbuckled his baby seat and pulled the squealing baby into her arms.

"Ya." Eva swiped a wet cloth over Junior's cheek, catching the blob of baby food that had escaped his mouth. "Be *gut* for *mammi."*

Junior squealed again and wrapped his arms around *Mamm*'s neck.

Mamm laughed. "Oh, Junior. You remind me so much of your *dat."* Her voice wobbled. "He would have adored you."

Tears threatened Kayla's eyes as *Mamm* carried Junior into the addition where he and Eva lived. She glanced at the counter where Eva had just started filling the sink with water and soap. She waited for Eva to say something about Simeon or to wipe her eyes, but she continued to work as if *Mamm* hadn't mentioned him at all. Was Eva masking her emotions? Or did it not bother her when someone mentioned him?

Eva turned toward Kayla and smiled. "I'll wash and you dry, okay?"

"Ya." Kayla gathered glasses from the table and carried them to the counter. She studied her sister-in-law, but she didn't find any sign of grief.

She considered Eva as she continued to

clear the table. She always seemed to have her emotions in check. She was kind and sweet, and nothing ever upset her. Of course, Eva had sobbed the day Simeon died and during the service. She had also broken down frequently in the weeks following the funeral and again four months later when Junior was born.

Yet one morning a few months ago, Eva awoke happy, and her pleasant mood had continued as she doted on her son and worked at the restaurant. Kayla was constantly astounded by Eva's fortitude.

Eva broke into Kayla's thoughts as she scrubbed a serving bowl. "Was Simeon as eager to become a firefighter as Nathan is?"

"*Ya,* he was." Kayla wiped crumbs from the tablecloth into her hands. "He and his best *freinden* from his youth group all signed up for training together. They were inspired after the *haus* down the street burned down. Simeon and I had the youth gathering here that day, and they all went down the street when the fire department arrived. They watched the entire scene unfold, and Simeon said they were fascinated by how the members of the fire company worked together. The man who lived there at the time was injured, but overall he was okay."

Crossing the kitchen, Kayla brushed the crumbs from her palm into the trash can. "One of the men volunteering was Amish. When they talked to him, they realized they wanted to help people in the community too."

Eva set the serving bowl in the drain board. "Simeon told me he liked the brotherhood of the fire company too. He enjoyed being with the other firefighters. It was like another family to him."

"*Ya,* he told me that once." Kayla grabbed a dish towel and began to dry the bowl. "He truly loved volunteering."

"*Ya,* he did." Eva sighed as she washed a platter. "I was so taken by him when I met him at that youth group gathering over in Lititz. He was so handsome and he had the most electric smile. When he talked to me, I thought he was more interested in *mei freind* Ellie, but he said he liked me." She set the platter in the drain board and started on the plates. "That feels like a lifetime ago now. So much has changed."

A comfortable silence fell between them, and the sound of *Mamm* singing to Junior as he squealed in the bathtub came all the way through to the kitchen from Eva's apartment. Kayla lost herself in thoughts of Simeon and Eva — when they first began dating, their engagement, and their wedding. Kayla had admired their easy relationship. They often joked and laughed when they were together. Would she ever find a special relationship like that?

Eva set a plate in the drain board and began to wash another one. "I think Junior looks like him. He has his smile. Sometimes I look at *mei sohn* and I'm sure I see Simeon staring back at me." She glanced over at Kayla and chuckled. "You must think I'm *narrisch.*"

"No, I see it too." Kayla dried a plate and set it in the cabinet as she considered all Eva had gone through since marrying Simeon three years ago. "Do you regret staying with us instead of moving to Western Pennsylvania with your parents after Simeon died?"

"No." Eva turned toward her, her smile gone. "Why would you think that?"

Kayla shrugged. "I guess I thought you might miss your parents."

"I do miss them sometimes." Eva returned to washing the dishes. "But I love working in the restaurant and living in the apartment I shared with Simeon. It's comforting to be here and around you, and I know having Junior here helps your parents deal with losing their *sohn.*"

"I'm so *froh* you're here."

"I am too." Eva wiped her hands on a dish towel and hugged Kayla. "You're the *schweschder* I never had."

Kayla laughed as tears stung her eyes. "It's funny you say that. I've always thought the same about you."

SEVEN

"Mei bruder is talented when it comes to attracting *maed,"* Jamie said to Noah as he leaned back against the pasture fence.

They'd both noticed Mark sitting between two young women on the Riehls' back porch. They were both watching him with rapt attention as he told some story. How had his younger brother learned how to attract so many women while Jamie hardly knew what to say when he found himself in a conversation with one?

It was Sunday night, and since it was an off-Sunday without a church service, the Riehl family had invited friends to supper. Jamie took a long draw on his bottle of homemade root beer.

Noah leaned against the fence beside Jamie and lifted his own bottle. "I guess your *bruder* was the only one to inherit that talent, huh?"

Jamie started to laugh, began to choke,

and spit out a mouthful of root beer.

"Well, I'm certain all the women sitting nearby would be impressed by the disgusting sight of you choking on your drink." Noah chuckled.

"*Danki,* buddy." Jamie swiped the back of his hand over his mouth.

Noah's wife, Elsie, rushed over with their toddler. Christian was squirming in her arms. "Are you all right?"

"*Ya,* I'm fine." Jamie pointed at Noah. "Your husband decided to make a joke while I was drinking."

"He's *gut* at making jokes at the worst time." Elsie set Christian on the ground, and he took off running toward the porch. "I better follow him." She hurried after the boy.

"He's always so busy. He keeps us running."

"I see that."

Christian stomped up the porch steps, where Laura sat with her boyfriend, Rudy Swarey, along with her best friend, Savilla Lambert, and Savilla's husband, Allen. When Christian dashed to Savilla and held up his arms, all the women on the porch broke out in a chorus of "Aw." Savilla lifted him onto her lap and rocked the boy against her protruding abdomen as Elsie sank down in the rocker beside Laura.

"I suppose Savilla will have her *boppli* soon," Jamie said.

"*Ya,* I guess so."

"It's hard to believe Savilla is going to be a *mamm.* I remember Laura's first day of first grade. She sat next to Savilla and declared them best *freinden* for life. It seems as if it's going to work out that way too. They're just as close as they were when they were seven."

"And we've known each other that long too."

"That's true." Jamie set his empty bottle on the ground.

"Do you think Laura will get married soon?" Noah jammed his thumb toward where Laura and Rudy were laughing. "They've been together a long time, haven't they?"

"*Ya,* I think it's three years now. I'm sure he'll ask *mei daed* permission to marry her before too long, and then Laura will be the first of us Riehl *kinner* to get married and bring a grandchild into the world." *And I'll still be single.*

Noah turned toward him. "When are you going to settle down? You're not getting any younger."

"You sound like Mark, but his advice is

110

ironic since he has the attention of all the *maed* in his youth group but doesn't want to pick one to settle down with."

"Has Mark been giving you a hard time about dating?"

"He always does." Jamie picked up his bottle and reached for Noah's. "Would you like another one?"

"I'm not done with this one yet, and I'm not done with our conversation." Noah lifted his eyebrows. "I know you. In fact, I probably know you as well as you know yourself. You're going to tell me you don't have time to date. But it's worth it."

"It may be worth it, but I have so much responsibility here on the farm." Jamie made a sweeping gesture. "I'm the oldest, and I'll take over this dairy farm someday. I need to show *mei dat* I can handle it, prove to him how serious I am about keeping this farm a success. Right now he won't even go on a vacation with *Mamm* because he thinks I can't manage the farm without him. Not even with Mark's help."

"Everyone knows how serious you are. You've never done anything reckless." Noah grinned. "Except if you count running into burning buildings. I suppose people could say that's reckless."

"That's another issue. I also volunteer

111

once a week. I can't add anything else to my life right now. How could I give a *maedel* the attention she'd expect?"

"I've made it work. I have a job and volunteer."

Jamie shook his head. "You're not a dairy farmer."

"So you think being a carpenter is less work?"

"No, I didn't say that."

"Jamie, just hear me out." Noah stood up straight and faced him, his dark eyes serious. "I know it seems like you can't find balance with dating and the other demands in your life, but you need to. You'll be *froh* you did." He nodded toward the porch, where Elsie was now rocking Christian. "Marrying Elsie and having Christian are the best decisions I've made in my life. I thank God every day for *mei fraa* and *mei sohn.* If you took the time to find the right *maedel,* you'd be just as *froh* and fulfilled as I am."

Jamie frowned. "Are you done lecturing me?"

"*Ya,* I think so." Noah took the last drink and handed his bottle to Jamie. "I'll take another one."

Jamie snatched two fresh bottles of root beer from a cooler by the porch and carried them back to Noah. "Here you go."

"Danki." Noah opened the bottle and stuck the cap in his pocket. "I heard Willie Dienner's barn raising is Tuesday. One of the guys at my store told me Willie was already able to get the lot cleared and the supplies ordered. I'm surprised he did all that quickly, but apparently he has *freinden* who pulled some strings for him. Are you going to help build the new barn? I'm planning to."

"It's on Tuesday?" Jamie asked and Noah nodded. "*Ya,* Mark and I will be there. *Dat* said he'd keep things going here so we can go, and I'm not on duty at the fire station then either." An image of Kayla filled his mind as he recalled his last conversation with her at the restaurant.

"You have a strange expression on your face. What is it?" Noah raised his eyebrows.

"I was just thinking about Kayla." Jamie leaned back against the fence again as he opened his bottle. "Mark and I saw her last week. We went to Dienner's Family Restaurant, but I didn't know her family owns and runs it." He gave Noah the gist of what happened there. "She doesn't want me to talk to Nathan, but I feel compelled to help out at the barn raising. Not only was Simeon a fellow firefighter, but we're supposed to help each other."

Jamie turned his gaze toward the porch. Cindy was handing out plates with pretzels.

"And you like her."

"What?" Jamie spun toward Noah.

"You like Kayla." Noah took a long draw on his root beer.

"No, I don't." Jamie shook his head. "I suppose I do like her as a *freind,* but that's it."

Noah grinned, and frustration boiled inside of Jamie.

"Would you like some pretzels?" Cindy arrived and offered each of them a plate. They both thanked her and Noah smiled as he took one. "I'm surprised you're not with your youth group tonight."

She fingered her black apron. "I didn't feel like going since I knew we were having company."

Jamie took the other plate from her, and he was thankful for the distraction from his conversation with Noah.

"How's the store doing?" She swiped a pretzel from Jamie's plate.

"It's *gut.* We're getting a lot of orders for bedroom suites, and that keeps us busy." They discussed the most popular items he, his father, and brother sold at their furniture store before their moving on to friends and acquaintances in their district. Soon the sun began to set, painting the sky with vivid splashes of red, pink, yellow, orange, and purple.

Elsie sidled up to Noah with Christian fast asleep on her shoulder. "I think it's time to go."

"*Ya*. It looks like he's worn himself out." Noah held out his hands and Elsie handed the boy to him. Christian continued to sleep, burrowing into Noah's shoulder as he adjusted himself. "*Danki* for having us over. I'll see you on Tuesday, Jamie."

The four said good night, and then Elsie climbed into the buggy before taking Christian from Noah's arms. As they started down the driveway, Jamie picked up the two empty bottles and walked with Cindy toward the porch. Cindy hurried up the steps ahead of him, gathered dirty dishes, and carried them into the house.

Jamie climbed the steps and waved to his siblings and their friends. *"Gut nacht."* He yanked open the back door and started into the mudroom.

"You're going to bed?" Mark called after him.

"It's late."

"*Ya,* I know, but we're having a *gut* time. You should stay here and talk to us." Mark

115

lifted his plate of pretzels. "Have another snack."

"*Ya*, join us," Franey said. She was one of the young women sitting with Mark.

"*Ya,*" Ruthann chimed in from his brother's other side.

"No, *danki.*" Jamie shook his head. "I have a lot of work to do tomorrow."

"You need to relax and have more fun." Mark stood and gestured for Jamie to sit in the empty chair beside Franey. "Come sit with us for a while. The night is young."

Jamie pressed his lips together and swallowed back the frustrated words that threatened to jump from his lips. Instead, he took a deep breath. "I'm going to bed. Work comes early in the morning."

"*Ya*, I know." Mark shrugged. "We'll get all our work done."

"*Gut nacht.*" Jamie nodded to the crowd on the porch and went inside. After saying good night to his parents, who were just leaving the family room for their own bed, he climbed the stairs to his bedroom.

As he undressed and got under his sheets, his mind swirled with a list of everything he had to do the following day.

Kayla yawned as she walked from the bathroom toward her bedroom. She stopped when she reached Nathan's room, where a soft glow peeked out from under the doorway. Guilt crept over her. Nathan hadn't said much to her since their conversation at supper Wednesday night. He had not only accused her of never letting him talk about firefighting, but he'd reminded her she wasn't his mother. Ever since he had given her only one-word answers when she attempted to speak to him, and he glowered every time she looked at him.

She blew out a sigh. She couldn't bear the distance that had grown between them since the barn burned down. Kayla wanted to protect Nathan, but she didn't want to lose his friendship in the process. After all, he was her only living brother. She wanted to have a relationship with him long after they both were married and had families of their own.

That is, if she could ever give her heart to a man.

She started to knock on the door but hesitated, her hand suspended in the air. If she attempted to clear things up between them, she had to do her best not to lecture him. She had to let him talk and to respect his point of view, even if she didn't agree with it.

Squaring her shoulders, she knocked.

"Come in," he called.

She opened the door and stood in his doorway. "Hi."

Sprawled on his double bed and clad in shorts and a white T-shirt, he sat up straighter, leaned back on two pillows propped up against his headboard, and set a book down beside him. "Are you heading to bed?"

"Ya." She folded her arms over her robe. "Do you have a minute?"

"Well" — he gestured around his large bedroom — "I'm not very busy right now." When Simeon married Eva and moved to the apartment downstairs, Nathan jumped at the chance to move from his smaller bedroom. The larger room gave him the opportunity to have a double bed and add a second dresser and a nightstand.

She glanced around the room as memories of Simeon filled her mind. It seemed as if it was only yesterday he knocked on her door when she overslept and told her to hurry up so they could open the restaurant on time. She missed the days when he was still around to be her big brother and remind her to greet the customers as they arrived in the restaurant, fill the drink orders quickly, and keep smiling even when patrons complained.

Understanding suddenly punched Kayla in the stomach as she realized she had picked up where Simeon left off as the older sibling. She had become just as bossy toward Nathan as Simeon had been toward her.

"Kay?"

"What?" She snapped her gaze to Nathan's as he lifted an eyebrow.

"You look a bit lost in thought. Is everything okay?" A smile slowly spread across his lips, and relief flooded her. He was actually smiling at her for the first time since the barn burned down. Maybe they would be okay after all.

"*Ya.*" She squared her shoulders again. "I was wondering if we could talk."

"What do you want to talk about?"

"I'm sorry for upsetting you the other night." She touched the tie on her robe as she spoke. "I know you have your heart set on being a firefighter, but I'm worried about you. I don't want to lose *mei* only *bruder.*"

His smile faded as his eyes narrowed. "I know that already, but —"

She held up her hand. "Let me finish. I know you're frustrated with me because you think I'm acting like *Mamm* or *Dat,* but I just realized Simeon used to treat me the same way. He also acted like he was my third parent."

His expression softened. "Really?"

"*Ya.* I guess that's what older siblings do when they care. Maybe that's what I'm supposed to do to keep you safe."

"But you can't be the one to keep me safe forever. I have to grow up sometime, Kay. I have to learn to keep myself safe."

Kayla nodded. "*Ya,* I guess you do."

"*Danki,* I guess, for caring about me."

She laughed. "*Gern gschehne. Gut nacht.* We have to get up early tomorrow. Monday is one the busiest days at the restaurant."

"Every day is one of the busiest days there. And it's going to be even busier since we have to make food for the barn raising on Tuesday."

As Kayla turned to leave the room, her gaze moved to Nathan's row of shelves on his far wall. She spotted a firefighter radio and crossed the room to pick it up.

"Is this Simeon's?" She held it in her hands, and memories of the radio echoing throughout the house as it announced various calls — from medical to accidents to fires — appeared in her mind. It seemed as if it was only yesterday that Simeon was rushing out the door in response.

"*Ya.*" He scooted to the edge of his bed. "Brody told me I could keep it as a way to remember him."

"That was really nice of him." She set the radio on the shelf and walked to the door. "You'd better get some sleep."

"Ya, Mamm." He drew out the words with dripping sarcasm.

She turned toward him, and to her surprise, he smiled.

"See you bright and early." She stepped backward into the hallway.

"Gut nacht." Nathan scooted under his sheets and flipped off the Coleman lantern on his nightstand.

Kayla closed his door and made her way to her room. As she slipped into bed, her thoughts spun with memories of Simeon and his last fire call. It was late that night when Brody came to the house with the tragic news. The sound of *Mamm*'s sobs filled the house and woke both Kayla and Nathan.

They ran down the stairs, and when they reached the bottom step they found *Mamm* sobbing in *Dat*'s arms as Eva sobbed in Brody's arms. Brody explained what had happened, and Kayla felt as if the wind had been punched out of her lungs. Her older brother being crushed under a burning house sounded more like a nightmare than a true story.

The next few days passed in a blur as they hosted the visitation in their home and then buried Simeon in a nearby cemetery.

Kayla sniffed and wiped her cheeks as she rolled onto her side and faced the wall. She closed her eyes and tried to shove away the heartbreaking memories of the days that followed her brother's death.

Soon her thoughts moved to James and his family. He'd told her he'd begun volunteering when he was sixteen, and he shared with Nathan that he'd had some frightening experiences. Did his family ever worry about him? Did they pray every time he went to the firehouse to serve? She rubbed her forehead. Of course they worried about him. They were his family and they loved him the same way she loved her brothers.

As Kayla settled under the covers, she continued to think about James. Would she see him at the barn raising? He and Mark had promised to come, hadn't they? And as much as she hated to admit it, she secretly longed to talk to James again.

EIGHT

Kayla balanced a large tray of sandwiches as she stepped onto the back porch. She glanced toward the wooden skeleton beginning to look like a barn. The naked wood stretched up toward heaven with an azure sky as its backdrop, and she counted at least twenty men lined up on the top of the structure. They were hammering in the boards for the roof. Another thirty or so were on the ground cutting boards, building walls, and supervising the hard work.

Voices shouted over the noise as the men worked in unison with the hot sun beating down on them, and her heart swelled with gratitude for all the volunteers who had come out to help her father rebuild.

It was close to noon and time to deliver lunch to the line of tables Nathan had set up for the food they'd prepared.

She noticed a man walking up the rock path leading toward the house. From where she stood, he looked tall, but his face was hidden in the shadow cast by the rim of his straw hat. She crossed the porch and started slowly down the steps, ready to greet him.

As Kayla reached the bottom, her foot slipped. She lost her balance and stumbled, falling into the hard chest of the man, who was suddenly there. She dropped the tray, and sandwiches went tumbling to the ground as he grabbed her arms and righted her.

"Are you all right?"

She looked up and gasped as James Riehl's ice-blue eyes searched her face. "I-I'm so sorry. I didn't mean to —"

"It's all right." He laughed as he released her arms. "Are you hurt?"

"No." Her cheeks blazed as hot humiliation flooded her face. She bent to retrieve the sandwiches peppering the path.

"Wait." He grabbed her arms again.

She stood up straight, startled. *"Was iss letz?"*

"We've done this before and we both wound up with headaches." He chuckled, a deep and sweet melodious sound that sent more warmth roaring through her veins.

Whoa. Where did that come from?

"Let me." He bent and handed her the tray. "You hold the tray, and I'll get the sandwiches."

"Okay." She held out the tray as he piled the soiled sandwiches on it. Then he smiled at her, and her cheeks flamed even hotter.

"*Danki* for your help," she muttered.

"*Gern gschehne*. So why do we keep meeting like this?" He raised his dark eyebrows. "Do you feel the need to keep throwing food and drinks at me?"

"Oh, well, I . . . um, I didn't mean to . . ." She racked her brain for an explanation for her clumsiness. How had James Riehl managed to steal her ability to speak clearly?

"I'm kidding." He held out his hands. "Would you like me to carry this back inside for you?"

"That's not necessary, but *danki*." She turned and started up the steps, hoping her face would return to a normal temperature.

"Actually, I was wondering if I could use your bathroom."

She craned her neck and peeked over her shoulder. He still stood at the bottom of the steps, leaning his tall body against the railing. "Come inside, and I'll show you where it is."

He hurried up the steps. "Let me get the door for you."

"*Danki*." She walked through the mudroom and stepped into the large kitchen. *Mamm* and Eva turned and greeted James as he walked in behind her.

"It's so *gut* to see you," *Mamm* said.

Eva nodded. "*Danki* for coming out today to help."

"It's nice to see you both too." James glanced at Kayla and raised his eyebrows.

Kayla pointed to the family room. "The bathroom is just through there, to the left."

"*Danki.*" James gave her a little nod before disappearing through the doorway.

"What happened there?" *Mamm* asked as Kayla set the tray with the pebble-and-dirt-covered sandwiches on the counter.

"I slipped on the steps and dropped the tray." Kayla lifted the lid of the trash can and began tossing the sandwiches.

"Don't worry about it," Eva said. "I have more rolls. I'll start making new ones. Did you fall?"

Kayla tossed the last of the spoiled food. "No. James caught me."

"He caught you?" *Mamm*'s tone made Kayla look up, and she saw that her eyes had widened. "How did he manage that?"

Eva stepped over to the counter. "He caught you in his arms?"

"Shh." Kayla looked toward the doorway, hoping James wasn't standing there listening. "Be quiet or he'll hear you."

"Why are you blushing?" *Mamm* asked.

"Please stop teasing me," Kayla pleaded with them. "It wasn't a big deal. I started to fall, and he happened to be there and caught me."

"That sounds kind of coincidental." Eva rested her elbow on the counter and set her chin on her palm. "Tell me more."

Oh, how Kayla wanted to silence her mother and sister-in-law. She bit back the frustrated words that wanted to roll off her tongue.

Eva suddenly stood up straight and smiled at someone behind Kayla.

"Can I carry something outside for you? That way I can make sure you don't stumble again."

James had stepped back into the kitchen. Kayla opened her mouth to tell him she was perfectly capable of walking down the steps when she heard the screen door click shut. Three women appeared in the kitchen doorway, each holding large trays.

"*Mamm!* I'm so *froh* you made it." James walked over to the eldest woman and took the tray from her hands. "This is Kayla Dienner, and her *mamm,* Marilyn. This is her sister-in-law, Eva." Then he motioned toward his mother and the younger women. "This is *mei mamm,* Dorothy, and *mei schweschdere,* Laura and Cindy."

So he has two schweschdere. Kayla held out her hand to Dorothy. "It's so nice to meet you. *Danki* for coming." Then she shook Laura's and Cindy's hands, marveling at their eye color. It was so similar to James's.

Eva and *Mamm* followed suit, greeting each of their guests. "We're so *froh* you're here today," *Mamm* said. "It was such a shock to lose our barn, and we appreciate everyone who's taken the time to help us."

"We wouldn't miss an opportunity to help neighbors." Dorothy pointed to the serving tray James placed on the table. "*Mei dochdern* and I made sandwiches — ham and cheese and turkey and cheese." Then she pointed to the serving platters her daughters held. "We also have some *kichlin* for dessert."

Laura nodded toward her brother. "Jamie insisted we make peanut butter *kichlin.* They're his favorite."

Jamie?

Kayla turned toward James as he shrugged. "It's your own fault for making such *appeditlich kichlin.*"

Kayla studied him as the name rolled around in her head. *Did his family call him*

Jamie? Why did he introduce himself as James?

"You'd better not eat them all," Cindy scolded him. "They're for everyone."

"We'll keep an eye on him, right, Kayla?" Eva grinned.

Kayla longed to hide under the table. Was Eva going to tease her all day?

"Why don't we go ahead and take the food outside?" *Mamm* suggested, and Kayla was thankful for the distraction.

Eva examined the tray Dorothy had been holding. "These sandwiches look *appeditlich.*" She glanced at Kayla. "Especially since *someone* managed to drop a tray full of the sandwiches I spent nearly all morning preparing."

"It wasn't her fault," James chimed in. "I witnessed her fall."

"You fell?" Concern filled Laura's expression as she turned toward Kayla. "Are you all right?"

Kayla longed to get out from under the microscope her mother and sister-in-law had trained on her. "*Ya.* I didn't fall. I stumbled, and James grabbed me before I actually fell. The sandwiches took all the damage." She lifted the tray of sandwiches from the table. "I'll carry these out. I'm sure the men are getting hungry. They've been working in the hot sun since early this morning."

"Let me carry that." James took the tray from her. "We don't want to take any chances with *these* sandwiches," he deadpanned.

Kayla ignored him. She spotted a jug of iced tea and a package of plastic cups on the counter. "I'll bring the iced tea."

James raised an eyebrow. "Are you sure you can handle all that without stumbling? If my hands are full, I might not be able to catch you this time."

Kayla pressed her lips together as frustration boiled through her. When would she stop being the butt of their jokes? She picked up the jug and cups.

James's smile faded. "I'm only kidding. You carry those, and I'll take the sandwiches."

"Great." Relief flooded Kayla. Maybe the jokes would stop after all.

She followed him out to the porch and down the steps.

"How have you been?" he asked as they headed to the tables her family had set up near the building site.

"Fine." She glanced up at him and, for the first time, noticed his wide chest and broad shoulders. Had farm work given him such a muscular physique? Or perhaps he was a carpenter? "How are you?"

"I'm *gut.*" He paused for a moment as if he were contemplating what to say next. Before they reached the tables, he halted.

She stopped walking, too, and turned around to see why.

"Listen. I feel like we started off on the wrong foot. I never meant to overstep my bounds by encouraging Nathan to join the fire department as a volunteer. I really would like to start over with you and would like to be your *freind.* How would you feel about that?"

He stilled as if her response meant the world to him, and happiness fluttered in her chest.

"I'd like that."

"Great." They reached the tables and she set the iced tea and cups beside the napkins, plates, and utensils she'd carried out earlier.

He put the tray next to the iced tea. "Would you like to eat lunch with me?"

Surprised, she took an involuntary step back. But then she jammed her thumb in the direction of the house behind her. "I need to bring out the rest of the food."

"I think they've taken care of that." He nodded toward the house. She turned to see their mothers, Eva, and his sisters walking toward them, their arms full.

"Oh." She waited until all five women arrived. As they set all the food on the tables, Kayla sidled over to Eva and lowered her voice. "Do you need my help with anything?"

Eva swiveled toward her. "I think we have it handled." Her eyes narrowed. "Why do you ask?"

"James asked me to eat lunch with him."

Eva's face brightened and she grinned as she glanced over Kayla's shoulder toward James.

Kayla gritted her teeth. "Stop looking at him."

Eva touched Kayla's arm. "Relax. I think it's great he wants to have lunch with you. Go have fun. His *mamm* and *schweschdere* offered to help us carry out these desserts, and now we're all going to make more sandwiches. We'll be fine."

"*Danki.*" Kayla walked back to James and picked up a plate. "Eva said they have plenty of help with the food since your *mamm* and *schweschdere* are here. I guess I can eat with you."

"Great." He grinned. "Let's eat by that big tree over there."

"That would be nice." She filled her plate with a sandwich, a scoop of pasta salad, and a handful of potato chips as he filled his own plate. After they each poured a cup of iced tea, she followed him over to the tree and sat down on the grass, facing him.

After a silent prayer, they began to eat.

"I didn't realize you were here. When did you come?" She lifted her turkey and cheese sandwich.

"I wanted to get here earlier, but I had to take care of some chores first. I think we got here about an hour ago." He picked up a chip.

"Oh. Did your *daed* and *bruder* come with you?"

"Just Mark. *Mei daed* stayed behind to run our farm." He bit into the chip.

So he's a farmer. "What kind of farm do you have?"

"Dairy." He pointed toward the line of men now serving themselves lunch. "Some of *mei freinden* came to help too. *Mei* best *friend,* Noah, is there next to Mark, along with Laura's boyfriend, Rudy, and Rudy's best *freind,* Allen. We all wanted to help your family."

Her heart warmed. "That's really nice that you all came. *Danki.*"

"*Gern gschehne.*" He shrugged. "That's what we do in this community."

They ate in silence for a few moments,

and she considered what else to ask him about his life. She suddenly felt compelled to ask if he had a girlfriend, but she didn't dare.

"How long did you say your parents have owned the restaurant?" His question broke through her racing thoughts.

"Thirty years, ever since they were married." She fingered her cup. "*Dat*'s older *bruder* took over their *daed*'s farm, and *mei daed* never really had an interest in farming. His *daed* thought he was *narrisch* for wanting to open a restaurant, but it was his dream. His *mammi* taught him how to cook.

"Then *Dat* met *mei mamm,* and they say it was love at first sight." She pointed to her house. "*Mamm*'s parents had passed away and left her this *haus* and some money. She was their only *kind*. When *mei daed* mentioned opening a restaurant, she loved the idea. They found the perfect site in Bird-in-Hand and opened Dienner's Family Restaurant. *Mei daed* says his *daed* didn't think the restaurant would last. But it's still going strong."

"That's a great story." He lifted his cup as if to make a toast. "The food is fantastic. Do you like working there?"

"*Ya.* It's fun talking with the customers. I usually waitress, but sometimes I get to help cook." She took a sip.

"Do you like to cook?"

"I do." She set her cup on the grass. "How did you get into firefighting?"

He bent one of his knees and rested his arm on it. "When I was sixteen I was at a youth gathering one Sunday afternoon. I was playing volleyball with *mei freinden* when we heard this tremendous crash. It sounded like a bomb went off."

"What was it?"

His lips formed a thin line. "It was a bad accident. A bus full of people from a nearby church had crashed. The driver ran off the road and hit a tree. *Mei freinden* and I rushed to the scene and tried to help the people until the fire department and EMTs arrived. So many people were hurt and needed assistance. It made such an impression on us that *mei freinden* and I became volunteers. We wanted to help the people in our community. I've been a volunteer ever since."

She leaned closer to him, interested by how similar his story was to the one she'd told Eva about Simeon and his youth group friends. "I can understand how that would affect you. What else do you like about it?"

He gave her a shy smile, and she couldn't help but think he was adorable. "I enjoy the brotherhood." Kayla remembered how Simeon told her the same thing.

"I know that sounds juvenile," James added, "but I enjoy the *freinden* I've made through the department."

"Like Brody?"

"Ya." He paused for a moment. "You know Brody well because he was Simeon's chief."

"That's right. He was there when Simeon died, and he actually came to the *haus* and told us what happened." She cleared her throat against the emotion threatening to bubble up.

"I'm sorry."

"Danki."

"I started out volunteering at the station here in Ronks, but I moved to the Bird-in-Hand station about a month ago when there was an opening."

"That station is near the restaurant. It's closer to our *haus,* too, even though our address is Ronks." She picked up another chip from her plate.

"Ya, that's right."

Some of the firefighters and EMTs from that fire station still came into the restaurant for meals while they were on duty, even though Simeon was no longer there to greet them when he was off duty. Would James frequent the restaurant now too?

She pushed the ties from her prayer covering over her shoulder. "So when you were —"

"May I join you?"

Kayla tented her hand over her eyes as she looked up at Mark, standing over her with a plate. "Hi, Mark. *Ya,* you can join us." She patted the ground beside her.

Mark sank down and grinned at James. "Now I see why you ran off and left us working at the barn."

James frowned at his brother and then looked at Kayla. "What were you saying before *mei bruder* so rudely interrupted you?"

"Oh." She gave a little laugh. "I don't remember." She glanced over at James's other friends, sitting on the grass under another tree. "Why are the rest of your *freinden* sitting over there?"

Mark scooped up a spoonful of pasta salad. "They said they didn't want to bother you —"

"But you, of course, *didn't* mind bothering us," James finished.

Kayla bit back another laugh.

"I never mind bothering you, Jamie." Mark smirked as he shoved pasta salad into his mouth.

There's that nickname again. She made a

mental note to ask James about it later.

"So, Kayla," Mark began, "you have to have some great stories about working in the restaurant. What's the funniest customer story you can think of to tell us?"

"Hmm." She rubbed her chin. "I've had some funny questions from tourists."

"Oh *ya*?" James leaned forward. "Like what?"

"One time a tourist asked me how we cook without electricity. She thought we used a fire pit instead of a stove and never used an oven. I had to explain we have propane stoves and don't cook outside like someone who is camping." She laughed, and James and Mark joined in.

"Another time a customer asked me if we supply our own milk from our cows." She smiled. "As if we have time to run both a dairy farm and a restaurant."

James chuckled. "That would be an amazing feat."

She shared more stories and soon their plates were empty.

"I suppose we'd better get back to work." James gestured toward the barn, where most of the men had returned to work.

"I'll see you later." Mark hopped up and set off toward the barn, dropping his plastic dinnerware into a trash can on the way.

James stood and held out his hand to Kayla. She hesitated but then grabbed it. When their skin touched, electricity sizzled through her arms, and she bit back a startled gasp. He lifted her to her feet as if she weighed nothing. She stared up at him, wondering if he'd felt the electricity too. Had she imagined it? She'd never felt anything like that when Abram held her hand.

"I enjoyed lunch." His voice cut through her thoughts.

"I did too." She took his plate, utensils, and cup from him. "I'll toss these for you."

"Danki." He fiddled with his suspenders. "I guess I'll see you later."

"Ya." She started toward the house and then spun, remembering what she'd wanted to ask him. "James!"

"Ya?"

"I noticed your family calls you Jamie."

He shrugged. "*Ya,* that's my nickname."

"But when you introduced yourself to Nathan and me the night of the fire, you said your name was James."

"*Ya, mei freinden* and family call me Jamie, but I refer to myself as James in more formal settings, like when I'm on duty." He gave her a sheepish smile. "I know it's kind of *gegisch.*"

"Oh." She paused. "What should I call you?"

"You can call me Jamie." He smiled and then turned toward the barn.

As he walked away, Kayla's pulse fluttered, and she tried to ignore it. *No, no, no! I don't want to have feelings for a firefighter! I can't let him steal my heart. It won't end well.*

A groan escaped Kayla's lips. She'd vowed to never let another man hurt her the way Abram had. She couldn't allow herself to trust Jamie only to have him let her down and break her heart.

But it was too late. She was already falling for Jamie Riehl.

NINE

"You and Kayla were getting awfully cozy at lunch," Mark quipped as he picked up a sheet of plywood and handed it to Jamie.

"Getting cozy?" Jamie narrowed his eyes. "I don't see how eating lunch together is getting cozy." He set the plywood against the barn's wall frame and held it steady with his left forearm while holding a nail between his finger and thumb.

"She was very friendly with you." Mark stood behind him, and Jamie ignored him as he began to hammer the nail. "In fact — I'll say it again — I think she likes you."

With that, Jamie lost his concentration and missed the nail, sending a shockwave of pain from his thumb, through his hand, and up his arm. Sucking in a deep breath, he dropped the hammer and began to dance around. Shaking his hand and stamping his foot, he groaned and tucked his hand under his arm.

Mark grinned. "Did that hurt?"

Jamie bit his lip. "I'm fine."

"Did you break it?" Mark lifted another sheet of plywood.

Jamie examined his thumb, now bright red. He moved it and the pain flared. "I don't think so." He shook his head as the pain continued to throb. "Okay, that hurts."

"Did I say something wrong?" Mark placed the plywood against the wall frame and balanced it with his forearm.

Jamie ignored his brother's teasing tone and turned his attention to his task. He lined up the sheet of plywood again and lifted the hammer, careful to aim for the nail and not his throbbing thumb. He hammered it in and then started on another one. He hoped the subject would change, and relief washed over him when Mark began nailing a sheet of plywood beside him. They worked in silence until both sheets were firmly attached to the frame.

As Jamie picked up another sheet of plywood from the pile and began lining it up, Mark leaned back against the wall beside him, lifted his straw hat, and swiped the back of his hand over his sweaty brow. "You like her too."

So he's still not going to drop the subject. "Sure I do." Jamie lined up his nail. "I like her as a *freind.* But that's it. We're just *freinden.*"

"No, it's more than that."

Jamie closed his eyes and released a long, frustrated breath. "Why won't you let this go?"

"Because I don't want to see you miss out on this opportunity. You've finally found a *maedel* you like, and she likes you too. You need to go for it before it's too late."

Jamie smacked the nail into place and glanced over at Mark. "Don't you think you need to take a look at your own life instead of worrying about mine?"

Mark stood up straight. "What's wrong with my life? Plenty of *maed* like me."

"Exactly." Jamie pointed the hammer at him. "Why haven't you bothered to pick one instead of leading on nearly every *maedel* in your youth group?"

"I don't lead anyone on. I haven't made any promises to any of them. They know where I stand."

"Do they?" Jamie leaned against the plywood. "Is that why Franey and Ruthann were both vying for your attention Sunday night?"

Mark's lips pressed into a thin line. "They both know I'm not looking for anything serious."

"Do they truly know that? Then why do they hang on your every word? They're waiting for you to ask them out. They both think they have a chance at marrying you."

"Marrying me?" Mark scoffed. "I never said I wanted to get married."

"Maybe I don't want to get married either." Jamie turned back to his work.

"Well, you're twenty-five, and I'm only twenty-three," Mark continued. "You need to start thinking about getting married. Don't take a chance at messing this up."

Jamie hammered in a nail in an effort to drown out his brother's words. He didn't need or want a lecture about dating Kayla. Now wasn't the time for him to think about dating and getting married. He had too much to do and too many responsibilities.

"Hey, I was talking." Mark stepped over to Jamie. "You know she likes you, so what are you waiting for?"

"Who likes Jamie?" Noah appeared, flanked by Rudy and Allen. Each man held a hammer.

"No one does." Jamie looked toward the far end of the barn where the three men had been working. "You've all been busy, huh? You're further along than we are."

"Are you talking about the *maedel* you were eating lunch with?" Rudy picked up a sheet of plywood.

"You don't need to worry about that." Jamie nodded toward the pile. "Do you need help carrying supplies?"

"Are you avoiding the subject?" Rudy turned to Allen. "It looks like Jamie finally found himself a girlfriend."

Jamie craned his neck to glare at his brother. "*Danki* for bringing this up."

"What?" Mark gave him a mock innocent expression. "I have no idea what you're talking about."

Mark shot Noah a grin, and suspicion simmered in Jamie's gut. Why was Mark pushing him to date Kayla, and why was Noah getting involved?

"Let's get the plywood," Allen said. "We have plenty to do before the sun goes down. No time for chatting."

"Mark and I will help you," Jamie offered.

A few minutes later Jamie and Mark were once again working in their own area, this time in silence. Jamie was grateful for the opportunity to concentrate on the work without receiving a lecture.

"Jamie," Mark suddenly said.

"What?" Jamie lifted his hat and swept a palm across his sweaty brow.

"I'm not trying to tell you what to do, but I'm worried about you." Mark gestured

145

toward the farmhouse. "Kayla seems great. I think you should see if your friendship can become something more." He groaned and looked up toward the sky. "That sounds so sappy, but you know what I mean." He shrugged and took another sheet of plywood from the pile. "It's just a suggestion."

Jamie glanced toward the house and felt a tug on his heart. Could his brother be right about Kayla? He banished the thought and picked up his next nail. A list of unfinished chores filtered through his mind as he tried to ignore thoughts of Kayla and her beautiful smile.

Kayla gathered the empty serving trays, stacked serving utensils on top of them, and started up the path toward the back porch. When she reached the top step, she stopped and looked toward the barn. Jamie and Mark were close enough that she could spot them, and they seemed to have fallen into a rhythm as they hammered sheets of plywood onto the barn's wall frame.

"I think the men enjoyed lunch."

Kayla swiveled. Laura Dienner stood at the bottom step, her fingers looped through the handles of four plastic iced tea containers, all drained dry.

"*Ya,* I think you're right." She lifted the

trays. "All the food is gone."

"*Ya.*" Laura paused for a moment, a smile growing on her lips. "I've heard a lot of *gut* things about you."

"You have?"

Laura pointed two of the empty containers toward the barn. "Mark said he and Jamie ate at your restaurant the other day, and the meat loaf was fantastic. He also said you and Jamie are friendly."

"He did?"

"*Ya.*" Laura shrugged. "Jamie is sort of shy with *maed,* but don't let that fool you. I think he's fond of you."

"Really?" Kayla loathed the desperation in her voice. She cleared her throat. "He seems very nice."

"*Ya,* he is. He's kind of serious, too, and he needs to be reminded to have fun. But he's a really *gut* man."

Kayla considered the Riehl family as more questions rolled through her mind. "Is Jamie the oldest?"

"*Ya.* He's twenty-five." Laura set the empty containers on the railing. "Mark and I are twenty-three, and Cindy is the youngest. She's seventeen."

"Are you and Mark twins?"

"*Ya,* we are. I'm five minutes older than he is." Laura rolled her eyes. "Sometimes it

147

feels more like five years. You know how *buwe* can be."

Kayla laughed. "*Ya,* I do." She nodded toward the barn where Nathan stood talking to her father and a few of the volunteers. "Have you met *mei bruder,* Nathan? He's fourteen."

"No." Laura's eyes followed Kayla's. "I haven't met him. You'll have to introduce me. Mark told me Nathan really took to Jamie. Apparently they bonded over firefighting. He said Nathan wants to volunteer too."

"*Ya,* that's true." Kayla frowned. "He's determined to become a firefighter."

Laura's smile faded. "I heard about Simeon too. I'm very sorry for your loss."

"*Danki.*" Kayla liked Laura. She seemed straightforward and thoughtful.

Eva appeared and climbed the steps, holding all the unused utensils, plates, and cups. "I think we got everything off the tables."

Cindy came up behind her with the tablecloths, and they both climbed the steps. Cindy gave Kayla a shy smile.

"I'll fold up the tables after I carry in the trays," Kayla said.

"Nathan can do it later." Eva nodded toward the door. "Would you please open that, Cindy?"

"I've got it." Laura scooted over, set down two of her jugs, and wrenched it open.

"Danki," Eva and Kayla both said. Kayla followed Eva into the kitchen and set the serving trays on the counter. She glanced around. "Where's *Mamm*?"

"I think our mothers are in your sewing room upstairs." Cindy stepped into the kitchen and dropped the tablecloths on the table. "I heard them talking about quilting earlier and your *mamm* offered to show mine a few of her designs."

Kayla began to fill one side of the sink with hot, soapy water. "I didn't see them come inside."

"Do you quilt?" Cindy stepped over to the counter beside Kayla.

"*Ya*, but not very well." Kayla nodded toward Eva. "She's a much better quilter than I am."

"That's not true." Eva wagged a finger at Kayla. "You're a *gut* quilter. You just don't quilt very often." She rested her hand on her hip. "Honestly, I don't know how *Mamm* finds the time to quilt. We're so busy at the restaurant and then we get home late in the evening."

"I think it's her favorite way to relax after cooking all day." Kayla began to wash one of the serving trays.

149

"I'm going to go check on Junior." Eva started toward the doorway that led to her apartment. "He should be waking up from his nap."

"May I come with you?" Cindy offered. "I'd like to meet your *sohn.*"

"I'd like that." Eva gestured for Cindy to follow her into the apartment, and they disappeared through the doorway.

Laura deposited her empty iced tea containers on the counter, sidled up to Kayla, and picked up a dish towel. "How about I dry?"

"That would be great." Kayla finished washing the first serving tray and set it in the side of the sink she'd filled with clean water for rinsing. "Cindy seems very sweet."

"*Ya*, and she's also very shy and soft-spoken." Laura grinned. "I guess we're sort of opposites. She doesn't go to her youth group gatherings that often. We're trying to encourage her to go, but she likes to stay home with the family."

"I'm sure she'll find her place in the youth group soon. Does she have a boyfriend?"

Laura shook her head. "No, she doesn't. Do you?"

"No." Kayla briefly considered telling Laura about Abram and how he broke her heart, but she decided not to share something so personal. At least not yet. "I heard your boyfriend, Rudy, came to help today."

"*Ya,* he did." Laura finished drying the serving tray and set it on the counter. "I'll have to introduce you to him."

"I'd love to meet him. How long have you been together?" Kayla began on another tray.

"Three years." Laura smiled. "He's a very nice man. His *daed* owns a hardware store."

Kayla set the tray in the rinse water. "I appreciate your family and *freinden* coming today."

"We're *froh* to help." Laura started drying the second serving tray. "Eva is your sister-in-law, right?"

"*Ya,* that's right."

"She was married to your *bruder* Simeon."

"*Ya.* He died before their *sohn* was born."

"*Ach,* that's *bedauerlich.*" Laura frowned. "That had to be so difficult for you all."

"*Ya.*" Kayla wanted to change the subject. "So do you help your *mamm* quilt?"

Laura nodded. "Sometimes. Cindy is a much better quilter, but I do help. What are your most popular dishes at the restaurant?"

They chatted about recipes, and soon the serving trays and utensils were done and stowed in cabinets. They were wiping down the counters when Eva and Cindy re-

151

appeared in the kitchen. Cindy was holding Junior.

"He just woke up." Cindy rubbed Junior's head as he rested his cheek on her shoulder. "He's so sweet."

"Danki." Eva glanced around the kitchen. "You cleaned everything up already."

"Ya. And we were discussing recipes." Laura leaned back against the counter. "We'll have to set a time to bake together."

"I would like that." Kayla smiled, happy to have a new friend.

"I think Jamie would like it if we invited you over." Laura gave Kayla a knowing smile, and Kayla's cheeks heated.

Footfalls on the stairs announced *Mamm*'s and Dorothy's descent from the sewing room.

"Marilyn, you have some *schee* patterns. I just love them," Dorothy was saying.

"Oh, *danki.* If only I had more time to quilt, then maybe I could sell some of my work."

"I definitely think you could sell them. Your quilts are just gorgeous." Dorothy entered the kitchen with *Mamm* close behind her. She walked over to Cindy and smiled at Junior. "Why, hello there."

Junior moaned and snuggled closer to Cindy. Everyone laughed.

"He just woke up from his nap." Eva rubbed small circles on Junior's back. "He's a little cranky."

Junior looked up at Eva and then stretched out his arms.

"Kumm, mei liewe," Eva murmured to the baby as she took him and held him close to her chest.

"I guess we should get going." Dorothy picked up her purse from one of the kitchen chairs. "Our driver should be here. I have to get started on supper soon."

"Danki for helping us today," *Mamm* said. "It was really generous of you all to come and bring food."

"Gern gschehne," Dorothy said. "We had a great time."

"Ya, we did." Laura hugged Kayla before retrieving their serving trays. "I hope we see each other again soon."

"Ya, I do too."

Kayla followed the three Riehl women out to the porch. She waved as they climbed into the van waiting in the driveway and drove off. Kayla turned toward the barn. Now it was almost entirely enclosed with outer walls, and the roof was coming along. Men crouched on top, hammering shingles, as others continued to attach sheets of plywood to the wall frame.

153

Mamm and Eva joined her, and *Mamm* rested her hands on the porch railing. "They are such a *wunderbaar* family."

"*Ya,* they are," Eva agreed, balancing Junior on her hip. "I really enjoyed talking with them. You seemed to bond with Dorothy."

"I did." *Mamm* smoothed her hands down her black apron. "We talked about quilting and then about our childhoods. She grew up close to where I did in Lititz. We know some of the same people. We talked about maybe having a quilting bee sometime, but I'm not sure how I can fit it into our crazy schedule."

She touched Junior's head and looked over at Kayla. "I'd like to see Dorothy again soon. We can figure something out. You seemed to have gotten to know Laura well."

"*Ya,* I did. She's great." Kayla picked at a loose piece of wood on the porch railing as she considered a friendship with Laura. But would spending time with her make an already blossoming friendship with Jamie grow?

She couldn't take that risk. She had to keep a cover over her heart. Why did she even agree to have lunch with him?

"It looks like we're going to have a barn before nightfall." *Mamm* turned her attention to the volunteers. "Your *daed* said he was going to see if he could convince a crew to come back tomorrow to start painting. We're going to have to run the restaurant without him tomorrow, but the barn will be done."

"That will be *wunderbaar.*" Eva switched Junior to her other hip. "Our community certainly is a blessing."

Kayla nodded in agreement as her focus landed on Jamie. He was still working beside his brother. A pang of worry slammed through her.

He and his family were finding a place not only in her heart, but in the hearts of all the Dienners.

TEN

A week later, Jamie slung his duffel bag over his shoulder before rushing down the stairs. He was late! Why had he allowed himself to oversleep on a Wednesday morning? He never overslept, but adding extra chores to his usual list yesterday must have worn him out.

After cleaning the dairy barn in the afternoon, he'd spent hours repairing the wire fencing surrounding the chicken coop. Then he remembered he'd promised Mark he'd help him repair the barn doors. They finished that project after supper and then it was bedtime. He was sore when he climbed into bed, and the soreness was worse today. Now he had a twenty-four-hour shift at the firehouse before he came back to the farm to all the chores he still hadn't completed.

The delicious aroma of breakfast food made his stomach gurgle as his foot hit the bottom step. If only he had time to eat, but his driver had already been sitting in the driveway for ten minutes. It would be rude to ask him to wait any longer.

Jamie waved to his mother and Cindy as he hurriedly walked toward the mudroom. "Have a *gut* day. I'll see you tomorrow."

"Wait!" *Mamm* called after him, making him turn around. "Aren't you going to eat?"

"I don't have time. I'm late."

"I'll pack something for you," Cindy said. "Give me a moment, and I'll put together a plate. You can eat on your way."

"All right. *Danki.*" Jamie watched as she scurried around to put scrambled eggs, bacon, home fries, and a roll on a paper plate.

He glanced at the clock on the wall. It was 5:50, and his shift began at six. He might be late, but Brody would understand. His focus moved to the counter. Glass jars were lined up near the stove. "Are you going to can today?"

"*Ya.*" *Mamm* gestured toward the large pot on the counter. "Laura is going to spend the day with Savilla, and Cindy and I are going to can vegetables."

Jamie glanced toward the basement door and then groaned, looking up toward the ceiling. "The banister. That's what I forgot. Mark and I were going to fix it earlier in the week, but we got so sidetracked harvesting the hay Saturday and Monday. Then I had to repair the chicken coop and the barn doors. I'm so sorry." He huffed out a deep sigh as self-deprecation weighed heavily on his already-sore shoulders. He had to stay more focused. How could he be so irresponsible?

"Didn't you buy the supplies for the banister a couple of weeks ago?" Cindy carried the plate of food to him. She had covered it with cling wrap and set a napkin and plastic utensils on top.

"*Ya,* we did." Jamie frowned. "I'm so sorry. Mark and I will get on it first thing tomorrow."

"Can't Mark and *Dat* fix it today?" Cindy suggested.

"No." Jamie shook his head with emphasis. "I promised to do it, and I will keep that promise. *Dat* was complaining yesterday that his back was sore, and I don't want him to strain himself. Mark has too much to do when I'm at the firehouse. He and I will take care of it tomorrow. I'll put it at the top of my list."

Maybe if he took on more of the chores, *Dat* would have enough confidence to leave him in charge of the farm and take *Mamm* to Pinecraft after all for a much-needed

158

vacation.

Cindy continued to frown, but *Mamm* smiled. "That sounds fine."

"I'll be sure to remind you," Cindy chimed in. "And I'll tell Mark the banister is your top priority tomorrow."

"Okay," Jamie agreed. "Just do me a favor and please be careful on the stairs."

"We will." *Mamm* touched his arm. "You be careful today too."

"I will." He smiled at Cindy. "*Danki* for breakfast. Have a *gut* day." He looked back at his mother once more and then rushed out to the waiting truck.

The fire engine came to a stop in the large apparatus bay in the station, and Jamie climbed out of the passenger seat and massaged his neck with his fingertips. Exhaustion covered him like a dense fog, weighing down his steps as he walked into the kitchen.

"I hope that's our last call." Leon spoke Jamie's thoughts aloud as they walked through the door. "What was that — our sixth medical call of the day?"

"Day?" Jamie pointed toward the window where the setting sun painted the sky with bold hues of vivid colors. "It's nighttime now." He dropped into a chair and rested his forearms on the table. Every muscle in his body ached from his neck to his feet. "We haven't had more than fifteen minutes to rest all day long. I'm wiped out."

Yawning, Jamie rubbed his dry eyes and then covered his face with his hands as another yawn overtook his body.

Brody came into the kitchen. "Are you actually tired, Riehl? I didn't think you ever stopped moving. Do you want a Coke? It should help you wake up."

"Yeah, thanks." Jamie stifled another yawn. "I may not be worth anything the rest of the night if I close my eyes."

"Here." Leon set a can of Coke and packet of peanut butter crackers in front of Jamie and sat down beside him. "Have a snack."

"Danki." Jamie opened the can and took a long drink, relishing the cool carbonation on his parched throat.

"I heard the Dienner family rebuilt their barn last week." Brody sat down across from Jamie and Leon with his own Coke and packet of crackers. "Did you help at the barn raising?"

A vision of Kayla's beautiful face and bright smile filled Jamie's mind. Had it really been a week since he'd seen her? He thought about her frequently and considered going to visit her at the restaurant. Chores at the farm had taken priority, though, and he had a sudden and over-whelming feeling of regret. Did he actually miss her? She was more of an acquaintance than a friend. How could he miss someone he hardly knew?

"Jamie?" Brody leaned forward, his eye-brows raised. "Did you hear me? I asked if you helped at the barn raising."

"Sorry. I was lost in thought." He cleared his throat. "I did. My brother, Noah, and a few of our friends helped too. My mom and sisters took food and helped serve lunch." Jamie was aware he had easily slipped into only English. He still wasn't as used to speaking *Dietsch* around Brody as friends like Leon sometimes did — even though he knew his chief was comfortable with it.

"That's nice." Brody lifted a cracker from the package. "I wanted to help, but I was working."

Leon ripped open his package of crackers. "I couldn't get time off from my father's store. I heard they painted the barn last Wednesday, and it came out really nice."

Jamie sipped his Coke. "I wanted to go back and help on Wednesday, too, but we were too busy on the farm. I couldn't take another day away." *But it would have been nice to see Kayla again.*

Brody pushed back his chair and stood. "I'd better get started on the paperwork. I may need your help with the details since we've had so many calls today." He picked up his Coke and crackers and then walked toward the offices on the other side of the station.

"Just call us, and we'll help you." Jamie bit into a cracker.

"Thanks."

Leon crunched on a cracker too. "You really do look like you need a nap."

"I'm fine." Jamie swallowed another yawn. "It's just been an especially busy week at the farm. We had to harvest the hay, and stuff to repair. I just need a little caffeine, and I'll be fine."

Leon popped the last cracker into his mouth and stood. "Would you like more crackers?"

"Sure. *Danki.*"

Leon rooted around in the cabinets. "Have you seen Noah this week?" He dug out two packets of crackers and tossed one to Jamie, who immediately pulled it open.

"No, I was just wondering —"

The alarm cut through his words, followed by a voice blaring from the speaker in the kitchen. "All available units respond to 1836

162

Beechdale Road, Bird-in-Hand, fifty-two-year-old female. Serious fall with injury to the neck and head."

Jamie froze with his hand in the air and his blood ran cold. Had he heard that call correctly? His gaze locked with Leon's. "What was that address?"

Leon gaped, his eyebrows raised.

Brody appeared in the kitchen, his eyes wide. "Jamie, don't you live at 1836 Beechdale Road?"

The voice came over the loudspeaker again and panic grabbed Jamie by the neck. The voice clearly said, "1836 Beechdale Road, Bird-in-Hand . . ."

Mamm! *No, no, no!*

Jamie shot up from the table, knocking over his chair as he grabbed his gear and raced to the fire engine. He jumped into the passenger seat, adrenaline pumping through his veins. Brody and Leon joined him and the engine roared to life, siren blaring.

As Brody steered the truck down the street, Jamie switched on the radio and waited for more information to come through. He drummed his fingers on the door of the truck as worry and fear clashed within him. His heartbeat sounded loud in his ears.

"Jamie," Leon said, leaning forward and

yelling over the siren. "Jamie, it will be fine. Everything will be fine."

Jamie waved off his friend's platitudes.

Mamm *is hurt.*

"Units are responding to a fifty-two-year-old female, fall from staircase," the voice continued. "Patient is unresponsive and bleeding from head wound."

Jamie's lungs clenched and stole his breath. His mother was unresponsive. Would they arrive in time to help her? He turned to Brody as the fire truck approached an intersection. "Can we hurry?"

"We're almost there." Brody kept his eyes trained on the road ahead as they roared through the intersection and turned onto Beechdale Road. "Everything will be fine. We'll help her."

Jamie braced the door handle, ready to launch himself from the truck when they arrived. When the farmhouse came into view, his heartbeat spiked. Flashing lights from two ambulances reflected off the house.

"EMTs are here," Leon said, stating the obvious. "She's in *gut* hands."

As soon as the truck slowed, Jamie wrenched the door open and jumped from the moving truck. He took off running across the rock driveway and up the porch steps. The back door was already open and he pushed inside and through the mud-room.

At the far end of the kitchen, Mark was embracing Laura. She was sobbing on his shoulder. Increased alarm shot through Jamie. He scanned the room for his father, but he didn't find him.

"What happened?" Jamie approached his brother and sister.

"She fell." Mark's eyes were red and puffy, and his voice was hoarse. "She was carrying canning jars down to the basement and she must have stumbled. The banister gave way, and she fell over the side. She broke her —" He cleared his throat. "She broke her neck, Jamie."

The banister. No!

"Where's *Dat*?" Jamie's voice shook.

Laura pulled away from Mark and wiped her eyes. "He's down in the basement with the EMTs."

"Jamie." Brody rested his hand on Jamie's shoulder, causing him to jump. "I'll go see what's going on. You stay here."

Jamie shook his head. "No. I'll go."

"Jamie." Laura reached for his arm and pulled him back. "Let Brody go."

"I'm going." Jamie tried to pull away from her, but she held fast to his arm.

Tears rolled down her cheeks. "Jamie, you don't want to go down there. Trust me." Her voice cracked.

"It's bad," Mark whispered with tears glistening in his eyes.

Jamie yanked his arm out of his sister's grasp and hurried to follow Brody down the basement stairs. A lump swelled in his throat as the sounds of sobs filled his ears. Glancing to the right, he took in the splintered wood poles that had once held up the flimsy banister. His stomach twisted.

The sobs grew louder, and he stopped dead in his tracks as his eyes moved to the concrete floor where four EMTs hovered around his mother. She was lying with her neck twisted at an odd angle and a pool of blood trickling from under her *kapp.* Glass from broken jars littered the floor like macabre confetti as Brody approached the EMTs. They all spoke in hushed tones.

In one corner, Cindy sobbed as she pressed the side of her face into *Dat*'s chest. *Dat* rubbed her back as tears poured from his own eyes. Jamie couldn't remember a time he'd ever seen his father cry.

A strange calmness hovered over the situation. He had to be dreaming. This couldn't be happening. Any minute he'd wake up and find his mother working in the kitchen, making breakfast for him.

Jamie's heart began to pound, and then reality smacked him in the gut, knocking the wind out of him. He sank down onto a step. The EMTs weren't loading *Mamm* onto a gurney and rushing her to the hospital. That could mean only one thing.

After a moment, he stood, wobbled, and made his way down the rest of the steps.

"Brody." Jamie's voice sounded high and foreign to his own ears. "Brody."

Brody spun toward him, and shook his head. "I don't know how to tell you this." He put a hand on Jamie's shoulder. "They tried CPR and did an EKG, but she doesn't have any heart activity. I'm afraid she's gone, and there's nothing we can do." His eyes glistened with tears. "I'm so sorry."

Jamie's breath came out in a whoosh as tears stung his eyes.

"It's your fault!" Cindy came at Jamie, her finger wagging at him. "You did this! You killed our *mamm!*"

Jamie held up his hands and shook his head. "No, I never . . . I didn't . . . I would never . . ." His mind swirled with grief and confusion.

Dat came after her. "Cindy, stop. Cindy." He reached for her, and she stepped back, keeping her vehement eyes trained on Jamie.

167

Cindy continued to furiously shake a finger at him with a murderous glare. "You bought the supplies to repair the banister weeks ago, but you didn't do it! You promised you would, but you didn't. I told you this morning that Mark and *Dat* should do it, and you said no. Now-now . . ." Fresh tears streamed down her face. "Now she's gone. You did this. You *murdered* her!"

Jamie staggered backward until he stumbled over the bottom step.

Cindy choked on a sob, and *Dat* pulled her into his arms and held her against his chest. "Shh, *mei liewe,*" he murmured into her prayer covering, his voice shaking. "Just calm down."

Jamie's chest squeezed, sucking all the air out of his lungs. He glanced at his mother's lifeless body, and blood roared in his ears as Cindy's accusation hit home.

Cindy is right. This is all my fault. I killed our mother.

He needed air. He couldn't breathe. The basement walls were closing in on him.

He wiped his eyes and ran up the stairs, through the kitchen and mudroom to find the back door.

"Jamie!" Mark yelled. "Where are you going?"

Ignoring his brother, Jamie ran until he

reached the pasture fence. He leaned forward on the slats and sucked in the fresh night air. His body shook like a leaf in a windstorm, and he gripped the slats in a vain attempt to calm himself.

I killed my mother. I killed my mother. I killed my mother.

His stomach churned and acid burned his throat. Then Jamie bent at his waist and vomited.

ELEVEN

Jamie straightened and breathed in deep gulps of air, attempting to stop his body from shivering. Cindy's convicting words and the image of his mother's lifeless body echoed through his mind, over and over.

The blare of sirens crashed through his thoughts and drew his attention toward the rock driveway. The flashing lights from two police cruisers cast eerie shadows on the side of the house as the cars came to a stop behind the fire engine. Two officers leapt out and went into the house. Jamie knew it was protocol to call law enforcement to investigate when someone is found dead on arrival.

Dead on arrival.

His mother's death.

Jamie's stomach began to roil and acid again erupted in his throat. Sucking in more deep breaths, he leaned back against the fence.

"Jamie?" Brody stepped out of the shadows. "Are you okay?" He cringed. "That's a really stupid question."

"I don't think I'll ever be all right again." Jamie sniffed as tears welled up in his eyes.

"Cindy didn't mean what she said." Brody held up his hands as if to calm Jamie. "She's distraught. She was the first to go to your mother. She had to leave her and run for your father. Mark called nine-one-one, and there was nothing they could do but wait. You happened to be the one to take the brunt of Cindy's grief. But she didn't mean it. She'll apologize to you after she calms down."

Jamie wiped away a tear and then gripped the fence slat behind him as his body continued to tremble. "She doesn't need to apologize. She's right. It is my fault. It's *all* my fault." His could hear his voice growing thin and reedy.

"No, it's not your fault." Brody squeezed Jamie's shoulder. "Right now you can't see through the thick haze of your grief. It was an accident. Stop blaming yourself."

"Brody." Jamie ground out his name. "I was supposed to fix that banister two weeks ago. I kept forgetting, and when Cindy reminded me this morning, I told her not to let my dad and Mark do it. I said I would

171

do it tomorrow. And now it's too late."

"But you didn't plan for this to happen."

"That doesn't matter. It happened, and now she's gone." Jamie sank down to the ground as the weight of what he'd done settled on his shoulders. "Why didn't I at least repair that banister the day she told me it needed it? That would have been better than nothing. Then I could have replaced it as soon as I got the materials. Why didn't I make my mother's safety a priority?" He covered his face with his hands as he fought back another wave of nausea.

"Jamie?" Noah was here. "What happened? I heard the call come through and got here as soon as I could."

Jamie shook his head as words stalled in his throat. How could he say the words aloud? His mother was dead. Gone. This had to be some sort of cruel nightmare, but the pain that squeezed at his heart was real and tangible. He braced himself as Brody gave Noah a quick explanation of what happened. Noah gasped.

To avoid his sympathetic expression, Jamie looked across the driveway. A crowd of neighbors had gathered.

"Do you want me to go talk to everyone?" Brody offered.

"Yes." Jamie's voice croaked. "Thanks."

"Call me if you need me." Brody started across the driveway just as Leon stepped onto the back porch, holding a lantern. Brody met him at the steps and they both began talking to the neighbors.

"Do you want me to leave you alone?" Noah asked.

"No." Jamie cleared his throat past the thick cold knot forming there. "I need to talk." He told him about his conversation with Cindy and his mother that morning before he left for his shift. He told him how the accident was all his fault.

Noah blew out a deep gasp of air. "Jamie, I am so sorry. But it's not your fault."

"Please. Don't patronize me." Jamie rubbed his eyes where the beginning of a migraine pounded. When would he wake up from this nightmare? His thoughts turned to his father and siblings. He was certain the police officers were following procedure and interviewing them to find out exactly what happened. He rubbed his forehead as the pain throbbed, resembling a vice squeezing his brain.

"I'm not trying to patronize you." Noah's words were soft and measured. "What happened was God's will. You know that as well as I do."

"But I broke a promise to *mei mamm,* and

it ended her life. How can I live with that?"

"Lay your burden's at God's feet. He will heal your heart."

Tears began to well up as he tried to accept Noah's assurances. But as much as he wanted to believe his friend, the words seemed empty. His life and his family would never be the same without *Mamm.* How would he ever move on?

TWELVE

Kayla hummed as she took breakfast platters to a couple seated near the front of the restaurant. "Enjoy," she told them. "And please let me know if you need anything else."

When the bell on the door announced new customers, she spun and found Brody and Leon waiting, making her smile. This was a surprise. Brody and Leon hadn't been in since Simeon's death. Maybe coming had been Jamie's idea. But her good mood faded as she realized he wasn't with them.

She hadn't heard from him since the barn raising more than a week ago. She'd hoped he would come to the restaurant when he was on duty at the fire station. Honestly, she'd hoped he would visit her at her house, but that was a silly notion. She and Jamie hardly knew each other, and the idea of getting to know him was preposterous. After all, if he liked her he wouldn't have allowed this much time to pass before making time to see her.

Besides, she wasn't ready for another relationship. Heat rose to her face as she remembered every time she had to tell someone Abram stood her up again. Still, it would be nice to have Jamie as a friend. And maybe he wasn't on duty today. She didn't know his schedule.

"Good morning." She took two menus from under the stand. "It's good to see you. How are you doing today?"

Brody and Leon nodded, but she noted neither seemed as friendly as usual.

"Follow me." She led them to a table. After sharing the specials, she took their drink order and headed to the beverage station. As she headed back with two cups of coffee, she heard Leon mention Dorothy Riehl. Her footsteps slowed.

"I still can't believe what happened to Jamie's mother last night," Leon was saying. "I just talked to her the other day when I saw her at the market. It was such a tragic accident. It feels almost surreal, you know?"

"What did you say?" Kayla's pulse raced as she set the coffee on the table. "Did something happen to Dorothy?"

Brody and Leon startled at her voice. "Yes." Brody hesitated. "We actually came to tell your family the news. We got the call last night while Jamie was on duty. His mother fell down their basement steps and broke her neck. She died instantly."

"What?" Kayla gasped, crossing her hands across her heart. "Dorothy's dead?"

"Ya." Leon took a big breath. "She was carrying canned tomatoes down to the basement, and she apparently stumbled and grabbed the banister. It gave way, and she fell over the side. Cindy was in the kitchen and heard her *mamm* scream. When she got there, it was too late to help her."

Kayla's throat dried as a tear trickled down her cheek. She grabbed a handful of napkins from the holder in the center of the table and wiped her face as more tears fell. *"Ach,* no," she managed to say. "The family?"

"About what you'd expect." Brody swiped a finger over his eyes. "We were there until about midnight. They're all in shock. Viewing will be today and tomorrow, and then the funeral on Saturday."

"How's Jamie?"

Leon's expression was grave. "He's a mess."

Grief welled up inside of her as she tried to stop crying. "I'm so sorry to hear this."

She managed to take their order and then

hurried to push through the swinging kitchen doors. She leaned back against a wall and took deep breaths as her mind swirled with concern for Jamie and his family.

"Kayla?" Eva's voice sounded from nearby. *"Was iss letz?"*

"Brody is here, and Leon is with him," Kayla began as her parents and Nathan joined them. "They came to tell us Dorothy Riehl died last night." She repeated the story of Dorothy's fall as her family listened with stricken expressions. "Leon said the family is in shock. I just can't believe it. We just met Dorothy and Jamie's *schweschdere* last week. How can she be gone?" Fresh tears came to Kayla's eyes.

"*Ach,* no!" *Mamm* sank into the closest chair. "Dorothy was such a lovely woman. I was looking forward to getting to know her better. What a tragedy."

"Her poor family." Eva sniffed. "That's just so *bedauerlich.* Losing someone suddenly is incredibly difficult." She hugged Kayla. "I'm so sorry. When is the funeral? We have to go."

"Leon said the viewing is today and tomorrow, and the funeral will be Saturday." Kayla wiped her eyes.

"We'll close the restaurant a half day

tomorrow and Saturday so we can go to both the viewing and funeral," *Dat* said. "We'll cook tonight and take some food. I want to do something nice for the family." *Dat* rubbed *Mamm*'s shoulder. "I really appreciated Jamie's and Mark's help at the barn raising. We need to support their family."

Nathan looked just as upset as the rest of his family. "Was Jamie on duty when the call came in?"

Kayla nodded. "He was."

Nathan's shoulders fell. "It was probably terrible for him to respond to an accident at his own *haus.*"

"My heart goes out to them." Eva squeezed Kayla's hand. "We know how hard it is to lose someone you love in a horrible accident."

The bell on the front door rang and Kayla snapped to attention. She wiped her face with a napkin and tossed it into the trash. She had to get herself together. "We have more customers to seat."

"I'll do it." Eva touched Kayla's arm. "Do you need a break?"

"No, I'll be fine." Kayla pointed toward the coffeepot, then took her notepad out of her pocket. "Here's Brodie and Leon's order, *Dat.* I need to see if any customers need a refill." Squaring her shoulders, she picked up the coffeepot and left for the dining room.

After Brody and Leon left, Kayla somehow managed to get through the day, even if she was only going through the motions. But more than once she asked God to help her family bring some measure of comfort to their new friends.

The following afternoon Kayla balanced an aluminum foil pan with meat loaf in one hand and smoothed her hand down her black dress with the other. Then she followed her parents and Eva up the back-porch steps of the Riehls' home. Nathan trailed close behind Kayla with a basket of rolls. *Mamm* carried a peach pie.

Kayla, *Mamm,* and *Dat* had stayed late at the restaurant the night before and made this meal for the Riehl family. Kayla suggested they make a meat loaf since Mark and Jamie had enjoyed it the day the two men came to the restaurant for lunch.

As Kayla walked across the porch toward the back door, she glanced at the long line of buggies stretched along the pasture fence. The azure sky was cloudless, and the sun was bright — a cruel irony on such a sad day.

She gripped the pan as her thoughts turned to Jamie. She'd spent most of the night tossing and turning while contemplating how he and his family were coping after losing Dorothy in such a horrific accident. Staring at the dark ceiling in her bedroom, her mind had replayed Simeon's visitation and funeral. She could still hear her mother's and Eva's sobs as they stood in their family room next to her brother's coffin, doing their best to greet members of the community who had come to pay their last respects. Today was the Riehl family's turn to endure a similar tragic event.

Kayla begged God to give her both the strength and right words to comfort Jamie and his family.

She followed her parents and Eva through the mudroom and into the kitchen, where they found a sea of unfamiliar faces. A low murmur of voices filled the air as she surveyed the counters, already clogged with food for the family. The aroma of offerings such as chili, baked chicken, and freshly baked bread overpowered Kayla's senses as *Mamm* moved two serving platters aside to make room for their contributions. Kayla set her pan next to *Mamm*'s and then looked around for members of the Riehl family.

The kitchen was hot and stuffy despite

the open windows. Junior squirmed and moaned in *Dat*'s arms and then reached for Eva, who took him and held him close despite the heat. Kayla followed her parents through the doorway to the family room — also hot, stuffy, and full of people.

A middle-aged man stood at the far end of the room between Mark and Cindy. Kayla assumed he was Vernon Riehl. Next to them was the open casket. Kayla slipped closer and thought Dorothy appeared as if she were sleeping soundly. She clutched her chest and bit her lower lip, quickly dismissing more unbidden memories of her brother's visitation and turning her focus back on Dorothy's husband. Although his hair was a lighter brown than Jamie's, the family resemblance was plain. He had the same striking blue eyes.

Her breath caught in her throat as she took in the sadness etched in the man's pale face. His eyes were red and puffy as he shook an elderly man's hand. Mark's eyes looked the same as he nodded and listened to an elderly woman. Cindy gripped her father's arm. She resembled a frightened little girl, not a young woman.

Kayla blinked against threatening tears as she scanned the crowd for Jamie. Where could he be? The line of mourners waiting to talk to Mark and his father snaked around the room. She and her family took their places at the end of the line, but Kayla was determined to find Jamie. She peered across the room through the open windows. People were sitting on the front porch. She touched Nathan's arm. "I'm going to look for Jamie."

Nathan nodded. "All right. But I want to talk to Mark. He was really nice to me the day of the barn raising."

Kayla wove through the crowd, nodding at those who greeted her, and then slipped out the screen door to the front porch. Laura sat on a swing beside Rudy. A couple who also looked to be in their mid-twenties sat on rockers beside them.

"Kayla!" Laura leapt to her feet and pulled Kayla against her for a tight hug. "I'm so glad you're here."

"Oh, Laura." Kayla's vision blurred as she held on to her. "I'm so sorry. Brody and Leon came to the restaurant yesterday and told us what happened."

"Danki." Laura gestured to the young man on the swing. "Kayla, you remember Rudy." She gestured toward the couple. "This is my best *freind,* Savilla Lambert, and her husband, Allen."

"Hi." Savilla gave her a little wave. Kayla

noted she looked at least six months pregnant.

"Hello." Allen gripped Savilla's hand.

Kayla nodded before turning back to Laura. "I've been thinking of you all since Brody and Leon told us. I just can't believe it."

"I know." Laura wiped her eyes. "I had spent the day with Savilla. We did some shopping and then sewing for her *boppli*. I invited Cindy to come with me, but she wanted to stay home and help *Mamm* can." Her voice quaked. "I got home just after it happened. I keep thinking if I had been here, maybe —" She choked on a sob and Rudy jumped to his feet.

"*Ach,* Laura." He pulled her against his chest. "You couldn't have done anything. Stop blaming yourself."

Laura rested her cheek on his shoulder as tears trailed down her face.

Kayla cleared her throat and scanned the front yard, where dozens more community members stood talking. She searched each face for Jamie, but he was nowhere in sight. "Where's Jamie?"

Laura's expression grew grim. "He's in the basement."

"The basement?" Kayla tilted her head to the side. "I don't understand."

"He's replacing the banister." Rudy took a fresh tissue offered by Savilla and handed it to Laura.

"Why would he do that now?" Kayla searched their faces in an attempt to understand what they were saying.

Laura looked up at Rudy as if asking him to explain.

"Jamie blames himself for Dorothy's fall. He knew the banister had to be replaced and he didn't do it right away." Rudy spoke in a hushed tone. "Mark tried to convince him to wait until after the funeral, but he refused. He insisted it had to be done today. We couldn't get him to come upstairs."

Laura's expression suddenly brightened as she reached out and touched Kayla's arm. "Maybe you could convince him to stop. He likes you. Maybe he'll listen to you."

"I don't know," Kayla hedged. "We don't know each other very well. I don't see how I can help at a time like this."

"Please try." Laura's eyes pleaded with Kayla.

Kayla nodded. "*Ya,* of course I will."

"*Danki.*" Laura pointed toward the front door of the house. "The basement door is right off the kitchen. You might hear him hammering."

"I'll do my best." Kayla went into the house and wove through the knot of mourners as she made her way to the kitchen. She saw more than one door, all closed. Listening intently, she could hear hammering even above all the voices, and she went to the door that seemed to be the way down.

She gripped the knob, closed her eyes, and silently prayed she could be a blessing to Jamie.

THIRTEEN

Kayla hesitated and took a deep breath as she continued to grip the cool doorknob. Despite her prayer, doubt invaded her resolve. Was she the best person to talk to Jamie? She didn't know him well enough to offer her condolences and comfort at a time like this, did she?

Then Kayla remembered the desperation in Laura's eyes. She'd promised her new friend she'd do her best to help Jamie. She couldn't let Laura down. Her stomach clenched as she opened the door and stepped onto the basement stairs. She quietly pulled the door shut behind her and placed her hand flat on the wall as she negotiated the first three steps. Her eyes moved to take in the expanse of the basement.

It was full of shelves holding a variety of canned goods, boxes, random pieces of furniture, and tools. Splintered pieces of wood — surely remnants of the broken banister — littered the gray cement floor. A pile of new wood, along with nails and tools, sat next to the splintered pieces.

Jamie was hunched over the bottom step, hammering one of the pieces of wood that lined the steps, ready to serve as the base for the new banister. He looked up, and when his gaze locked with hers, she held her breath. His normally bright eyes were dull and red-rimmed, and his mouth was pressed into a thin line. He placed the hammer on the bottom step and pushed his hand through his hair. "Kayla."

Suddenly speechless and wringing her hands, she took a fresh breath and searched her mind for something to say. "I'm so sorry."

"Danki." He gave her a curt nod and then hesitated. "How did you know I was down here?"

"Laura told me." She waited for him to say something, but he remained silent, his eyes fixed on hers. "Do you want to talk?"

He shook his head.

"Okay. Is it all right if I keep you company while you work?"

He hesitated, but then said, "*Ya,* that's fine."

She sank onto the step, tucking the skirt

of her dress behind her legs. Then she rested her elbows on her knees and calmed herself as Jamie returned to hammering.

For several minutes, he continued working, adding another piece of wood between two of the posts already there. She studied his bleak expression, silently willing him to open up to her. He looked as if he carried the weight of the world on his broad shoulders.

"It's my fault," Jamie suddenly said, his voice sounding small and unsure as it echoed in the large basement. He stepped back from the staircase and gestured toward it. "If I had done this weeks ago, *mei mamm* would still be alive."

"That's not true," Kayla insisted. "Whatever happens is God's will, and there's nothing you could have done."

"That's what Noah said, but I have a difficult time believing that." He set the hammer on the bottom step and looked up at her. His voice shook and his eyes shimmered with tears. "When the call came over the radio, I was at the fire station. We'd had a busy day, and I was exhausted. When I heard my address, at first I thought I had imagined it." He went on to describe everything that happened, including Cindy's reaction and when Noah tried to reassure him he wasn't to blame for his mother's accident.

As Kayla listened to his story, her throat dried and her eyes filled with fresh tears. She held her breath in an attempt to keep herself from crying.

He jabbed his chest twice with one finger. "I know it's my fault. I told Cindy I would fix the banister first thing the next morning, but now *mei mamm* is dead and *mei schweschder* hates me." The pain in his face nearly sliced her heart in two.

"Your *schweschder* loves you," she said, her own voice quavering. "She's just upset and she took her grief out on you. I was broken when Simeon died and I took my emotions out on other people. I remember lashing out at Nathan more than once, but I love Nathan. Cindy doesn't hate you."

"*Ya,* she does. She hasn't looked at me or spoken to me since it happened, and I don't blame her because I hate myself too." His voice broke and his handsome face crumpled as a choked sob escaped. He sank to his knees and covered his face with his hands.

Kayla launched herself down the stairs, and, without thinking, knelt on the hard floor to wrap her arms around his neck, pulling him against her. At first, his body

190

went rigid, but he suddenly relaxed against her, burying his face in the crook of her neck as he sobbed.

"I'm so sorry," she murmured as she held him close, tears pouring down her cheeks. "I'm so sorry."

After several minutes, he stopped crying and drew back. She released his neck, and he stood up straight and rubbed his eyes. He reached for her hand and pulled her to her feet. Although she longed to console him, she resisted the urge to reach up and wipe the tears from his cheeks. After all, she'd already been much too forward and bold, but how could she not comfort a grieving friend?

"I've been holding that in since it happened." He glanced at the corner and then brought over two folding chairs. After opening them, he tapped one. "Would you please sit with me?"

"*Ya,* of course." She lowered herself onto the chair as he sat down across from her.

"I'm so glad you're here." He cupped his hand to his forehead. "It's been a horrible couple of days. I keep thinking I'm going to wake up and find this is a bad dream, but it isn't." He folded his hands in his lap as he looked at her. "You should be at work."

She shook her head. "We closed the restaurant this afternoon."

"Your parents closed the restaurant for my family?"

She nodded. "Of course we did. We're *freinden,* right?"

"Ya." Jamie stared down at his hands, and she sensed his unbearable sadness and grief. Kayla longed to take away his pain. She reached for his hand but then pulled her arm back. She'd already been too brazen, and she didn't want to give him the wrong idea. If only he would tell her everything going on in his mind, she could try to help him.

"Jamie," she began, and his eyes snapped to hers. "Please talk to me."

"I don't even know what to say." He folded his arms over his wide chest. "I'm so confused."

"It might help you if you talk about how you're feeling."

He looked over at the stairs, and his eyes glistened with unshed tears. "I asked *Mamm* and Cindy to be careful on the stairs that day, but I never imagined the loose banister would cause something like this. Mark and I bought the supplies weeks ago, and we meant to fix the banister more than once. But other chores took priority. If I had only known what would happen, I would have replaced it the day we bought the wood and nails. Now it's too late."

"You have to stop punishing yourself." She pointed to the basement ceiling. "You should come upstairs with me. Have you eaten?"

He shook his head. "I haven't been hungry."

"Let's go get something to eat." She stood and held out her hand. "There's all kinds of food upstairs. The kitchen smells wonderful."

He shook his head. "No, I can't go up there."

"Why not?" She continued to hold out her hand in the hopes he'd take it. "Hundreds of people have come to express their condolences. The community cares about you and your family."

"I can't face them. Besides, my family doesn't want me around."

"That's not true." She let her arm fall to her side. "Laura asked me to come down and convince you to come upstairs. You should be with your family."

His expression hardened. "That's why you came down here? You're just trying to help Laura?"

"No." She shook her head. "I was looking for you. I've been worried about you since

Brody and Leon told me what happened. When I couldn't find you in the *haus,* I asked Laura where you were. She told me you were down here. She did ask me to try to convince you to come upstairs, but I would have done that anyway."

The door opened and Kayla walked over to the staircase to see who was coming.

Nathan appeared on the steps and shut the door behind him. "I've been looking for you. Laura said to come down here." He looked at Jamie, his face expressing the empathy Kayla knew he felt. "I'm so sorry about your *mamm.*"

"*Danki.*" Jamie stood. "It was nice of you to come."

Nathan scanned the basement and then looked at Jamie once again. "Do you need help with the banister?"

Jamie's facial muscles tensed. "You want to help me?"

"Why not?" Nathan shrugged. "You helped rebuild our barn."

Jamie's expression softened. "I suppose that's true. I'd appreciate the help."

"Let's get started." Nathan pointed at the pieces of wood Jamie had nailed to the stairs. "I guess you're ready to put the banister on now. I'll hand you the nails while you hammer." He turned toward

194

Kayla. "Looks like you'll be the supervisor."

"*Ya,* I can handle that." She sat back down in the folding chair as her heart swelled with admiration for her younger brother. Nathan and Jamie set to work.

An hour later, Jamie surveyed the finished banister. He'd hoped replacing the banister would begin to repair the gaping hole in his chest, but it felt just as big as when he first walked down the stairs.

Mark had begged Jamie not to deal with the banister today, but Jamie couldn't bring himself to face their community. He also couldn't stomach the accusatory looks Cindy threw at him every time he looked at her.

"You don't like it." Nathan broke through Jamie's mental tirade.

"What?" Jamie rubbed the back of his neck in an attempt to loosen his tight muscles.

"I said you don't like it."

"I didn't say that. It's fine." Jamie ran his fingers over the homemade banister. It was simple but functional. Substantial. "I appreciate the help."

"I wasn't much help. Woodworking isn't really my gift." Nathan gave him a crooked smile, then turned to his sister. "I guess I'm better at washing dishes, right, Kay?"

"You're an expert at wiping down tables." Kayla said, laughing, and Jamie enjoyed the sweet sound.

"See?" Nathan said. "My true gift is working in a restaurant. I don't think that will impress the *maed* in my youth group, though."

"I suppose it will impress a *maedel* who doesn't like to cook." Jamie snickered despite the heaviness still in is chest.

"See, there's hope for you yet, Nathan." Kayla sidled up to Jamie and touched his arm. "It's *gut* to see you smile. I promise you life will look brighter in time. Just give yourself space to grieve."

"Danki." Jamie took in her porcelain skin and the golden hair peeking out from under her prayer covering. She was beautiful. More beautiful than he'd remembered.

Having her close was a welcome balm to his soul. He'd retreated to the basement to escape the crowd, but also to try to hide from the suffocating bereavement sucking the life out of him. He'd hoped replacing the banister would somehow help his soul. But, of course, it hadn't.

Jamie was afraid Kayla would flee from the basement when he started crying. Some people were uncomfortable with emotion from others. But instead she wrapped him in her arms and consoled him. It was as if she'd known exactly what he needed. He felt safe in her arms. Being with her felt natural, but he was a mess. If only his life were different, then maybe he *would* snatch her up before another man had the chance.

She tilted her head as she looked at him. "Are you all right?"

"*Ya.*" Jamie cleared his throat. "I'm really glad you and Nathan came today. *Danki* for coming down here."

"*Gern gschehne.*" She turned to her brother. "We've been down here for quite a while. I guess we should see if *Mamm* and *Dat* are looking for us."

Nathan pointed to the wood shavings, nails, and broken banister pieces on the floor. "Why don't I help clean this up before we head upstairs?"

Jamie shook his head. "No, don't worry about the mess. I can take care of it next week."

"I insist." Nathan began piling up the unused wood and nodded toward a broom in the corner. "Would you please sweep up, Kay?"

"No." Jamie touched her arm. "I don't want you to get your dress dirty." He turned to Nathan. "I appreciate the offer, but I'll take care of it next week. Mark will help me."

"All right." Nathan shook his hand. "If I can help with anything on the farm, just let me know. I can come over next weekend and give you and Mark a hand if you need it."

Gratitude swelled inside Jamie. "I appreciate that very much. You were a great help, and I think you can do more than wash dishes."

Nathan chuckled. "That means a lot. Hopefully I'll be fighting fires alongside you someday — if I can ever convince my parents to allow me."

Out of the corner of his eye, Jamie could see Kayla frown. That was still a sore subject. He braced himself for her disapproval, but to his surprise she remained silent. Was she considering changing her mind about Nathan's desire to become a firefighter?

"I hope to see you again soon. I'll go find *Mamm* and *Dat.*" Nathan started up the stairs.

Jamie swiveled toward Kayla. She was still frowning. They stared at each other, and he had the sudden urge to hug her. He longed to feel her warm embrace.

"Nathan was a great help to me," he

finally said, gesturing toward the banister.

"*Ya.* He's a *gut* young man." She hesitated for a moment. "When I lost *mei* older *bruder,* people offered a lot of platitudes and empty words to my family and me. I don't want to say anything that might sound empty and meaningless."

"You haven't. You've been really helpful."

"I'm glad." Her eyes glistened. "When I lost Simeon, I thought it would hurt forever. It still hurts, but the pain does lessen with time. Give your heart time to heal, Jamie. And if you need someone to talk to, please reach out to me."

"I will."

She took a step toward him, and he held his breath, certain she was going to hug him.

Instead, she gave him a sad smile. "Are you going to come upstairs? I'm sure my parents would like to see you before we go home."

He shook his head. "No, I think I'll stay down here."

"You might feel better if you're surrounded by your family and community." She gestured for him to follow her to the stairs. "Come up and have something to eat."

"No, *danki.* I'm fine." He forced a smile, but it felt more like a grimace.

"All right." She didn't look convinced, but she walked over to the stairs and climbed two steps before turning back toward him. "You take care of yourself."

"I will." As she disappeared up the stairs, he fought the overwhelming urge to ask her to stay.

When he heard the door close behind her, he glanced around the basement, taking in the mess he'd made. He decided to clean up the basement after all. He cut up the broken pieces of wood and placed them in a large trash can before piling leftover new pieces in the corner. After he swept up the wood shavings and put away the nails, he surveyed the basement again. The work was done, and he didn't have any more reason to stay downstairs alone. Besides, most of their visitors should have left by now.

Taking a deep breath, he climbed the stairs and entered the kitchen. A few women from his church district were scurrying around the kitchen, cleaning the counters and stowing food in the propane-powered refrigerator. The well-meaning women stopped chatting when he passed through the room. He nodded greetings and moved through the room quickly, determined to avoid awkward conversation.

He stopped in the doorway leading to the

family room. His father stood by the casket surrounded by his three siblings. Jamie looked at his mother's serene expression, and his eyes filled with new tears. Kayla's words echoed in his mind.

You might feel better if you're surrounded by your family and community.

Perhaps she was right. Perhaps he needed his family's support to help heal his broken heart. And maybe, just maybe, his family needed him as much as he needed them.

Jamie took a step into the family room, and Cindy's gaze snapped to his. Her sorrowful expression transformed into a hateful glare, and he halted. No, his family didn't need him. In fact, he was the last person Cindy needed right now.

Turning on his heel, he stalked toward the stairs and headed up to his room.

"Jamie!" Mark's voice echoed in the stairwell. "Jamie! Come back."

Jamie reached the top of the stairs and looked down at his brother. "I really just need to be alone right now." He headed down the hallway, entered his room, closed the door behind him, and sank onto the corner of his bed.

Mark pushed the door open and stood on the threshold. "You've been alone all day.

Come downstairs and be part of the family."

"I'd rather be alone."

Mark pointed in the direction of the stairs. "We're going to eat. Come and eat with us."

"I'm not hungry." Jamie kicked off his shoes and stretched out on his double bed, resting his head on his pillow.

Mark leaned a shoulder against the doorframe. "You're part of this family, Jamie. We should all be together right now."

"I don't think Cindy would agree with you. She looks as if she would like me to move out." Jamie folded his arms behind his head. "I might start building that *haus Dat* talked about letting me construct on the other side of the pasture once I found a *fraa*. I think it's time I had my own place."

Mark folded his arms across his chest. "I don't think now is the time for you to move out. Not after what we've just been through. We all need each other. Things will never be the same without *Mamm.*"

Jamie glared at his brother. "I know that."

"Look, you might feel like you need to be alone, but *Dat* needs us more than ever. Stop being so stubborn and come downstairs. Have something to eat and be with the rest of us." Mark took a step into the hallway. "Come on."

"No, *danki.*" Jamie closed his eyes. "I'm going to take a nap." He expected to hear his brother's footfalls heading toward the stairs, but instead there was silence. He opened his eyes and found Mark staring at him. "I told you I'm not going to join you right now."

Mark didn't move from the doorway. "Did you finish the new banister?"

"*Ya.* Nathan Dienner helped me."

"I would've helped you build it next week."

"It's done. Don't worry about it." Jamie closed his eyes. He waited for the sound of his brother's footsteps, but again it was quiet.

"You know, Jamie, if you let people in, you wouldn't be so lonely," Mark's voice was soft but firm.

Jamie opened his eyes as his brother disappeared into the hallway. Soon he heard Mark's footsteps echo down the stairwell. The silence in his bedroom roared in his ears as guilt threatened to drown him. The events of the past few days assaulted his mind, and his chest squeezed yet again with suffocating grief.

He again replayed his conversation with Kayla and the warmth of her arms as she consoled him. How he longed to have a woman like her in his life, but she deserved better. He was a failure to his family, especially his mother. He'd trained to become a firefighter to help people, and he couldn't even save his own mother. He wasn't worthy of the uniform or the title of firefighter.

Rolling to his side, he buried his face in his pillow. If only he'd done what he should have, none of this would be happening. His family would be intact, and he would be ready to start a relationship with someone like Kayla Dienner.

But he couldn't travel back in time, and he couldn't fix the mistakes he'd made. He had to find a way to push forward. He just had no idea how to start.

Tomorrow he would have to stand with his family and endure his mother's funeral. He didn't have the strength to say good-bye to her when it was his fault she was gone.

Jamie opened his heart to pray, but he couldn't form the words. He squeezed his eyes shut. Maybe God would guide him through the toughest day of his life, even if he didn't know how to ask.

FOURTEEN

Kayla held a tissue to her nose as she stood at the back of the crowd gathered around Dorothy's grave. Her stomach clenched and the scent of moist earth seemed overwhelming as she watched two sons shovel dirt over their mother's coffin.

The minister read a prayer as her heart broke for Jamie and his family. She was thankful for her tall stature, enabling her to see Jamie from where she stood between Nathan and her father. Eva had stayed home with Junior, but the rest of the family attended the funeral.

When the prayer ended, a murmur of conversation spread throughout the crowd. Kayla scanned the Riehl family from where she stood. Laura leaned on Rudy as she wept, and Cindy clung to her father's arm. Mark wiped his eyes as he spoke to Savilla and Allen. Jamie stood about a foot away from his family, as if he were only an acquaintance. The pain etched on his face as he stared at the freshly covered grave nearly crushed Kayla's soul. He needed a friend, and she longed to be that friend.

But would she be too bold if she approached him alone again today? Would he and the other members of the community brand her a brazen woman?

She banished those thoughts. Jamie needed a friend, and she could be that friend despite what members of the community might think of her.

Kayla touched her father's arm. "I'm going to talk to Jamie."

Dat nodded. "All right."

She wove through the crowd, moving past the knot of people gathered around the rest of Dorothy's family. She stepped behind Jamie, now a solitary figure at his mother's grave.

"Jamie." When he didn't respond, she spoke his name again. "Jamie."

He swiveled his head and met her gaze, and the pain in his eyes was almost too much to bear.

"Kayla." His voice sounded hoarse. "I didn't realize you were here." He craned his neck, looking past her. "Your parents and Nathan are here too?" He met her gaze again. "Did you close the restaurant again?"

"*Ya,* we did."

He shook his head. "Your family is losing two days of business for my family."

"No, we're going to open this afternoon. We only missed a half day yesterday, and it's a half day again today." She shrugged. "You and your family are more important than a day of work."

She tilted her head. "How are you?"

"I don't know. I'm just here." He looked toward his family and she did too. His siblings and father were still receiving hugs from community members. "*Mei daed* hasn't eaten much. I'm worried about him. I heard him crying in his room this morning. That was surreal."

He turned back to her. "Cindy is still upset with me. I tried to talk to her last night before I went to bed, but she wouldn't answer me. She walked away and went to her room. This morning I walked into the kitchen and she turned her back on me. I don't think she'll ever forgive me." His voice quavered. "I feel like I've lost *mei mamm* and *mei schweschder.*" His face crumpled and he cleared his throat again as if fighting to hold back his emotions.

"It will get better. I promise you." She longed to comfort him, but if she touched him in public, she risked embarrassing herself and earning a questionable reputation. "Give it time."

"Ya." He blew out a long sigh.

"Kayla." Laura appeared at her side and pulled her into a hug.

"I'm so sorry, Laura." Kayla hugged Laura tight.

"Danki." Laura released Kayla and touched Jamie's arm. "We'll get through this somehow."

Jamie nodded, but he didn't look convinced.

"Laura." Savilla looped her arm around Laura's shoulders and nodded at Kayla. "Hi, Kayla." She whispered something to Laura as she nudged her toward a group of young people.

Kayla turned her focus back to Jamie. "Can I do anything to help you and your family?"

"No, *danki.* We're supposed to just move forward, right?" He looked toward his father again, and Kayla did as well. Tears rolled down Vernon's face.

She reached out and touched Jamie's arm, despite the risk to her reputation. He needed her comfort. "Lean on your family and your *freinden.* Your community will help you through this."

He opened his mouth to respond to her,

but Noah, Leon, Brody, and a group of *Englishers* Kayla assumed were members of the fire department had walked over. They began shaking his hand.

"Jamie." Noah nodded a greeting to Kayla. "Hi, Kayla."

Kayla nodded in response.

A pretty woman sidled up to Kayla while balancing a toddler on her hip. "Hi, I'm Elsie Zook. Noah is my husband."

"I'm Kayla Dienner." Kayla touched the young boy's arm. "Who is this?"

"This is Christian." Elsie shifted him on her hip, and he buried his face on the shoulder of her black dress. "He's ready for a morning nap."

The boy had dark hair and eyes, like his parents.

"He's a handsome *bu*." Kayla rubbed his arm. "How old is he?"

"Eighteen months." Elsie touched his pink cheek. "He's heavy."

"Would you like me to hold him?" Kayla held out her arms.

"Oh, no, *danki*. He's fine. I'm building up my muscles, right?" Elsie nodded toward Jamie, who was still talking with the group of men. "How is he doing?"

Kayla frowned and lowered her voice. "I don't think he's doing well at all. He told me Cindy won't talk to him. She blames him for the accident."

Elsie clicked her tongue. "Noah mentioned that to me too. I hoped Cindy would have realized by now we can't change God's will. It wasn't Jamie's fault." She rubbed Christian's back. "I'm so sorry they're going through this. It's just so painful."

"Have you known the Riehl family a long time?"

"*Ya.* Noah, Jamie, and I are the same age. We went to school together and we were in the same youth group." She rested her chin against Christian's head. "I've known the Riehl family nearly my whole life. Dorothy was like another mother to me. It's difficult to believe she's gone." Her bottom lip quivered. "I'm worried about Jamie. He always keeps his feelings bottled up. I'm glad he has you. You'll help him through this."

Kayla held up her hands. "Oh, you have the wrong impression. We're not a couple."

Elsie raised her eyebrows. "Noah told me Jamie likes you. I could see it earlier when he was talking to you. You're just what he needs right now."

"No, it's not like that at all. Jamie and I don't really know each other that well."

Christian started to moan, and Elsie

210

shifted him on her hip once again. His moans transformed into sobs as he rubbed his eyes.

"He definitely needs a nap." Elsie stepped over to Noah and touched his arm. "I think we need to get Christian home."

"*Ya,* it looks that way." Noah took his son from Elsie.

"It was nice talking to you," Elsie said before she and Noah made their way through the crowd to the waiting horses and buggies.

Kayla hugged her arms to her chest as she turned toward Jamie, still surrounded by friends. She scanned the multitude of mourners and spotted her parents talking with Vernon. She made her way to where Nathan spoke to Mark. Like Jamie's, Mark's eyes were bloodshot, and his face was lined with bereavement. An overwhelming empathy for him almost made her stumble.

"Hi, Kayla." Mark shook her hand. "It was nice of you to come today."

"I'm so sorry, Mark."

"*Danki.*"

"How are you holding up?"

"I guess we're just going through the motions right now." Mark gestured toward his brother. "Jamie's been keeping to himself. I tried to talk to him last night, but he wanted

211

to be alone. It was *gut* to see him talking to you."

"I'm not sure how much I helped him." She looked toward Vernon, who was still talking to her parents. "Jamie said your *daed* is having a tough time."

"Ya." Mark cringed. "It's been hard watching him grieve. I don't know what to do for him."

"When Simeon died, I felt that way with Eva. I just offered my shoulder when she needed to cry."

"*Ya,* that's about all you can do," Nathan offered. "Just be there when he needs someone to listen. If you need help with anything at the farm, let me know. I can come over and help you with chores."

Mark smiled at Nathan. "*Danki.* I think Jamie and I can handle it, but I appreciate the offer."

An older couple approached Mark to offer their condolences, and Kayla and Nathan moved to where their parents now waited for them. Kayla had hoped to offer her condolences to Vernon, but a crowd had gathered around him. She followed her family to their horse and buggy.

As she climbed in, she looked back toward Jamie, and Elsie's words echoed through her mind. Could Kayla be the friend he would need in the coming days?

The scent of rain wafted over Jamie as he stepped out of the barn Tuesday night. The cool mist that brushed his cheeks was a welcome change from the brutally humid days. He turned his face up toward the dark sky and relished the soothing raindrops for a moment before heading to the back porch.

He spotted a silhouette sitting in the glider. As he climbed the steps, his father's face came into view.

"I didn't realize you were out here," Jamie said when he reached the top step. "I just took care of the animals."

"Gut." Dat patted the rocker beside him. "Sit with me."

Jamie sat down and stretched his aching legs out in front of him. He'd been on his feet all day as he completed chores on the farm. His shoulders were tight, and his arms were sore. He hadn't slept more than a few hours each night since his mother passed away. He hoped he'd sleep tonight. His weary bones needed the rest.

The silence stretched between Jamie and his father as the mist transformed into rain and began a steady cadence on the porch roof above them.

"She wanted to go to Niagara Falls. And

see the Grand Canyon," *Dat* suddenly said, breaking through the silence. "I promised her I would take her someday, but someday never came."

Jamie turned toward his father. "It's not your fault you didn't get to go."

Dat rested his hands on his lap. "That's not entirely true."

"What do you mean?"

"I told her we'd go once you and Mark were old enough to run the farm." *Dat* stared out toward the pasture. "You and Mark have been capable for quite some time now, but I guess I didn't want to admit you could do it without me. So I never took her. Last fall her best *freind* went to Florida for a month. Your *mamm* wanted to go, but I told her we had too much to do here on the farm. I should have let you and Mark manage and just taken her." Painful regret reverberated in *Dat*'s voice.

Jamie's heart lodged in his throat like a chunk of ice, and he couldn't speak.

"I should have made the time to take your *mamm* where she wanted to go." *Dat* rested his ankle on his opposite knee. "Money wasn't the issue. We always saved well, and I could have afforded the trips."

"You didn't know this was going to happen." Jamie's voice sounded strained even

214

to his own ears. "No one could have imagined we'd lose her like this. Don't punish yourself."

Dat angled his body toward Jamie. "I forgot tomorrow is never promised, Jamie. Don't live your life the way I did. Don't wait to do the things you dream of doing. You never know what God has planned for you, *sohn*. Don't live with the regrets I have. Live your life to the fullest."

A flash of Kayla's beautiful face as she spoke with him at his mother's grave filled Jamie's mind. The care and understanding in her attentive eyes had warmed his soul when he'd opened up to her. When he was with Kayla, all the walls he'd built to shield his heart came tumbling down. Just looking into her eyes gave him courage to let someone in.

Jamie rejected his thoughts about Kayla. How could he think about her when his father was reaching out to him through his cloud of grief? Now wasn't the time for Jamie to concentrate on his own broken heart. He needed to put his father's emotions before his own. *Dat* lost the love of his life. He needed Jamie to carry the load of the farm. It was time for Jamie to take charge as the older son.

"Why don't you take some time off?"

Jamie suggested. "You can visit your favorite cousin in Middlefield. You always said you wanted to go out there and spend some time with him."

Dat frowned. "You're missing my point, James."

Jamie bristled at his formal name. "How am I missing the point?"

"I've already missed my chances to make those special memories with your *mamm.* Going to see Jeremiah isn't going to give me back those chances." His expression softened. "You're still young, and God willing, you have many years ahead of you. You should grab those opportunities when you can. Don't wait until it's too late."

Jamie swallowed against his suddenly bone-dry throat. "I'm so sorry, *Dat.* If I had only replaced that banister —"

"It's not your fault." *Dat* patted Jamie's arm. "Stop blaming yourself. I didn't ask you to sit with me to make you feel bad. I don't blame you for anything that happened." He pushed himself up from the glider. "It's getting late. We should go inside."

"All right." Jamie stood and opened the door. When they stepped into the kitchen they found Laura staring at a piece of paper on the counter. *"Was iss letz?"*

216

She looked at them and wiped a tear away. "I found her shopping list. We were supposed to go grocery shopping after we finished the laundry yesterday." She sniffed and held up the piece of paper. "I think I'm going to keep this." Her voice caught as tears ran in rivulets down her flushed cheeks.

"Come here, *mei liewe.*" *Dat* pulled her into his arms.

Jamie's lungs seized with memories of his mother. Her warm smile as she sang "Happy Birthday" and carried one of her delicious homemade cakes to the table. Her laughter when *Dat* made a silly joke. Her patient ear when one of her children needed her quiet, sage advice.

Grief punched another gaping hole in his chest. He needed to get out of there before he melted into a puddle on the floor. He headed up the stairs and stopped dead on the landing when he nearly bumped into Cindy.

"Cindy," he said. "Can we talk?"

She backed away from him toward her bedroom door. "I have nothing to say to you."

"Please talk to me," he pleaded, following her down the hallway. "We're siblings, and *Mamm* is gone now. We need to take care of each other."

She lifted her chin as she backed into the bedroom she shared with Laura and slammed the door. A moment later, the lock on the doorknob clicked.

He hung his head as he leaned against her doorframe. He lifted his hand to knock but then let his arm fall to his side. Maybe she just needed to be alone. Kayla said the pain would subside over time. He needed to give Cindy space to heal, and then perhaps she would realize she needed her siblings as much as they needed her. Even him.

He started down the hallway and stopped in front of Mark's closed bedroom door. For a moment, he considered sharing his conversation with *Dat.* Certainly Mark would agree they should tell *Dat* to take a break while they ran the farm. Jamie lifted his hand to knock but then again let it fall to his side. He wasn't in the mood to talk. He'd rather be alone with his confusing feelings and drowning bereavement. He could tell Mark what *Dat* said tomorrow.

Jamie went to this room and changed into shorts and a T-shirt. Then he dropped onto his bed and stared up at the ceiling as his conversation with *Dat* rolled through his mind. His father's regrets sliced through his soul like sharp knives.

It was Jamie's job to make things right now that *Mamm* was gone. He would carry the load of running the dairy farm, and he would convince *Dat* to take some time for himself.

As he rolled to his side and faced the wall, *Dat*'s words echoed in his thoughts.

You're still young, and God willing, you have many years ahead of you. You should grab those opportunities when you can. Don't wait until it's too late.

His thoughts turned to Kayla. Was *Dat* suggesting he should pursue a relationship with her? Could she be his future?

No, he couldn't worry about his future now. He had to be *Dat*'s strength. *Dat* was too embroiled in his own sadness to be the head of the family. It was his job to take care of his family and be the best emergency responder he could be. If he couldn't help his own mother, he had to at least do his best to help others in his community.

He wasn't emotionally ready to take on a relationship.

But then why couldn't he keep Kayla from invading his thoughts?

FIFTEEN

Jamie jolted out of bed when he read the clock the next morning.

Six fifteen.

He gasped and rubbed the sleep from his eyes. He'd overslept again. After staring at the ceiling for hours, sleep had found him around two in the morning. He'd planned to get up at five and feed the animals before his father got out of bed. But those plans were dashed when he'd forgotten to set his alarm.

After getting dressed, he rushed down to the kitchen. Laura and Cindy were cooking, working side by side. They'd had so many gifts of food, and had all been grieving in their own ways, they'd not sat down for a meal together since *Mamm*'s accident. The familiar aroma of eggs, home fries, bacon, and fresh rolls filled the kitchen and made his stomach gurgle.

Laura spun toward him and smiled, but

her smile was more forced than genuine. *"Gude mariye."*

"Gude mariye." He glanced at Cindy, who was flipping scrambled eggs in a large skillet. *"Gude mariye,* Cindy." He held his breath and waited for her to look at him, but she kept her back to him and her eyes focused on the frying pan. Deflated, his shoulders dropped.

Jamie turned toward the table, set for five. Staring at the bare space where *Mamm* had always sat, he suddenly felt as if his heart had been ripped from his chest.

He was alarmed to see dark circles rimming Laura's eyes as she placed a platter of home fries on the table.

"How are you?" Jamie asked.

Laura shrugged. "I'm all right."

"Did you sleep last night?"

"Maybe an hour or two." She turned toward the counter. *"Kaffi?"*

"I need to take care of the animals." He started toward the mudroom. "I'll have some *kaffi* when I get back."

"Mark already went out to take care of the animals." Laura poured a mug of coffee and handed it to him. "He should be on his way back anytime now. He went out at five."

He frowned as guilt seeped through him. He was supposed to take care of things, but he couldn't even get out of bed on time. He needed to step up and start acting like the older son.

"Danki." He took a long draw on the mug. The coffee was strong and rich, just the way he liked it.

The back door opened and clicked closed, and then Mark stepped into the kitchen. "The animals are fed." He crossed the kitchen to wash his hands in the sink. "Breakfast smells *appeditlich.*"

"Danki." Cindy looked at him. "I hope you're hungry."

"You know I'm always hungry." Mark dried his hands with a paper towel.

Jamie's shoulders clenched. Cindy would acknowledge Mark, but she wouldn't even look at him. How long would her resentment last? When would she even discuss her anger with Jamie? He pushed away his frustration and focused on his brother. He owed Mark an apology.

"I'm sorry," Jamie said. "I was going to handle the chores this morning, but I forgot to set my alarm."

"It's fine. We always share the chores, right?" Mark tossed the used paper towel into the trash can in the corner and stepped over to the table.

Laura placed a basket of bread and a platter of bacon on the table. "What are we missing?" she muttered, fingering the hem of her black apron.

"Laura, let me help you. I'll pour the *kaffi.*" Jamie filled three mugs with coffee and handed two to her. He'd pour *Dat*'s in a minute.

"Danki." Laura set them by two of the plates.

Cindy scraped the eggs onto a platter and set it on the table.

"It looks like *Dat* is going to sleep in for a while." Laura rested her hand on the back of her chair and then glanced toward the doorway leading to the family room. The doorway that led to their parents' bedroom was there. "We should eat and I'll reheat the food when *Dat* gets up."

"That's a *gut* idea." Cindy pulled out her usual chair, across the table from Jamie's, and sank down on it. "We should eat and then get started on our morning chores."

Mark sat down as Laura did the same across from her twin. Jamie lingered, standing behind his chair as he stared toward the doorway. It was unusual for *Dat* to sleep past six. What if he was ill?

"Jamie?" Mark looked up at him, his eyebrows lifted. "Are you going to eat?"

"Should we go and check on *Dat*?" Jamie

nodded toward the doorway.

"I think we should let him sleep." Laura tapped her plate. "Sit. The food is getting cold."

Jamie dropped onto his chair, folded his hands, closed his eyes, and opened his heart, silently begging God for guidance.

Please, God. Make me the sohn mei daed *deserves and the* bruder *my siblings need. I'm lost. Show me how to get through this devastatingly painful time. Help my family to heal and move on without our beloved* mamm. *Amen.*

Jamie opened his eyes, and when he saw Mark move in his peripheral vision, he sat up straight and began to fill his plate with food. Soon they were all eating, but not only did Cindy continue to reject him, his siblings were silent. Jamie couldn't remember a time when his family had eaten a meal in complete silence. Would their lives ever return to normal?

Several painful moments passed before *Dat*'s footsteps echoed from the family room. He appeared in the doorway sporting dark circles under his eyes that mirrored Laura's. Gone was the mirth Jamie had known since childhood. *Dat* took his usual spot at the head of the table.

"Gude mariye." *Dat*'s voice sounded gravelly.

Jamie and his siblings echoed the greeting.

Dat filled his plate but then picked at the food. It dawned on Jamie that his father hadn't cleaned his plate since *Mamm* passed away. *Dat* had always praised *Mamm*'s cooking and eaten every morsel of it. Jamie's hands trembled as a fresh wave of grief shook him.

Silence continued to hang over the room like a thick fog. Jamie glanced around the table and found his siblings and *Dat* staring at their plates as they moved the food around on their plates. No one seemed to have a big appetite. After several minutes, the silence began to grate on his already-frayed nerves. He needed to break the deafening silence.

"I have duty tomorrow," he blurted, causing everyone but Cindy to snap their gazes to him.

"Oh." *Dat* lifted his mug and took a sip of coffee. "That's *gut.*"

"I don't have to go in," Jamie offered. "I can tell Brody I need to stay home to help with chores. He'll understand I need to be here for my family."

"That's not necessary." Mark swiped a roll

225

from the basket. "I can handle the chores while you're on duty."

"You don't have to do all the chores, Mark," *Dat* countered. "I'll help you."

"You don't need to help." Mark's tone was insistent as he sliced open the roll. "You can rest."

Dat frowned at Mark. "We'll discuss this later." Then he looked at Jamie, his expression softening. "You don't have to skip duty. We'll handle things here."

"All right." Jamie scooped a forkful of home fries into his mouth and chewed slowly as guilt settled on his already-tight shoulders. He needed to help his family, but he also had an obligation to his community. And maybe, just maybe, helping someone in the community would ease the culpability he carried for not protecting his mother.

"Enjoy your meal." Kayla placed the roast beef sandwich platter in front of an *Englisher* who had come to the restaurant for lunch. "Please let me know if you need anything else."

"Thank you." The middle-aged man lifted half the sandwich and dug in.

She glanced toward the front of the restaurant as she walked toward the kitchen.

Another wave of disappointment washed over her. Every day she hoped to see Jamie walk through the front door. His beavered face had haunted her since the funeral, and her constant thoughts and prayers had been filled with hope for his family. As the days since the funeral had worn on, her worry for the Riehls had grown. More than once she'd considered stopping by the fire station to see if Brody had spoken to Jamie or his siblings.

As she stepped into the kitchen, an idea took hold. She looked toward her parents. *Mamm* was wiping down a counter while *Dat* flipped a burger on the grill.

"Mamm. Dat." She crossed the kitchen, and they both turned toward her, their expressions filling with curiosity. "I've been worried about Jamie and his family."

Mamm frowned. "I have too."

"Have you heard from him?" *Dat* asked.

"No, I haven't, and I think about him and his family constantly." Kayla perched on a stool beside her mother and ran her finger over the cool steel edge of the counter. "I was thinking about taking a tray of sandwiches over to the fire station and asking Brody if he's heard from him. The restaurant is quiet since the lunch rush is over. Only two customers are out there, and they

227

both have their food." She assumed the burger was for *Dat.*

"That's a great idea." *Dat* pointed to the counter. "Why don't you make the sandwiches and include that bag of chips? You can grab a gallon of iced tea too."

"Take a few pieces of pie with you as well," *Mamm* suggested. "I'll cut and wrap them."

"Danki." Kayla began pulling out the supplies to make a few sandwiches. As she worked, she silently prayed Jamie would be at the station so she could talk to him.

"Do you need help with anything?" Eva sidled up to Kayla.

"Would you please wrap this sandwich?" Kayla cut the first roast beef sandwich in half. "I'll start making another one."

"Okay." Eva grabbed the cling wrap. "Who are these sandwiches for? Do we have a take-out order?"

"No. I want to see if Brody has heard from Jamie, so I'm going to take them over to the fire station." Kayla began making a ham and cheese sandwich.

"You're going to the fire station?" Nathan appeared in the doorway holding the plastic washbasin he used to clear tables. "Can I come with you?"

Kayla turned toward her mother, who

228

nodded. "*Ya,* Nathan can go with you, if it's okay with Eva." *Mamm* placed five wrapped pieces of pie into a box. "Are you comfortable running the dining room alone while they're gone?"

"*Ya.* I don't mind at all." Eva picked up one half of the sandwich and began to wrap it. "If Jamie is there, please tell him he and his family are in all our prayers."

"I will." Kayla and Eva finished making sandwiches and then added them to the box with the chips and pie.

Kayla carried a jug of tea and Nathan carried the box down the block to the fire station. She followed Nathan inside the bay area, where they found Brody talking with Leon next to one of the fire engines.

"Hi, Brody!" Nathan called as the chief waved to them.

"Hi!" Brody said. "It's good to see you two."

Kayla greeted both men.

Leon smiled and waved as he walked over. *"Wie geht's?"*

Nathan lifted the box. "We brought you food."

"Thanks so much. Let me help you." Brody took the jug of iced tea from Kayla's hand. "I've been meaning to get over to the restaurant this week, but we've been busy

229

with training. How are you both doing?"

"Fine." Kayla glanced toward a door in search of Jamie. Then she looked back at Brody. "How are you doing?"

"Great." Brody gestured toward the same door. "Why don't we go inside?"

Kayla followed the men into their kitchen, where they set the food and iced tea on a long table.

"It's so nice of you to bring us food." Leon peered into the box. "Can you stay for a little bit or do you have to rush back to the restaurant?"

"We have a few minutes." Nathan leaned on one of the chairs. "We were wondering if you've seen Jamie or have talked to any of his siblings."

Kayla added, "We've been worried about them."

When Brody looked concerned, her heart thumped. He nodded toward a doorway. "Jamie is in the sitting room. He's been really quiet all day."

Leon shook his head, his smile fading. "He hasn't said much since he reported for duty this morning. Why don't you take some food back to him?" He pulled out a sandwich and piece of pie. "I'm sure he'd enjoy seeing you."

"All right." Kayla turned to her brother.

"Do you want to come with me?"

When Nathan hesitated, Leon jumped in. "Why don't you stay here and talk to us for a few minutes, Nathan."

"Oh." Nathan divided a look between Leon and Brody, and something passed among the three men. Were they conspiring to get Kayla to visit Jamie by herself? Maybe they believed she could cheer up Jamie if she saw him alone.

Maybe they were right.

Nathan turned toward Kayla. "Go on and see Jamie. I'll stay here and talk to Brody and Leon. I'll come and get you when it's time for us to go. We probably shouldn't stay away more than about thirty minutes. The late afternoon crowd will be at the restaurant before we know it, and we still have to get ready for them."

"All right." A strange combination of excitement and anxiety coursed through her at the idea of seeing Jamie. She opened the bag of chips. "I'll pour a cup of tea for him too."

"Let me get you a plate." Brody got a plate and stacked a fork and napkin on it. He also poured iced tea into a plastic cup. "Do you think you can carry all this?"

"Are you kidding?" She chuckled as she placed food on the plate. "I'm a waitress, remember?"

"That's true." Brody smiled. "I'm glad you came by. If anyone can cheer up Jamie, it's you."

"Thanks." Kayla's cheeks heated. She smoothed her hands over her purple dress and then touched her prayer covering before she balanced the plate in one hand and the cup in the other. She hesitated. Should she insist Nathan go with her?

Brody pointed again. "The sitting room is right through that doorway, down the hall. You remember, right?"

"Yes, I know where it is." Kayla visited Simeon at the station more than once when he was a volunteer there. She held her breath as she started forward. Doubt suddenly stole her confidence. What if Jamie would rather be alone? What if she said something that upset him instead of consoling him?

She blew out a deep breath and silently prayed.

Lord, please make me the freind *Jamie needs. Guide my words and help me offer him comfort. Amen.*

Kayla stepped into the hall and stopped at the doorway to the sitting room. It was furnished with a sofa, four recliners, and a large, flat screen television. Jamie sat in a recliner reading. His eyes were focused on his book as if he were deep in thought. Should she leave him alone? No, she had to be strong.

She cleared her throat and forced a smile on her face. "Knock, knock. Hello, Jamie? Would you like some company?" Her pulse raced as she awaited his response.

SIXTEEN

Jamie glanced up from the devotional he'd been reading. His eyes widened when he saw Kayla standing there. "Kayla. Hi. Wh-what are you doing here?"

"Surprise." She held up the plate and plastic cup. "I brought you some food from the restaurant."

He admired her beautiful face and gorgeous eyes. She gave him a shy smile, a balm to his battered soul. Was he dreaming or was she truly standing in front of him?

"Did I come at a bad time?" Her smile faded as she took a step back. "I can leave if you'd like."

"No, no. Please sit down." He gestured toward the recliner beside his.

"Okay." She stepped farther into the room and held out the plate. "I brought you a roast beef sandwich. I promise I won't drop it on you this time."

He laughed, and something inside of him

broke apart, releasing a fraction of the grief and stress he'd been holding on to so tightly since his mother passed away. Tears filled his eyes, and he wiped them away.

Kayla gnawed at her lower lip. "Oh no. I've already managed to say the wrong thing. Maybe I should go."

"No, no, no. That was funny." He wiped his eyes. "I was laughing. It's the first time I've laughed since . . ." He cleared his throat. "*Danki* for the food."

"*Gern gschehne.*" She paused. "How are you? Tell me the truth."

He blew out a deep breath. "I'm a mess."

"I'm so sorry," she whispered, her eyes shimmering.

He pointed toward the chair again. "Have a seat. It's so *gut* to see you."

"It's *gut* to see you too. I've been worried about you. Here you go." She handed him the plate and then sank into the chair. She put the cup on a nearby table.

"*Danki.*" After a silent prayer he unwrapped the sandwich. "Have you eaten?" He took a bite and savored the flavor.

"*Ya,* I have. I took a lunch break about an hour ago." She fingered the tie on her prayer covering. Was she nervous? "How is your family?"

He chewed and swallowed as his appetite

suddenly evaporated. He set the sandwich on the plate and tried to gather words.

Kayla's eyes widened and she held up her hands in defense. "If this is too personal —"

"Stop." He reached out and touched her hand, enjoying the warm softness of her skin. "It's not too personal. I'm just having a tough time choosing the words to describe how I feel."

"Take your time." She pointed to the sandwich. "Eat. You need your strength."

A smile overtook his lips. She truly cared about him, and the realization warmed his heart.

He lifted a chip. "I'll only eat this chip if you have some too."

"But it's your lunch. I don't want to eat your food."

He raised an eyebrow, and she laughed. He cherished the sweet sound.

"Fine." She picked up a chip from his plate, popped it into her mouth, and crossed her arms over her middle. "Now, you eat."

He ate the chip and then picked up another and ate it. "*Mei haus* is so quiet. No one spoke at breakfast yesterday, and it happened again at lunch and dinner. I don't ever remember the kitchen being that quiet during a meal. We used to all talk at once

— like we were all fighting to get *Mamm* and *Dat*'s attention. But now all I hear is the sound of our utensils hitting the plates, and no one finishes their food." He looked down at the pile of chips to avoid her concerned eyes. "It's like we're all walking around in a fog. No one knows what to say. To make matters worse, *mei schweschder* still won't speak to me, and it really hurts."

"*Ach,* Jamie. I am so sorry. But I promise you it won't last forever."

"I'm starting to think it might." His shoulders sagged. "I've bickered with my siblings in the past. One time, when I was eighteen and Mark was sixteen, Mark went out with his buddies and didn't do any of his chores. I was left with all the work and he didn't even thank me. I was bitter, but I forgave him after an hour or two. Cindy's anger toward me is completely different. It's like she can't stand the sight of me. I would never hold a grudge against one of my siblings for this long. I feel as if she will never forgive me."

"You know that's not true. Cindy will forgive you. It's our way to forgive. She'll realize she's sinning by blaming you, and she will apologize for making you feel so bad. Just give her time. Rely on God, and he will carry you through this." She sniffed and wiped her eyes. "Your family is hurting. My family went through the same pain when we lost Simeon, but we eventually found a way to move on."

"How?" He hated the desperation in his voice, but he craved her reassurance to the very marrow of his bones.

She glanced up at the ceiling as if contemplating the question thoroughly. "I don't know. I suppose it just got easier one day. There's no set time line for grieving, but one day it will get easier." She paused for a moment. "Is there anything I can do to help you through this?" She pointed to the sandwich he'd hardly touched. "Bringing you a meal doesn't seem like nearly enough."

"Just be *mei freind.*" Inwardly, he cringed at his own anguish. He'd never felt so weak or eager for someone's approval.

"That's easy. I thought we were already *freinden.*" She pointed to his plate. "You need to eat. You need all your strength in case that alarm goes off and you have to respond to a difficult call."

"I will, but only if you help me eat these chips. I feel guilty eating in front of you." He held the plate out to her.

"You shouldn't feel guilty, but I will help you out." She took a few chips and raised her eyebrows. "Now, you eat the sandwich." Her eyes suddenly widened. "Or do you not like it? I thought you liked roast beef, but maybe I was wrong."

He smiled, and her expression relaxed. "What man doesn't like roast beef?"

"Oh, *gut*. I had this horrible feeling you were stalling because you don't like it but you didn't want to hurt my feelings." She popped a chip into her mouth.

"So how have you been?" He took a drink of iced tea.

"I've been fine. My family is *gut* too. We've all been thinking of you, which is why Nathan and I brought food over."

"Nathan is here too?"

"*Ya,* he's talking to Brody and Leon." She gestured toward the doorway. "He should be back to see you in a few minutes. Has it been busy today?"

He shook his head as he finished chewing and swallowing another bite of the sandwich. "No, we were doing some training this morning. I was just resting this afternoon." He took another bite.

She took a few more chips and then looked up at him. "You look like you need the rest. I'm sure you haven't been sleeping well."

"No, I haven't." He wiped his mouth with

239

the napkin. "This sandwich is *appeditlich,* especially since you didn't throw it at me."

She laughed and her cheeks flushed bright pink. When she stopped laughing, her eyes locked with his and something in the air shifted between them. The urge to hold on to her friendship grabbed him by his shoulders and shook him.

I need Kayla in my life. I can't lose her.

The thought was so sudden he swallowed a gasp. What was happening to him?

Nathan appeared in the doorway and gave Jamie a little wave. "Hi, Jamie. *Wie geht's?*" He crossed his arms over his chest and leaned against the doorframe.

Jamie shook himself from his thoughts and forced his lips to form a smile. "I'm managing. How are you?"

"Gut, gut." Nathan shrugged.

Kayla turned to meet her brother's gaze. "Is it time to go already?"

"Ya." Nathan jammed his thumb toward the kitchen. "We need to get going so we can get ready before the late afternoon crowd comes. Eva can't do it alone."

"I know." When she faced Jamie again, a frown had clouded her pretty face. "I feel like I just got here. I hate that I have to go."

"I know." Jamie placed the plate on the table next to his chair. "I appreciate the visit and the food. *Danki* for coming to see me."

"Gern gschehne." She stood. "You make sure you finish that sandwich."

"Kay," Nathan said with a groan. "He's not your little *bruder.* He'll decide what he wants to eat."

She bit her lower lip. "I'm sorry. I didn't mean to order you around."

"Don't let her kid you," Nathan muttered. "She's very good at giving orders."

"Nathan!" she gasped. "That isn't nice."

Jamie stifled a snicker. "It's fine. I have *schweschdere,* so I understand. And, honestly, I appreciate the concern."

"We need to get going." Nathan stepped into the room. "Take care."

"Thanks for stopping by." Jamie stood and shook his hand.

"Gern gschehne." Nathan walked to the doorway and tapped the doorframe. "I'll meet you outside, Kay."

"All right. I'll be right there." After Nathan disappeared into the hallway, she shook her head. "I'm so sorry. He can be so rude with his comments. I hope that didn't offend you."

"No, it didn't offend me. I have younger siblings, remember?" He held out his hand, and she took it. But instead of shaking her hand, he held it, enjoying the intimacy of

241

her touch. "I'd like to see you again."

She nodded. "I would like that very much."

"Great." He released her hand. "Have a *gut* afternoon."

"You too." She smiled and left.

Kayla felt as if she were walking on a cloud. She said good-bye to Brody and Leon and then followed Nathan out to the sidewalk. Her thoughts were spinning with excitement after her conversation with Jamie. While her heart broke for him and his family, it swelled with the possibility of getting to know him better. Her breath had caught in her throat at the intensity in his eyes when he told her he wanted to see her again. Surely that meant he liked her.

Her lungs seized with a mixture of betrayal, worry, and alarm as a memory surfaced. Abram arrived late one night to see her, and after spending an hour talking on the porch, she walked him to his buggy. She expected to receive his usual quick kiss good-bye, but when she leaned in, he moved away and put his arm up to halt her.

"We were just being *freinden* tonight, Kayla." Then he shook her hand, said good night, and climbed into his buggy. As he disappeared into the night, his rejection crushed her heart and her spirit, stealing her confidence in its painful wake. Not long after that, he broke up with her.

Would Jamie play with her heart the same way Abram had?

"Hello? Kayla?"

Her gaze snapped to her brother's puzzled expression as they walked down the block toward the restaurant.

"You didn't hear a word I said, did you?" He raised his eyebrows.

"I'm sorry. What were you saying?" She tried her best to hide her embarrassment.

He stopped walking and swiveled toward her. "You really like him, don't you?"

She pressed her lips together. "Please don't tease me. I'm not in the mood." She started walking again, and he grabbed her arm, tugging her back.

"I'm not teasing you." His smile seemed genuine. "I think it's great. Jamie is really nice. I'm glad you're not still hung up on Abram."

She cringed at the sound of her exboyfriend's name. "We need to go. I'm sure *Mamm* and *Dat* are anxious for us to get back to work. You know how busy it gets."

"Really, Kay. I think it's *wunderbaar* how you've both moved on."

"Who's moved on? Abram?"

"*Ya.* I heard your *freinden* Katie and Lillian talking about him when they stopped by for lunch yesterday."

"What did they say?" Try as she might, Kayla couldn't stop a blush from creeping up her face. She could feel it.

"They mentioned he was seeing someone. Who was it?" He snapped his fingers. "That's right. Bena Smoker."

She cringed. "Bena Smoker?" She wasn't Abram's type at all.

She started walking again in an attempt to leave any thoughts of Abram there on the sidewalk. "We've already been gone too long. Let's go."

Before Nathan could respond, Kayla hurried to the restaurant and slipped in the front door. She redirected her thoughts to Jamie and his family as she crossed the dining area. Eva was setting a sandwich platter in front of a customer, but then she hurried over to Kayla and walked with her to the kitchen. Nathan was right behind them.

"Did you get to talk to Brody?" *Mamm* asked as they came in.

"*Ya,* we did." Nathan crossed the room and began to pull on his apron. "Brody and Leon appreciated the food."

"Did you get an update on the Riehl family?" Eva asked.

"*Ya.*" Kayla rested her hand on the counter. "I actually got to see Jamie." She summarized what he shared about his family, leaving out the personal information about his strained relationship with Cindy.

Her parents and Eva listened as frowns darkened their expressions.

"I've been keeping the family in my prayers." *Mamm*'s eyes shimmered. "I'm so sorry for all they're going through."

"*Ya,* I am too." *Dat* patted *Mamm*'s arm. "It has to be difficult for Vernon. I'm sure he feels lost right now."

Kayla folded her arms over her chest as an idea took root in her mind. "I was thinking maybe Eva and I could take them a meal."

"*Ya.*" Eva snapped her fingers. "I love that idea."

"I do too," *Mamm* chimed in. "We can come up with a nice menu, and I'll take care of Junior for you."

"Great." Kayla rubbed her hands together. "If it's okay with them, let's take the meal to them tomorrow night."

Kayla's stomach flip-flopped. She was going to see Jamie again. And soon.

SEVENTEEN

Later that evening Jamie climbed from the fire truck and secured his helmet. Red strobe lights reflected off the slate-gray paint on the small house as smoke poured out of the right-side windows. A petite woman who looked to be in her mid-thirties stood on the dark front lawn in jeans and a light-blue T-shirt. She was coughing into a dish towel.

Jamie rushed to her and then glanced over his shoulder in search of the ambulance. *Where is it? It should be here by now!*

"Ma'am, are you okay?"

She nodded as she continued to cough. Her eyes were bloodshot and tears streaked down her pale cheeks. After a moment, she caught her breath and wiped her face with the towel.

"Thank you for coming so quickly." She pointed toward the house, her hand shaking. "I was warming up some soup, and I fell asleep. When I woke up, the house was full of smoke."

"Is there anyone else in the house, ma'am?" he asked.

The woman shook her head. "No, my husband is out of town."

"Any pets?" he asked as Leon appeared beside him.

She shook her head. "No. No one else and no pets."

"Brody's handling the scene size-up. I'll let him know," Leon offered before jogging over to the truck where Brody was speaking into his radio.

"All right." Jamie opened his mouth to speak to the woman but stopped as the blare of sirens filled the air. She wouldn't be able to hear him.

An ambulance and the Ronks Fire engine parked beside the Bird-in-Hand truck.

"There's the ambulance."

The woman began to cough again, and when she swayed Jamie grabbed her arms and held her upright. Her body wilted in his arms.

He turned toward the ambulance. "Could I get some help, please?"

Two paramedics jumped out and took a gurney from the back of their vehicle.

"They're going to help you, ma'am." Jamie held her steady.

The paramedics brought the gurney, and Jamie helped the woman lie down. Then the paramedics took her to the ambulance.

"Is she all right?" Leon asked as he returned.

"I think she has smoke inhalation." Jamie pointed toward the house. "Are we going to go in?"

Leon gestured toward the Ronks company as four men in turnout gear walked over to them. "*Ya.* I think they're going to stay and see if we need any help, though, since Noah's not on duty tonight. It's just you, me, and Brody."

"Sounds *gut.*" Jamie greeted the four firemen, and then Brody approached the group.

"All right. Two in and two out. Who wants to go in first?"

Leon smacked Jamie's arm. "We'll do it, right, Jamie?"

"*Ya.*" Jamie put his mask over his face. "Let's go." As he turned toward the house, he spotted a flash of metal, a reflective vest, and a small light that resembled a lantern moving near the road.

"Jamie?" Leon asked.

"Look there." Jamie nodded toward the road. "It looks like someone on a scooter."

Leon nodded slowly. "Why would someone be out on a scooter in the dark?"

"Are you two going in or what?" Brody snapped.

"We'll go," one of the firemen from Ronks said, turning to another. "You ready, Cooper?"

"Yeah." Cooper put his mask on and started toward the house.

The chief from the other station walked over to Brody and began to discuss the scene. Jamie started toward the road.

"Where are you going?" Leon hurried after him.

"I'm going to tell this person he's going to get hit by a car if he continues to ride his scooter outside in the dark. It's dangerous to ride a scooter at night, even if you have on a reflective vest and carry a lantern."

As Jamie approached the road, the scooter steered into the driveway.

"Jamie?" the rider asked as he steered the scooter over to him and Leon.

"Nathan?" Jamie couldn't believe his eyes. "What are you doing here?"

"I heard the call, and I thought I'd come in case you need extra help." Nathan lifted a radio from the basket on the front of the scooter. Then he pointed behind him. "I don't live far from here. I figured I'd head over and check things out."

"Where did you get that radio?" Jamie asked.

"It was Simeon's," Leon answered for Nathan. "Brody let him keep it as a memento."

Jamie's shoulders tensed.

"I just want to help." Nathan pointed toward the house. "I thought since I live close —"

"Are you saying you often go on calls close to your *haus*?" Jamie couldn't keep his voice from rising with alarm.

"No!" Nathan shook his head, looking surprised at the question. "This is the first time."

"Are you telling me the truth?"

"*Ya.*" Nathan nodded with emphasis.

Jamie jammed his thumb toward the Ronks fire engine. "So if I ask the Ronks chief, he won't tell me you've been coming to scenes to offer your help?"

"No, he won't. This is the first time." Nathan took a step back. "I'll just go back home."

"No, don't go back out on that road. It's too dark. I don't want you to get hit." Jamie gestured toward his station's fire engine. "You can wait in the truck. We'll take you home when we're done here."

"Okay." Nathan nodded. "I can watch

250

how you fight the fire."

"You won't see anything too exciting," Leon offered. "It's a stove fire. I'm pretty sure they have it out already."

A call for a fan came over the radio.

"Just as I said. It's out." Leon hurried back toward the truck. Brody was still there with the Ronks chief.

Jamie turned toward Nathan. "Does anyone in your family know you've left the *haus*?"

"No, they're all asleep."

Jamie cringed. "You realize your *schweschder* is going to be furious when she finds out you're here."

"*Ya,* I know." Nathan blew out a deep sigh. "It's not just Kayla, though. *Mei mamm* and *dat* won't be *froh* either."

"You know sneaking out to try to help us won't help convince them to let you start training."

Nathan's expression was solemn. "You're right."

"Let's head over to the truck." Jamie made a "let's go" gesture. "You can sit in there, and I'll find out what's going on with the fire."

They walked past the ambulance, where the resident was receiving an oxygen treatment. When they reached the fire engine,

251

Jamie opened the back door and Nathan climbed inside.

"Obviously, don't touch anything."

"I'm fourteen, not four," Nathan dead-panned.

Jamie bit back a smile. "I'm sorry. I didn't mean to insult you."

Nathan crossed his arms over his blue shirt.

"I'll be back soon." Jamie joined Brody, Leon, and the other chief. "What's going on?"

"The fire is out, and we're running fans to clear out the smoke," Lance, the Ronks chief, said. "Everything is fine."

"How is the woman?" Jamie looked toward the ambulance.

"I think they're going to take her to the hospital to be checked out," Brody said. "They're worried about smoke inhalation."

Jamie shook his head. "I hope she has relatives she can call since her husband is out of town."

"They're working on that," Lance said. "Her sister lives nearby."

Brody folded his arms over his jacket. "Leon told me Nathan Dienner is here."

"Ya." Jamie lifted his helmet. "I didn't know you'd given him Simeon's radio."

"Is that Simeon Dienner's younger

brother?" Lance asked.

"Yeah." Brody leaned on the bumper of the Ronks fire engine. "I thought it might help him feel a connection to his brother if he had his radio. I didn't know he'd use it to follow us to calls."

"He wants to volunteer," Leon chimed in.

Brody's expression brightened. "He should."

"But his mother and sister don't want him to, so his father won't give him permission to train." Jamie glanced back toward the truck.

"Makes sense." Lance kicked a stone with the toe of his boot. "I'm sure they're worried about something happening to him."

"I'm going to talk to him about not coming out on calls," Jamie said. "We can drop him home on our way back to the station. I don't want him out on the road in the dark. It's too dangerous."

"I agree," Brody said.

Lance gestured toward the house, where the smoke was now minimal. "You can go. We have it under control."

"All right." Brody shook Lance's hand. "Take care. I'm sure we'll see you and your company again soon."

Jamie and Leon said good night and headed to the truck. Jamie got in the back with Nathan and Leon slipped into the passenger seat beside Brody.

"How are you, Nathan?" Brody craned his neck to look at him.

"I'm okay. How are you?" Nathan looked sheepish as he ran his hands over his trousers as if anticipating a lecture.

"I'm doing well. I didn't expect to see you twice today." Brody smiled. "How's your family?"

"Fine." Nathan cleared his throat. "They're sleeping, actually."

"So no one knows you're here." Brody angled his body so he was facing Nathan. "Do you realize how worried your family would be if they woke up and realized you were gone?"

"We've already discussed that," Jamie cut in. "Right, Nathan?"

"Yeah." Nathan looked down at his lap. "I won't do it again."

"Great." Brody started the engine and steered it to the road.

When Brody brought the fire engine to a stop in front of the Dienners' farmhouse a few minutes later, Jamie climbed out and helped Nathan gather his scooter, lantern, and radio.

Jamie walked up the back porch with Nathan and shook his hand. "It was *gut* seeing you. Please tell your family I said hello."

"Danki. Gut nacht." Nathan leaned the scooter against the porch posts and Jamie started down the path to the truck.

"Nathan?"

Jamie spun at the sound of Kayla's voice. She stood in the doorway, holding a lantern. She had on the same blue robe and purple scarf she'd worn the night of the Dienner barn fire. Her eyebrows drew together as she studied her brother.

"What are you doing outside this late?" Her gaze moved to the fire truck in the driveway and she gasped. "What's going on?"

"Everything's okay." Jamie walked up the path.

"Jamie?" She smoothed her free hand down the terrycloth belt tied at her waist. "I didn't see you there." She looked over at the truck and then back at Jamie once again. "What's happened?"

"We just brought Nathan home." Jamie held up his hands to calm her. "Nothing happened. Nathan just came out to one of our calls nearby."

Kayla faced Nathan. "You what?" She paused for a moment as if contemplating what Jamie had said. "So you heard it come over Simeon's radio, and what? You thought you could help?" Her lips formed a deep frown. "Why would you do that?"

Nathan stared at the toes of his shoes. The frustration in his expression tugged at Jamie's heartstrings. The boy had already been lectured by Jamie and Brody.

"It's fine." Jamie leaned on the porch railing. "He knows what he did was dangerous. I don't think he'll do it again."

Nathan met Jamie's gaze and his scowl relaxed. "I'm sorry I woke you up, Kay." Nathan pulled off his reflective vest. "You should go back to bed."

Marilyn appeared behind her. "I thought I heard a diesel engine. Nathan? Why are you outside?" She looked at Jamie. "Oh, hello, Jamie. Is there a fire close by?"

Kayla pointed to her younger brother. "Nathan went out to one of their calls, and they brought him home."

Marilyn blinked. "You what?"

Nathan blew out a deep sigh as he climbed the porch steps. "Can we please talk about this tomorrow?"

"What do we need to talk about tomorrow?" Willie joined the family in the doorway.

Jamie took a step back, not wanting to intrude in a family matter. *"Gut nacht."* He waved. "I'll see you soon."

"Wait!" Kayla called, holding up her hand. "Would you like a snack?"

"That's a great idea," Marilyn said. "Is Brody in the truck? Invite him and anyone else with you too. I can put on some *kaffi*, and we have desserts from the restaurant. You can visit before you go back to the fire station. I know how hard you volunteers work."

"That sounds great." Jamie smiled at the idea of visiting with Kayla for the second time today. "I'll go get Brody and Leon."

Jamie sat in the Dienners' kitchen as Kayla filled his mug with hot coffee. The women had rushed away to get dressed before Marilyn brought out a variety of individually wrapped whoopie pies, a chocolate cake, and a shoofly pie. Eva had joined them and placed a pitcher of milk and a sugar bowl in the center of the table.

"Danki." Jamie glanced up at Kayla, and she gave him a shy smile, causing his pulse to speed up. While she was always attractive, she somehow seemed even more beautiful than usual. Perhaps it was the low light of the lanterns making her eyes an even deeper shade of blue.

"Gern gschehne." She began to fill Leon's mug beside his.

"Have you had a busy night?" Marilyn cut the chocolate cake and set a piece on Jamie's plate.

"No, actually," Jamie said. "This was our first call today." He forked a piece of the chocolate cake into his mouth and savored the sweet flavor. "This is *appeditlich. Danki.*"

Marilyn nodded toward Kayla. "She's the expert chocolate *kuche* baker."

"That's not true." Kayla's cheeks flushed, and she was even cuter. "You taught me how to bake."

"*Ya,* and you're *gut* at it." Marilyn placed a piece of cake on Brody's plate.

Kayla filled Brody's mug and then put the percolator back on the stove.

Jamie glanced toward the doorway that led to the family room. Willie stood with Nathan, speaking in a hushed tone. After a few moments, Nathan disappeared and footfalls echoed up a staircase. Willie entered the kitchen with a scowl. He stepped over to the counter and retrieved a mug from the cabinet.

"*Kaffi?*" Kayla asked her father.

"*Ya.*" He smiled, but his eyes reflected a serious mood. "*Danki.*"

She filled his mug and he sat down at the table beside Brody.

"So what call were you responding to?"

Willie took a sip as Marilyn slipped a piece of chocolate cake on a plate for him.

As Brody told them, Jamie finished his piece of chocolate cake and then chose a pumpkin whoopie pie from the tray. As he began to eat it he looked toward the kitchen counter, where Kayla stood with her mother and Eva. She smiled at him, and his thoughts spun.

For the first time in years, Jamie felt the urge to date. He hadn't dated since he was nineteen, and even then, the relationship was brief and more superficial than deep and meaningful. But he didn't crave a superficial relationship with Kayla. No, he wanted a true relationship with her. Still, he couldn't fathom how he would fit Kayla into his chaotic life and crazy schedule. Did he have time to have a meaningful relationship with a woman as special as Kayla Dienner?

Besides, why would he even deserve a relationship after the way his mother died? The familiar guilt suddenly overwhelmed him. How could he even consider romantic feelings for Kayla after what he'd done? When his family needed him?

"Right, Jamie?"

"What?" Jamie's gaze snapped to Brody's. "I'm sorry, but I didn't hear what you said."

A swift, sharp burst of pain exploded in

259

Jamie's ankle as someone kicked him under the table, and he barely suppressed a yelp. Had Leon kicked him? He'd address that mystery later. He remained stony-faced and focused on Brody.

"I said we've had a fair share of stove fires." Brody lifted his mug.

"*Ya, ya.* That's very true." Jamie cleared his throat and hoped his cheeks didn't betray his effort to conceal his embarrassment. "They're the most common fire calls lately."

"Exactly." Brody looked over at Willie. "How is the restaurant doing? The parking lot is always full when I drive past it."

"*Ya*, it's very busy." Willie rested his hands on his mug. "The summer tourists seem to enjoy our menu."

Jamie swallowed a sigh of relief as Willie discussed their authentic menu and Brody listened with interest. He caught Leon watching him in his peripheral vision and he turned toward his friend.

"You all right?" Leon's question was barely a whisper.

"I'm fine. Why?" Jamie kept his response quiet.

"Just checking." Leon raised his eyebrows as he lifted his mug to his lips.

"More *kaffi*?" Eva asked, carrying the

percolator to the table.

"Oh, no, *danki.*" Jamie shook his head. "I might not sleep tonight if I drink too much caffeine."

"Of course." Eva turned to Leon.

"No, thanks." Leon placed his hand over the rim of his mug. "I won't sleep either."

"I understand." She placed the percolator on the table and gestured toward the shoofly pie. "Would you like some pie? I can cut it for you."

"No, *danki.*" Jamie shook his head. "The whoopie pie and chocolate *kuche* were outstanding, but I'm full."

"*Ya,* they were." Leon patted his abdomen. "*Danki* for the *appeditich* snack. It really hit the spot."

"*Gern gschehne.*"

Kayla stepped over to the table. "I'll put these whoopie pies in a container for you to take back to the station."

"You don't need to do that." Jamie shook his head. "You already brought us a meal earlier today, and you fed us tonight. You don't need to send food with us too."

"I don't mind." Kayla found a container in one of the kitchen cabinets and placed all the whoopie pies inside.

"You can give them the shoofly pie too," Marilyn suggested. "Eva said she'll bake a

261

fresh one for the restaurant in the morning."

"You're spoiling us, Marilyn," Brody said.

"We enjoy doing it, right?" Marilyn looked around at her family.

"*Ya*. We're happy to support the volunteer station that has helped us so much," Kayla said.

"*Ya*, that's true." Eva walked over to Brody. "Would you like anything else to eat?"

"No," Brody said. "Everything was great."

"We'll wrap it up then." Kayla brought cling wrap from the pantry and began to cover the pie plate.

Willie patted Brody on the shoulder. "We'll always find ways to help you."

"Thank you." Brody glanced across the table at Jamie and Leon. "Are you two ready to head back to the station?"

"*Ya*." Leon pushed back his chair. "We should get some rest in case the radio goes off again." He glanced over at the women. "*Danki* again for the *kaffi* and dessert. It was nice visiting with you."

"Yes, it was." Brody stood. "I'll be sure to come by the restaurant again soon."

Willie stood too. "I'll walk you out."

The three men walked toward the mudroom, and after a moment, the screen door opened. Marilyn trailed after them with the container of whoopie pies and pie plate in her hands. "Don't forget the food."

As Jamie began to gather plates, out of the corner of his eye he spotted a silent conversation between Kayla and Eva, complete with animated expressions and arm gestures.

Kayla walked over to him a moment later. "You don't need to do that. I've got it."

"I don't want to leave you and your *mamm* with this mess." He lifted the plates. "Let me at least put these on the counter for you." He carried the stack to the counter and then faced Kayla and Eva.

Eva looked at each of them and then gestured toward a door. "I'm going to go check on Junior in our apartment. It was nice seeing you, Jamie." She shook his hand. "I hope you have a quiet night at the station."

"*Danki.* It was nice seeing you too."

Jamie turned toward Kayla after Eva left the room. "*Danki* for inviting us in."

She folded her arms over her green dress. "It was the least I could do."

"What do you mean?" He crossed the room and stood in front of her.

"I appreciate how you took care of *mei bruder* tonight."

"I really didn't do much."

Kayla gestured toward the ceiling as if indicating her bedroom above them. "I woke up to the sound of the diesel engine, and I thought the worst. When I looked out the window and didn't see lights, I felt a little better, but I was still concerned. I'm thankful it was a friendly call." She lowered her voice. "*Mei daed* is going to speak to Nathan alone later. He said he's going to take the radio away from Nathan if he responds to a call again."

"I don't think he will." Jamie rested his forearms on the back rung of the kitchen chair and leaned forward. "I talked to him, and Brody did too. I'm sure your *daed* will drive the message home."

"*Gut.*" A deep frown pulled at her mouth. "I can't stand the thought of Nathan sneaking out and running the risk of getting hurt."

"I think we can have faith in him." He folded his hands together as he studied her face. He yearned to ask if he could visit her tomorrow night, but his days at the farm after being on duty were always extra busy. And he would most likely go to bed earlier for lack of sleep. He would have to wait for another night. But the notion of not seeing her for a few days sent a pang of regret lancing through him. How had he become so

264

attached to Kayla so quickly?

"Would it be all right if Eva and I brought a meal over to your family tomorrow night?"

Jamie was so startled by the question that he stood up straight. It was as if she'd read his thoughts and offered a solution. "That would be *wunderbaar.*"

"Great." She rubbed her hands together.

Leon stuck his head into the kitchen. "Are you coming with us, Jamie?"

"*Ya.*" Leon left and Jamie stepped toward the door. "Thanks again."

"*Gern gschehne.*" She smiled. "I look forward to seeing you tomorrow, then."

"I look forward to seeing you too." Jamie followed Leon outside and said good night to Marilyn and Willie.

As Jamie walked with Brody and Leon to the fire engine, Brody's phone began to ring. He answered it, and Leon motioned for Jamie to slow his pace and allow Brody to move ahead of them.

"I'm sorry I kicked you earlier." Leon's voice was soft.

"Why did you?"

"Because you were so busy staring at Kayla you didn't even hear what Brody was saying to you." Leon stopped and faced him. "It's obvious you and Kayla like each other. It just wasn't the best time to bring that detail to light."

Jamie nodded. "You're right."

"I didn't mean to upset you." Leon held up his hand. "I think it's great you've finally found someone. She's an amazing *maedel*. Don't let her slip through your fingers. If you do, you'll regret it."

"Hey!" Brody called from the fire engine. "Are you two riding or walking back to the station?"

"Let's go." Leon began to lope back to the fire engine.

As Jamie fell into step beside him, he contemplated what Leon said. He'd never expected to fall for Kayla so quickly.

He made a decision. Somehow, he would do his best to hold on to her friendship — if she was truly interested in him.

A tiny spark of hope took root in his heart. And if she was, maybe, just maybe, their friendship could evolve into something more.

EIGHTEEN

"I'm going to talk to Nathan and make him understand what he did tonight was reckless and completely unacceptable." *Dat*'s voice echoed from the mudroom. His tone held a hard edge of irritation that sent a shiver down Kayla's spine as she busied herself with filling one side of the sink with hot, sudsy water, and the other side with rinse water.

"I want to be there when you talk to him," *Mamm* sounded determined. "I have a few things to say to him myself."

"Fine. I'll call him down and insist he talk to us now. It can't wait until morning."

Kayla glanced over her shoulder as her parents walked through the kitchen. Frustration radiated off them. They would give Nathan an emotional castigation, and as much as she longed to chime in and help them get Nathan's attention, she had to stay out of it. She was his sister and not his parent, but she couldn't stop herself from worrying about his safety.

Her heart had lodged in her throat when she looked out the window earlier and saw the fire truck. Even though she thought her own family was safe in their beds, she'd thought the worst — about Jamie. The memories of the night Simeon died came rushing back to her like a suffocating tidal wave. She would never forget that icy, hollow feeling that overcame her when Brody delivered the news.

"Nathan Paul! Your *mamm* and I want to speak with you. Come down now." *Dat*'s voice cut through her harrowing memories. Besides, Brody wouldn't come here if anything happened to Jamie. He'd be at the Riehl home.

She cringed at both her father's stern tone and his using her brother's full name. After a few moments, she heard Nathan coming down the stairs. She turned her attention to washing the dishes.

"Do you need help?"

Kayla jumped at Eva's question. "I didn't hear you come back."

"I'm sorry. I didn't mean to startle you." Eva sidled up to her and started drying the dishes.

"Is Junior okay?" Kayla finished rinsing

the last plate and put it in the drain board.

"*Ya.* He is fast asleep." Eva gave Kayla a sideways glance. "I didn't know if Jamie was still here."

"He's been gone for a few minutes." Kayla lifted a mug.

"Why did you go to that call tonight?" *Dat*'s voice boomed from the family room. "You could have been hurt or killed. Why would you risk your life after your *mamm* and I told you that you can't volunteer right now?"

Eva sucked in a breath. "Your *daed* is upset," she whispered.

"I know." Kayla finished washing the mug and dropped it into the rinse water.

"I want an answer, Nathan," *Dat* barked. "Why would you sneak out late at night to help at a fire when you haven't had any training? We didn't know you were gone. What if you'd been hurt on your way to the scene? We would've had no idea where to even begin to look for you."

A few moments of painful silence passed as Kayla rushed to finish washing the mugs. She started on the utensils while Eva dried and put items away.

"Nathan, please answer your *daed.*" *Mamm*'s voice sounded more anxious than angry.

"We should hurry," Kayla whispered to Eva as she finished washing a tray. "I feel like I'm eavesdropping on a very private conversation."

Eva nodded. "*Ya,* I agree. I'll wipe off the table and put away the milk."

Kayla went to work on the peculator and Eva grabbed a cloth and headed toward the table.

"I just wanted you and *Dat* to be proud of me." Nathan's voice was thin and weak, a tone Kayla hadn't heard from him since the days after Simeon's death.

"We are proud of you," *Dat* responded, his tone softer. "We're proud of all our *kinner.*"

"It's not the same," Nathan insisted, his voice louder. "I want you to be just as proud of me as you were of Simeon."

Her brother's words stabbed at Kayla's heart. She turned to look at Eva. Her eyes shimmered.

"*Ach,* Nathan. We are so, so proud of you." *Mamm*'s voice cracked.

Eva tossed the cloth she'd used to wipe the table onto the counter and looped her arm around Kayla's shoulder. "Let's go talk in my apartment."

"*Gut* idea." Kayla let Eva steer her past the family room doorway, but she got a

270

glimpse of her mother hugging Nathan and *Dat* wiping his eyes.

Inside the apartment, Kayla quietly closed the door behind them and looked around. She'd always liked this place. She stepped into the small family room, furnished with a sofa and two chairs. Off the family room was the eat-in kitchen, a bathroom, and doors to two bedrooms. A small mudroom and separate entrance were beyond the kitchen.

Memories of when her brother and Eva first moved in settled over Kayla as she trailed her fingers on the back of the sofa. The apartment was supposed to be temporary when they were first married, but Eva fell in love with it. She'd once told Kayla she didn't want to build a separate house until they truly outgrew the apartment because she loved being so close to Kayla and the rest of the family.

"We can talk in the kitchen." Eva crossed the family room and Kayla followed. "Would you like a cup of tea?"

"*Ya. Danki.* I'll get the mugs."

"Great." Eva filled the kettle and, after lighting a burner, put it on the stove.

Kayla dropped a tea bag into each mug before setting them on the counter.

"Let's sit." Eva gestured toward the table

271

and they sat down across from each other. She touched her tan headscarf, adjusting it on her light-brown hair. "Did you have a *gut* talk with Jamie?"

"Ya." Kayla shrugged as if it weren't a big deal, even though her lips threatened to betray her with a wide smile.

"He seemed to want to talk to you alone." Eva nudged Kayla with her hand.

Kayla traced a heart on the yellow tablecloth with her finger. When she realized what she'd drawn she froze. Was she falling in love with Jamie? But she hardly knew him. She'd been so determined to fall in love that she'd said "I love you" to Abram before he said it to her. She'd been humiliated when Abram had been silent in response. Would she make the same mistake with Jamie? Tell him her feelings before he was ready to share his with her?

"Kayla?" Eva leaned forward on the table. "What's on your mind?"

Kayla sat up straight and glanced toward the stove. "The water for our tea should be almost ready. I'll get it." She stood, and Eva grabbed her wrist.

"I'll get the kettle when the water boils. Sit down and relax." Eva released her wrist. "Talk to me. You like Jamie, and I think it's *wunderbaar.* He obviously likes you too."

Kayla sank back into her chair. "*Ya,* I think he does. When Nathan and I went to the fire station earlier today, he asked if he could see me again."

"I'm so *froh* for you. He seems like a *gut* man." Eva smiled. "And he's handsome."

"He is." Kayla spotted a notepad and pen on the counter, and she popped up to get them. "And he said we could take his family supper tomorrow night. Let's make a list for our menu." She sat down and poised the pen in her fingers. She glanced up, and Eva gave her a knowing smile. Eva could see right through her lame attempt at changing the subject. Still, Kayla didn't want to discuss Jamie when she had such conflicting emotions about the possibility of a relationship with him.

"I was thinking about that earlier," Eva said. "What if we made Swedish meatballs and egg noodles?"

"That's a great idea." Kayla wrote it on the notepad. "We could also take a salad and homemade dressing. And a pie for dessert."

"That's *gut.*" Eva tapped her finger on the table. "We can make rolls too. Maybe a cherry pie?"

"*Ya.*" Kayla wrote on the notepad. "I haven't made a cherry pie in a while."

The kettle began to whistle, and Eva jumped up. She brought the filled mugs to the table, followed by a pitcher of milk.

"I keep thinking about Nathan." Eva cradled the mug in her hands. "It broke my heart to hear him say he wants your parents to be as proud of him as they were of Simeon. Of course your parents are proud of him. He's just hurting because he misses his *bruder.* He has a hole in his life." She looked down at her tea. "We all do."

"*Ya,* we do. If I only knew how to help him." Kayla lifted her mug and took a sip.

"We're still all sort of floundering around, trying to figure out how to go on with our lives without him." Eva looked up at Kayla, and her hazel eyes were glassy. "Sometimes I cry when I'm alone in my bedroom at night. I miss him so much. I touch the sheets beside me, and the emptiness and coldness go straight to my heart. That's when I beg God to help us all through this."

"I had no idea. You always seem so strong."

Eva gave her a gentle smile. "I try to be strong, but I'm only human. I break down too. Sometimes I have no idea how to go on, but I have to be strong for Junior."

"You don't have to face this alone. We have each other." Kayla touched Eva's hand. "We're taking care of one another."

"That's true." Eva squeezed Kayla's hand. "You recently asked me why I chose to stay here after Simeon died. The truth is I feel closer to your parents, Nathan, and you than I ever felt to my own parents. I love them, but I have a stronger bond with your family. After I lost Simeon, I knew your family would give me more emotional support than my parents would."

"We're so *froh* you stayed, and we'll always be here for you." Kayla's thoughts meandered to the Riehl family. "And we can do the same thing for Jamie and his family. We can offer them support too."

"Ya." Eva pointed to the notepad. "Early tomorrow, let's make sure we have everything we need for our menu."

"If not, then I'll run to the market after the breakfast rush." Kayla contemplated seeing Jamie again tomorrow evening. She couldn't wait.

The two women talked about Kayla's newest cherry pie recipe as they finished their tea. Once her mug was empty, Kayla said good night and slipped out of the apartment. Nathan and *Dat* were still in the family room. *Mamm* must have gone to bed.

"Please don't take the radio from me," Nathan pleaded with *Dat* as he sat on a chair across from him. "I want to keep it. It's all I have from Simeon."

Kayla kept her eyes focused on the floor as she crossed the room and headed toward the stairs.

"Can I trust you not to go on anymore calls if I let you keep the radio?" *Dat* asked.

Kayla stopped in the stairwell and held her breath as she awaited Nathan's response.

"Ya," Nathan insisted. "You can trust me, *Dat.* Let me prove myself to you."

Kayla released the breath she'd been holding and started up the stairs. As she made her way to her room, she silently vowed to be a better sister to Nathan and not treat him like a child. She could help him see how important he was to the family without sneaking out of the house on fire calls. He didn't need to. They were already proud of him. Very proud.

The delicious aroma of breakfast food wafted over Jamie as he entered the mudroom and dropped his duffel bag on a bench. Yawning, he slipped off his boots and closed his eyes, taking a moment to gather the emotional strength to face his family.

He could do this. He could be strong. And he had something to look forward to tonight

— another visit with Kayla. She'd promised to bring a meal, and that would keep his mood positive, no matter how Cindy treated him today.

With a smile plastered on his face, Jamie walked into the kitchen. His siblings and father were already eating.

"Jamie." *Dat*'s face was pale, and dark circles rimmed his eyes as if he hadn't slept in months. "*Gut* to see you. How was your shift?"

"It was *gut.*" Jamie nodded at his siblings as he crossed the kitchen to the sink. *"Gude mariye."*

Cindy stared down at her plate, but Jamie kept his chin up. He would stay positive and keep Kayla's advice close to his heart. As he washed his hands, he recalled what she'd told him yesterday at the fire station.

Cindy will forgive you. It's our way to forgive. She'll realize she's sinning by blaming you and she will apologize for making you feel so bad about it. Just give her time. Rely on God, and he will carry you through this.

Yes, he would rely on God. Things would get better soon.

Jamie sat down in his usual place at the table, already set for him. He glanced toward his mother's empty spot, and yet another ache spread throughout his chest.

277

How could things get better without *Mamm*? She was the center of their lives. The house was hollow without her presence.

Grief melted away his hopeful mood.

After a silent prayer, he filled his plate with scrambled eggs, bacon, and home fries. Then he glanced across the table at Laura. "*Danki* for breakfast."

"*Gern gschehne.*" Laura raised an eyebrow. "Cindy and I make it every morning."

He looked at Cindy across from him. "*Danki,* Cindy." He waited for her to acknowledge him, but she kept her eyes focused on her plate as she moved her fork over some home fries. He fought the urge to frown and shoved a forkful of scrambled egg into his mouth.

"Tell us about your shift." *Dat* lifted his coffee cup. "Was it busy?"

Jamie shook his head as he chewed and swallowed.

"So you just hung out and napped while I did all your chores?" Mark pointed his fork at Jamie with a feigned glare.

Jamie ignored him and got up from the table. "We had one call." He described the stove fire and Nathan's arrival.

Jamie filled his mug with coffee and sat back down. "But Brody and I talked to him about how dangerous that was. The Ronks department took over the call, and we took Nathan home on our way back to the station. The Dienners invited us in and gave us a snack."

Mark's handful of bacon froze in midair as he studied Jamie. "You saw Kayla last night?"

"*Ya,* briefly." Jamie pretended he didn't see his brother's grin. "And she said she and Eva are going to bring us dinner tonight."

"Really?" *Dat* forced a smile. "How nice."

"That's *wunderbaar.*" Laura turned toward Cindy. "We can make those pork chops tomorrow."

"*Ya.*" Cindy took a roll from the basket in the center of the table. "That's really kind for the Dienners to do."

Jamie nodded as a small glimmer of hope took root deep inside of him. Was Cindy finally going to forgive him? Oh, how he prayed she would!

"It will be *gut* to see Kayla and Eva," Laura continued, oblivious to Jamie's inner turmoil. "I really enjoyed meeting them at the barn raising. I felt like I bonded with Kayla."

"I felt the same way about Eva." Cindy buttered the roll. "She was really nice to me."

279

"And I'm sure Jamie is looking forward to seeing Kayla again." Mark turned to his brother and smirked. "I'm sure she'll be *froh* to see you too."

"Is that right?" *Dat*'s eyebrows lifted. "So you like Kayla? She seems like a sweet *maedel.*"

Jamie wasn't in the mood to hear his family's opinion of Kayla. He looked at Mark. "Did you already take care of the animals?"

"*Ya.*" Mark speared home fries with his fork. "After we finish cleaning the dairy barn, we need to muck out the stalls. After the milking, I thought we could start painting the chicken coop. It's needed a fresh coat of paint for a while. Do you agree?"

"*Ya,* absolutely." Jamie welcomed the idea of being busy today. It would make the day go by faster. He just hoped it would keep his mind occupied too. Sitting in the kitchen without *Mamm* still hurt.

But he would see Kayla later today, and that would help lift his mood.

Once their plates were empty, Laura and Cindy began gathering the dishes.

Dat stood by the table and touched his beard. "I think I might go take a nap. I just don't have the strength to work outside today. Would that be all right, *buwe*?"

"That's fine." Mark stood and pushed his chair in. "You rest, *Dat*. Jamie and I will take care of the chores today." He turned toward Jamie, who nodded in agreement.

"We'll take care of everything," Jamie agreed. "I'll be out in a minute, Mark."

Mark headed outside and *Dat* left the kitchen. Jamie heard a door click shut, indicating his father had gone into his bedroom. His heart squeezed with concern.

"He's not doing well at all." Laura set the mugs on the counter. "I heard him crying last night when I came downstairs for a glass of water. His bedroom door was open a crack. I'm so worried about him."

"I am too." Jamie piled the platters and started toward the counter with them. "How are you doing?" he asked Laura when he reached the counter.

"I don't know." Laura's eyes began to well up with tears. "I keep expecting to see *Mamm* in the kitchen. I came downstairs this morning, and the *haus* was so empty, so cold without her. She was always in the kitchen before me — even if I came down early." Her voice shook. "She'd always greet me with a big smile and sometimes even a hug. But now she's gone, and I don't know how to go on. I don't know how to be a *dochder* without a *mutter*." A tear trailed down her cheek. "It's like a piece of me died with her."

Jamie heard Cindy sniff, and saw she was staring down at the table.

"I know." Jamie touched Laura's sleeve. "I feel the same way. She was everything to us."

"Exactly."

He needed to stay busy to keep his grief from exploding inside of him. He nodded toward the sink. "Let me help you clean up."

Laura cleared her throat and shook her head. "You can go. Cindy and I will take care of the dishes."

"I don't mind helping." Jamie put the plug in the drain and added dish detergent before turning on the hot water.

Laura set the dishes on the counter and touched his arm. "Go help Mark."

"You and Cindy always do the dishes. I'll help today." He set the stack of plates in the sink.

Laura studied him, her eyes narrowing. "What are you up to?"

"Nothing. Would you like me to wash or dry?"

Laura glanced toward the table and Jamie followed her lead. Cindy still lingered there, slowly putting utensils in a mug. Then Laura swiveled back to Jamie, placed her hand on her hip, and lowered her voice. "Just talk to her."

"I've tried." Jamie hated the thread of desperation in his voice.

"Try again. Washing dishes isn't going to help." When Jamie hesitated, Laura shoved him toward their younger sister. "Go on."

Jamie crossed the room and stood in front of Cindy. "I can't stand this silence between us any longer. Would you please talk to me?"

Cindy kept her eyes focused downward.

"Please, Cindy," he pleaded with her. "We're family. We need each other, especially now."

To his surprise, Cindy looked up and met his gaze. "I just can't right now." Her voice wavered. "I need time." Then she picked up the mug of utensils and headed to the sink. In another few seconds she was washing dishes.

Jamie stared after her, silently debating what to do.

Shaking her head, Laura pointed toward the mudroom as if to tell him to let it go for now.

Jamie left with disappointment and regret bogging his every step.

NINETEEN

Kayla's stomach flip-flopped as she stood on the Riehl family's back porch between Eva and Nathan. She gripped a bowl of salad in her hands and lifted her chin as Nathan knocked on the door.

The day had flown by at lightning speed at the restaurant. Between the breakfast and lunch rushes, she and Eva had prepared the Swedish meatballs and then baked them in one of the restaurant ovens in the afternoon. Kayla and Eva were ready by the time the restaurant closed and their driver arrived. Kayla's parents started cleanup before going home with Junior for the evening. They said they didn't mind, even though Nathan had asked to join Kayla and Eva so he could see Jamie again.

It seemed Nathan really had become attached to Jamie, just as she had. Kayla smiled at the thought before a wave of alarm came over her. She couldn't set herself up for heartache, especially if there was a chance Nathan would get hurt in the process. She couldn't deny she was happy to see Jamie again, but she had to keep their relationship a friendship only, no matter what her family thought.

After a few moments, the door opened. Laura stood before them in a green dress, a black apron, and a bright smile. The sight of her new friend calmed Kayla's apprehension.

"*Wie geht's? Danki* for bringing supper."

"*Gern gschehne.* We're *froh* to be here," Kayla said. "I hope you and your family like Swedish meatballs and egg noodles."

"And cherry pie and rolls and salad," Eva chimed in. She was holding the pan with the Swedish meatballs and egg noodles. Nathan had the pie and rolls.

"Oooh!" Laura clapped her hands. "That sounds amazing! I haven't had Swedish meatballs in a long time."

"It smells amazing too," Nathan added. "My stomach has been growling since we left the restaurant."

Laura chuckled as she held out her hands. "What can I carry for you?"

"We have everything." Kayla took a step toward the door. "We might just have to warm up the Swedish meatballs and egg

285

noodles a little bit."

"I'll turn on the oven." Laura motioned for them to step inside. "I've been looking forward to this all day long. Please come in."

Kayla followed Laura into the kitchen, where Cindy was setting the table. "Hi, Cindy."

Cindy smiled. "*Wie geht's?* It's so *gut* to see you!" She took the bowl from Kayla and turned toward Eva and Nathan. *"Willkumm!"*

"How are you?" Eva asked.

"I'm okay, *danki.*" Cindy set the bowl on the counter. "How are you?"

"Gut, gut," Eva said. "Busy, right, Kayla?"

"*Ya,* that's true," Kayla agreed as she took the pie plate from Nathan.

"Is Jamie outside?" He jammed his thumb toward the back door.

"*Ya.* He's with *mei daed* and Mark in the barn. You can go see them."

"Danki." Nathan turned toward the door and then looked at Kayla. "Let me know when it's time to leave."

"Time to leave?" Laura raised her eyebrows as she looked at Eva and then Kayla. "Aren't you staying to eat with us?"

Kayla glanced at Eva. They had discussed delivering the meal and then leaving, not wanting to intrude on the Riehl family's

286

time together. But secretly Kayla had hoped they would invite them to stay. They'd brought plenty of food.

Cindy's eyes widened. "Were you going to just drop off the meal and leave?"

"We didn't want to impose," Kayla said.

"Don't be *gegisch*!" Laura exclaimed. "We all have been looking forward to a visit."

Has Jamie been looking forward to seeing me? Kayla fingered her apron.

"We want you to stay," Laura continued. "We always have a place at our table for our *freinden*."

"*Ya.*" Cindy's eyes seemed to plead with Kayla. "Please say you'll eat with us."

Kayla turned toward Eva, who nodded in agreement, and then she looked back at Cindy. "We'd love to stay for supper."

"*Gut.* It's settled then." Laura pointed to the table. "We were just about to grab some extra chairs."

"Nathan can get the chairs for you before he goes out." Kayla turned toward him. "Right?"

"*Ya,* of course." Nathan stepped toward the table.

"*Danki.*" Cindy motioned for Nathan to follow her to a room off the kitchen. "We keep the extra chairs in the laundry room."

Laura slipped the meatballs and noodles into the oven. "Did you have a busy day at the restaurant?"

"*Ya,* we did." Kayla walked over to the counter and leaned against it. "We had a bus stop by with a large group of tourists."

"Really?" Laura folded her arms over her apron. "How many were in the group?"

"I think there were about two dozen, right, Kayla?" Eva asked, and Kayla nodded.

Laura clicked her tongue. "I'm sure you were hopping with their orders."

"We were." Kayla pointed to the cabinets. "May we put out drinking glasses for you?"

"*Ya,* that would be great." Laura showed Kayla which cabinet to open, and Kayla and Eva set glasses on the table just as Cindy and Nathan returned with three chairs.

"Do you need me for anything else?" Nathan asked after the table was set.

"No, you can go," Kayla told him.

Nathan disappeared into the mudroom and they heard the back door open and close.

Laura chuckled. "He couldn't stand one more moment with the *maed,* could he?"

Kayla laughed. "No. He begged my parents to let him come too. I think he wants to talk some more with Jamie about firefighting."

Eva gave Kayla a sad smile. "*Ya,* and I think he misses Simeon."

"That's true too." Kayla sighed. *We all do.* "Can we do anything else to help?"

"How about bowls for the salad?" Eva suggested.

"*Ya,* I'll get them." Laura pulled the bowls out and Eva set them on the table.

Laura set the rolls in a basket and brought them to the table as well. "I think we're all set. Let's sit for a few minutes and then I'll check on the meatballs." She gestured toward the table.

Kayla chose a seat near the center of the table and looked at the chair to her right. Would Jamie sit beside her? Her pulse skittered at the thought of sharing a meal with him. Maybe they'd share many more in the near future. She gnawed her lower lip as hope grew no matter how many times she warned herself.

Laura slipped onto the chair to the left beside Kayla, and Cindy sat down across the table, next to Eva.

Eva folded her hands on the tabletop. "So how are you all doing really?" She looked at Cindy and then Laura. "How are you coping?"

Laura pushed the ribbons from her prayer covering over her shoulders. "We're taking it day by day. It's difficult because the loss is so palpable. I keep expecting to see *Mamm* behind me or hear her voice. I feel her loss. The *haus* is just too big and too empty, but I'm trying to keep moving forward."

She paused. "But at the same time, I'm trying to be strong for *mei daed.* He's taking it so hard. I heard him crying last night and he napped most of today. I can see the grief in the lines of his face. He only left the *haus* a little while ago to see what Jamie and Mark were doing outside. We have to keep the *haus* running and try to bring some sense of normalcy for him." She reached across the table and touched Cindy's hand. "Right, Cindy?"

Cindy sniffed. "Excuse me." She rushed out of the room and soon they heard a door click shut.

"*Ach,* no." Eva gasped, cupping her hand to her mouth. "I didn't mean to upset her. I shouldn't have said anything."

"It's okay." Laura shook her head and wiped her eyes. "Cindy is having a really tough time. I've tried to talk to her about what happened, but she won't even discuss it."

Kayla's eyes stung, and she cleared her throat. "I'm so sorry, Laura."

"*Danki.*"

"I didn't mean to intrude." Eva grabbed a napkin from the holder in the center of the table and wiped at her own eyes. "I know how hard it is to lose someone. I lost my husband last year, and I always appreciated it when people listened."

"I'm so sorry about your husband." Laura shook her head. "That had to be so difficult for you, especially since you were expecting a *boppli*."

"It was, and it still is." Eva wiped away another tear trickling down her cheek. "Some days are more difficult than others." She paused and took a deep breath. "I didn't mean to make things awkward tonight by bringing up the subject. I was only trying to be a *gut freind* and offer my sympathies."

"I know that, and Cindy does too." Laura touched Kayla's arm. "We appreciate your friendship. I'm so glad God brought you all into our lives." She squeezed Kayla's arm and then released it. "I mean that."

"I am too." Kayla also took a napkin as tears trailed down her cheeks. "I think about you and your family often. Jamie has shared how he's been struggling."

"He blames himself for *Mamm*'s accident, and Cindy hasn't made it any easier telling him it was his fault." Laura fingered the

291

edge of the table as she spoke.

"Why does he think it's his fault?" Eva asked.

While Laura explained about the banister, Kayla stared at her lap and tried to hold back tears. She recalled the pain and heartbreak she'd witnessed in Jamie's eyes and heard in his voice as he spoke about his mother that day in the basement, and again at the funeral. How she longed to help him through this difficult time.

"Jamie tried to discuss it with Cindy earlier today, but she told him she wasn't ready to talk to him." Laura kept her voice soft. "I tried to talk to her after Jamie went out to do his chores, but she wouldn't talk to me either. She ran off to the bathroom, like she just did."

Laura ran her thumbnail over the edge of the table. "I can't stand the tension in the *haus.* My siblings and I have had our disagreements, but it's never been like this. I feel like I should fix it since I'm the older *maedel,* but I don't know how if Cindy won't talk to me. We used to be able to talk about anything, but she's completely shut herself off. I thought about discussing this with *mei daed,* but he's grieving too. We all are, and he doesn't need any extra stress right now. It's just so tough."

"Jamie shared with me how Cindy won't talk to him." Even to her own ears, Kayla's voice sounded thin. "I promised him it would get better, but I know from experience the words feel so empty when you're the one who's suffering."

"They're not empty." Laura smiled at Kayla. "It will get better, and you're helping Jamie more than you know."

"You think so?" Kayla could hear the thread of hope in her voice.

"*Ya,* I do. I can tell your friendship means a lot to him, and I'm thankful he found you."

"I am too," Eva chimed in with a smile.

Laura pushed her chair back. "I'm going to go check on Cindy. I'll be right back."

"I'll see if the meatballs are ready." Kayla started toward the oven. She hoped their supper would in some small way help the Riehl family heal.

Jamie stepped out of the barn and breathed in the warm evening air. He looked toward the pasture fence, where *Dat* and Mark stood talking to a neighbor. Turning toward the back porch, he grinned as Nathan ambled down the steps and waved.

Nathan is here, which means Kayla is here.

"Hi, Nathan!" Jamie waved.

"Wie geht's?" Nathan shook his hand. "Kayla, Eva, and I brought supper over."

"That's *wunderbaar. Danki.*" Jamie rested his hands on his suspenders. "I'm glad you came with them."

"Laura and Cindy invited us to stay for supper."

"I'm so glad to hear it." Jamie smiled at the prospect of talking to Kayla alone again. "How was the rest of your night? Did you have any more calls?"

"No, we didn't." Jamie sat down on a bench by the garden, and Nathan plopped down beside him. "It was an unusually quiet night. I actually got some sleep."

"That's *gut.*" Nathan looked out toward the pasture, and his smile faded as if he were contemplating something.

"Is there something you want to discuss?" Jamie prodded.

Nathan gave him a sheepish smile. "My parents were really upset with me last night. *Mei daed* threatened to take away Simeon's radio."

"Oh." Jamie paused, considering how to approach the topic without alienating Nathan. "You do understand why he wanted to take the radio, right?"

Nathan nodded. "*Ya.* What I did was reckless and dangerous. You don't need to

294

remind me."

Jamie ran his finger over the arm of the bench. "I have an idea that will satisfy both you and your parents."

Nathan raised his eyebrows. "I'm listening."

"You can visit me anytime you want, and I'll answer all your firefighting questions — on one condition." Jamie held up his index finger.

"Okay." Nathan lifted his hands. "What's the condition?"

"You only come to see me at the station and not on calls."

Nathan's lips formed a flat line. "That point has been made very clear to me. Is that it?"

"No, that's not it. Your parents have to know where you are. I can tell you when I'm on duty, and you can come to the station as long as your parents say it's okay. I'm sure Brody and the other guys would enjoy seeing you too. You're always welcome there."

"Danki." Nathan leaned his back against the arm of the bench. "That sounds *gut.*"

"Great." Jamie glanced toward the house. "How are your parents doing?"

"Fine. They told me to tell you and your family hello. They've been thinking of you."

"That's nice." Jamie turned toward the pasture. Mark and *Dat* were still talking to the neighbor. "We appreciate that."

"They said they want to visit sometime soon. They couldn't come tonight because they had to stay behind and clean up the restaurant after we left. *Mamm* is taking care of Junior too."

"I understand." Jamie rested his right ankle on his left knee. "It's very generous of you, Eva, and Kayla to come."

"It was Kayla's idea to bring the meal."

Jamie couldn't stop a smile. He looked down at the ground and then over at Nathan.

Nathan crossed his arms over his tan shirt and studied Jamie for a moment. "Do you like *mei schweschder*?"

Jamie was caught. There was no point in evading the question. "*Ya,* I do. I like her a lot."

"*Gut.*"

"*Gut?*" Jamie was stunned by the comment.

"*Ya, gut.* Kayla likes you too." Nathan's expression darkened slightly. "Her last boyfriend broke up with her just two months after Simeon died. It was really tough on her."

Jamie gaped. "That's horrible. Why would

he do that to her?"

"I don't know what Abram was thinking, but it was . . . What's the word she used? Devastating. Yeah, that's what I heard her tell Eva. I'm *froh* she has you for a *freind.*"

Jamie was so overwhelmed by Nathan's words that his own were trapped in his throat for a moment. He simply nodded in response.

"Nathan!" *Dat* called as he and Mark joined them by the garden. *"Wie geht's?"*

"How are you?" Nathan waved to them.

"It's *gut* to see you." Mark shook Nathan's hand. "I heard you brought us supper."

"*Ya,* I hope you like Swedish meatballs and egg noodles," Nathan offered.

"Oh, that sounds perfect," *Dat* said, and Mark agreed.

"Do you cook at the restaurant?" Mark asked.

Nathan shook his head. "Not much. *Mei daed* and *mamm* are starting to teach me how to make a few of the meals, but I mostly bus tables and wash dishes."

As Nathan continued chatting with Mark and *Dat,* Jamie's thoughts swirled with the information Nathan shared. Kayla dated someone named Abram who broke her heart shortly after Simeon died. Jamie had to tread lightly with her heart, but he also had to work on showing her how he felt about her. He would try to get her alone tonight and ask if he could visit her. He didn't deserve a chance at happiness when his family was going through such a hard time, but he couldn't fend off the hope that filled him at the thought of making Kayla his girlfriend.

After a few minutes, Laura appeared on the porch. "Supper is ready!"

"Let's eat," Mark said.

Jamie walked with the other men into the mudroom, and the aroma of Swedish meatballs wafted over him. Through the doorway to the kitchen, he could see his sisters, Eva, and Kayla waiting by the table.

Mark and *Dat* went in and greeted their guests, but Jamie lingered in the doorway, his eyes locked on Kayla. She was wearing a dusty-rose-colored dress that complemented her cheeks. He leaned his shoulder against the doorframe and memorized her face. His conversation with Nathan echoed through his mind. How could this Abram break up with a woman as kind, sweet, and beautiful as Kayla? Jamie would be blessed to have a woman like her in his life.

She looked toward the doorway, and when her gaze met his, her lips turned up in a gorgeous smile. His heart melted. "Hi."

"Hi." He took a step toward her. "How are you?"

"I'm *gut.*" She rested her hand on the back of one of the chairs. "How about you?"

I'm better now. "I'm fine." Jamie looked at the table, taking in the large serving platter of meatballs and noodles. "Dinner looks fantastic."

"Eva really was the one who made it."

He tilted his head and studied her sheepish expression. He had the distinct impression she wasn't one to take credit for things.

"Let's sit down and enjoy this *wunderbaar* meal," Laura announced.

"Where are you going to sit?" Kayla asked him.

"Beside you, hopefully."

"Gut," she said with a smile.

Jamie took his usual seat at the table and tapped the chair beside him. Kayla sank onto the chair, and when their knees brushed, a thrill moved down his spine.

After a silent prayer, they filled their plates and conversations bubbled up all around the table. Laura, sitting across from Kayla, kept her engaged in a discussion of recipes, and *Dat* and Eva talked about dairy farming. Nathan and Mark discussed the most common causes for stove fires.

Jamie took in the bustling scene around

him as he ate the delicious meal. A thought caught him off guard — Kayla and her family seemed to fit with his family. It was as if they'd known each other their whole lives.

Does this mean we belong together?

Hope lit a tiny flame in his chest. Maybe Kayla did belong with him, but only time would tell.

If only Mamm *were here.*

Unexpected grief sent a pang through him and stole his bright mood.

"Everything was *appeditlich.*" *Dat* leaned back in his chair and rubbed his abdomen. "*Danki* so much for bringing it over."

"*Ya,* it was fabulous." Jamie turned toward Kayla. "That was the best cherry pie I've ever had."

"I'm so glad you liked it." Kayla stood and began to gather plates. "Eva and I can help you clean up before we head home."

"*Ya.*" Eva lifted the serving dish and pie plate.

"No, no." Laura shook her head. "You did all the cooking. Cindy and I will clean up the kitchen. You can leave if you'd like. I imagine you have to be up early tomorrow."

"Are you sure?" Kayla asked.

"Of course." Cindy took the plates from Kayla's hands. "We just so appreciate the *appeditlich* food and the visit. I had a *wunderbaar* time."

"I did too," Mark said. "You need to come more often."

"I'm sure we will." Eva raised her eyebrows at Kayla.

Kayla nodded before looking down at the green tablecloth. Was she embarrassed?

"We should call our driver," Eva suggested.

"I'll do it." Kayla turned to Jamie. "Would you walk me out to your phone?"

"Ya." Jamie stood. "The shanty is out by the barn."

"Great." Kayla looked at Eva. "I'll tell Eric to come now."

"I'll wash our serving dishes while you're gone." Eva headed to the sink.

Jamie led Kayla to the mudroom, where he picked up a battery-operated lantern and turned it on. Then he held open the back door for her. The air was warm and humid, and the sun was beginning to set, staining the clear sky with explosions of purple, orange, magenta, and yellow. He breathed in the clean air and smiled. It was the perfect night.

They fell into step beside each other as they descended the porch steps. When they reached the path leading to the phone shanty, they both began to speak at once and then laughed.

"You go first," he insisted as they strolled toward the phone shanty.

"Okay." She stopped walking and pivoted toward him. "You were quiet during supper. *Was iss letz?*"

"Nothing is wrong. I was just enjoying our supper together and observing the conversation. You and Laura were enjoying your discussion of recipes, and I didn't want to intrude. You've really bonded with *mei schweschder.*"

She smiled brightly. "*Ya,* I have. Your family is great. I'm so *froh* we came over tonight."

"I am too." He lost himself in her eyes for a moment as a tornado of emotions swirled in his gut — longing, grief, excitement, anxiety, fear. He didn't want the evening to end, and he loathed the thought of her going home. He wanted to sit beside her on the porch glider and talk all night long. But the sky was getting dark, and work would come early tomorrow morning for them both.

"You're quiet again." This time her smile was coy. "What would I learn if I could read your thoughts?"

The question caught him off guard, and

302

he laughed.

She raised her eyebrows as her smile faded.

"I was just thinking we didn't have enough time together tonight," he admitted, and her smile returned. "May I see you again tomorrow? I think I can get away from the farm for a little while." He held his breath, anxiously awaiting her response.

"*Ya,* I'd like that very much."

"*Gut.*" He felt relieved.

Kayla pointed toward the phone shanty. "I better call our driver before our parents start to worry."

"*Ya.*" He held up the lantern, and Kayla stepped into the shanty.

Kayla dialed the phone and spoke to her driver, and Jamie found himself already looking forward to spending time with her tomorrow.

Minutes later, Jamie helped carry their serving dishes outside. When the van arrived, he helped their guests load it. Eva and Nathan climbed inside after their good-byes, but Kayla stood with him a few moments longer.

"*Danki* again for coming tonight."

"*Gern gschehne.*" She smiled, a little shyly. "I'll see you tomorrow."

"I can't wait." He touched her arm. "Have

a *gut* night."

"*Gut nacht.*" She climbed into the van, and he waved to Eva and Nathan before closing her door.

When the van's taillights had disappeared, Jamie jogged up the porch stairs, his pulse racing. He'd just spent a wonderful evening with Kayla and he would see her again tomorrow. His chest swelled and a smile curved his lips.

He stepped into the kitchen and stopped dead in his tracks. His siblings were already elsewhere, but his father sat at the table, wiping away tears.

"*Dat.*" Jamie rushed to his side. "Are you all right?"

Dat shook his head and mopped his face with a paper napkin. "I was just thinking about how much your *mamm* would have enjoyed this supper."

Jamie sank down into the chair beside his father and rubbed his shoulder. He silently kicked himself for putting his happiness before his father's needs. How could he even think about Kayla when his father was so much pain?

TWENTY

Disappointment crawled up Kayla's spine and tightened her shoulders as she wiped down tables for the last time. Jamie had invaded her thoughts throughout the day as she looked for his visit. He hadn't specified a time, but surely he meant to come for lunch or maybe even supper and then stay to keep her company for a while. But he never appeared. She doubted he would.

The restaurant was closed, and soon she would head home with her family. Knots of disappointment filled her stomach. Why had she allowed herself to get so attached to Jamie so quickly? Her resolve to remain only friends with him had disappeared as soon as she saw him in his kitchen doorway the night before.

Why would you expect Jamie to keep his promise? He was bound to let you down. He's just like Abram.

Kayla shoved away the negative voice in

her head and began to scrub another table.

"Maybe he'll be waiting for you at the *haus* when we get home."

Kayla blinked and then looked across the room to where Eva was cashing out the register. Could her sister-in-law read her thoughts?

"Don't give up. The night isn't over yet." Eva returned to counting and humming.

Kayla grimaced. As much as she wanted to believe in Eva's words, doubt had crept into her mind and it wouldn't be so easy to get it out again.

They worked in silence for several moments as her frustrated thoughts swirled. And then another thought hit her. What if Jamie had to fill in at the fire station and responded to an emergency call — and been injured? What if he'd been in an accident like Simeon's?

Icy fear slithered up her spine and froze her insides.

The bell on the front door rang.

Kayla frowned. Hadn't the person realized they were closed? They had a sign in the window, but they must have forgotten to lock the door. She turned toward the entrance and gasped as Jamie leaned on the hostess podium. He and Eva were both smiling. Speechless, she stared at him, fear and worry untangling in her chest.

"I know you're closed, but I was wondering if now is a good time to visit." He lifted his straw hat and pushed his hand through his thick, dark hair. "I had hoped to see you earlier, but I kept getting caught up with chores at the farm. I hope it's not too late."

"No, it's not too late." Relief replaced her doubt, worry, and fear as grateful tears stung her eyes.

"Gut." His gaze moved to Eva. "Hi."

"Hi, Jamie." Eva was still smiling. "I'm so glad you made it tonight."

"Danki." Jamie walked over to Kayla. "Maybe I can help you with your chores and then give you a ride home."

"That would be really nice." Happiness blossomed in Kayla's chest as she wiped away a tear.

He tilted his head and his smile faded. "Why are you crying?"

"At first I thought you'd stood me up, but then I was worried you had responded to a call and got hurt." She sniffed. "I'm just so thankful you're okay."

"I'm sorry. I didn't mean to worry you."

"It's fine." She blew out a relieved breath. "You're here now."

He rubbed his hands together. "So put me to work!"

"Oh, don't be *gegisch.*" She waved off the offer. "You don't have to help."

"I want to. The sooner the chores are done, the sooner we can leave, right?" He lifted an eyebrow.

"*Ya,* that's true." She handed him the paper towels and a bottle of cleaner, hoping he wouldn't mind the smell of ammonia. "You can help me clean off the tables. I'll go get another bottle and start on the other side of the room."

"Sounds *gut.*" He took the paper towels and got to work.

After finding another bottle of cleaner and a roll of paper towels in the supply room, Kayla stepped into the kitchen. Her parents were scrubbing the counters and Nathan was washing pans.

"Jamie's here." Her words came in a short burst as she fought to catch her breath. "He came to see me, and he wants to take me home. Is that all right with you, *Dat*?" She chewed her lower lip, hoping her father would agree.

"Of course it is," *Dat* said. "I like Jamie. I'm glad he came by."

"*Ya,* I am too," *Mamm* said.

"Jamie's here?" Nathan's face lit up. "I want to see him before you leave."

Kayla held up the cleaning supplies.

"Okay, but right now he's helping me clean tables."

"You've found a man who'll clean?" *Mamm*'s eyes got big. "You better hold on to him. Men like that are difficult to find."

"Excuse me?" *Dat* asked. "What am I doing right now?"

Mamm jammed one hand on her hip. "You have to clean, Willie. It's your restaurant."

Kayla took a step back toward the dining room. "I need to get back."

She found Jamie hard at work. He glanced at her. "We'll be done in no time."

Her heart felt as though it had turned over in her chest. She took in the breadth of his wide shoulders and his muscular biceps as he leaned over a table and scrubbed. When she realized she was staring, she set to cleaning a table.

Kayla felt someone watching her. She craned her neck to look over at Eva, who gave her a thumb's up. Kayla shook her head and looked over at Jamie, grateful he hadn't seen the gesture.

"How was your day, Kayla?" Jamie kept his focus trained on the table he was cleaning.

"It was *gut.* We had another tour group for lunch." *But the day dragged as I waited for you.*

"*Ya,* that was a surprise," Eva chimed in. "I told *Dat* he should ask the local tour companies to let us know when they plan to eat here. It would help if we were ready for them."

"That's very true." Kayla finished one table and started on another one. "How was your day, Jamie?"

"*Gut.* Mark and I got a lot of chores done." Jamie talked about mending some pasture fencing as they finished cleaning the tables. Then they placed all the chairs on the tabletops so Nathan and *Dat* could sweep and mop the floor.

Kayla made sure the front door was locked and then she, Eva, and Jamie moved to the kitchen. Her parents and Nathan were finishing up in the kitchen.

"How are you, Jamie?" *Dat* shook his hand.

"I'm fine. How are you?"

"I'm doing well."

"*Danki* for the *appeditlich* meal you sent to my family last night. We enjoyed it."

"*Gern gschehne.* And it was kind of you to help Kayla with her chores tonight." *Dat* gestured toward *Mamm.* "Marilyn is impressed you would help clean tables. She said Kayla should hold on to you for that reason alone."

310

"Dat!" Kayla gasped.

"I was kidding," *Mamm* said. "And your *daed* is too."

Jamie chuckled. "I don't mind helping. Actually, Willie, I want to ask your permission to take Kayla home in my buggy. Would it be all right? We'll go straight there."

"*Ya,* of course," *Dat* said. "I think she'll like that."

Kayla was certain her cheeks were going to spontaneously combust. "Would it be okay if we left now?"

"*Ya,* it's okay with me," *Mamm* said, turning toward *Dat,* who nodded in agreement.

When Junior began to moan from his play yard in the office beyond the kitchen, Eva hurried to him.

"Junior is ready to go home," *Mamm* quipped. "He's been fussy today."

"Would you like me to take Eva and Junior with us?" Jamie offered.

"No, no," *Mamm* said. "You two can go on to the *haus.* We'll be ready to leave soon."

"Hi, Jamie." Nathan came around the corner from the large sinks. He had two mops in his hands and pushed a bucket filled with water on wheels with one foot. *Dat* took one of the mops and leaned it against a counter.

"Wie geht's?" Jamie shook Nathan's hand.

"Are you going to be at the fire station next week?"

"*Ya,* but I'll have to look at my calendar at home to see what day I'm working. I can't remember off the top of my head."

Nathan wiped his hands down his white apron. "I was wondering if I could stop by and see you."

Jamie glanced at *Dat,* who nodded. "*Ya,* it's fine with me as long as it's okay with your *daed.*"

"*Ya,* that would be fine," *Dat* said. "As long as your chores at the restaurant are done."

Nathan nodded. "Great."

Kayla pointed to the back door. "I think we should get going."

"Be safe going home," *Mamm* said. "We'll see you soon."

Jamie waved to Kayla's family and then followed her outside.

They stepped into the parking lot, and seeds of uncertainty took root. But she shoved those thoughts away. She was going to go on her first ride with Jamie, and they would be alone. Excited butterflies flitted in her belly. Would he ask her to be his girlfriend? And if so, should she say yes?

They walked side by side to his waiting horse and buggy, and Kayla's pulse galloped. Despite her hesitation about having a relationship with him, she wanted to savor every moment of this ride with Jamie.

Jamie opened the passenger side door of the buggy, and Kayla climbed in.

"*Danki.*" She smoothed the skirt of her purple dress over her legs.

"*Gern gschehne.*" Jamie jogged around the buggy and slipped into the driver's side. Then he guided his horse toward the road. "I'm sorry I got here so late tonight. I was thankful when I saw the gaslights still on in the dining room."

"Your timing was perfect." She folded her hands on her lap. "You even got to help me clean."

"That was a bonus." He waggled his eyebrows, and she giggled.

She stared out the windshield toward the road ahead of them as he halted the horse at a red light. He recalled her tentative expression when he and Nathan mentioned a visit at the fire station and suddenly felt the urge to explain why he'd suggested it. He didn't want to risk any misunderstandings between them.

"You're probably wondering why I told Nathan he could visit me at the fire station."

She shrugged. "I thought maybe you

discussed it with him last night. He was eager to see you, which I'm sure is why he wanted to help Eva and me deliver the meal."

"*Ya,* we did talk about it, but I wanted to tell you exactly what we talked about." Jamie angled his body toward her. "I told Nathan I would answer any of his firefighting questions as long as he came to see me at the station and not on calls. I thought that would help inspire him to be safe. I explained he has to get permission from your *daed,* and he's not to sneak off anymore. He has to let his family know where he is."

"*Danki.* That was a *gut* idea."

"*Gern gschehne.*" The light turned green, and he guided the horse through the intersection. "I want Nathan to make *gut* decisions, but I didn't want you to think I was going behind your back. I'm not going to encourage him to register for training without your *daed*'s permission."

"I trust you."

The words were simple, but they touched him deeply.

"I think he has gravitated toward you because he misses Simeon so much," she continued, no doubt unaware of how her words had affected him. "I think you remind him of Simeon, and he misses having a *bruder.*"

Jamie nodded while keeping his eyes focused on the road ahead. Her comparing him to her older brother, whom he'd known to be a fine man, was so overwhelming he didn't know how to respond.

"How is your family today?" she asked.

He shrugged. The grief still hung over them like a dark cloud. "Not much has changed, really."

"Has Cindy spoken to you yet?"

The question caught him off guard, and he cut his eyes to hers. "No, she hasn't."

"I'm sorry to hear that." She sighed. "Cindy got upset last night."

"Did she get upset with you?" He gripped the reins tighter. "What did she say?"

"No, no. Cindy didn't get upset with me. She didn't say anything." She touched his arm, and the gesture sent warmth that extinguished his irritation. "We were getting ready for supper, and Eva asked Laura and Cindy how they were doing. Laura talked about how difficult it's been, and Cindy rushed off to cry by herself. Laura shared a little bit of what you've been going through with Cindy, and that she'd tried to encourage Cindy to talk to you. She said Cindy hasn't been able to talk about what happened at all. She's really having a tough time."

He kept his focus trained on the road as an ache radiated through his chest. "I guess Cindy finally came back since she had supper with us."

"*Ya,* Laura went and talked to her. I don't know what she said, but she convinced her to join us. Cindy was quiet, but she seemed okay." She turned to look at him. "Eva felt so bad. She thought she could try to help your *schweschdere* because she's knows how difficult it is to lose someone, but she never meant to hurt Cindy."

"It wasn't anything Eva said. I hope she knows that." He halted the horse at a stop sign and once more angled himself toward Kayla. "Cindy's just different now that *Mamm* is gone. It's like she can't keep her emotions in check. But we're all different now. *Mei daed* hasn't had the strength to help with chores. I've never seen him so run-down and depressed. Mark tries to crack jokes, but I can tell how deeply this is affecting him too. We're just not the same without *Mamm.*" When a knot of emotion swelled in his throat, he paused, gathering his thoughts. "I'll talk to Eva and tell her she shouldn't feel bad."

"That's not necessary." Her gaze was

warm. "I'm worried about you and your family. How are you coping?"

"I guess I just go through the motions every day."

"That's how I felt when we lost Simeon. On the bad days, I tried my best to recall this verse from the gospel of Luke. Jesus said to the Samaritan, 'Rise and go; your faith has made you well.' " She tapped his arm. "Your faith will heal your heart and make you well again."

Her deep faith and kindness warmed his battered heart. What Nathan told him about her ex-boyfriend echoed in his mind, and confused him. How could a man break up with someone as special and thoughtful as Kayla? He would be blessed to call her his girlfriend.

The notion sent his heart tripping over itself. Did he have the confidence to ask her to be his girlfriend?

"Turn here." She pointed toward her street. "Our farm is down this road."

"I know."

She laughed and shook her head. "I'm sorry. I forgot you probably know your way around Lancaster County better than I do since you volunteer for the fire department."

"It's okay. I don't mind the reminders." He gave her a sideways glance. "Tell me more about your day."

"Oh." She looked surprised by the question. "I met a nice couple from New Jersey today. They came here for the week."

She talked about some of her customers as they rode the rest of the way to her farm. When they reached the driveway, he guided the horse up to the porch, and disappointment crept in. The evening had gone by too quickly. He wasn't ready to say good night and make the long journey home alone. He needed more time with her.

Kayla turned toward him and fingered her apron. "*Danki* for giving me a ride home."

"*Gern gschehne. Danki* for allowing me to give you a ride home."

She glanced toward the porch and then looked back at him. "Are you in a hurry to get back?"

"No."

"*Mei daed* made root beer. Would you like to visit on the porch for a while?"

"I'd love to." Relief overtook his disappointment.

"Great. I'll get the root beer." She climbed out of the buggy and rushed up the porch steps to the house.

He tied his horse to the fence lining the driveway and then made his way to the glider on the back porch. He was gently pushing it back and forth when she re-appeared with two bottles of root beer and a lantern. He jumped up, took the lantern from her, and set it on the porch floor.

She handed him one of the cold bottles. "Would you like a snack too?"

"Oh, no." He shook his head. "I don't want you to go to any trouble."

She lifted an eyebrow. "My parents own a restaurant. It's no trouble." She pointed toward the door. "Do you want some pretzels or chips?"

"No." He made a sweeping gesture toward the glider. "I want you to sit and talk to me."

She hesitated. "Really, it's no trouble."

"Please sit."

"Okay." She sank down onto the glider, and he sat down beside her. "What did you want to talk about?"

"Anything." He took a long draw from the bottle, relishing the cool carbonation on his throat. "This root beer is fantastic."

"*Ya. Mei daed* makes the best root beer. I told him he should sell it at the restaurant, but he insists he couldn't keep it stocked. It's a lot of work." She took a drink. "Tell me about your *freinden.*"

"*Mei freinden?*" He rested the bottle on the arm of the glider. "Well, you've met Brody, Leon, and Noah. Noah and I have been *freinden* for years. He's married and has a *sohn.*"

"Oh *ya.*" She angled her body toward him. "I met Elsie and Christian." Her smile suddenly faded.

"Was iss letz?"

"I met them the day of the funeral."

"It's okay." He gave her a gentle smile. "I'm glad you got to meet them."

"I've met Savilla, Allen, and Rudy too."

"That's *gut.*" He took another drink. "What about you? Who are your *freinden?*"

Kayla fingered the condensation on her bottle. "I have a few *freinden* from my youth group. But Eva is my best *freind.* She's like the *schweschder* I never had."

He took another gulp of root beer as his thoughts moved to Abram. He longed to ask her about him, but he didn't know how to bring up the subject.

"Do you have a girlfriend?" She kept her eyes trained on her bottle as she asked the question.

He swallowed a laugh. "Do you think I'd be here if I did?"

She bit her lower lip as she shrugged, her eyes still focused on the bottle. "No, I don't think so."

"I don't have a girlfriend." *At least not yet.* "And do you have a boyfriend?"

"Not anymore." She shook her head. "My ex-boyfriend broke up with me shortly after Simeon died."

"I'm sorry. That had to be difficult." He gripped the root beer bottle waiting for her to share more.

"It was." She gazed out toward the new barn as she spoke. "His name is Abram Blank. We met through our youth group. We dated for about a year."

He sat up straight, surprised by that news.

Her shoulders hunched. "We'd been having issues before he broke it off." She ran her fingers over the bottle. "When we first started dating, he was attentive, and things seemed great. I did my best to be a *gut* girlfriend. In fact, I grew apart from some of *mei freinden* because I always made sure I had time to spend with him. But then I found myself waiting for him to visit me and he wouldn't show up. When I asked why, he'd tell me he was with his *freinden.* I never came first in his life. I tried to explain how I felt, but he never made an effort to change. I was frustrated, and I was planning to confront him, but then Simeon died and my world fell apart. My family and I were all so distraught. I was having a difficult time dealing with everything. He wound up breaking up with me. He said he wasn't ready for a serious relationship."

"It sounds like Abram had a lot of growing up to do if he couldn't put you first in his life. I'm sorry he did that to you."

"Danki." She finally met his gaze and then took a draw from her bottle. "What about you? Have you dated much?"

"No." Jamie set the bottle on the arm again. "I dated a little bit when I was a teenager, but it wasn't anything serious. I'm not *gut* at relationships."

"That's not true. I think you're *gut* at relationships."

"Would you like to have a relationship with me?" His shoulders and back tensed as he awaited her response.

"Ya. I'd like that very much."

"Gut." Relief flooded him, loosening his tense muscles. "Do you have church tomorrow?"

She shook her head. "It's an off Sunday for my church district."

"Would you like to come to church with me?"

"Ya, that would be fun."

Jamie smiled. "I'll look forward to it."

"I will too."

Kayla was almost certain she was dreaming. She and Jamie sat on the porch for nearly an hour talking as if they were old friends, and to her surprise, he'd asked if she would like to be more than friends. This was too good to be true! Surely she would wake up from the dream soon and realize it wasn't real.

When her family arrived home, she and Jamie greeted them and then continued to talk on the porch alone. Soon it was dark, and Kayla began to worry about his trip home.

"As much as I want to talk all night, I want you to be safe." She pointed toward the dark sky. "You should probably head home."

"Ya." He gave her a reluctant smile. "Do you think your *daed* is still awake?"

"He should be." Ripples of excitement ran through her veins. Was he going to ask her father's permission to date her? "Walk inside with me, and we can check."

He carried his empty bottle and the lantern toward the door. He balanced them in one hand and held the door open for her.

"Danki," she said as she entered. In the kitchen they found her parents sitting at the table with Eva.

"It was nice to see you all." He held up his hand. *"Gut nacht."*

"Are you heading home?" *Mamm* asked.

"*Ya*. It's getting dark." Jamie turned toward *Dat*. "I was wondering if I could speak with you, Willie."

"*Ya,* of course."

"Could you walk outside with me?"

"Sure." *Dat* stood and came to his side. Jamie touched Kayla's arm. "*Gut nacht.* I'll see you tomorrow."

"Be safe going home." Kayla gripped the back of one of the kitchen chairs as Jamie and *Dat* went outside.

"Is everything all right?" *Mamm* asked after the men were gone.

"*Ya.*" Kayla couldn't stop her grin. "He asked me if I wanted to date him. I think he's asking *Dat*'s permission."

Eva squealed as she jumped up and hugged Kayla. "That's fantastic! I knew it was coming."

"I'm so *froh* for you," *Mamm* said.

"*Danki*. I'm just so *naerfich.*" Kayla shook her head.

"Why?" Eva asked.

"Everything went wrong with Abram." Kayla wrapped her arms around her waist as apprehension and happiness warred inside of her. "I don't want to make those same mistakes."

Mamm stood and rubbed Kayla's arm. "Jamie is a different man. Abram wasn't ready for a true relationship. You didn't do anything wrong."

Kayla nodded, but she didn't entirely agree with her mother.

"Just take it slow," Eva said. "Get to know Jamie and take your time."

"Exactly," *Mamm* agreed.

The back door clicked shut, and *Dat* entered the kitchen as the clip-clop of a horse echoed from the driveway.

Kayla bit her lower lip as she waited for her father to speak.

"Jamie asked if he can date you." He smiled at her, and her chest constricted.

"What did you say?" Kayla's voice sounded tiny, as if she were a little girl.

"I said it's fine with me as long as it's fine with you. Was that the answer you'd hoped for?"

"Ya. Danki." Kayla blew out a relieved breath as *Mamm* and Eva smiled.

Dat touched her arm. "He also said you agreed to go to church with him tomorrow, and I'm certainly okay with that too. Well, I'm going to bed. Get some sleep. It's late." He turned to *Mamm.* "Are you ready too?"

"Ya." Mamm turned to Kayla and Eva. *"Gut nacht."*

"Gut nacht." Kayla and Eva responded in unison.

"Everything will be fine," Eva told Kayla after her parents left. "Jamie is a great guy, and he really likes you. I have a *gut* feeling."

"Danki. Gut nacht." Kayla hugged Eva. "I'll see you in the morning."

As Kayla climbed the stairs to her room, she imagined what it would be like to be Jamie's girlfriend. She just hoped this relationship would go better than the one with Abram.

TWENTY-ONE

"Stop fidgeting. You look *schee*."

Kayla pivoted from the kitchen window toward her mother as she fingered the blue skirt of her best dress. It was too early for Jamie to pick her up for church, but she was having a hard time settling down. *"Danki."* If only she felt as confident as her mother's smile.

"Why are you so *naerfich*? You looked like you had a *wunderbaar* time with Jamie last night."

"I'm going to see his *freinden* at church. I've only met them briefly once. What if they don't like me?"

Mamm chuckled. "Of course they'll like you." She pointed to Kayla's uneaten plate of eggs, toast, and bacon. "You should eat."

"I can't." Kayla placed her hands on her abdomen. "My stomach is in knots."

"Don't be *gegisch*. You don't want your stomach to growl during service. If it does, then his *freinden won't* like you." *Mamm* grinned.

"That's not funny." Kayla sat down at the table, and after a quick prayer, grabbed a piece of toast and bit into it. It tasted like sand.

"Gude mariye," Eva sang as she stepped into the kitchen with Junior on her hip.

"Gude mariye." *Mamm* held out her hands, and the baby squealed as she took him in her arms.

"Gude mariye." Kayla echoed before taking another bite. If she finished the toast, maybe she wouldn't run the risk of her growling stomach scaring away Jamie's friends.

Eva sat down across from Kayla, bowed her head in prayer, and began to scoop up eggs. "Oh, Kayla. You look so *schee.*"

"Danki." Kayla hoped Jamie would agree and then dismissed the thought. Vanity was a sin.

"Are you excited to go to church with Jamie and his family?" Eva asked.

"She's afraid his *freinden* won't like her even though they've already met her." *Mamm* slipped Junior into his baby seat attached to the high chair. He clapped his hands when he saw the food on the table.

328

Eva raised an eyebrow. "You can't be serious."

"She's serious." *Mamm* sat and fed him baby food from the jar that Eva had brought to the table.

"*Mamm,* I can speak for myself." Kayla picked up a second piece of toast. "But you're right. I am worried about his *freinden.*"

Eva leveled her gaze on Kayla. "Jamie really likes you, and that means his *freinden* will too. You have nothing to worry about."

"Exactly," *Mamm* added as she gave Junior another spoonful of food.

Kayla finished the toast and then hurried off to brush her teeth. When she stepped back into the kitchen, the clip-clop of a horse sounded from outside, and she tried to ignore the wild thumping of her heart. "I think he's here. I'll see you later."

"Have fun." Eva waved.

"Bye," *Mamm* called.

Kayla hurried down the back porch steps to where Jamie stood by his buggy. He looked handsome dressed in his Sunday suit with his black trousers, crisp white shirt, and black vest. *"Gude mariye."*

"Gude mariye." He opened the passenger side door. "You look *schee.*"

"Danki." She climbed into the buggy,

smoothed her hands over her dress, and then touched her abdomen. Hopefully the toast would hold her until lunch. Her stomach was still a ball of nervous knots.

Jamie slipped into the driver's side and took the reins. "It's a gorgeous day. It's hard to believe next week will be July."

"*Ya.*" Kayla gazed out at the beautiful cerulean sky as he guided the horse to the road. "The summer is going by too quickly. Where is church this morning?"

"It's at the Beilers' farm. Not far from *mei haus.*" He gripped the reins tighter as he kept his eyes on the road.

Kayla could feel the anxiety vibrating off him. What was wrong? What a silly question. He and his family were grieving, and this would be their first Sunday service without their mother. Of course he was a ball of nerves. She had to remember to be patient and offer him the same grace she needed after she'd lost Simeon. She prayed his family would feel God's love and comfort today.

They rode in silence for a few minutes.

When he halted the horse at a red light, Jamie suddenly looked at her, his expression somber. "I spoke to your *daed* before I left your *haus* last night."

"I know." She held her breath. Was he going to officially ask her to be his girlfriend?

"I asked him if I could date you. So now I need to ask you. Would you consider being my girlfriend — officially?"

"I'd love to."

"Gut." A smile lit up his attractive face.

The light turned green and he guided the horse through the intersection. "Laura is excited you're coming this morning. She can't wait to see you."

"I'm eager to see her and Cindy too." She gave him a sideways glance when she said Cindy's name, but he didn't show any outward reaction. "Will Rudy, Savilla, and Allen be there too?"

"Ya, they will." He talked about his friends during the remainder of the ride to the Beilers' house. When they reached the farm, she climbed from the buggy and met him at the back. "I'll see you after the service."

"Ya." He touched her arm. "I'm glad you're here."

"I am too." She squared her shoulders, took a deep breath, and nodded at the men standing by the barn before heading toward the large farmhouse. That's where the women always gathered before a church service.

Kayla found them in the kitchen standing in a large circle, talking. She scanned the

331

unfamiliar faces, and her shoulders loosened when she spotted Cindy and Laura in the far corner of the room. They were with Savilla and Elsie, who had Christian balanced on her hip.

"Kayla!" Laura waved for her to join them.

"Gude mariye." Savilla held out her hand.

"It's *gut* to see you again." Kayla shook her hand and then shook Elsie's hand. "It's nice to see you again too." She touched the little boy's back. "Hi, Christian."

"I'm so glad you could come to church with us today," Elsie said.

"Wie geht's?" Cindy shook Kayla's hand. The sadness in her eyes nearly broke Kayla's heart.

"It's *gut* to see you," Kayla told Cindy.

Laura hugged Kayla. *"Mei bruder* told us you were coming." She moved closer and lowered her voice. "Did he ask you to be his girlfriend yet?"

Kayla nodded as she felt a blush crawling up her neck.

Laura smiled. "That's *gut.*"

"It's about time," Savilla quipped. "He's been alone too long."

"I agree," Elsie added.

Laura took Kayla's hand and led her toward the circle of women. "I want you to meet some of the members of our district."

After introductions, the clock chimed nine and Kayla exited the house with the Riehl sisters, Elsie, and Savilla. In the barn, the warm, heavy aroma of animals and moist earth wafted over her.

"We'll see you after the service," Savilla said softly as she and Elsie went to sit with the married women.

"You're going to sit with Cindy and me, right?" Laura whispered.

"*Ya,* of course. Where else would I sit?" Laura took her arm and led her to where the other unmarried young women sat. Kayla sank onto a backless bench between Jamie's two sisters and nodded at a few more of the women in the community.

When she turned toward the rows of unmarried young men, she found Jamie sitting between his brother and Rudy. Kayla kept her eyes focused on Jamie as he spoke to Mark. When his gaze met hers, a smile lit his face. A fluttering started deep in her stomach as she smiled in returned. She felt breathless.

Be careful with your heart, Kayla.

The thought surprised her and sent uncertainty her way, but she kept a smile on her face as Jamie stared at her. Were she and Jamie moving too fast? Should she have insisted they get to know each other better before officially dating? She had quickly agreed to be Abram's girlfriend when he asked, but they had known each other for years. Was she heading down the same heartbreaking path she'd traveled with Abram?

And was Jamie jumping into a relationship with her to avoid the pain of losing his mother? That last question sent a new thread of worry coiling in her chest.

Rudy said something to Jamie, and he broke their gaze and turned.

Kayla looked at Laura and found her wiping her nose with a tissue. Reaching out, she touched her hand.

"It's difficult." Laura sniffed and pushed the tissue into the pocket of her dress. "It felt strange climbing into the buggy without her this morning. And everyone was silent during the ride here. It's like we were all trying to comprehend how she could be gone." She nodded toward the other side of the barn. "Now I keep looking across at the married women and expecting to see her, but she's not there." Her body shuddered as she took a deep breath.

Kayla rubbed her arm. "I'm so sorry. I promise it will get better, but it's definitely difficult. It will hurt for a long time. I'm here if you need someone to talk to."

"*Danki.* I'm sure it will." Laura gave her a watery smile. "I meant it when I said I'm *froh* Jamie asked you to be his girlfriend. I'm certain you can help him with his grief. Rudy has been helpful to me. Jamie has a difficult time opening up to people, but I've noticed he talks to you. You're a blessing to him."

Kayla swallowed against her dry throat. "I hope I can be."

"I'm sure you will. He needs you."

Speechless, Kayla looked down at the hymnal in her lap. When Laura turned to say something to the woman beside her, the tension in Kayla's back released. She glanced over at Cindy, who was staring down at her own hymnal and running her fingers over the cover. Worry nipped at Kayla as she took in Cindy's anxiety. Was there anything she could do to help her? She racked her brain for something comforting to say that wouldn't upset Cindy.

"The Beiler family seems nice. I met Lizzie," Kayla said, referring to the family who was hosting the service.

"*Ya.*" Cindy looked up at her and gave a tentative smile. "I went to school with their *dochdern.*" She nodded her head toward two brunettes sitting one row in front of them. "They're nice. Their *daed* is a butcher, and they work at his counter in the farmers market in Bird-in-Hand."

"Oh. That's nice." Kayla was relieved. She'd found common ground with Cindy. "If you need someone to talk to, I'm here, okay?"

Cindy nodded as she glanced down at the hymnal once again. *"Danki."*

The service began and Kayla joined in as the congregation slowly sang the opening hymn. As she expected, this district's services were much like her own. A young man sitting across the barn served as the song leader. He began the first syllable of each line and then the rest of the congregation joined in to finish the verse.

While the ministers met in another room for thirty minutes to choose who would preach that day, the congregation continued to sing. During the last verse of the second hymn, Kayla's gaze moved to the back of the barn just as the ministers returned. They placed their hats on two hay bales, indicating that the service was about to begin.

The chosen minister began the first sermon, and Kayla tried her best to concentrate on his holy words. But her thoughts turned to Jamie and his family. She hoped she could be the blessing Laura insisted she could be. Is that what God intended her to do? Her eyes moved toward the young men across the aisle. Jamie sat with his head bowed, focusing on his hands in his lap. Was he thinking about his *mamm*?

She redirected her thoughts to the sermon, taking in the message and concentrating on God. She wondered what God had in store for her. Would Jamie become her future? She felt excited and hopeful at the thought.

The first sermon ended, and Kayla knelt in silent prayer between the Riehl sisters. She closed her eyes and thanked God for her new friends. She also prayed for Jamie, asking God to send healing and comfort to him and his family. After the prayers, the deacon read from the Scriptures, and then the hour-long main sermon began. Kayla willed herself to concentrate as the deacon preached from the book of Acts.

Relief flooded Kayla when the fifteen-minute kneeling prayer ended. The congregation stood for the benediction and sang the closing hymn. While she sang, her eyes moved again to Jamie. She wondered if he could feel her watching him, but he didn't look her way.

When the service ended, Laura touched Kayla's and Cindy's hands. "Let's go help serve the meal."

"Ya." Kayla glanced toward Jamie and saw

him talking to two other young men. She considered walking over there, but she didn't want to appear too eager in front of his sisters and friends. She followed the Riehls out of the barn to the house.

"Why don't we fill *kaffi* cups?" Laura suggested.

Kayla liked that idea. She might have the opportunity to talk to Jamie at his table.

After the service, Jamie and the other men in the congregation had converted the benches into long picnic tables by setting them into wooden stands. Now he stared toward the entrance to the barn as he sat between Mark and Noah, hoping for another glimpse at Kayla.

Mark leaned over and lowered his voice. "It was strange not having *Mamm* at service with us. I kept expecting to see her sitting with Elsie and Savilla."

Jamie closed his eyes and nodded as the gloom that had plagued him during the service came back in a sudden rush. "I was thinking the same thing."

"I'm concerned about *Dat.*" Mark kept his voice low as he nodded to where their father sat across their table, down at the other end. He was staring at his empty cup. "I saw him wiping tears during the service."

"I noticed that too." Anxiety gripped Jamie. "We need to encourage him to keep resting. We have to give him time."

"I know." Mark sighed.

"So, Allen," Rudy began, "have you been busy at the carriage shop?"

Jamie lost himself in his thoughts as the men around him talked. Jamie had done his best to concentrate on the ministers' holy words during the service, but his attention kept cutting to *Dat* and then to Kayla. He was plagued with concern for his father but also distracted by Kayla. He once again felt guilty. Maybe bringing Kayla here was a bad idea when his family was still reeling after losing his mother. Maybe he'd asked Kayla to be his girlfriend too soon. His grief was still so raw, so all-consuming.

Perhaps he should have grieved for his mother before he asked Kayla to be part of his life. But how could he let Kayla slip through his fingers when his feelings for her were so strong and overwhelming?

He needed Kayla in his life. And when he spotted her talking to Cindy before the service, he wondered if Kayla could help his sister heal after such a devastating loss. His heart warmed with the hope that someday Cindy would forgive him. During the prayers, he asked God to help his family, and he prayed Cindy would act like his sister again, not his adversary.

Jamie covered his mouth as a yawn gripped him. He'd had difficulty falling asleep last night. He kept thinking about Kayla and then about his mother. *Mamm* would have been delighted to know Jamie had asked Kayla's father if he could date her.

Oh, Mamm, *I'm so sorry you're not here to share this moment with me.*

"Kaffi?"

Jamie glanced up at Kayla smiling down at him. "Hi. You snuck up behind me." He held up his cup and she started filling it.

"You looked like you were lost in thought."

"Allen and Rudy, you remember Kayla," Jamie told his friends.

"Hi." She gave a little wave before filling Mark's cup too.

"Glad you could come to our service today," Mark said.

"It's nice to see you again," Allen chimed in from across the table.

"*Ya,* Laura can't stop talking about you," Rudy added.

"Danki." Kayla filled Noah's cup next and greeted him.

"I'll see you later," she told Jamie before moving down the table.

Jamie looked across the table just as Rudy and Allen nodded their approval of Kayla.

"You need to snatch her up before she finds someone else," Mark said.

"I know." Jamie lifted his cup. "That's why I asked her to be my girlfriend this morning."

"So it's official, huh?" Noah asked.

"*Ya,* it is."

"*Gut.*" Noah pounded him on the shoulder, almost making him spill his coffee. "You'll be married before you know it."

Jamie's throat tightened at the thought. How could he think about settling down? He'd only just decided he could find a way to fit dating into his life.

"Don't look so terrified." Noah snickered. "It will happen when the time is right."

"How will I know when the time is right?" Jamie's question took even himself by surprise.

"I can't tell you exactly when." Noah shrugged. "You'll just know."

Jamie let Noah's conviction roll around in his mind, but the thought of marriage seemed too much right now.

"*Danki* for being such a *gut* influence for Nathan," Willie told Jamie later that evening as they stepped out of the barn and walked toward the house.

Jamie halted and looked at Willie. The afternoon had gone by quickly. After the service and lunch, he'd brought Kayla home, and she invited him to stay. He'd spent the afternoon talking to the family, although Nathan was out with his youth group. Jamie stayed for supper and then accompanied Willie outside to help with chores.

Even though he enjoyed his time with Kayla's family, he worried that he should have been with his own family instead. The despondency in his father's face during the service and lunch flashed through his mind. Had his father spent the afternoon alone in his bedroom? Had his siblings tried to comfort him? If so, could they have used Jamie's help?

Willie chuckled. "You look confused."

Jamie swallowed back his guilt and forced a smile. "Is it that obvious?"

"*Ya,* it is." Willie pointed to the porch. "Let's sit for a few minutes."

Jamie followed him up the steps and sat down on a chair beside him.

Willie leaned back and stared out toward the dark pasture. "Your friendship means a lot to Nathan, and Marilyn and I appreciate your encouraging him to visit you at the fire station instead of sneaking out to calls."

"Nathan's friendship means a lot to me." *And Kayla's does too.* "I enjoy spending time with him." Jamie rested his elbows on the arms of the chair and breathed in the warm night air. The sun had set and the cicadas sang through the darkness. They sat in an amicable silence for a few moments as Jamie considered what to say next.

"It's been tough since we lost Simeon," Willie suddenly said, looking at Jamie. "I know you understand that."

Jamie nodded, rubbing his fingers over the arms of the chair.

"Nathan has had difficulty adjusting to not having Simeon around, and then you came into our lives. You're helping Nathan heal from the loss, and Marilyn and I appreciate it. So *danki* for being a *gut freind* to both Kayla and Nathan."

Jamie cleared his throat as the weight of Willie's words settled over his chest. "*Gern gschehne,* but I feel the same way about Kayla and Nathan."

"*Gut.*" Willie's expression filled with concern. "How are you handling everything since your *mamm*'s accident?"

Jamie folded his hands in his lap. "It hasn't been easy. *Mei daed* is taking it hard, and I don't know how to help him. We all really

343

missed her today at church. I feel like a piece of my life is missing."

"I understand that," Willie said. "Grief is tough. It has a way of sneaking up on you. Sometimes I'll be in the kitchen at the restaurant cooking, and suddenly I'll be transported back to a memory of Simeon. It takes my breath away, and I feel like I can't function. Some days I'll think of something Simeon said and I'll laugh."

A smile passed over Willie's face as if a memory had found him for a brief moment. "And then sometimes I look at Junior and feel like I'm looking into Simeon's face when he was a *boppli.* I try not to cry because I don't want to upset Marilyn or Eva."

Willie shook his head. "But it took a while to get to that point. I'm certain your grief is too new now. Is there anything you need to get off your chest? I'm *froh* to be a sounding board if you have something you feel like you can't share with your family."

Jamie considered sharing the thoughts that had haunted him last night, or the issues between him and Cindy, but both felt too personal, too intimate to share with Kayla's father. "How do you get through the tough times?"

"Prayer helps a lot. If I feel like I'm going

to fall apart, I pray for strength, and it helps."

The screen door opened and Kayla joined them on the porch. She looked at each of them. "Did I interrupt something?" She pointed toward the door. "Should I go back inside?"

"No, no." Willie popped up from his chair. "I was just going inside to check on your *mamm.*"

Jamie stood as Willie disappeared into the house. "Hi."

"Hi." Kayla leaned against a porch post. "I didn't mean to interrupt your conversation. But you and *Dat* have been outside for quite a while."

"I didn't realize it had been that long." He indicated the chair Willie had been sitting in. "Would you like to sit down?"

"I was wondering when you're leaving."

"You're kicking me out?" he said, teasing her.

"No." She smiled, then pointed to the dark sky. "But I can't help but worry about you heading home too late."

"You're worried about me." He took a step toward her.

"Of course I am."

Suddenly he felt an overwhelming urge to kiss her pretty pink lips.

345

"It's after eight," she continued, oblivious to his thoughts. "Eva just went to put Junior in bed."

"So you *are* kicking me out."

"You're not listening." She harrumphed and folded her arms over her chest. "I'm worried about your safety because I want you to come and visit me again very soon."

"I promise you I won't be able to stay away from you for long."

"*Gut.* I will hold you to that promise." Her smile was back, and his heart thudded.

"I suppose you're right. I should get going."

She lifted her chin. "I'm always right."

He chuckled. She was adorable.

"Well, I should say good-bye to your family before I leave."

Inside he thanked her parents for supper and said good night. Then he and Kayla walked out to his buggy. He hitched the horse as she stood nearby.

"I guess this is *gut nacht* since you kicked me out."

"Stop saying that." She paused as she studied him. "What were you and *mei daed* talking about?"

Jamie hesitated as he adjusted his hat on his head.

"You don't have to tell me."

"No, I'll tell you." He rested his hand on the buggy door. "We were talking about grief. He thinks my friendship with Nathan is helping him deal with losing Simeon."

"I think so too. In fact, I think you're helping all of us." She paused and her eyebrows drew together. "Is my family helping you at all?"

He nodded. "Your *daed* and I talked a bit about that. Your family is definitely helping my family. I think our families are helping each other."

"Gut."

As she looked up at him, a tendril of her golden hair floated in front of her face. He reached out and pushed it away, and then without thinking he leaned down and brushed his lips across her cheek. She sucked in a breath at the contact.

"I can't wait to see you again," he whispered against her cheek. *"Gut nacht."*

"Gut nacht," she whispered.

Jamie climbed into the buggy and waved as he guided the horse toward the road.

Kayla felt as if she were floating as she bounced up the porch steps. She touched her face where Jamie's lips had been and sighed.

Astonishment had pushed the air from her

lungs when he kissed her cheek, heat flooding her body at the sensation of his touch. She was tempted to kiss his lips, but that would have been too forward.

She had enjoyed every minute of their time together today. Whenever she thought about Jamie, her heart took on wings, and a smile turned up the corners of her mouth. His handsome face permeated her thoughts constantly.

As she entered the house, a thought slammed into her. She was falling in love with him. A whirlwind of emotions churned in her gut — excitement and happiness, but also fear, anxiety, hesitation. It was too soon! She was opening herself to hurt, and she'd promised herself she wouldn't do that.

But how would she ever know she could trust Jamie if she didn't give him the chance?

She gasped as her feet hit the threshold separating the mudroom from the kitchen.

"Kayla?" *Mamm* called. "Is everything okay?"

"*Ya.*" Kayla rested her hand on the door-frame.

"You look worried." *Mamm* walked over. "Please tell me what's wrong."

Kayla paused, trying to put her confusing thoughts into words. "I think I'm falling in love with Jamie."

"Oh, that's *wunderbaar.*" *Mamm* clapped her hands. "I'm so *froh* for you. He's such a nice man. Just last night your *daed* and I were discussing what a blessing he's been to your *bruder* and you." Her smile faded. "Why aren't you *froh*?"

"I guess I'm scared. It's all happening so fast." Kayla folded her hands over her chest as if to guard her heart. "I don't think my feelings for Abram were this intense this quickly."

Mamm pointed to the table. "Sit. Let's talk."

Kayla slipped into her usual seat and *Mamm* sat down beside her.

"When I met your *daed,* I had just had my heart broken by a man I dated for a few years."

Kayla's eyes widened. "You never told me this."

"I didn't think you needed to know, but maybe I can help you by sharing my heart-break with you."

"So you understand how I feel about what happened between Abram and me," Kayla concluded.

"*Ya,* I do." *Mamm* touched Kayla's arm. "I was worried about having my heart broken, but your *daed* and I just clicked. It

349

was as if we'd known each other for years because our friendship was so easy. We quickly became best *freinden,* and in less than a year we were engaged. One of *mei freinden* said your *daed* and I were moving too fast, but it worked for us."

She gestured around the kitchen. "Look at us now. If you're comfortable with Jamie, let the relationship progress at a comfortable pace."

Kayla moved her thumbnail in a circle as she looked down at the table and contemplated her confusing feelings. "Something else is bothering me too."

"What is it?" *Mamm* leaned forward.

Kayla thought she heard a door click closed, but she kept her eyes focused on the table.

"Talk to me," *Mamm* prodded her. "I can't help you if you don't."

"It scares me that I'm this attached to Jamie already." Kayla's eyes filled with tears as the truth punched her in her chest. "He's a firefighter. I'm afraid of losing him like we lost Simeon."

"What happened to Simeon won't necessarily happen to Jamie."

Eva's voice took Kayla by surprise.

Kayla looked up at her sister-in-law. She was standing in front of the door that led to her apartment.

"Eva, I'm so sorry. I-I didn't mean —"

"It's okay." Eva sat down on Kayla's other side. "You can't let what happened to Simeon make you doubt how you feel about Jamie. You can't stop living your life because Simeon died in a fire."

Kayla sniffed as tears stung her eyes.

"Look at Brody," Eva continued. "He's been fighting fires much longer than Jamie has, and he's fine." She covered Kayla's hand with hers. "Live your life, Kayla. I think Jamie loves you. Follow your heart and trust God's plan for you."

"Danki." Kayla hugged Eva as a tear slipped down one cheek. "I will."

TWENTY-TWO

"You should take this table." Eva placed her hand on Kayla's shoulder. "Trust me. I think they're *gut* tippers."

Kayla pivoted toward her sister-in-law's wide smile. "What do you mean?"

"Look." Eva pointed to a table nearby.

Kayla grinned and her pulse zinged when she saw Jamie sitting with Brody, Leon, and Noah. Jamie lifted his hand and waved.

"Go." Eva nudged her forward.

Kayla's smile faded. "I need to check on the order for table five. It should be up now."

"I've got it." Eva nodded toward Jamie's table. "Go see your boyfriend."

"Danki." Kayla's steps sped up as she approached the four men. She hadn't seen Jamie for three days, and her heart had been aching for him. Despite Eva's encouraging words, she worried about him at night, praying he'd be safe when he was on duty at the

fire station and went on calls. Relief stole over her as she looked into his eyes. "Hi."

"Wie geht's?" Jamie responded with a grin. "I heard the food is *gut* here. What do you recommend?"

Kayla gave them the specials and they gave her their order. "I'll get your drinks right out."

"Danki," Leon said before he turned to Noah and Brody. "So when is that hazmat class again?"

As the three men began discussing their training schedule, Jamie reached for her hand and threaded his fingers with hers. She enjoyed the feel of his warm skin against hers.

"I've missed you," he said softly. "How are you?"

"I'm fine. I was wondering when I'd see you again."

"I know." He frowned. "I tried to get out to your *haus* Monday night, but I had a lot of chores. Last night I had to get to bed early since I'm on duty today." He squeezed her hand. "Can I come see you tomorrow night?"

"Ya, that would perfect."

"Gut." Jamie released her hand. "I look forward to it."

"I'll be right back with your drinks." Kayla

grinned as she made her way toward the kitchen.

Jamie hammered another new slat on the pasture fence. Then he set the hammer on the ground and swiped his hand over his sweaty brow.

"Do you realize what time it is?"

Craning his neck, Jamie glanced over his shoulder. His father was watching him with intense eyes. "No. What time is it?"

"It's after seven." *Dat* gestured toward the driveway. "I thought you were going to see Kayla tonight."

Jamie cringed. Where had the time gone? He looked down the length of the fence. "I can't go until this is done."

"Who told you that?"

"What?" Jamie stood up straight, stretching his aching back.

"Who said you can't go until the fence is done?"

"I did." Jamie pointed toward the far end. "This fence has needed to be repaired for months."

"What's another day?" *Dat* shrugged. "The work will still be here tomorrow. You need to make time for fun. Go see Kayla before she thinks you forgot about her."

Jamie eyed his father with suspicion. *Dat*

resembled someone Jamie didn't recognize. In the past, *Dat* insisted all their chores had to be done before Jamie and his siblings could visit their friends.

"Don't you remember what I told you after your *mamm*'s funeral?"

Jamie's chest tightened at the mention of both his mother and the funeral.

"Life is fleeting, James." *Dat*'s voice shook. "You need to enjoy it while you can. Fix the fence tomorrow or fix it next week. Just don't fix it tonight when you could be with your girlfriend."

"No, I need to get this done." Jamie picked up the hammer. "I'm volunteering again on Friday, and I have a list of chores that need to get done this week. I can't let the fence go or it will never be fixed."

"So what? The horses and cows haven't run away on us yet. Don't let life pass you by like I did. If I'd known I was going to lose your *mamm,* I would have made time for more fun. Now she's gone and it's too late to make those precious memories."

Jamie shook his head. "Kayla will understand if I delay our date for a couple of days." He pointed the hammer toward the fence. "The farm has to be my priority for now."

Dat rested his hand on Jamie's shoulder.

"Don't put your chores first. Let Kayla know she comes first in your life. If you don't, you'll regret it." With a deep frown, he turned and started toward the house.

Jamie's thoughts turned to the conversation he'd had with Kayla about how Abram had hurt her. *Dat* was right. He couldn't allow Kayla to believe he would take her for granted. He would leave her a message and explain. He had to let her know he cared for her, but he had to concentrate on the farm tonight.

He headed toward the phone shanty and dialed Kayla's number. After a few rings, her father's voice sounded through the phone.

"You've reached the Dienners. To leave a message for Marilyn and Willie, press one. For Eva, press two. For Kayla, press three, and for Nathan, press four."

Jamie pressed three and then cleared his throat as a long beep sounded. "Kayla, this is Jamie. I'm sorry, but I'm not going to make it over to your *haus* tonight. I got wrapped up in a project here, and I have to get it done because I'm volunteering again tomorrow. One of the other volunteers had to change his schedule, so I offered to take his shift."

His father's words about regret echoed

through his mind, and guilt grabbed him by the throat. "Kayla, I'm really sorry. Please forgive me. I promise I will see you soon. I miss you. Take care and tell your family hello for me. Good-bye."

As he hung up the phone, he recalled her beautiful smile yesterday when he promised to visit her. He swallowed a groan. Would she forgive him? Of course she would. He would show her how much he cared for her when he saw her.

He stepped out of the phone shanty and started for the fence. His thoughts spun as once again his father's warning echoed through his head. But *Dat* was too steeped in grief to see all that had to be done on the farm. His eyes scanned the fence. It had to be repaired, and there was no time like the present.

He picked up the hammer and continued working. He longed to see Kayla's beautiful smile, but he would have more time for her later.

An image of *Mamm* suddenly filled his mind. She was smiling and laughing as *Dat* hugged her in the kitchen. *Dat* would never get to do that again, and it was all Jamie's fault.

No, he couldn't allow his thoughts to go down that road. He had to work, and he'd keep working until he was too tired to see straight. That was when he could finally go to bed without more of these painful memories keeping him awake all night long.

Hard physical labor was his only escape.

Kayla gazed at the gorgeous sunset. She'd been sitting on the porch for an hour now, and there was still no sign of Jamie. She was worried. Had he been in an accident? Or been hurt while on duty?

Eva's warning to not let fear hold her back filled her mind. No, no, she had to force those thoughts away. Jamie was fine. He was just running late. Surely that was it. But maybe . . .

"Kay!" Nathan jogged up the porch steps. "There's a message for you on voice mail. You should go listen to it right away."

"Who is it from?" Anticipation pricked her spine.

"You know I don't listen to your personal voice mails," he huffed. "But I wanted you to know it's waiting for you." He slipped past her to go into the house.

"Oh. *Danki* for telling me." Kayla's heartbeat spiked as she headed to the phone shanty at the top of the driveway.

As Jamie's voice sounded over the recording, she blew out a deep sigh and her heartbeat slowed. She leaned forward on the desk as she listened to his message.

He wasn't hurt, but his voice was shaky, as if he was nervous. Her heart swelled with concern for him and his family. He said he'd been caught up with something at the farm, but had Jamie also had a bad day? Or had his father had a bad day? She clearly recalled how her mother's and Eva's grief had cut her to the bone after Simeon died. Maybe Jamie had to spend the evening helping his father or siblings cope.

The muscles in Kayla's shoulders tightened. Jamie had promised to see her soon. She would hold on to that promise and say extra prayers for him and his family tonight.

After deleting the message, she made her way back to the porch and gathered the peach salsa, tortilla chips, and bottles of root beer she'd set out for Jamie's visit. As she managed to open the screen door and entered the mudroom, a niggling of doubt, along with a headache, began at the base of her neck. But Jamie deserved her understanding, not doubt.

She pushed her concern away. Jamie wouldn't let her down.

Just inside the front door of the restaurant, Jamie watched Kayla deliver an order to a young *English* couple. Warmth filled his chest. Oh, how he'd missed her. She smiled and nodded at her customers before stopping at the next table and speaking to an elderly couple eating their lunch. Then she made a beeline for the kitchen and disappeared.

"Jamie!" Nathan was wearing his usual white apron and carrying a plastic tub full of dirty dishes. "How are you?"

"I'm fine. How are you?"

"Gut, gut." Nathan set the plastic tub on top of the podium. "Kayla told me she got your message last night. She was really disappointed you didn't come."

Jamie cringed as blame settled heavy and tense on his back. "I feel terrible about that. I wanted to, but I was repairing the pasture fence and I had to get it done."

"I understand. I think she did too."

"I want to apologize to Kayla, but I just saw her go into the kitchen." Jamie walked around the podium. "Could I go see her?"

"She should be right out. We've run out of lunch meat and a few other things. She was going to run to the market for supplies before the dinner rush."

"Oh. I wonder if I could go with her."

"Sure. I don't see why not." Nathan looked toward the kitchen. "You can ask

360

her yourself. See you later." He picked up the plastic tub and started toward another table to clear.

Jamie looked toward the kitchen doors just as Kayla came out with a purse slung over her shoulder. When their gazes collided, her expression brightened, sending relief soaring through his veins.

"Hi." He smiled. "How are you?"

"I'm fine." She suddenly looked at him intensely, as if she were assessing him. "I've been worried about you. How are you and your family doing?"

"We're okay."

Her eyebrows lifted. "Are you telling me the truth?" Her expression softened. "You can talk to me."

"*Mei daed* is still having a tough time." He lowered his voice as a couple moved past them. "He helps with the chores sometimes, but he gets emotional when we mention *Mamm.*" His throat dried. "It's been hard. Cindy's about the same."

"I'm so sorry."

The care and concern in her eyes was almost too much for him. He had to change the subject before he got emotional in public.

He nodded toward the front door. "Nathan said you had to go to the market for supplies. Would it be all right if I came along? I could help you carry the bags."

"Do you have time?" Kayla hesitated, her gaze moving up and down his attire. "You're on duty. Are you allowed to go that far from the station?"

"*Ya*, it's fine." He patted the radio on his belt. "I can rush back to the station if I have to." He paused to gather his confusing thoughts. "I really missed you last night, and I want to spend time with you. I'm so sorry I had to cancel. Please let me go to the market with you."

"Okay. It will give us a chance to get caught up."

His shoulders relaxed as he held open the door for her.

Kayla walked beside Jamie as they made their way down the sidewalk to the Bird-in-Hand Farmers Market. Although she appreciated his apology, she still couldn't shake the doubt that had taken root in her heart the night before, no matter how many times she told herself Jamie wouldn't let her down. She glanced over at him. He looked more handsome than usual, and somehow appeared taller and more confident than he had on Sunday. Maybe it was the uniform.

She was attracted to him and cared deeply

for him. She might even be falling in love with him. But she couldn't dismiss the feeling that something was going to go wrong. Why did she allow Abram's mistakes to cloud her feelings for Jamie? It wasn't Jamie's fault her relationship with Abram had fallen apart.

"What's on your mind?" His question was timid, as if he dreaded the answer.

She fingered the strap on her purse as she considered her response. She wanted to be honest, but how could she tell him she was afraid of another breakup?

He stopped walking and faced her. "Kayla, you are very important to me. I'm sorry about last night. Please forgive me?" His eyes pleaded with her, and something inside of her melted.

"Of course I forgive you."

"Are you still my girlfriend?"

"*Ya.*" She smiled as the tension in her spine released. "I would never give up on you that easily."

His jaw muscles visibly loosened. *"Danki."*

"*Gern gschehne.* We can talk more later." She pointed toward the farmers market. "I need to do this shopping and hurry back to the restaurant before it gets busy again."

"I understand." He held out his hand, and she took it. "Let's go."

They made small talk as they picked up the items on her shopping list. After she paid for the groceries and supplies, they carried the bags back to the restaurant.

"*Danki* for your help," she said as they stepped inside, this time through the back door. She set her bags on a counter in the supply room off the kitchen and he laid his bags beside hers.

"*Gern gschehne,* Kayla. I had a *gut* time."

"You had a *gut* time shopping?" She lifted an eyebrow.

"Anytime with you is a *gut* time." He opened his mouth to say more but was cut off by his radio.

"All available units respond to accident with injuries at Old Philadelphia Pike at North Ronks Road," the voice said.

"I have to go." He touched her arm. "I'm sorry."

"When will I see you again?" She hated the whine in her voice.

"How about tomorrow night?" he asked, raising his voice to be heard over the radio repeating the call.

"*Ya,* that would be fine."

"Great. I look forward to seeing you again." He squeezed her hand.

"Be safe!" she called after him.

"I will!" he responded just before the door

clicked shut behind him.

Kayla wanted to believe he would keep his promise to see her tomorrow night and relieve the doubts that taunted her heart.

TWENTY-THREE

"The animals are fed," Jamie announced as he stepped into the kitchen the following evening.

"Are you going to see Kayla now?" Laura stood at the counter, drying the dinner dishes.

"Ya." Jamie started up the stairs.

"You'd better hurry," she called after him. "It's getting late."

"I know, but I need to get cleaned up." He hurriedly grabbed clean clothes from his room before getting into the shower. After he shaved and dressed, he rushed down the hallway toward the stairs.

The crackle of his radio made him freeze.

"All available units respond to 1742 Beechdale Road, Bird-in-Hand, seventy-four-year-old man," the voice over the radio blared. "Chest pains. Possible heart attack."

"1742 Beechdale Road," he whispered as he rushed into his room and retrieved the radio from his nightstand. That was right up the street.

The call came through again. "All available units respond to 1742 Beechdale Road, Bird-in-Hand, seventy-four-year-old man . . ."

He sprang into action. Gripping the radio, he ran down the stairs and through the kitchen toward the back door, nearly knocking Mark over as he stepped into the mudroom.

"Whoa!" Mark held up his hands. "Slow down. Where's the fire?"

"Medical call up the street," Jamie explained. "A man is having a heart attack. I have to help." He slipped past Mark and out the door.

"Jamie! Jamie, wait!" Mark rushed after him. "You said you were going to see Kayla tonight."

"I can see her later. I have to help this man." He dashed toward the road on foot.

"Jamie!" Mark yelled after him. "Even if you answer every single call it won't bring *Mamm* back!"

Jamie gritted his teeth and kept running.

Kayla stood up from the glider and walked to the end of the porch. The sky was dark, and the only sounds were the singing cicadas and the rumble of engines from cars on nearby roads.

Still no sign of Jamie. Where was he? She pushed away thoughts of his being hurt. Maybe he had decided something else was more important to him tonight. Or maybe he forgot about her.

Or maybe he was hurt.

She picked up the lantern from the porch railing. Worry mixed with frustration shoved her off the porch and sent her hustling to the phone shanty, hoping for a voice mail message. She dialed the number and the electronic voice said, "You have no new messages."

She closed her eyes and released a long, shaky breath. Where was he and why didn't he call her to tell her he was okay? What if he wasn't okay? But if something had happened to him, wouldn't Laura have called?

What if he was in an accident and Laura is too distraught to call me?

The thought sent gooseflesh surging down her arms.

No, no, no. Jamie has to be fine. He's probably just busy with his family. They've endured a lot of heartache lately. He needs my patience and grace. And I have to believe he wouldn't forget his promise.

Swallowing back the lump swelling in her

throat, she made her way back to the house. Her mother was writing on a notepad at the kitchen table.

Mamm looked up and smiled. "Is Jamie here?"

"No." Kayla turned off the lantern and set it on the counter. "He didn't show up and he didn't leave me a message this time. I don't know what to think or believe."

"Oh." *Mamm*'s smile dissolved. "Maybe something came up."

"Maybe."

"Sit down." *Mamm*'s voice was gentle.

Kayla sank into the chair beside her. "Are you making a shopping list?"

"*Ya,* but that's not what I want to discuss." *Mamm* touched Kayla's hand. "Talk to me. What are you feeling right now?"

Kayla set her elbows on the table and rested her chin on her palms. "I'm frustrated, but I'm trying to give Jamie the benefit of the doubt. I'm worried something happened to him or he and his family are having a hard time tonight. I know I need to be patient and give him time to heal after losing his *mamm,* but there's something else bothering me too."

"What is it, *mei liewe*?"

"When he apologized for not coming last night, he said he truly cares about me. But I

369

don't understand why he wouldn't at least call tonight if he can't make it. After all, he did the other night. Why not tonight?" She cringed. "Does that sound terrible?"

Mamm paused as if contemplating Kayla's words. "I believe Jamie does care about you very much. I think he will have an explanation."

"I'm sure he will, but it still hurts."

"Why?"

Kayla paused. Should she be honest or keep her fears to herself?

"Kayla, you can talk to me. I'll listen without judgment." *Mamm*'s eyes were warm and comforting.

"I know I shouldn't believe the worst about Jamie. He's a *gut* man. But I still remember the humiliating feeling of sitting on the porch and waiting for Abram to come, only to find out he chose his *freinden* over me. I promised myself I would never do that again. What if Jamie is choosing something over me? If not his *freinden,* then something else?"

"I understand what you're saying, but Jamie isn't Abram." *Mamm* took Kayla's hand in hers and gave it a gentle squeeze. "You do need to give him the benefit of the doubt. His family is going through a tough time. What if his *daed* needed someone to talk to and Jamie was there at the right time? You would understand that, wouldn't you?"

Guilt, hot and stinging, sliced through Kayla's chest. "*Ya,* of course I would. We know firsthand how hard it is to lose someone."

"Exactly. You shouldn't make a judgment until you've heard the entire story. Jamie went out of his way to visit you at the restaurant yesterday. I believe he was genuine." *Mamm* released her hand. "Wait and see what Jamie has to say and then decide if he's not the man for you."

"Okay." She cupped her hand against a yawn.

"You're exhausted. Why don't you go to bed? You'll feel better in the morning."

Kayla stood and pushed her chair in. "Are you going to bed?"

"Soon. I just want to make a list of everything we're running low on at the restaurant. You picked up the most urgent supplies yesterday, but I'm going to need to go shopping again soon." *Mamm* looked up at her. "I'll go shortly. We have church in the morning, so we both need our sleep."

Kayla started toward the stairs, but then turned and faced her mother again. "*Danki* for talking with me."

"You know you're always welcome. I enjoy our talks."

"I do too. *Ich liebe dich, Mamm.*"

Mamm smiled. *"Ich liebe dich, mei liewe."*

As Kayla climbed the stairs, her heart turned to the Riehl family. She couldn't imagine not having her mother's love and support when she needed someone to listen and offer advice.

"Let's stop in at the Dienners' restaurant before we go to the hardware store," Jamie said to Mark as they rode in their driver's van. He turned to the driver. "Would that be all right, Blake?"

"That sounds fine to me." Blake steered into the restaurant's parking lot. "I need to get a few things at the farmers market anyway. We can meet in the hardware store parking lot."

"Perfect." Jamie took a deep breath. He hoped he could find the right words to apologize to Kayla for missing another date.

They decided to meet in an hour, and as soon as the van came to a stop, Jamie leaped out and hurried toward the entrance.

"What's the rush?" Mark jogged to catch up with him.

"I need to talk to Kayla and we don't have much time. I haven't talked to her since

Friday. Remember? I had to go on that medical call Saturday night. I have to tell her why I missed our date."

"Are you saying you didn't call to tell her why you didn't show up?"

"No, I didn't." Jamie reached for the door, but his brother pulled his arm back. "What are you doing, Mark?"

"Today is Monday," Mark spoke slowly as if Jamie might not be able to understand the language.

"I realize that."

Mark held his hands up as if to surrender. "Don't you think she's going to be upset and feel like you forgot about her? Why didn't you call her and explain what happened?"

"I meant to, but I didn't get home until late Saturday night and I just fell into bed. Then we had visitors all day yesterday, and like you and our *schweschdere,* I was keeping a close eye on *Dat.*" Irritation bubbled up inside of him. "That's why we're here now. I can tell Kayla what happened and apologize. Hopefully she'll understand."

When Mark frowned, Jamie spun toward the door and pulled it open. He stepped into the lobby, where an *English* couple stood waiting for a table. The dining room was filled with customers and the delicious aroma of breakfast foods.

Eva waved at Jamie and Mark before leading the couple away.

"There she is," Mark said under his breath.

Jamie looked across the restaurant where Kayla spoke to some customers at a table near the kitchen. She nodded as she wrote on her notepad. Then she turned and walked toward the kitchen. Eva came up behind her and put her hand on Kayla's shoulder. Eva whispered something in Kayla's ear and Kayla's shoulders stiffened. She turned toward the front of the restaurant and looked at Jamie. When their gazes clashed, her lips tightened. And then she looked away.

"She looks upset," Mark said.

Jamie glared at Mark, who held up his hands and took a step back. Then Jamie looked back at Kayla as anxiety churned in his gut. Mark was right; Jamie should have made time to call her. He made a huge mistake and now he had to convince her to forgive him — again. His throat dried at the thought of losing her.

"I don't think she wants to talk to you," Mark muttered under his breath.

Jamie cupped his hand to the back of his neck as the weight of his mistakes made him mute. Was he too late? Had he lost her for good this time?

"You'd better make it clear you're sorry." Mark jammed his thumb toward the front door. "Do you want me to wait outside?"

"No." Jamie shook his head. "You can stay."

Mark raised his eyebrows. "For emotional support?"

Maybe. Jamie swiveled back to where Eva and Kayla were still talking. He could see Kayla's expression, and it was anything but friendly. After a few moments, Kayla handed Eva her notepad and Eva disappeared into the kitchen. Kayla ambled toward the podium.

"Gude mariye."

"Gude mariye, Kayla."

"I'm glad to see you're okay. I thought something might have happened to you."

Jamie's shoulders hunched. "I'm sorry for worrying you."

She took two menus from under the stand. "May I seat you for breakfast?" She kept her eyes focused on Mark as she spoke.

"No, actually," Jamie said, his voice sounding more confident than he felt, "I'd like to talk to you."

"This really isn't a *gut* time." She gestured toward the dining room. "As you can see,

375

I'm very busy."

"I know that, but I only need a few minutes." Jamie rested his hands on the podium. "I promise it won't take long."

Mark took a step back. "Jamie, I'm going to go to the hardware store. I'll meet you there. It was nice seeing you, Kayla."

Jamie kept his eyes trained on her. "Please, Kayla. I want to apologize about Saturday night."

"Why didn't you call to tell me you weren't coming?" Her voice was thick. "I was afraid you might have been injured."

"I'm so sorry." He folded his hands as if to beg for her forgiveness. "I never meant to worry you like that."

"Then I was worried about your family." Her voice shook. "I just didn't know what to think." The pain in her voice stabbed at his gut.

"I should have called you." He reached for her, but she took a step back.

A couple sitting at a table behind her turned and looked at Jamie, their eyebrows raised as they stared.

"Let's go somewhere to talk in private, okay?" He worked to keep his voice low. "People are looking at us."

"Let them stare. I have nothing to hide. What happened Saturday night?"

"I wasn't in an accident, and my family is fine." He sighed. "As I was leaving for your *haus,* a medical call came over my radio for an elderly man who lives on my street. He was having chest pains, so I ran over to stabilize him until the EMTs arrived. He was pretty scared, so I stayed while the EMTs checked him out and prepared him for transport. Then I told his *fraa* I'd check on their animals for them before I went home so she could go to the hospital without having to worry about them. I guess they don't have any family around, and their neighbors didn't seem to be home."

Her eyes widened. "Was he all right?"

He nodded. "*Ya,* he had a mild heart attack. I talked to his *fraa* yesterday, and he's going to be okay."

"*Gut.* What a blessing." She studied him for a moment and then her expression hardened again. "So you weren't even on duty, but you responded to a call. Why didn't you at least phone and explain what happened? If not Saturday, then sometime yesterday."

"I'm so sorry. I really am. Please forgive me."

"You still haven't answered my question." Her voice rose, and the people sitting behind her continued to stare. "Why didn't

377

you call?"

Guilt and regret dug their claws into him. "You're right. I should have called you."

"Why didn't you?" Her voice was small, sounding like an unsure child.

He rubbed at a knot in his shoulder. "First I was focused on trying to save that man and helping his *fraa*. When I got home, it was late and I was completely worn-out. And then yesterday members of our church district came to see how we're doing without *Mamm*. We had visitors all day, and I was concerned about how *Dat* would handle talking about *Mamm*." He paused and took a deep breath. "Kayla, I'm sorry I got involved in a medical call, but that doesn't mean I forgot about you. I really care about you."

"I know you and your family are going through a lot right now, and I'm very sorry. But I have to tell you how I really feel." Her voice trembled. "Why should I believe you want to have a true relationship with me if you didn't let me know you weren't going to make it? I feel like I don't matter to you, no matter what you say now."

"That's not true at all." His answer came out with more force than he expected, and she jumped with a start. "I'm sorry. I didn't mean to yell. I *do* want to have a relation-

378

ship with you. Please give me another chance."

Her hesitation sliced at his soul. "I don't know. I've already had my heart broken once. I don't need it broken again."

"Please don't compare me to Abram." He reached for her, and she took a step back. "I will make this up to you."

"How?"

"I have to go to the hardware store and finish up chores today. What if I come back to see you at closing?"

The bell on the door rang and a group of five *English* women stepped into the restaurant.

"See, Lola," one of the women said. "I told you this was an Amish restaurant."

"Please," Jamie pleaded, lowering his voice in an attempt to keep their conversation private. "Give me another chance. Let me come see you tonight."

Kayla glanced past him and smiled at the women behind him. "Good morning. Welcome to Dienner's Family Restaurant. I'll be with you in a moment."

She briefly turned her focus back to him. "Fine. Be here at closing." She bent, picked up three more menus, and smiled brightly as she addressed the women. "Table for five?" She stepped away from him and led the women away.

Jamie went outside and found Mark sitting on a bench.

"I thought you were going to the hardware store."

"I didn't know how long you'd be, so I figured it was best to wait for you." Mark stood and they started down the street. "How did it go?"

"Fine." Jamie's stomach tightened. "She said I can come back to see her tonight."

"Do you really care about her?"

Jamie stopped and pivoted toward him. "*Ya,* I do. I care about her a lot."

"Then you need to hold on to her, Jamie. You should do everything in your power to show her how you feel about her. You need to start putting her first."

"Really, Mark?" Jamie quipped. "You're going to give me dating advice?"

"What's that supposed to mean?" Mark's eyebrows lifted.

"You can't even date just one *maedel,* but you're telling me how to make it work between Kayla and me." He shook his head as he started walking again.

"You can ignore me, but you know I'm right," Mark called after him.

"Let's buy the supplies and get back to the farm. We have a lot to do today." Jamie squared his shoulders and tried to turn his focus to the task in front of them, but Mark's words stayed with him.

In his heart Jamie was certain Mark was right. He would do better with Kayla. He couldn't risk losing her. He needed her in his life, and he would prove that to her somehow.

TWENTY-FOUR

Kayla hung a pair of her father's trousers on the line as the humid August air kissed her cheeks. She reached for another pair as Eva stepped out onto the porch. "Hi."

"Need some help?" Eva fished two clothespins from the bag hanging by the clothesline and handed them to Kayla.

"Danki." Kayla pushed the clothespins over the material and then moved the clothesline down to make room for more clothes. "I thought you were going to give Junior a bath this evening."

"Mamm insisted on bathing him. She enjoys playing with him in the water." Eva gave Kayla another pair of *Dat*'s trousers. "Is Jamie coming tonight?"

"No. He's on duty." Kayla attached the trousers to the line and then pushed it along.

"Are you okay with that?" Eva lifted one of *Dat*'s shirts from the basket and gave it to Kayla.

"*Ya,* I am." Kayla smiled as she hung up the shirt. "I still worry about him when he's on duty, but I've found prayer gets me through."

"That's *gut.*" Eva gave her another shirt as a coy smile turned up her lips. "Does your smile mean things are going well between you and Jamie?"

Kayla hung the shirt and then turned to face Eva. "Things have been going pretty well."

"You've been seeing him for a month now, right?" Eva gave her another shirt and two clothespins.

"*Ya,* and the weeks have passed by quickly." Her smile faded as she contemplated their relationship.

"Was iss letz?"

"Nothing is really wrong, but I guess things aren't exactly the way I thought they'd be." She lifted another shirt from the basket and hung it on the line to avoid Eva's curious expression. "He hasn't missed a date since the time he went to help the man who was having the heart attack, but we still don't see each other as often as I'd like. I understand he's busy and has a lot of demands on his time. I just wish I could see him more."

383

"Maybe you will with time. You know he's still going through a lot. He only lost his *mamm* six weeks ago." Eva gave her another shirt. "Just let the relationship grow naturally."

Kayla nodded. She wanted nothing more than to be the support Jamie needed.

The bright blue, cloudless sky shone bright above Kayla as she hefted her purse onto her shoulder and marched down the sidewalk. She stepped into the farmers market, chose a shopping cart, and steered it toward the deli section. She'd asked her father if she could pick up supplies. She needed to get out of the restaurant and have some time alone with her thoughts.

For the past three days, she'd jumped every time the phone rang in the restaurant, hoping to hear Jamie's voice on the other end of the line. Perhaps to ask her on another picnic like the one they'd been on last week. But every time she answered the phone in the restaurant or listened to the voice mail messages at home, she'd been disappointed.

The anticipation and frustration became more and more overwhelming as each of those three days had passed. She tried her best to suppress her chagrin, but it still reared its ugly head, along with heartache. Eva's words from Monday night were still fresh in her mind, and she wanted to give Jamie the time and space he needed to work through his grief. But on the other hand, she wanted so desperately for Jamie to become a part of her daily life.

Now it was Thursday afternoon, and she hadn't heard from him since he briefly stopped by the restaurant after his shift ended Tuesday morning. Was she asking for more than he was capable of giving? Would he ever be able to give her a more permanent commitment?

"May I help you?" The Amish man behind the deli counter smiled.

"Hi." Kayla glanced down at the case of meats and cheeses, gave him her order, and watched as he sliced the meat and packaged it up for her. After she paid him, the man handed her two bags and she thanked him. She started down one aisle, but halted when a man's voice called her name.

"Kayla!" he called again. "Kayla Dienner!"

She spun and swallowed a gasp. Abram walked toward her, smiling and waving. He looked the same — still handsome with sandy-blond hair and bright hazel eyes.

"Kayla, hi. How are you?"

"I'm fine. How are you?" She gripped the handle of the shopping cart with one hand as she looked up at him. Unexpected guilt washed over her. What would Jamie say if he knew she was talking to her ex-boyfriend?

"I'm fine." He pointed to the two bags in the grocery cart. "I guess you're here getting supplies for the restaurant."

"*Ya,* that's right. What are you doing here?"

"*Mei mamm* asked me to pick up a few things. She's hosting a dinner tonight at the *haus.*" He fingered his suspenders. "How's your family doing?"

"Everyone is fine. How's yours?"

"*Gut.*" He leaned on her grocery cart handle. "*Mei schweschder* just got engaged."

"Really?" She smiled. While she and Abram had always had their issues, she'd quickly fallen for his family, especially his sister. After Abram broke up with her, she had a moment of clarity. Perhaps she'd loved his family more than she'd ever loved him. "To Daniel?"

"*Ya,* they're going to get married in November."

"That's *wunderbaar.*"

"How's Eva?" he asked.

"She's well. Junior, *mei bruderskind,* is getting so big. It's difficult to believe he's six months old already."

His smile faded. "Oh. So Eva had a *bu*."
He hesitated. "Can I walk you back to the
restaurant?"

"Don't you need to get the supplies for
your *mamm*?"

Abram grinned. "Would you wait a minute? I'll pick up what she needs and then
walk you back." He gnawed his lower lip
and studied her as if hoping she'd say yes.

Alarm bells screamed in Kayla's head and
she had a quick conversation with herself.
*Don't do it. What would Jamie think if he saw
you with Abram? Walk away! Don't risk hurting Jamie.*

"I don't think that's a *gut* idea. I really
need to get back to the restaurant before
the supper rush starts." She forced a pleasant smile on her lips. "It was *gut* seeing you.
Take care." She started toward the door,
but he called her back.

"Kayla! Wait." He rushed to her side. "I
want to talk to you."

Gripping the cart handle, she braced
herself. *Be strong, Kayla!*

"I'm so sorry for hurting you," he said.

"*Danki,* but it's okay. You don't need to
apologize. It was a long time ago, and I'm
over it now. Have a *gut* day." She turned to
go, but he touched her arm. She squeezed

her eyes shut for a moment, dreading what was coming next.

Walk away, Kayla!

"Please wait. I'm not done." Abram's frown was full of emotion. "I miss you."

"Abram, I don't think we should discuss —"

"I wasn't a *gut* boyfriend to you. I took you for granted. I was more interested in being with *mei freinden* than with you. I should have been more attentive and more supportive. It's all my fault our relationship fell apart." He touched his chest. "When you needed me most, I broke up with you and walked away. I was immature and thoughtless, and I'm so sorry. You deserved better. If I could, I would go back and fix things between us."

Speechless, she stared at him. Had she just imagined such an admission?

Abram chuckled. "You look stunned."

"I am." She scowled as she remembered what her brother told her a little more than a month ago. "What would Bena Smoker say if she heard what you just said to me?"

"Bena Smoker?" His brow furrowed. "What does she have to do with any of this?"

"Isn't she your girlfriend?"

"No. Who told you that?"

"Nathan overheard Katie and Lillian talking about you and Bena at the restaurant."

"It's not true. I'm not dating anyone." He shook his head as if shooing away the rumor. "Look, I've done a lot of thinking, and I realize I missed my chance with you. But I'd love to be *freinden.* You were a *gut freind,* and I miss that." He placed his hand on her shopping cart. "Would you consider being *mei freind*?"

She shrugged. "*Ya,* of course."

"*Gut.*" He smiled as he released the cart. "Maybe I'll see you sometime soon?"

"*Ya.* Maybe." She started to push the cart toward the exit. "Tell your family hello for me."

"Abram apologized to you?" Eva's eyes had widened as they stood by the podium and talked.

"*Ya.* I still can't believe it. He actually admitted he was immature and wasn't there for me when I needed him most."

The dining room was half full, so Kayla was careful to keep her voice low. She didn't want to draw attention like she had that day with Jamie.

"He said he wants to be your *freind*? Do you think he'll come visit you?"

Kayla groaned. "*Ach,* no. I hope not."

Eva cringed. "How would Jamie feel if he

389

knew your ex-boyfriend wanted to recon-
nect with you?"

"I don't know what to think about Jamie."
Kayla leaned back on the stand. "When he
came to see me Tuesday morning after his
shift, he said he'd call me and set up a date
to get together. Today is Thursday, and I
still haven't heard from him. I don't know if
I'll see him this week or not. It's tearing me
up to go days without seeing him. What if I
don't see him for another week?"

"Why are you giving up on Jamie so easily?" Eva frowned. "You know all the stress
he's under at home. Why aren't you giving
him a chance to prove himself to you?"

"I'm just so confused. He tells me he cares
and then he doesn't call for days. I want to
be first in his life, and I want to know he
cares for me as much as I care for him."
Kayla couldn't stop tears from welling.

Eva grabbed a tissue from beneath the
stand and handed it to her. "I'm so sorry."

Kayla wiped her eyes. "I think I'm in love
with him, but I don't think he loves me
back."

Eva opened her mouth but closed it again
when the door to the restaurant opened. A
group of six *English* women clad in T-shirts
and shorts walked in.

Kayla stuffed the tissue in her pocket,

grabbed six menus, and plastered a smile on her face. "Welcome to Dienner's Family Restaurant."

Jamie spun his fork in his spaghetti as he sat beside Leon at the fire station's long table Saturday night.

"It was incredible. The pickup rolled down the embankment and landed on its wheels." Brody gestured with his arms as if showing how the vehicle had rolled. "The driver walked away with just cuts and bruises, but the bed of the truck was bent and the windshield was busted. That driver was definitely blessed."

"Wow." Leon stabbed a meatball. "The hand of God saved that guy."

Jamie shoved the spaghetti into his mouth and chewed.

"You're awfully quiet, Riehl," Brody quipped. "What's going on?"

"I'm fine." Jamie cut a meatball in half and then forked it. "Just tired."

"How are things going at the farm?" Leon asked.

Jamie shrugged and swallowed before answering. "It's the same. Busy." *I can't keep up.*

"I was surprised when Brody mentioned you volunteered to take another shift," Leon said. "This is your third one this week."

Jamie wiped his mouth with a paper napkin. "Brody said he was down one man since Swanson is out of town on vacation. I thought I'd help out."

Leon raised an eyebrow. "Don't you think you're taking on too much?"

Jamie shook his head. "I'm happy to do my part for the station."

The door opened, and when Nathan appeared, Jamie froze. He craned his neck, looking behind Nathan for Kayla. But she wasn't there. Disappointment and regret transformed the spaghetti in his stomach into a heavy rock.

"Hi, Nathan," Brody called. "How are you?"

"Have you eaten?" Leon asked. "We have plenty of spaghetti and meatballs. Brody always makes too much."

"Thanks, but I only have a few minutes." Nathan sat down across from Jamie.

"Hi," Jamie said. "How are you?"

"I'm fine." Nathan removed his straw hat and placed it on the chair beside him. "You haven't been by the *haus* all week, and I missed you when you stopped by the restaurant Tuesday morning. I thought I'd check on you."

"I'm all right." Jamie dipped his fork into

the pile of spaghetti. "How's your family?"

Nathan shrugged. "Fine. I think *mei schweschder* misses you, though. She's been really cranky and mopey. Where've you been since Tuesday?"

Jamie felt Brody and Leon staring at him, and heat slithered up his neck. "I've been busy. *Mei bruder* and I are adding on to one of our barns. It's turned into a much bigger project than we anticipated."

"Oh." Nathan nodded slowly. "How have things been here? Have you had any exciting calls?"

"Brody, tell him about the car accident you responded to yesterday," Leon said.

Jamie continued eating while Brody shared the story, but Brody's words were only background noise to his loud thoughts. He missed Kayla, but soon after their picnic last week, taking time he didn't really feel he could spare, he'd begun to realize the truth — he didn't know how to fit her into his life.

Every day he witnessed the pain in his family's eyes and knew he was the reason for their pain. Every day he fought hard to push himself forward, working long days to ensure his siblings and especially his father knew they could count on him. And he worked hard for another reason too. He needed to keep his guilt and grief over his mother's death at bay, allowing him to get at least a little sleep at night before he couldn't even function as a good firefighter.

He was so tired.

But he cared about Kayla, deeply. He had tried to give her enough attention. And he usually felt better after spending time with her because she was a good listener and he knew she cared about him, just as he cared about her. After the picnic, he went home to all his responsibilities, already so worried about how he'd carve out time to see her again that he worked even more to bury that guilt too. He'd had to force himself to see her Tuesday morning, knowing the turmoil in his soul.

How could he be a good boyfriend when his life was a complete and utter mess?

Kayla was better off without him.

He was better off without her.

But then why did the idea of not having her in his life hurt so deeply? Still, he didn't think he could avoid the issue much longer. It wasn't fair to either of them.

Brody shared a few more stories before Nathan stood up from the table.

"I need to get back to the restaurant." He slipped his hat back onto his head as he looked at Jamie. "Stop by the *haus* or the restaurant soon."

"I will," Jamie said before Nathan left.

"I cooked, so you two get to clean up." Brody carried his dishes to the sink. "I'm going to see if any games are on television." He disappeared into the hallway that led to the large sitting room.

Jamie gathered the leftover spaghetti and meatballs and carried them to the counter and scraped them into plastic containers.

"Did you and Kayla break up?" Leon brought their drinking glasses.

"What?" Jamie spun toward him. "No, we didn't break up."

Leon raised his eyebrows. "If you didn't break up with her, then why haven't you seen her since Tuesday?" He returned to the table for the remaining plates and utensils.

"I have too many demands on my time right now. *Dat* still isn't up to par, and the farm needs a lot of work. I'm here at least once a week. I feel like I can never get caught up, even though Mark is certainly doing his fair share."

Jamie stowed the food and began filling the sink with water and soap. Leon grabbed a container of bleach wipes from the pantry. He moved to the table and began wiping it down.

Jamie scrubbed a bowl in the hot water and suddenly decided to confide in Leon. "I don't think I can fit a relationship into my life right now. It's just not the right time."

"Do you want to know what I think?" Leon offered.

"I have a feeling you're going to tell me whether I want to hear it or not."

Leon pointed a bleach wipe at him, and Jamie grinned. "I think you'd be *narrisch* to let a *maedel* like Kayla slip through your fingers. If I were you, I'd do everything in my power to hold on to her."

Jamie was silent as he washed the next bowl.

"You have nothing to say?" Leon asked.

Jamie shrugged. "I'm not sure what to say."

"I messed up with Susie Bontrager, and I regret it to this day. I heard she's going to marry Josh Chupp."

"Really?" Jamie recalled when Leon dated Susie. They met in youth group and dated for two years before going their separate ways.

"*Ya.*" Leon frowned. "It's too late for me and Susie. Don't be like me. Fix things with Kayla before it's too late."

Leon's words settled over Jamie as he

worked at the sink. If only he knew how to fit Kayla into his life, then he could make things right. But that seemed like an impossible task.

TWENTY-FIVE

"How's Kayla?"

Jamie closed the devotional he'd been reading and looked up at Laura. She was standing in the doorway to the kitchen. "I don't know. I haven't seen her since Tuesday morning."

"And now it's Sunday? Why not?" She crossed the room and sat down on the sofa across from him.

"I've been wrapped up in projects here, and when I'm not here, I'm at the fire station working." He paused. "I just don't know if I can make this relationship work, Laura."

"You aren't making time for Kayla, Jamie. And I don't understand why." She frowned. "You two are great together. She cares about you, and you care about her. You could be at her *haus* right now. What's the problem?"

He pursed his lips. "The problem is I'm

overwhelmed trying to keep this farm running and help the members of our community as a first responder."

"You say that like you're the only person working on this farm or at the fire station."

He blinked at her. "What do you mean?"

"I mean you're not the only person who lives here." She gestured around the room. "Mark is here, too, and *Dat* is getting his strength back. None of you needs to be working day and night for the farm to succeed. Cindy and I keep the household running. Brody, Leon, and Noah are only a handful of the other firefighters at the station. The farm and the firehouse won't come to a screeching halt if you visit your girlfriend a few times a week."

Jamie stared at her.

"You seem so *froh* when you're with Kayla." Her expression softened. "With what our family has been through, you need someone more than ever." She paused. "We all miss *Mamm,* Jamie. You can't bury your grief with work. We're all broken because she's gone, and the only way we can get through this is if we're surrounded by people who love us. I'm sure Kayla loves you, and whether or not you realize it, you love her too. Let her help you heal."

Her words touched him deep in his soul.

He longed to respond, but he felt as if he had a rock in his throat.

"Kayla is perfect for you," she continued. "She's strong and loving. I could see her standing by your side through thick and thin, but you have to put the effort into building a relationship with her."

"You're right." His voice sounded foreign to his own ears.

"I know I am." She stood. "But if you agree with me, then why are you sitting here? Go tell her how you feel."

He stood and dropped his book on an end table. "I'll see you later."

"Tell her I said hello," she called after him as he strode out of the room. Maybe he could find a way to make this relationship work after all. Laura was right. Kayla was worth it.

"A buggy just came up the driveway. Someone's here!"

Kayla spun toward the mudroom as *Dat* called from the back door. A moment later, the screen door clicked shut, and her heartbeat galloped as she set a serving platter in a cabinet.

Mamm nudged her. "Go see who it is."

Had Jamie finally come? Kayla froze as she stared at her mother. "What if it's

400

Jamie? What do I say to him? He hasn't even called me in days." A mixture of irritation and hope warred inside of her.

"If it's Jamie, then you say hello and let him talk." Eva pointed toward the door. "Go on. Be brave."

Kayla wiped her hands on her apron and padded out to the mudroom. She peeked out the screen door and her shoulders dropped with disappointment. Her father was talking with Abram as they stood by his horse and buggy.

Jamie hadn't come, but Abram had.

Dat said something, and Abram laughed. The familiar sound sent memories and confusing emotions spinning. Part of her wanted to rush out and greet Abram, and another part of her longed to hide in her room.

Eva's words echoed through Kayla's mind: *Go on. Be brave.*

Yes, Kayla could be brave. She was courageous to her core. She could sit and talk to her ex-boyfriend without allowing him to hurt her again.

Taking a deep breath, she pushed open the screen door and stepped onto the porch. The door clicked shut behind her.

"Hi, Abram!" She waved when he turned toward her. "I didn't expect to see you tonight."

Dat said something to him and then walked toward the barn. Would *Dat* think she was going to get back together with Abram? Did she want to get back together with him?

Her stomach soured. No, she had intense, deep feelings for Jamie. She just didn't know if he had the same feelings for her.

"Hi." Abram walked over to the porch. "Would it be all right if I visited with you for a little bit?"

"*Ya*, I suppose so." She pointed toward the kitchen. "Do you want something to eat?"

"No, *danki.*" He touched his abdomen as he climbed the steps. "I ate too much at supper."

"Oh." She turned toward the glider and frowned as memories of Jamie's last visit came to mind. He had rested his arm behind her and touched her shoulder while he poured out his heart about how much Cindy's rejection continued to hurt him. She couldn't sit on the glider with Abram. That was Jamie's spot. She sat down in the rocker beside it and smiled up at Abram. "Have a seat."

"*Danki.*" He folded his lanky body into the

rocker beside her. "How has your Sunday been?"

"*Gut*. We visited with another family this morning and then rested this afternoon. How has your Sunday been?" She folded her hands in her lap.

"It was nice. We had church in our district and then rested." His expression grew serious, and he leaned forward. "Kayla, I wanted to say something else to you at the farmers market, but I didn't have the courage. I need to get it off my chest before I go *narrisch*."

Panic gripped her. Was he going to ask her to be his girlfriend again? Oh no. She couldn't handle this, not when her heart still belonged to Jamie. Plus, technically, she was still Jamie's girlfriend — even if she had no idea what he'd been doing or feeling for the last few days.

"Would you like some lemonade?" She popped up from the rocker, and Abram sat back with a start. "*Ya,* I'll go get some lemonade and pretzels."

Before he could respond, she rushed into the house. Her mother and Eva sat at the kitchen table, drinking from mugs.

"Is Jamie here?" Eva grinned.

"No." Kayla shook her head. "It's Abram."

Mamm gasped. "Abram? Why is he here?"

"You didn't tell your *mamm* you ran into him at the market?" Eva asked.

Mamm divided a look between them. "What happened? What did he say?"

"I can't explain now." Kayla held up her hands. "I told him I would get us a snack."

"I'll fill *Mamm* in." Eva waved Kayla off.

Kayla crossed the room to the refrigerator and pulled out the container of lemonade. After pouring two glasses, she grabbed a bag of pretzels, loaded it all onto a tray, and went back to the mudroom. Squaring her shoulders, she stepped onto the porch. She was brave. She could be strong and guard her heart no matter what Abram said to her.

She handed him a glass, and when their fingers brushed, she felt nothing. There was no electricity. No excitement. Her body didn't respond to him like it did to Jamie.

"*Danki.*" He took a long drink. "You still make the best lemonade."

"*Danki.*" She sat on the rocker beside him and opened the bag of pretzels. After scooping out a handful, she gave him the bag. She popped a pretzel into her mouth as she waited for him to speak.

He took a handful of pretzels, too, and then set the bag on the chair beside him. He ate in silence for a few moments and then turned toward her. "I told you *mei schweschder* got engaged."

"*Ya*. That's *wunderbaar.*" She lifted her glass and took a long drink.

"Seeing her get engaged made me realize I've made some mistakes in my life. Big mistakes. And the biggest mistake I made was losing you."

She started to choke. She coughed and her eyes watered as she struggled to swallow the sweet liquid.

"Calm down." He took the glass from her and began patting her back. "Take a deep breath."

She coughed until she was able to breathe again. She wiped her eyes with the back of her hand.

"Are you okay now?" Concern was etched on his face.

She nodded. "It went down the wrong way, but I'm fine." She took another drink.

"I'm glad." He cleared his throat. "As I was saying, I made a mistake when I broke up with you, and I want to apologize again." He paused. "I also want to say I really miss you."

When her hands started to shake, she set the glass on the floor beside her chair. This was confusing.

An awkward silence stretched between them like a great chasm.

"Kay?" He gave a nervous laugh. "Please say something. Anything."

"I don't know what to say."

"Okay." His face clouded with a deep frown. "You don't feel the same way, do you?"

She shook her head as confidence surged through her, straightening her spine as if a steel rod had been inserted. "No, I don't feel the same way. You hurt me badly. You took me for granted every time you left me sitting on this porch waiting for you. You chose your *freinden* over me again and again. I skipped youth gatherings waiting for you, and then you didn't come. I lost close friendships because of you. You never put me first in your life. And then you broke up with me when I needed you most."

She leaned forward. "How could I ever trust you again?" Relief flooded her as a giant weight disappeared from her shoulders. Oh, it felt good to get her feelings out in the open.

"You're right." Abram rested his elbow on the arm of the chair. "I was selfish. I should have been the boyfriend you needed, but I wasn't." His expression softened. "Why don't we start over? I'll do better this time. What do you think?"

Kayla's mouth dried as her thoughts

turned to Jamie. But Abram was sitting next to her, and Jamie was nowhere to be found.

Pure dread flowed through Jamie's veins as he stared at Kayla's back porch. He wanted to believe he was dreaming, but he wasn't. Kayla sat on a rocking chair next to another young man, drinking something and talking. Alone. Kayla hadn't even heard his horse and buggy coming up the drive.

What Leon told him would happen was unfolding in front of his eyes — Kayla had found someone else. He was too late.

"Jamie? Is that you?" Kayla had seen him. She stood and rushed to the edge of the porch.

For a moment he couldn't speak. He gripped the reins tighter with shaky hands. The coward in him wanted to flee, but the strong man buried deep inside his battered soul propelled him out of the buggy and onto the rock driveway. He cleared his throat and mustered all the strength he could find.

"Kayla," he called. "Could I speak to you a moment?"

"*Ya.*" She fingered the ribbons on her prayer covering as she turned to the man. "I'll be back in a moment."

He nodded at her and then glared at

Jamie. The animosity in the stranger's face sent bile bubbling in Jamie's throat. Who did this man think he was spending time with Kayla? After all, she was Jamie's girlfriend, not his.

But I haven't seen her in nearly a week. How can I justify calling her my girlfriend?

Jamie balled his hands into fists as Kayla descended the steps and hurried over. "Could we walk down the driveway for some privacy?" he asked. He swallowed the sourness in his throat.

"*Ya.*" She walked next to him, and the frustration radiating off her was palpable.

When they reached the bottom of the driveway, he spun toward her. "Who is he?"

She lifted her chin, her face twisted in a frown. "That's Abram Blank."

His mouth fell open as her words punched him in the stomach. Hard. "You're seeing Abram again?"

"It wasn't planned. I ran into him at the market on Thursday, and he just showed up tonight."

"He hurt you. Why didn't you tell him to leave?" His voice rose.

"I haven't seen you or even heard from you in days. Where have you been?" Her voice was thick as her eyes glistened in the light of the setting sun.

"I'm sorry," he began. "Mark and I have been busy harvesting hay."

"I see. Did you think of me at all last week?"

"Of course I did."

"And were you busy all afternoon today, a Sunday?"

"I —"

"Do you care about me, Jamie?" The pain in her eyes slashed through his soul.

"Of course I do. You're my girlfriend."

"I don't feel like your girlfriend." She shook her head, and her eyes watered.

"What do you mean?"

"I've waited to hear from you since that few minutes I saw you on Tuesday. I think about you every day. When you're on duty, you're a block from where I work, right?"

"That's right."

"Yet you told me you were volunteering for an extra shift."

He cringed. "I volunteered on Saturday too."

Her blonde eyebrows drew together. "Were you too busy to stop by the restaurant to see me on either day?"

He paused, and her face crumbled.

"Maybe we should take a break." Her voice was wobbly.

This is it. She's breaking up with me. His

insides went cold as he held up his hands. "I don't want to break up with you."

"I think maybe this relationship is too much for you right now. Perhaps we should just be *freinden.*" She swiped the back of her hand over her eyes. "I care about you and your family very much, but I don't think our relationship is working."

Jamie closed the distance between them. He'd been thinking the same thing. But between Leon and Laura's encouragement, he'd found a new determination. "Please give me another chance. Let me explain —"

She shook her head as she stepped away from him. "We need a break."

"Please don't give up on me," he pleaded with her. "I'm so sorry."

"I am too," she whispered. "Good-bye, Jamie."

As Kayla walked away and he followed her, a churning ball of anxiety in his chest felt like a heart attack.

How could he have let this happen?

Kayla climbed the porch steps, then turned to see Jamie's horse pulling his buggy down the driveway. She sucked in a deep breath as her heart shredded into a million pieces. Tears trickled down her hot cheeks and she brushed them away. She couldn't allow herself to fall apart in front of Abram.

Abram came up behind her. "Are you okay?"

"*Ya.*" Her voice sounded weak to her own ears.

"Who was that?"

"*Mei freind* Jamie." She wiped her eyes again and then turned toward him. "We sort of had an argument."

"Did my being here cause a problem between you?"

"*Ya.*" She shook her head. "I mean, no. It's more complicated than that." She paused and took a shaky breath in an effort to stave off more tears. "I'm sorry, but I think I need to go inside."

"I understand." He studied her for a moment. "I didn't mean to cause you any problems."

"It's okay. The problems between Jamie and me have been brewing for a while." She set the glasses on the tray and added the bag of pretzels. "It was nice seeing you. *Gut nacht.*" She started toward the door.

"Wait."

Kayla gritted her teeth. She was tired of men telling her what to do. She turned toward him. "*Ya?*"

"May I see you again?" The hopeful expression on Abram's face was nearly too much for her to endure.

"What I really need right now is a *freind*. If you can handle being only *mei freind,* then, *ya,* you can see me again." She gripped the handle and pushed open the screen door without waiting for a response.

"Gut nacht," she called over her shoulder as she stepped into the house. After the screen door clicked shut, she set the tray on a bench. When she heard Abram walk down the steps and start across the rock driveway, she closed the inner door too, leaned against it, and sobbed.

Jamie trudged up the porch steps after stowing his horse and buggy. The weight of his mistakes bogged his steps as he entered the mudroom, kicked off his boots, and hung his hat on the peg beside Mark's. He was a failure. He had failed his mother, his family, and now Kayla. It was probably only a matter of time before he failed as a firefighter too. His life was in shambles.

He stepped into the kitchen and leaned his back against a wall, scrubbing his hands down his face. He wanted to sob. He wanted to scream. But he just rubbed his eyes as grief and regret swallowed his insides.

"Jamie?"

He opened his eyes, expecting to find

Laura standing in front of him. But Cindy was there, and he froze.

"Are you hurt?" She looked scared. "What happened?"

He stared at her, unable to say a word. The agonizing pain of losing Kayla coupled with the shock of Cindy's sudden willingness to speak to him were overwhelming.

"Please answer me." Her eyes brimmed with tears. "Are you okay?"

"No, I'm not okay." He pushed off the wall, went to the table, and dropped onto a chair. He set his elbows on the table's surface and covered his face with his hands. Dread pooled low in his gut.

He heard the chair beside him scraping the floor, followed by the rustling of clothing.

"What happened?" Her voice was right next to his ear.

"Kayla broke up with me, and it's my fault." His hands muffled his voice.

"I'm so sorry." Her tone rang with sympathy. "Please tell me what happened."

He turned to look at her. "I'm confused. Why are you talking to me now? It's been weeks and weeks. You've done nothing but rebuff me since we lost *Mamm.* Why do you suddenly care?"

Her face crumpled. "I'm so sorry. I never

413

should have lashed out at you or blamed you. I've just been so lost without her."

"I know." He blew out a deep sigh. "I am too."

"I've been blaming myself. I kept thinking if only I had been the one to carry that last batch of jars down the stairs, she'd still be alive. I couldn't live with the blame, so I took it out on you. But I was so wrong. It wasn't your fault or mine that she died."

She took a napkin from the holder in the center of the table and wiped her eyes. "It was God's will, and I need to accept that. It was a sin for me to take it out on you, especially for so long." She sniffed as more tears spilled down her cheeks. "I hope you can forgive me."

A small sound escaped her throat, and she began to sob.

He pulled his sister into his arms, and she collapsed against his shoulder. "Of course I forgive you. I hope you can forgive me too." He rubbed her back until she calmed down.

"I'm so sorry," she whispered. "You're *mei bruder,* and I never should have treated you so badly."

"It's forgiven and forgotten." *If only it could be this easy with Kayla.*

"Please tell me what happened with Kayla."

414

Jamie rubbed the bridge of his nose as he gathered his thoughts. Then he told Cindy everything. How he had treated Kayla. How overwhelmed he'd felt by his responsibilities at the farm and the firehouse. How Laura had made him realize he'd been trying to bury his own grief and guilt with overwork. How even the duty he felt as a firefighter had clouded the other important things in his life. He finished with what happened when he went to see Kayla tonight.

Cindy clicked her tongue. "I'm so sorry."

"Thanks." He slumped back in the chair. "I made a huge mistake, and now I've lost her."

"Not necessarily."

He turned toward her, his eyebrows raised. "Why would you say that?"

"She cried, right?" she asked, and he nodded. "That means you hurt her."

"I already figured that out. I don't see how that's a *gut* thing. In fact, that's why she broke up with me." He pushed his chair back. "*Danki* for listening, Cindy. It felt *gut* to get all that off my chest. But I still have a lot of thinking to do. I'm going to bed."

"Wait." She grabbed his arm, pulling him back. "Just hear me out. If you hurt her that badly, that means she loves you. If she loves you, then you can win her back. We just need to figure out how."

"I don't think she'll give me another chance. How am I supposed to prove I'm trustworthy when she's lost all faith in me?"

"Give her something to have faith in." She shrugged as if the answer was simple. "She obviously feels very deeply about you. She believes in you. Show her you care about her and you're not going to give up that easily."

"Okay. I'll try that." But he knew how half hearted he sounded. "I'm going to go to bed now. *Danki* again for talking with me."

"I hope it helped."

"It did. *Gut nacht.*"

"*Gut nacht. Danki* for forgiving me."

"*Gern gschehne.*"

But as Jamie climbed the stairs, a flicker of faith took root deep in his soul. He managed to get his sister back. Perhaps he could get Kayla back too.

Twenty-Six

Jamie stared at the Closed sign in the window of Dienner's Family Restaurant the following morning. A knot of emotion tightened in his chest. He tented one hand above his forehead, leaned forward on the cool glass door, and peered inside. Kayla and Eva were setting small vases with a daisy on each table. As he watched Kayla, his stomach twisted and renewed regret flowed through his veins.

He hadn't slept more than a couple of hours the night before. He'd stared at the ceiling and contemplated what Cindy said. She was right; he had to prove himself to Kayla. Begging for her forgiveness was the best start to showing her how he felt about her.

This morning he'd rushed through his chores, and since he'd left a message for Blake last night, his driver was ready to take him to the restaurant at six thirty this morning. And now he stood there with his heart on his sleeve and words stuck in his throat. The restaurant wouldn't open for another fifteen minutes, and this was his only chance to get Kayla alone — if she agreed to talk to him.

Lifting his trembling hand, he knocked three times. Kayla jumped with a start and swiveled toward the door. She stared at him, looking surprised. He didn't blame her.

She turned to Eva, said something, and hurried over. After flipping the lock, she wrenched open the door. "What are you doing here?"

"*Gude mariye.*" He lifted his hand in greeting. "*Wie geht's?*"

She blinked at him and he took in her face. Purple circles outlined the bottom of her eyes. Had she lost sleep over their breakup too? The notion gave him a thread of hope that they could work this out.

"What are you doing here?" she repeated, her words measured.

"I was hoping we could talk." He could hear the desperation in his voice. "Please. I only need a few minutes."

She craned her neck to look toward her sister-in-law. "Eva, I'll be back in a minute, okay?"

"Take your time. We're ready for the

breakfast rush," Eva called before waving at him. *"Gude mariye."*

"Hi, Eva." A glimmer of hope flittered through his gut at Eva's friendly tone. He pushed the thought away and nodded toward the bench near the door. "Would you like to sit for a minute?"

"Ya." Kayla stepped over to the bench and sat down.

He sat down beside her and cleared his throat in an attempt to sound more confident. *"Danki* for talking to me."

"I'm surprised to see you." She touched the hem of her black apron.

"Did you think I would give up on you that easily?"

She shrugged and turned her attention to her apron.

"Please look at me."

She did. "What do you want from me?" The question was simple, but it cut him to the quick.

"I want to try to make this work. I want to apologize. I want you back."

She shook her head, and her eyes glistened in the early morning sun. "I think it would be best if we were just *freinden.*"

"Are you seeing Abram now?" He inwardly cringed as he waited for her response.

"No." She shook her head. "I told you the truth last night. I ran into him at the farmers market last week and we spoke briefly. Then he stopped by unexpectedly, and I told him the same thing I'm telling you — I only want to be *freinden.*"

So Jamie was in the same category as Abram. An ex-boyfriend. The realization turned the knot of emotion in his chest to ice.

"I need to go. We're opening soon, and Mondays are usually busy." She stood and started for the door.

He grabbed her hands, stopping her. "Please stay for another minute."

She stared down at him. "Please let me go." Her voice broke, nearly breaking his heart once again.

He released her hand, and she stepped away. Panic consumed him. He couldn't let her go. He jumped up from the bench. "Wait!"

She spun and faced him. "Jamie, I don't think —"

"Please listen to me." He walked over to her. "You said you'll be *mei freind.* Did you mean that?"

She nodded. "*Ya,* of course."

"If I prove to you that I can be a *gut freind,* would you give me another chance as your

420

boyfriend?"

She hesitated as she studied his eyes, and he hoped she could sense his sincerity. Then she seemed to relax just a little.

"*Ya.*"

"*Gut.*" Relief flowed through him. "May I see you tonight?"

Gripping the door handle, she studied him again. "Be here at closing."

"I will. *Danki.*"

She gave him a curt nod and disappeared into the restaurant.

Jamie hurried to the van with a spring in his step.

Jamie rushed down the stairs and into the kitchen. Cindy and Laura were still cleaning up after dinner.

"You're going to meet Kayla at the restaurant now?" Cindy asked as she dried a dish.

"*Ya.* She told me to be there at closing. I have thirty minutes to get there." He patted his trouser pockets and found them empty. Where was his wallet? He needed to take it in case he could convince her to go out for ice cream. He glanced around the kitchen but didn't see it.

"*Was iss letz?*" Laura asked.

"Have you seen my wallet?" He moved a

421

stack of papers on the counter but didn't find it.

"No. Have you checked your room?" Cindy asked.

Jamie jogged up the stairs and down the hallway to his bedroom. The wallet was sitting on his dresser. As he slipped it into his back pocket, his radio crackled to life, and he stopped to listen.

"All available units respond to accident with multiple injuries at Old Philadelphia Pike at Beechdale Road," the voice over the radio said.

He stilled. The accident was on the route to the restaurant. He was taking his horse and buggy, but he could stop and make sure the victims were okay before he went to the restaurant to meet Kayla.

But I'm not on duty. If I'm late, she'll feel betrayed.

Still, I'm a firefighter. Simeon was a firefighter, too, so Kayla should understand my dedication. How can I not help people who need me?

Jamie rubbed his eyes with the heels of his hands as confusion coiled in a tight knot inside of him.

The call came through again, and he sprang into action, racing down the stairs.

"I guess you found your wallet?" Laura

grinned.

"*Ya.* I'll see you later." He made for the back door.

"Bye!" Cindy called after him.

Jamie launched himself into his buggy and guided the horse toward the intersection at Old Philadelphia Pike.

"He could just be running late, and he'll be here in a minute." *Mamm* touched Kayla's shoulder as they stood at the front window of the restaurant staring out toward Old Philadelphia Pike.

Kayla pointed toward the clock above them. "He's more than an hour late, *Mamm.* We've already had supper, and now we're going to leave to go home."

"Give him the benefit of the doubt," *Mamm* continued. "Maybe he had to finish something up at the farm, and he'll meet us at the *haus.*"

Kayla pointed to the kitchen. "Do you need any more help cleaning up?"

"It's all done. We can go." *Mamm* touched Kayla's arm.

As she walked with her family toward their waiting buggy, Kayla squared her shoulders. She could get through this, even though she felt as if her insides had just been ripped apart.

■ ■ ■ ■

Jamie knocked on Kayla's back door as thunder rumbled in the distance. The aroma of moist earth and rain filled his nostrils as he glanced down at his dirty blue shirt. It turned out his fire station was short-staffed today, and he'd spent nearly three hours helping a crew extract victims from the car accident and then clean up at the scene.

While he'd considered just passing by the accident, he couldn't bring himself to avoid it when he saw a baby seat in the back of one of the three smashed cars. He had to help the child, and he prayed Kayla would understand and forgive him.

He was just about to wonder if anyone was awake, when the inner door swung open. It was Kayla's father. He wore a robe, and Jamie realized just how late he'd come.

"Jamie, what are you doing here?"

"I'm sorry, Willie, but I really need to talk with Kayla."

Willie hesitated for a moment, but then nodded. "Why don't you wait here?"

Minutes later, the door swung open again. Kayla glared at him through the screen door and he swallowed against his suddenly bone-dry throat. "Hi."

She continued to stare at him with her arms folded over her robe, her hair covered by a scarf. He wasn't sure he'd ever seen her face with such a severe frown, and it scared him.

"I'm sorry." The words tumbled out of his mouth at a quick clip. "There was a bad accident at the intersection of Old Philadelphia Pike and Beechdale Road. You might have heard the sirens earlier. When I went past it, I saw —"

"Wait." She held up her hand, silencing him, and stepped out onto the porch. "You went on a call on the way to see me."

"Right. But I saw —"

"Once again, you weren't on duty, but you responded to a call instead of coming to me, right?"

"Let me explain —"

"No, I've heard enough." Her voice rose as a bolt of lightning lit up the porch, followed by a rumble of thunder. "A relationship more than *freinden* can't survive if you're not making it a priority in your life."

"Please listen to me." His voice shook as irritation boiled in his gut. "I had all intensions of coming to see you, but when I went by the accident, I saw a *kind* in a *boppli* seat. I couldn't just leave. I had to help. It's my duty as a firefighter to help people. I would imagine Simeon felt the same way. I'm sure there were times when his plans changed because he felt compelled to respond to a call."

"Don't bring *mei bruder* into this." Her eyes smoldered as she stepped onto the porch. He backed up a step as she shook a finger in his face. "He was a *gut* man, a *gut* husband, and he would've been a *gut daed*. Simeon always put his family first."

He held up his hands as if to surrender to her fury. "I know he was a *gut* man. I didn't mean to imply I was criticizing him."

Thunder boomed around them, and the sky opened up, sending buckets of rain crashing to the earth. Kayla jumped with a start, but then her eyebrows drew together and her glower twisted her face once again.

"Your problem is you put work and the fire department first. That's not what I want in a relationship." She jammed her finger in her chest. "*I* want to come first. And if that can't happen, then I never should have said you could see me tonight." Her eyes narrowed. "Even a *freind* would have more consideration than to break promises over and over again!"

Anger bubbled up inside of him as thunder rumbled once again. This wasn't about friendship, no matter what she'd said that

426

morning at the restaurant. It was about two people who deeply cared for each other. "You do come first."

"No, I don't. I'm the last person on your mind." She took a step back as her face crumpled. "I respect your schedule and your dedication to the fire station, but I want to be the one you rush to see when you're not on duty."

"You are." He reached for her hands, but she stepped out of his reach. "You're the one I want to be with. You're the one I want to build a relationship with. Why can't you see that?"

Her eyes narrowed with a glare. "Because actions speak louder than words. Your actions have proven to me that I don't matter enough to you. You would have to give more of yourself for a relationship to work."

Lightning streaked across the sky, followed by a tremendous boom.

"You're everything to me." He pleaded with her, almost yelling to be heard over the driving rain. "You have my heart." He tapped his chest. "You're the most important person in my life."

"No, I'm not." She folded her arms over her chest. "I want to be treasured."

"You are treasured." When she continued to glare at him, his shoulders hunched with

427

defeat. "I don't want to let you go. I want you in my life."

"I'm sorry." She sniffed as she took a step backward toward the door. "I can't let you hurt me any longer. It's over. You need to accept it and move on. Because I already have."

He opened his mouth to respond, but Kayla was already inside the house, slamming both doors shut in his face.

He stood rooted for several moments as her words soaked through his brain.

I can't let you hurt me any longer. It's over. You need to accept it and move on. Because I already have.

He closed his eyes as the thunder rumbled all around him.

It's over.

"No," he whispered. "No, it can't be."

He trudged toward the door and lifted his hand to knock, but then he suddenly stopped as her words echoed through his mind once more.

I can't let you hurt me any longer.

His hand dropped to his side. *She's right. I need to stop hurting her.*

Turning, he padded across the porch and down the steps into the pouring rain. He stood by his buggy as the rain dripped off his hat, drenching his shirt and trousers. He looked up just as a bright bolt of lightning split the sky, followed by a loud, booming crack of thunder.

And then it hit him like a bolt of lightning. He loved Kayla. For the first time in his life, he was truly in love. The realization choked him from the inside out, and a heavy pain settled in his bones.

I need her, I love her, and I can't live without her.

He removed his hat and looked up toward the sky, allowing the rain to soak his face. And then he began to whisper a prayer.

"God, I'm confused. I love Kayla to the very depth of my soul, but I ruined our relationship. The pain of losing her is too much for me to bear. Please help me win her back. Give me the words that will make her understand I will cherish her for the rest of my life. Help me be the man she needs so she and I can build a life together that's pleasing to you. In Jesus's holy name, amen."

Then Jamie climbed into his buggy and started the trek home in the pouring rain.

Kayla sank into a kitchen chair and grasped the edges of the seat. Tears spilled from her eyes and a crippling ache took hold of her, seizing up her lungs and throat. She felt as if she couldn't breathe.

"Kayla!" *Mamm* ran into the room and sat down beside her. "What is it?" She pulled a napkin from the holder in the center of the table and began to dab Kayla's face.

"It's over. I told him I can't do this anymore." Kayla told her what happened. "I'm going to give up on love."

"Don't say that." *Mamm* frowned. "It will work out for you one day. It just takes time. Unfortunately, breakups hurt terribly, but God will lead you to the right man. I promise you."

Kayla's bottom lip trembled as she recalled the pain in Jamie's eyes when she told him it was over. She'd hurt him, but she had to do what was right for her. He wasn't being realistic, so she had to be.

Footfalls on the stairs drew her attention to the doorway. Nathan walked into the kitchen and studied her. *"Was iss letz?"*

"Nothing." Kayla sniffed and wiped her eyes with another napkin.

"Obviously something is wrong." Nathan came to stand beside her and leaned on a chair. "What is it?"

"She'll be fine." *Mamm* gave him a pointed expression. "You can go."

He frowned, crossed to the kitchen to take a glass from a cabinet, filled it with water, and left again.

"Things will get better." *Mamm* rubbed Kayla's shoulder. "I promise you. Just give it time."

"But I love him," she whispered. She hugged her arms to her chest as if it would stop her heart from shattering. "If we're not meant to be together, why does it hurt so much? Why, *Mamm*?"

When her tears started again, Kayla leaned forward and cried on her mother's shoulder. Kayla wondered if the pain would ever stop.

TWENTY-SEVEN

Jamie felt as though each of his legs weighed two hundred pounds as he trudged across the apparatus bay. He hadn't slept more than a few hours over the past two days, and the exhaustion had caught up to him earlier when he was on his third medical call since he came on duty at six this morning.

All he wanted to do was sleep, but when his head hit the pillow, his brain replayed the scene from Monday night when Kayla broke up with him again. Then he was stuck awake while battling suffocating regret. Memories of his mother mingled with his misery over losing Kayla, and before he knew it, he was drowning in grief.

He hoped the calls would stop and he could sneak in a nap before he had to make supper. Why did it have to be his turn to cook when he didn't have enough energy or ambition to even plan a meal? Perhaps he could convince the crew to order pizza.

He reached for the fire station door and yanked it open.

"Jamie!"

He released the door handle and turned toward the voice. His eyebrows knitted together as Nathan crossed the bay toward him. "Nathan. Hi."

Nathan jammed his thumb toward the engine. "I saw you all come back. Busy day?"

"The busiest." Jamie pushed his hand through his sweaty hair. "What brings you here?"

"I want to talk to you." Nathan sat down on the bumper of the brush truck.

Jamie crossed his arms over his collared uniform shirt and leaned back against the wall. "About what?"

Mei schweschder.

Jamie stood up straight as if someone had pulled him upright. "Is she all right?"

When Nathan hesitated, Jamie took a step toward him as panic gripped him.

"Calm down." Nathan held up his hands. "She's not hurt or anything, but she's . . . Well, I heard *Mamm* says she's an emotional wreck."

I know the feeling. "Oh," Jamie hoped he sounded casual. "I'm sorry to hear that."

Nathan lifted an eyebrow. "Are you?"

Jamie shifted his stance on his feet. "What are you trying to get at?"

"Look, I know you two broke up, but *mei schweschder* is miserable. I have a feeling you are, too, even though you're trying to act like it doesn't bother you."

"Did she send you here to talk to me?" Jamie held his breath, hoping Nathan would say yes.

"No." Nathan rested his left ankle on his right knee and leaned back on the bumper of the truck. "I told my parents I was going to walk up to the bookstore, and I will go there." He nodded in the direction of the building across the street. "But they have no idea I'm here too." He frowned. "Monday night I walked into the kitchen to get a drink. It must've been right after you left. Kay was crying — no, she was sobbing — on *mei mamm*'s shoulder. She was really upset after what happened between you two."

Jamie glanced up at the ceiling as renewed anguish came calling.

"My bedroom is next to hers, and she cried herself to sleep Monday night and again last night."

"I'm sorry to hear that, but she broke up with me. This is what she wants." Jamie gave

434

him a palms up. "I have no idea what you want me to say."

"Are you *froh* that you broke up?" Nathan's eyes challenged him.

"No, I'm not *froh.*" Jamie leaned back against the wall. "It's not what I wanted, and I begged her to take me back."

"I can't stand to see *mei schweschder* this miserable."

"I don't know what else to do." Jamie let his hands drop to his sides. "I begged her to forgive me, but she insists all I do is hurt her."

"Then you need to stop hurting her."

"I have stopped hurting her. I'm staying away from her."

Nathan stood. "I just told you she's miserable without you."

"But she's miserable with me too. I make her miserable."

Nathan shook his head. "Don't you see that you two belong together?"

"You're not making any sense. If I make her miserable then why should I be with her?"

"How old are you?" Nathan crossed his arms over his chest and stood up straighter.

"I'm twenty-five. Why?"

"I'm eleven years younger than you and I've already figured this out."

"Please, enlighten me," Jamie dead-panned.

"You need to try harder." Nathan poked Jamie in the chest. "You and Kayla care about each other. Make it work. Don't take no for an answer. If she didn't love you, she wouldn't be crying and moping around."

"She's moping?"

"*Ya,* she's moping." Nathan rolled his eyes. "She's been horrible to live with. If you say the wrong thing to her, she yells or runs off to be alone. You need to keep trying. If she didn't care about you, then she wouldn't be such a wreck."

Jamie nodded. Nathan and Cindy had said the same thing. But they were too young to have experienced what he and Kayla were going through, so what did they know? Doubt covered him like an uncomfortable, scratchy blanket.

"Hey, Nathan." Noah came around the corner from behind the engine. *"Wie geht's?"*

Jamie eyed Noah with suspicion. Had he been eavesdropping?

Nathan pivoted toward him. "Hi, Noah. How are you?"

"Fine, fine." Noah hugged a clipboard to his chest. "Are you on a break from the restaurant?"

"Ya." Nathan pointed toward the street. "I

need to get over to the bookstore. It was *gut* seeing you." He swiveled toward Jamie. "I hope to see you soon."

Jamie gave Nathan a wave as he headed out. Once Nathan was gone, Jamie turned to his best friend. "How much did you hear?"

"All of it." Noah eyed him with interest. "So she broke up with you?"

"*Ya.* It's for *gut* this time." Jamie cupped his hand to the back of his neck. "She said I keep hurting her, and she doesn't want to see me anymore." He summarized their argument Monday night.

"And Nathan came over to tell you to keep trying." Noah looked toward the street. "I think he's right."

Jamie shook his head. "Kayla made it clear she doesn't want to see me. Why would I chase after her after she told me not to? That's considered harassment."

Noah turned toward Jamie, his expression stoic. "I heard everything Nathan said. He's right. If Kayla is an emotional mess, then she loves you."

Jamie's stomach flip-flopped at the word *love.*

"She wouldn't take the breakup so hard if you didn't mean something to her."

"That's what everyone keeps saying. But

she told me —"

"I know what she told you, but what she feels is completely different. Do you remember when Elsie and I got engaged?"

Jamie nodded. "*Ya,* I remember. You took her on a picnic by a lake, and you asked her there."

"Right. A few weeks before that, she told me she didn't want to see me anymore. We'd had a big fight over something *gegisch*. She was upset, and we each said things we regretted. She broke up with me and said she didn't want to see me again."

"Really?" Jamie's eyebrows lifted. "You never told me that."

"I kept it to myself." Noah shrugged. "I didn't speak to her for two days. I thought I was better off without her. I was petty and prideful. But by the third day, I was miserable. I went back to her, begged for her forgiveness, and we were engaged two weeks later."

Jamie gaped. "I had no idea you and Elsie had problems."

"All couples have problems. No one is immune. It's part of being human." Noah leaned against the fire engine. "Swallowing my pride and working things out with Elsie was the best thing I've done in my life. I can't imagine being without her." He paused as if contemplating something. "I'm going to tell you something I haven't told anyone else."

"What is it?"

"We're expecting another *boppli.*"

Jamie grinned. "That's *wunderbaar.* Congratulations."

Noah smiled. "*Danki.* Life is tough sometimes, but it's also *wunderbaar.* We all have ups and downs." His smile faded. "I know you don't need a lecture, but my point is you will regret it if you let Kayla walk out of your life. Take Nathan's visit as a clear sign you need to try again."

Jamie swallowed.

Noah tapped Jamie's arm with the clipboard. "Let's go do the paperwork for this last call before the radio goes off again."

As they headed inside the station and walked back to the office, Noah's words marinated in Jamie's mind. He was confused. Should he take Nathan's visit as a sign or should he give up?

His mind told him to give up. But deep in his heart, Jamie was certain he had to try at least once more.

"Kayla," Eva whispered as she came up behind her. "Abram is here. He asked if you would seat him."

Kayla spun toward the front of the restaurant. Abram held his hat in one hand and waved to her with the other. She bit back a groan. He was the last person she wanted to see, but at least he still made an effort, unlike Jamie.

For the past three days Kayla had kept an eye on the front of the restaurant, hoping Jamie would come for breakfast or lunch while he was on duty at the firehouse. But he never appeared. In the evening she walked past the front window at least four times, hoping to catch a glimpse of him in his buggy.

If only Jamie would come to tell her he loved her. She'd had plenty of time to remind herself how rough his life had been since his mother's death. She knew how responsible he felt about the farm and his duty as a first responder. She had also reconsidered his stopping to help the child in the car accident. Of course that's what Simeon would have done.

But she still wasn't sure if Jamie loved her. If only he would fight for their relationship.

I'm pathetic. Jamie never said he loved me. He only said he cared about me. Caring for someone is not the same as loving someone.

She gritted her teeth against the bitter disappointment rising in her throat.

Eva touched her arm. "Are you all right?"

"*Ya,* I'm fine." Kayla lifted her chin. "I'll seat him." She marched toward the front of the restaurant. Abram was smiling at her. "*Gude mariye.* Table for one?"

"*Ya.*" His grin seemed huge. "Unless you can take a break and eat breakfast with me."

"I'm sorry, but the restaurant is too busy right now." She lifted a menu. "Follow me, please."

"How have you been?" His voice was near her ear, and she fought the urge to swat him away. "Did you work things out with Jamie?"

Kayla cringed at the mention of Jamie's name. "We haven't had a chance to talk again." Lying was a sin, but her situation with Jamie was too painful and too personal to share. They reached a table not far from the front door, and she handed him the menu. "Here you go. The breakfast specials are on page two. Would you like some *kaffi*?"

He took her hand in his. "Would you join my family and me for supper tonight? I'd love for you to come."

"No, I-I don't think so." Why was he holding on to her hand? She was about to pull it away when the bell on the door rang, announcing the arrival of another customer. She glanced up and found Jamie standing in the doorway, staring at them. She gasped and yanked her hand from Abram's grasp. "Jamie," she whispered.

"What?" Abram spun, his eyes narrowing as he followed her line of sight.

Jamie's face contorted into a deep scowl and he backed out the door.

Panic surged through Kayla's veins. *I have to stop him!*

"Eva!" she shouted.

All the conversations around the restaurant stopped, and Kayla felt every set of eyes burning through her as heat crept up her neck.

Eva turned toward her. "What?"

"Please take care of the front. I'll be right back." Before Eva could respond, she bolted across the dining room and out the door.

When she hit the sidewalk, she spotted Jamie walking quickly toward the firehouse. Her pulse stampeded through her veins.

She had to stop him. She needed to know why he came. She couldn't let him leave. She still loved him.

"Jamie!" Kayla shouted as she held on to her apron and ran after him. "Jamie, please wait!"

Caustic jealousy burned in Jamie's blood. He heard Kayla calling to him, but he kept walking despite her pleading. She told him she didn't care about Abram. But if that was true, then why was she holding his hand? He saw it now. She'd used him to get Abram back. She'd lied to him. She'd played him like a board game, using tears to string him along until she got what she wanted. She never really cared about him. She'd fooled everyone, including her family.

"So I guess it's really over then, huh?" she yelled.

He stilled and spun toward her, his chest heaving with fury, unconcerned that any passersby would hear. "You mean it wasn't really over when you slammed your door in my face the other night? Was that just another one of your games?"

"One of my games?" She blanched as if he'd struck her. "What does that mean?"

"*Ya*, your games." He walked toward her, stopping a foot in front of her. "I thought I'd ask you to give me one last chance. Nathan came to see me yesterday and said you were miserable without me." He gestured toward the restaurant. "But I see you're already cozying up with Abram. So much for just being his *freind*."

Her blonde eyebrows drew together. "Nathan came to see you?"

"*Ya*, he came to the firehouse yesterday and said you've been crying yourself to sleep at night. He believes we belong together, but it's obvious you've already replaced me. I'm sure that's what you wanted all along."

She folded her arms across her chest and gave him a haughty sneer. "At least Abram keeps his promises."

"Is that so?" He glared at her as his body shook with betrayal and anger. "If he's so trustworthy, why did he break up with you when you needed him?" He paused, unable to stop a wry smile from overtaking his lips. "Oh, wait a minute — that's exactly what you did to me too. You dumped me even though I've been struggling after losing *mei mamm*."

Her mouth worked, but no words came out.

"Good-bye, Kayla. I have to get back to the station." He turned and hurried away.

"Fine, then!" she yelled after him. "Just go back to the firehouse. After all, that's your true love."

He stalked to where his driver waited. He'd delayed his ride home so he could try to talk to Kayla one last time. He'd contemplated Noah's advice most of last night and decided to try pleading with her and speaking honestly from his heart. He was even going to tell her he loved her. But when he saw her holding Abram's hand, something

444

inside shattered. Jealousy, hurt, and fury consumed him, and he couldn't think straight.

It was time for Jamie to give up on Kayla. There was nothing left for him to do. She'd made her choice, and now he had to live with it.

But how could he move on when he loved Kayla so deeply his heart ached for her?

TWENTY-EIGHT

Anger clung to Jamie like a second skin as he climbed from the van and marched up the back-porch steps. He'd spent the ride home staring out the windshield and contemplating how he was going to move on with his life without Kayla in it.

When he reached the top step, his sisters, who were hanging out the laundry, both turned toward him.

"You're home late. I saved breakfast for you. It's in the oven." Laura's smile faded. "You look upset. Did something happen while you were on duty?"

"Gude mariye." He waved her off and started toward the house. He was too exhausted to rehash what happened.

"Jamie!" Cindy scampered after him. "Wait. Tell us what's wrong. You look haggard."

"I am haggard, and I'm heartbroken." He blew out a deep breath through his nose. "I

446

don't want to talk about it."

"Is it Kayla?" Laura walked up behind Cindy. "Did you try to talk to her again?"

He gave up and collapsed into one of the rocking chairs on the porch. "*Ya,* I did." He told them about Nathan's coming to the firehouse yesterday, and then his conversation with Noah. "Noah convinced me to give it one more try, so I did this morning. But I was too late. She was holding hands with her ex-boyfriend in the restaurant. I feel like a complete idiot."

"Oh, no." Cindy cupped her hand to her mouth. "I'm so sorry."

Laura shook her head, her expression puzzled. "That doesn't sound like Kayla."

"It may not sound like her, but it's the truth. When I asked her if she was seeing him, she said at least he keeps his promises. That sounds to me like she's gone back to him." The words tasted bitter on his lips.

Laura scrunched her nose as if smelling something foul. "I can't see her going back to her ex-boyfriend so quickly after breaking up with you. She cares about you deeply. I could tell whenever I talked to her."

"*Ya.*" Cindy nodded. "I agree."

"I know what I saw, and she was holding his hand. I think deep down she always wanted him back. It's really over this time, and now I need to figure out how to move on." He got up and took a step backward toward the house. "I need to get a shower and start my chores."

"Wait." Cindy clamped her hand over his arm. "Why don't you cool down and then call Kayla at the restaurant later? Maybe you can have a *gut* talk after you've both had some time to think."

He sighed as he looked at his youngest sibling. Her heart was in the right place, but it was time to move on. "I appreciate the sentiment, but I think I need to accept it's over." *Even though I have no idea how I can accept it.*

His sisters exchanged knowing glances, but he didn't have the emotional energy to ask them what they were thinking.

Laura suddenly smiled. "I have *gut* news that will cheer you up. Savilla had her *boppli* last night."

"Really?" He felt his scowl relax. "What did she have?"

"A girl." Laura clapped her hands together. "They named her Mollie Faith."

"That's great." He was grateful to have something positive to focus on. "They must be thrilled."

"*Ya,* they are." Laura pointed toward the house. "Let me warm up breakfast for you."

"No, *danki.*" He shook his head. "I'm not hungry." His appetite dissolved when he saw Kayla with Abram. "How's *Dat* today?"

Laura's expression brightened. "He ate all his breakfast today and then went out to help Mark with the chores. I think they're in the barn."

"That's *gut*. That's progress. He said yesterday that he'd try to help Mark with the milking today." The tight muscles in Jamie's back loosened slightly.

"I'd hoped he'd have a lot more energy by now, but he's getting there slowly." Cindy's eyes shimmered.

"He will." Laura rubbed her arm. "It'll take time, but we'll all get through this. We just have to take care of each other."

"*Ya.*" Cindy wiped away a tear. "We just have to have faith God will heal our hearts."

Jamie cleared his throat in an attempt to keep his emotions at bay. "I'm going upstairs."

"I really think you should reach out to Kayla again," Laura called after him.

"*Danki* for your concern, but I think it's time to let it go." As he stepped into the house, he overheard his sisters whispering, most likely analyzing his situation with Kayla. He tried to shove away the fury and betrayal boiling inside of him, but he

449

couldn't shake them. Kayla's words echoed through his mind as he climbed the stairs.

Just go back to the firehouse. After all, that's your true love.

Her words made him cringe. Didn't she understand he had a duty to help his community? Simeon was a firefighter, so why didn't she understand why he felt an obligation to help people?

But I couldn't save my own mother.

Tension coiled in Jamie's back as he hit the top step. He squared his shoulders, climbed the stairs to his room, and tossed his duffel bag on the floor. He sank down on the corner of the bed. The frame creaked under his weight as he covered his face with his hands and blew out a deep sigh that felt as though it had originated in his toes.

A sinking despondency suffocated him as he flopped back and stared at the ceiling.

As Kayla delivered two slices of shoofly pie to a table, the bell on the front door rang. When she turned, she saw Laura and Cindy. Alarm gripped her. Was Jamie okay?

Kayla hurried over. "*Gude mariye.* Is everything all right?"

"*Ya,* of course it is." Laura pulled Kayla into a hug. "How are you?"

Kayla relaxed. "I'm okay. How are you?"

She hugged Cindy.

Cindy gave her a shy smile. "We're all right."

"What brings you out this way today? Are you doing some Saturday shopping?"

"We were just visiting Savilla," Laura said. "She had her *boppli* Wednesday night."

"She had a girl and they named her Mollie Faith," Cindy added. "She's so cute. They're doing really well."

"Oh, that's so *wunderbaar.*" Kayla clapped her hands. "I'm so *froh* for her and Allen."

Laura's smile faded. "So how are you really?"

Kayla gripped the edge of her apron as an image of Jamie's angry face entered her mind. "I'm fine."

Cindy and Laura looked at each other, and she was certain they were communicating without words. Kayla's neck stiffened with tension as she waited for one of them to speak.

"You can be honest with us." Laura touched Kayla's arm. "We know you and Jamie broke up. He's a mess, and we believe you two can work this out if you really try."

"*Ya,*" Cindy chimed in. "He's really *bedauerlich.* He's been sulking, and we're worried about him."

"We wanted to see if we can help get you

two back together," Laura added.

Kayla's stomach constricted with anxiety. "It's really nice that you want to help, but there's nothing more to discuss. It's over. We tried, and it just didn't work."

The sisters glanced at each other again, and Kayla longed to run to the kitchen and hide.

"Jamie isn't eating," Cindy said. "And I don't think he's slept much. He looks terrible."

Pressure clamped Kayla's chest as she imagined Jamie's pain. Not only had he lost his mother, but now he was dealing with the pain of their breakup. His words echoed in her mind.

Oh, wait a minute — that's exactly what you did to me too. You dumped me even though I've been struggling after losing mei mamm.

She shoved the thought away. But he had hurt her! She was suffering. She hadn't slept either, and she couldn't get her last encounter with Jamie out of her mind.

She needed to end this conversation. His sisters were wasting their time.

"I'm really *froh* to see you both, but I don't feel comfortable discussing this." Kayla gestured toward the kitchen. "I need to go check on my customers' orders." She took two menus from the shelf under the

452

stand. "Would you like breakfast?"

"No, we have to go."

Kayla took a step backward, but Laura grabbed her arm and stopped her.

"Please," Laura began. "Don't run off. We know Jamie has made mistakes with your relationship, but he hasn't dated much. And we've all been dealing with a lot after losing our *mamm.* He's had a tough time, and he needs you."

Kayla shook her head as Laura released her arm. "I know you want to help your *bruder,* but he hurt me too."

"Please give him another chance," Cindy said. "We know he cares about you. He's a *gut* man. He just needs a little patience."

Kayla blinked, stunned at Cindy's support of Jamie. Did this mean she and Jamie had worked out their differences? Her heart warmed at the notion.

"Do you care about him?" Cindy's eyes were bright and hopeful.

"I'm sorry, but I really need to get back to work." She took another step away. "*Danki* for stopping by. Please tell Savilla and Allen congratulations for me."

"You do care about him, don't you?" Laura challenged her.

Kayla's shoulders dropped. "*Ya,* I do, but it will never work between us."

Laura hugged her again. "I hope to see you again soon."

"*Ya,* I do too." Kayla hugged Cindy. "Take care."

Laura and Cindy headed out the door, and Kayla slouched against the podium as if her spirit had been drained from her body.

"I've been looking for you." Eva came up behind her. "What's wrong?"

"Laura and Cindy were just here. They wanted to say hi and tell me Savilla had her *boppli.* Savilla is Laura's best *freind.*"

"Oh. That's nice." Eva studied her. "But what's bothering you?"

"They were really here to talk to me about Jamie." Kayla's thoughts tangled as she looked at her sister-in-law's sympathetic expression. "I'm so confused."

"*Kumm.* Let's talk." Eva took her hand and led her toward the supply room off the kitchen. "Talk to me."

"I already told you what happened on Thursday when Jamie came into the restaurant," Kayla began, and Eva nodded. "Laura and Cindy were trying to convince me to give Jamie another chance, but it's too late. There's nothing left to save. I wanted to feel like I'm first in his life, but he always put the farm and the firehouse before me. He even responded to calls when he wasn't on duty. How can I have a lasting relationship with someone who doesn't put our relationship first in his life?"

Kayla fingered her apron as a knot of emotion clogged her throat. "I want a relationship like you and Simeon had. You never took each other for granted, and he always put you first."

Eva scanned the large supply room. She grabbed a step stool from the corner, opened it, and pointed. "Sit."

Kayla sank down onto the stool as Eva opened up another and sat down in front of her.

Then Eva leaned forward, resting her elbows on her knees. "You seem to believe Simeon and I had the perfect relationship and perfect marriage, but we had our problems like every other couple."

"What do you mean?"

"We argued, we disagreed, and we hurt each other." Eva smiled. "But at the end of the day, we always loved and forgave each other." She sat up straight. "Simeon made his share of mistakes. In fact, he was a lot like Jamie. He would volunteer to take shifts at the firehouse for his *freinden* and not check with me first. One time we were supposed to visit one of *mei freinden* over in Lititz for a birthday party. Simeon called me up from the firehouse and said he wasn't coming home because he agreed to take another shift for a *freind* who was ill. I was furious with him. I had told him about her party more than once, but he just completely forgot."

Eva laughed, her hazel eyes shimmering in the gaslight above them. "I had to go to the party with my dessert alone. I was so angry I didn't talk to him for a few days after that. But I forgave him." She touched her chest. "I knew from the very bottom of my heart he loved me. He just made a mistake."

Kayla shook her head. "I had no idea. You never told me."

Eva shrugged. "I didn't feel the need to. I think your *mamm* knew something was wrong, but she didn't push me to share it with her." She folded her arms over her apron. "I made mistakes too. I hurt Simeon's feelings and let him down at times, but he still loved me."

Kayla nodded as understanding wafted over her. "We're all human."

"*Ya,* that's right. We all make mistakes, which is why we're taught to forgive at a young age. No one is perfect." Eva's expression became somber. "Do you still care about Jamie?"

Kayla nodded as tears stung her eyes. "*Ya.* I love him so much, sometimes I feel like I can't breathe."

"I know what you mean." Eva's voice shook. "I still feel that way about Simeon." She paused for a moment, sniffed, and cleared her throat. "Simeon eventually found a balance between the firehouse and our marriage, and I believe Jamie can find that balance too. You just have to be patient with him."

"I don't know how to make it work. I've sent him away so many times." Kayla groaned. "He thinks I've moved on."

"What do you mean?"

"He thinks I got back together with Abram. Remember, he saw Abram holding my hand, and I let him think . . ." She rubbed her temple with her fists. "Why did I do that?"

"Maybe you wanted to hurt him because he hurt you?" Eva cringed. "I remember doing that to Simeon when I was really angry with him. I wanted him to know how I felt, so I hurt him too. We all do it as a defense mechanism."

"But what I did was worse." Kayla's throat dried and her eyes stung with tears. "He said I hurt him the same way Abram hurt me. I broke up with him and let him down

457

when he needed me most. He just lost his *mamm* and then I broke his heart." Tears sprinkled down her cheeks. "He's right. I'm just as thoughtless and callous as Abram was."

"You made a mistake, but he will forgive you." Eva reached over and squeezed her hand. "Just tell him how you feel."

"But he was so angry." She wiped the back of her hand over her eyes and cheeks. "I don't even know how to apologize."

"Just give it a few days. Let him cool down and then go see him at the firehouse. Tell him you still care about him. And pray for him."

"Ya." Kayla nodded. "I will."

"Gut." Eva stood. "We should go check on our tables."

Eva folded up her step stool and stowed it as Kayla leaned hers against the wall in the far corner.

"Eva." Kayla touched her shoulder as they exited the supply room. *"Danki."*

"Gern gschehne." Eva smiled. "And I truly believe everything will be okay."

"I hope you're right," Kayla whispered as they walked into the dining room.

Sweat pooled between Jamie's shoulder blades and trickled down his brow as he stood on a ladder. He was hammering shingles on the barn addition he and Mark had built. The only light came from a lantern sitting on the roof beside him.

The moist earth filled his nostrils as he worked, trying in vain to relieve the anger and heartache that hadn't stopped plaguing him in the days since he and Kayla broke up. He yawned, and his eyes stung with exhaustion. He needed to go to bed and try to sleep, but every time he closed his eyes, he recalled Abram holding Kayla's hand. And her biting words echoed through his mind on a near constant loop.

He was determined to find relief from his mental anguish, even if it meant doing chores twenty-four hours a day. His friends and family had tried to tell him he needed to work less, but they were wrong. This is what he needed.

"Jamie?"

He glanced down at his father standing by the ladder. "Hi, *Dat.*"

"You do realize it's nearly nine o'clock, right?"

"Is it?" Jamie set the hammer on the roof.

"Are you planning to get any sleep tonight?"

"I need to finish shingling the roof."

"In the dark?" *Dat* raised his eyebrows.

"Come down, *sohn*. Let's talk."

Jamie stuck the box of nails in his pocket. Then he picked up the hammer and lantern and climbed down the ladder.

"I'm worried about you." *Dat* rested his hand on the ladder. "I shared my regrets with you weeks ago, but I'm afraid you're still going to make the same mistakes I did. You need to find some balance." He pointed to the roof. "I don't expect you to finish all your chores and projects in one day. Some projects take days or weeks to complete. I once read a quote that said life is about the journey, not the destination. That means you have to enjoy each day to the fullest." He sighed. "Mark understands that. Why don't you?"

Jamie couldn't stop the chuckle that burst from his lips. Mark worked hard at the farm, but he wasn't the oldest son. The one with primary responsibility. The one who had taken *Dat*'s wife from him through a failure to prioritize. The one who had to keep busy so he wouldn't have time to think.

Dat took a step back. "You're laughing at me?"

Jamie didn't want *Dat* to feel as though he needed to do more. He wanted him to rest. "I'm sorry. I don't mean to be disrespectful, but I have to get the work done. That's just how it is." Jamie gestured around the farm. "I have to get caught up."

"Jamie, none of us will ever be caught up. That's the way it is on a farm, and that's okay." *Dat* paused, his eyes assessing Jamie. "Laura and Cindy told me you had a falling out with Kayla. I'm sorry to hear that."

Jamie blew out a deep sigh as he kicked a stone with the toe of his work boot. "*Ya*, well, it wasn't meant to be."

"May I ask what happened?"

Jamie licked his lips as he contemplated how much to share. "I guess you could say I messed up. I missed a few of our dates because I was either tied up here or I responded to calls. She was upset. I tried to apologize and beg for another chance, and she gave up on me. She said I should go back to the firehouse because it's my true love."

Dat was silent for a moment as he fingered his beard. "And what do you think about what she said?"

"I don't think it was a fair statement. I expected her to understand why I volunteer since her *bruder* was also a volunteer firefighter." When *Dat* didn't respond, Jamie lifted his eyebrows. "What do you think?"

"I think she's right. I think you need to make room in your life for a *fraa* and a fam-

461

ily. This farm can't be your everything, and neither can volunteering."

White-hot anger combined with betrayal surged through Jamie. "I can't believe you said that. I thought you would understand me better than anyone."

Dat held up his hands. "Wait a minute. I didn't mean that as a criticism."

Jamie folded the ladder and carried it toward the barn as his fury continued to boil.

"Jamie!" *Dat* called after him. "James!"

Jamie didn't stop. He entered the barn and leaned the ladder against a wall.

"Why are you so upset with me?" *Dat* had followed him and set the lantern and hammer on a workbench. "You asked for my opinion, and I gave it to you. I'm always honest with *mei kinner.* I think you're making a mistake by not taking time to enjoy life. If you work all the time, you'll never have a future beyond this farm."

"This farm *is* my future," Jamie snapped. He pointed to his chest. "I'm the oldest and it's my responsibility. That's why I have to make sure the animals are fed, the cows are milked, and the buildings are standing."

"*Ya,* and it was my responsibility for years and years and years, and I missed out on giving your *mamm* everything she wanted. I

462

was so focused on this farm that she died without ever doing the things she wanted to do."

"But I'm not married."

"And you will never be married if you don't stop and look around you." *Dat* held up his hands. "Life is passing you by. You're going to die alone if you don't take a breath. We're called to bear fruit, and you can't do that on your own. You're a *gut* man, James, and Kayla is a *gut* woman. Your *schweschdere* told me some of the things Kayla has been trying to tell you. Stop being so prideful. She wants to be with you. She cares about you. Why would you throw that away?"

Speechless, Jamie stared at his father.

"I was about your age when I met your *mamm.* I knew the moment I saw her that I would marry her someday." *Dat*'s voice quavered, and he swiped at his eyes with the back of his hand. "We had a *gut* marriage and we built a *wunderbaar* life. You and your siblings are our greatest blessing. We had some tough years when the farm didn't do as well as we'd hoped, but we were steadfast in our faith, both in God and in each other." He paused and took a trembling breath. "I can tell you're hurting, which to me means you love Kayla."

Jamie nodded as emotion grabbed him by the throat.

"If you love her, go after her. Work through your differences and build a life with her. You'll be so grateful you did." *Dat* patted Jamie's shoulder. "And cherish each and every day with her."

Dat started toward the barn doors. "I'm going to bed. Don't stay out too late. *Gut nacht.*" His boots crunched over the dried hay and he disappeared into the dark night.

Dumbfounded, Jamie stood in the barn, staring after his father as his words wrapped around his thoughts.

Suddenly, grief opened a hole in his chest and he sank down to his knees. All the sadness of losing his mother and losing Kayla rained down on him. He hugged his arms to his chest as he opened his heart and prayed.

God, I'm so lost and confused. I don't understand where you want me to go and what you want me to do with my life. Do I belong with Kayla? Am I even worthy enough to have a woman as special as she is? Please help me understand the path you've chosen for me and lead me toward it. Please, God, please.

Jamie stood and relief loosened the tension in his muscles. He closed the barn and headed into the house. After changing into his nightclothes, he climbed into bed. And for the first time in nearly a week, he fell right to sleep.

TWENTY-NINE

Jamie rubbed his eyes as he guided his horse the following evening. Although he'd slept last night, he still was bone tired after another day working on the farm. He'd kept himself busy, but his father's words had haunted him all day. He couldn't let go of the notion he had to try to work things out with Kayla or his heart would never heal.

And he couldn't wait another day. He prayed Kayla would still be up and talk to him when he arrived. He knew the family often retired early, but he wanted to talk to her at home, not at the restaurant. He hoped Kayla — and her parents — would understand.

As he turned onto Irishtown Road, the pungent odor of burning wood filled the buggy. When he spotted a plume of smoke rising above the rooftops, his pulse pumped and he snapped the reins to speed up the horse's pace.

He halted the horse in front of Kayla's house and took in the flames licking up the side of a large farmhouse across the street. Dark smoke poured from the roof and up into the night sky. He suddenly remembered. The day of the barn raising, Nathan mentioned an elderly widower named Amos Lapp lived alone in that house.

He leapt from the buggy and started running.

"Jamie!"

He spun. Nathan was dashing toward him clad in shorts and a T-shirt.

"Call nine-one-one!" Jamie shouted as he continued toward the house.

"What are you doing?" Nathan yelled back.

"Go call nine-one-one!" Jamie repeated.

Nathan nodded and sprinted up his driveway toward the phone shanty.

Jamie jogged up the front porch steps, and after taking a deep breath, went into the house. He stepped into the foyer and was immediately overwhelmed by heavy, unforgiving smoke.

"Amos!" Jamie shouted. "Amos! Are you here?" He went into the family room, searching for the silhouette of a body in the smoke-filled structure.

"Amos? Where are you? I'm here to help!"

467

He moved a few more steps forward and stumbled as his leg hit a piece of furniture.

Smoke filled his lungs, and he began to cough as his eyes stung. "Amos! Where are —" A coughing fit overtook him. He bent at his waist and dropped to his knees. He had to get out of the house. Without his gear, he was in danger, and he couldn't help Amos.

But what if Amos was injured? He had to try to save him. He couldn't allow the man to die alone.

Jamie covered his mouth and switched directions. He was lost. How could he help the elderly man if he didn't even know where to go? His pulse sped up. He needed oxygen, a radio, and his fire company. Where were the sirens? Surely Nathan had called and the fire trucks were on the way.

Think, Jamie. Think!

Taking deep breaths, he crawled in the direction of where he thought the doorway might be. His knees hit something wooden. Was it a threshold?

He moved forward and smoke filled his lungs once again. He gasped, sputtered, and collapsed on the floor. His thoughts spun with worry. He had to rescue Amos.

A siren sounded in the distance, and Jamie closed his eyes.

Please, God. Please send help before it's

too late.

The loud wail of a siren slammed Kayla awake. She yawned and rubbed her eyes. Was she dreaming? As the haze of sleep dissolved, her pulse began to pump with panic.

She leaped from her bed, moved the green shade on her bedroom window aside, and squinted against the bright red lights shining from the fire engine tanker parked across the street.

She gasped as she took in the flames racing up the side of Amos's house. Dark smoke poured from the roof.

"Oh no!" She pulled on her robe, grabbed shoes and a headscarf, and ran to Nathan's room. She needed him to call nine-one-one. "Nathan!" She knocked on his door as she slipped on the shoes. "Nathan, wake up! Amos Lapp's *haus* is on fire!"

When he didn't answer, she pushed the door open. "Nathan?" She flipped on the lantern on his nightstand and found his bed empty.

Panic crawled up her spine. Where was he? She looked out the window and white-hot fear clamped over her chest like a vise. Had he gone to help Amos?

"No, no, no!" She grabbed the lantern and ran down the stairs. She hurried through the family room and kitchen, searching for her brother. When she didn't find him, she banged on her parents' bedroom door. "*Mamm! Dat!* Wake up! Amos Lapp's *haus* is on fire, and I can't find Nathan."

In only a few seconds, *Dat* wrenched the door open. He looked stunned, and *Mamm* stood behind him, her shoes in her hands. "Nathan is missing?"

"*Ya.* I looked in his room and down here, and I can't find him." Kayla pointed toward the front door across the family room. "I'm going to go see if he's with the firemen."

"I'll go with you." Kayla waited while *Dat* pushed his feet into slippers.

"What's going on?" Eva appeared from the kitchen. "I heard sirens and then I heard you yelling."

"Amos Lapp's *haus* is on fire, and I can't find Nathan." Kayla's voice faltered. "The fire department is already here."

"Let's go see if he's outside." *Dat*'s tone sounded as if he was working to remain calm. "He could be just observing what's going on."

"*Kumm.*" *Mamm* tied her robe closed as she followed *Dat,* and then covered her hair with a scarf.

Kayla rushed past them out the front door, down the steps, and across the street, tying her scarf as she ran. A second fire engine was parked beside the first tanker, and a group of firemen was climbing out. Fire hoses from the tanker sprayed the flames. Two ambulances sat nearby.

"Nathan!" she yelled as fear twisted deep in her belly. "Nathan, where are you?" The thick, heavy smell of burning wood filled her lungs as she stood as near the burning house as she dared. In her peripheral vision, she saw someone rushing toward her.

"Kayla!" Nathan grabbed her arm, startling her. "I'm right here."

"Oh, thank goodness!" She hugged him. "I was afraid you'd gone in to help Amos."

"I didn't, but I think Jamie did, and I don't think he's come out yet." Nathan words came in a rush. "His buggy is over there." He pointed toward the road behind her, where a horse and buggy sat. "I guess he was coming to see you and he saw the *haus* was on fire. I had gotten up to use the bathroom when I saw the flames. I ran outside, and Jamie told me to call nine-one-one. When I came back from the phone shanty, he was gone." He pointed toward the house again. "I told Brody, and they're getting a team together to go in after him."

Her heart nearly pumped out of her chest. Suddenly, the anger and disappointment she'd harbored broke apart, and worry for Jamie overwhelmed her. She still loved him, and the thought of losing him shook her to her very core.

"He doesn't have any gear." Nathan looked grim.

"*Ach,* no!" She cupped her hand to her mouth as her body shuddered.

Brody, Leon, and Noah, all dressed in turnout gear, approached them.

"Jamie's in there." She turned to Brody, her voice shaking. "Please go save him and Amos."

"We will," Brody promised before he turned and began barking orders. "An elderly man lives alone in this house. Also, Jamie Riehl is in there without gear. We need to assume both Jamie and Amos need help."

"Nathan," *Dat* said as the rest of their family caught up to them. "We were afraid you were in the *haus.*"

"I'm the one who called nine-one-one." Nathan explained the situation as Kayla pressed her hands together and swallowed back tears. *Dat* looped his arm over her shoulder.

"Let's go," Brody said to Leon and Noah.

"They'll find Jamie and Amos," *Dat* whispered against her temple. "Have faith."

472

Closing her eyes, Kayla whispered, "Please God, keep everyone safe. Please assist Jamie's *freinden* as they help him and Amos, and bring them all out of the *haus* safely."

The three firefighters disappeared through the front door. Soon Kayla could hear the chatter over a nearby firefighter's radio.

"This is Morgan. Kitchen is engulfed in flames," Brody's voice crackled over the radio. "We need to get some hoses on the back of the house."

"Ten-four," another voice responded.

"This is King. Found the elderly man," Leon's voice rang out next. "Downstairs bedroom to the left past the stairs. He's nonresponsive. Need help lifting him."

"On my way," Brody called.

"This is Zook. I'm going to look for Riehl," Noah announced.

Kayla swallowed back threatening tears as Eva touched her shoulder. She had Junior in her arms.

"Don't give up hope," Eva whispered. "They'll find him."

"Paramedics stand by," a voice called over the radio. "We're bringing the occupant out through the front door."

Kayla turned to Eva. "I think that was Brody or Leon." Fear clogged her throat. "But where's Jamie?"

"He'll be fine. Have faith," Eva insisted. "He's strong and brave, just like Simeon."

Junior whined and nuzzled deeper into Eva's shoulder.

The front door opened, and two firefighters carried out Amos, each holding one of his arms. Amos was bent over and limp as the firemen lifted him down the steps and onto a waiting gurney. The paramedics rushed him toward the waiting ambulance.

The firemen lifted facemasks, and Kayla's stomach dropped. Why weren't they going back in to help Noah? *Where is Jamie?*

Behind her, the ambulance's sirens wailed as they left for the hospital. Fire licked across the roof at an alarming rate.

"This is Zook. I found Riehl," Noah's voice called over the radio.

"He found him," Kayla whispered, grabbing onto Eva's hand and squeezing hard. "He found him."

"Oh, praise God!" *Dat* exclaimed.

"He's awake but injured," Noah continued, his voice strong and even. "Need assistance. I'm on the first floor near the stairs. Brody, Leon, are you still in the house? I need a paramedic. Send in —"

Noah's voice was cut off as a loud crack thundered and the roof shifted. Kayla heard herself scream.

"Roof collapsed at the front of the house!" a voice yelled over the radio. "We need to get Zook and Riehl out of there!"

Kayla's blood ran cold, and a strangled sob escaped her throat.

"Zook?" A voice announced over the radio. "Zook? Where are you? Respond, Zook. Noah! Noah! What is your status?"

When the radio remained silent, Kayla swayed and her legs gave out. Strong arms caught her. She turned as *Dat* held her up.

"There's another way in!" Nathan yelled as he took off running toward Brody. "Brody! Follow me!"

"I need a crew to go with me," Brody yelled as he followed Nathan to the far right side of the house. Three more firemen in turnout gear ran after them.

"This is King," Leon announced over the radio. "The fire in the kitchen is partially out. I need a crew to follow me in through the back. I'm going for Zook and Riehl." Two more firemen in turnout gear ran toward the house.

"Zook? Noah, can you hear us?" someone called over the radio. "What's your status?"

Kayla held her breath as tears rained down her cheeks. *No, no, no. This can't be happening!*

Junior whimpered, and Eva rocked him as

she whispered in his ear.

A black fear swallowed Kayla's insides as she covered her face with her hands and sobbed. *Please, God. Please keep Jamie and the other firefighters safe. Please, God, protect them.*

Several moments passed as Kayla held her arms to her chest and cried. Eva squeezed Kayla's shoulder and gave her an encouraging expression as tears spilled from her own eyes.

"This is Brody," a voice called over the radio. "We're coming out the side door. Need paramedics ready. We have Jamie."

"Ten-four," someone said.

"Jamie!" Kayla yelled. "Jamie!" She took off running but skidded to a stop on the wet grass at the side of the house. Nathan stood there, waiting.

Paramedics from the second ambulance rushed past her with a gurney. *Mamm, Dat,* and Eva came to a stop beside her.

Suddenly Noah and Brody emerged from the smoky doorway, helping Jamie walk down the side steps. His face was covered in soot as he coughed uncontrollably, but the firemen clapped and cheered.

"Oh, thank you, Jesus!" Kayla cried.

Brody and Noah helped Jamie onto the gurney, and the paramedics covered him

476

with a blanket.

Relief mixed with jubilation shuddered through Kayla as she studied Jamie's face.

"You're a hero, Nathan." Brody smacked her brother's back. "You told me how to get in to help Noah bring Jamie out."

Nathan grinned. "I remembered the side door, and I thought it was worth a try." He looked at Noah. "Why didn't you answer the calls?"

Noah leaned against the fence as his shoulders hunched. "I lost my radio for a few minutes. I was trying to call to say we were trapped. Once the roof collapsed, the smoke and dust were like a thick fog. I couldn't find the way out." He pointed toward the side door. "I'm so grateful you thought of this door." He opened his coat and took deep breaths. "I'm going to rest for a minute."

The paramedics pushed the gurney toward the ambulance.

"Go," Eva said, nudging Kayla forward. "Go talk to Jamie before they take him to the hospital."

Kayla hugged her arms close to her chest as she followed Jamie to the ambulance. As the paramedics took his vitals and handed him an oxygen mask, she took in his haggard form. He looked exhausted as his body

477

wilted, but his eyes were bright and alert. His gaze met hers as he breathed in the oxygen, and she edged closer to him. Admiration blossomed in her chest. She missed him. She loved him, and she wanted to work things out.

"Riehl, do you realize just how dangerous and reckless your stunt was tonight?"

Kayla jumped as Brody's voice boomed from behind her.

"You could have been killed," Brody continued as he stopped beside Kayla. "What were you thinking when you ran into that burning house without any gear or any backup? Actually, you weren't thinking at all, were you?"

Jamie shook his head as he continued to breathe in the oxygen.

"I can't believe you did that." Brody crossed his arms over his chest. "You know better."

Jamie nodded.

"Brody!" someone called from near the house. "We need you!" Brody turned toward the firefighters congregating by the house. "I'll be right there." Then he faced Jamie again. "Go to the hospital and get checked out. I'll see you later. I'll send someone over to let your father know what's going on. They can give your family a lift to the hospital."

Jamie gave him a thumb's up.

Then Brody turned toward Kayla. "Be sure to tell Jamie how dense he was to attempt to save Amos by himself."

"I will," Kayla said as Brody walked away and she pivoted toward Jamie.

"Ma'am, you can climb up into the ambulance if you'd like," a young EMT said as he held out his hand. "I can help you up."

"Thank you." Kayla took his hand and allowed him to lift her into the back of the ambulance.

"How are you doing, Jamie?" the EMT asked him.

Jamie lifted the mask. "Better. Thanks, Rob." His voice was hoarse. "I can breathe now."

"That's a good sign." Rob grinned. "Brody was right, though. We have to take you to the hospital to get you checked out."

"I know." Jamie looked at Kayla. "I came over here tonight to talk to you."

Kayla's eyes filled with tears as she nodded.

Rob looked at Kayla and then Jamie. "I'll give you a minute, but then we need to be on our way." He jumped out of the ambulance and walked around the side.

Jamie held his hand out to Kayla, and she

took it. "Sit." He patted the space beside him on the gurney, and she sat. Pulling a handful of tissues from her pocket, she mopped the soot off his face and then set the tissues onto the gurney beside her.

"I was so scared when Nathan told me you were in the *haus* without any gear." Her voice broke and a sob clogged her throat. An overwhelming need to hug him came over her. She wrapped her arms around his neck and buried her face in his collarbone as all the raging emotions she'd kept locked up came rushing out. She breathed in his scent — smoke, soot, sweat. She basked in all that was him, and she wanted to hold on to him forever.

"I'm so sorry for scaring you all. I had a complete lapse of judgment," he whispered into her scarf. His voice was warm, comforting. Stronger now. "I saw the *haus* was on fire, and I remembered Nathan told me Amos lived alone. I reacted without thinking it through. I wanted to save him, but I forgot I couldn't do it by myself." He rested his chin on her head and ran his fingers over her back, sending electric pulses dancing up her spine. "I guess all the stress and lack of sleep got to me."

She looked up at him, and he ran a finger down her cheek, wiping away her tears. His blue eyes were warm, inviting, and they felt like home. She belonged with him.

Suddenly, all the pieces of her heart came back together. She loved him, and she needed him in her life. "Jamie, I have to tell you —"

"Jamie!" *Dat* appeared at the ambulance's open doors with *Mamm,* Nathan, and Eva. "How are you?"

"You really gave us a scare," Nathan said. "When Noah's radio went dead, we all thought the worse."

"It was Nathan's idea to go in the side door to look for you," Eva added as she held the now-sleeping Junior against her shoulder.

"Really?" Jamie grinned at Nathan. "*Danki.* You're a hero."

Nathan grinned. "You think so?"

"*Ya,* I do." Jamie coughed and put the oxygen mask back over his nose and mouth.

Eva turned toward *Mamm* and *Dat.* "I've been wanting to talk to you about that. I've been thinking about it, and I need to tell you how I feel about Nathan's wish to become a firefighter. It's not my place to tell you how to raise your *kind,* but I feel really strongly about this."

"What is it?" *Mamm* asked.

"I think it's time you let Nathan start

481

training. He has the drive in him." Eva touched Junior's back. "He reminds me of Simeon, and you know how Simeon felt called to help people."

"I don't know . . ." *Mamm* shook her head and turned toward *Dat.* "I don't know if I can do it."

Eva held up her hands as if to assure *Mamm.* "I know it's scary, but you can't live in fear. You have to trust God to keep him safe. You have to trust Nathan to train well, and learn how to be safe. I know that's difficult because we lost Simeon, but not every firefighter is injured. Even fewer lose their lives. It's obvious that Nathan wants to be a firefighter. I think you need to let him try."

Mamm frowned. "What do you think, Willie?"

Dat raised his chin toward Jamie. "Let's ask him what he thinks. What's your opinion, Jamie?"

Jamie removed the oxygen mask and hesitated. "I'm not sure it's my business."

"We want your honest opinion," *Dat* said. "Please tell us."

"Okay. I think Eva is right and you should let Nathan train. I was just like him when I was a teenager. The training is thorough, and we don't allow the teenagers to go into burning buildings until they are seventeen and we're convinced they're ready." Jamie met Kayla's gaze. "I'll look after him. I promise."

Dat and *Mamm* exchanged a look.

"Eva and Jamie are right," *Mamm* said. "It's time we let him follow his dreams."

"*Ya,* I agree." *Dat* turned back to Nathan. "Are you ready?"

"*Ya,* I am." Nathan beamed. *"Danki, Dat."* He hugged *Mamm. "Danki, Mamm."* He hugged Eva last. "*Danki,* Eva, for believing in me. I promise I'll be responsible and I'll follow all the safety policies and rules."

Kayla brushed away tears of happiness. Now if only the doctors would tell her Jamie would suffer no permanent damage to his lungs.

When Jamie started to cough again, she touched his arm. "You need to go to the hospital."

Jamie nodded as he took in more oxygen.

"I'll take care of your horse and buggy," Nathan offered.

"Danki," Jamie said before turning to Kayla. "I want to talk to you."

"I want to talk to you too." She squeezed his hand. "I'll come to the hospital as soon as I can."

THIRTY

"I'm here to see James Riehl." Kayla stood at the desk in the emergency room nearly an hour later. After she and her father dressed, a neighbor drove them to the hospital.

"What's your name, dear?" The middle-aged woman didn't seem at all welcoming. In fact, she was frowning.

"Kayla Dienner."

"Are you family?"

"No, but I'm a close family friend." Kayla tapped the counter. "He'll want to know I'm here."

When the woman didn't respond right away, Kayla quickly added, "Please ask if he'll see me."

"Please have a seat. I'll see if I can get a message to him, but it's very busy back there. Plus, you're not family." The woman looked at someone behind Kayla. "May I help you?"

"Let's sit." *Dat* took her arm and steered her to a sofa in the corner that faced a flat screen television. A news program was on. "Everything will be fine."

She dropped into one end the sofa and moved her finger over its arm. "She's not going to let us see him. Maybe we should just go home."

"Don't give up just yet," *Dat* warned. "If we don't hear anything in a little bit, I'll ask again."

Kayla was staring at the television screen when someone called her name. She gasped when she turned and saw Mark walking toward her. She leapt to her feet and rushed over to him, her father in tow. "Mark! How is he?"

"He's going to be fine. He has some smoke inhalation so they're going to keep him overnight. But he'll most likely go home tomorrow. I was just going to call *mei schweschdere* to give them an update."

"Oh, praise God he's okay!"

"That's *gut* news," *Dat* added.

"*Ya,* I agree," Mark said. "We're waiting for them to move him to a room upstairs. He's in *gut* spirits. He was cracking jokes earlier."

"Oh, I'm so *froh* to hear that." Kayla

squeezed *Dat*'s hand. "He really gave us a scare."

Mark pointed toward the emergency room door. "Would you like to see him, Kayla?"

"I'd love to." She turned to *Dat*. "Would you like to come too?"

Dat smiled as he shook his head. "You can give Jamie my regards. I'll wait here so you can have some privacy."

"He's going to be so surprised to see you," Mark said as she walked beside him.

Kayla's heart thudded. She had to tell Jamie how sorry she was for breaking up with him. She prayed he would accept her apology and take her back.

Jamie's chest ached and his eyes stung as he scooted straighter against two pillows, but he was thankful to be alive. The chest X-ray and blood test had shown minor smoke inhalation, but according to the emergency room doctor he'd most likely be able to go home tomorrow afternoon after more oxygen treatments and a few follow-up tests.

In the corner of the small room, *Dat* sat in a chair and thumbed through a magazine. Jamie was grateful Brody had sent one of the firefighters to get his family. *Dat* had convinced his sisters to stay home, but Mark promised to call them with an update.

The curtain closed against the hallway fluttered open, and Mark stepped in. When Kayla followed him, Jamie was thrilled.

"Kayla." He breathed her name and drank in the sight of her.

She'd changed into a rose-colored dress, a black apron, and a prayer *kapp*. Her cheeks were pink, and even though he knew she'd been without sleep for hours now, her eyes were bright.

"Hi, Jamie." She gave him a smile and then waved at his father. "How are you, Vernon?"

Dat nodded a greeting.

Kayla moved to the side of Jamie's bed. "I've been worried about you. How are you feeling?"

Jamie forced a smile. "I've been better, but I'm doing okay."

"Hey, *Dat.*" Mark beckoned for him to come to the door. "Let's go call Laura and Cindy and then get something to drink. I saw a vending machine room off the lobby. Willie is out there too."

"That's a *gut* idea." *Dat* stood and winked at Jamie before following Mark.

Jamie nodded toward the chair his father had been sitting in. "Pull that over, and let's talk."

"Okay." She dragged the chair over to his

bedside and sat down.

They started to talk at once, and then they laughed.

"You go first," she offered.

"No, you first." He touched her hand, and heat flooded his veins at the feel of her warm skin.

"Okay." She threaded her fingers with his. "I just can't tell you how thankful I am that you're okay." She shook her head as tears shimmered in her eyes. "I was so scared. When the roof collapsed, all I could think was that you were gone just like Simeon. My heart couldn't bear losing you."

The tears slipped down her face, and he pulled her hand toward him.

"Come here," he said.

They both leaned forward, and he hugged her close and breathed in the scent of her flowery shampoo. He rested his cheek on her head and closed his eyes.

"Oh, Kayla, I'm so sorry."

"I'm sorry too." She rested her head on his shoulder. "I've missed you so much."

"I've missed you too."

Then he recalled their last conversation. He believed her when she said she'd been worried about him, and even that she'd missed him. After all, over the last weeks they'd bonded as they shared their experiences with grief and sorrow. But was he only a friend to her? Did someone else have her heart?

He had to know.

"Kayla, are you in love with Abram?"

"What?" She pulled back from him and swiped the back of her hand over her cheek. "No, I was never in love with Abram. I'm not seeing him again."

"But you were holding his hand in the restaurant." He folded his arms over his chest. "You said he keeps his promises, so I thought you got back together with him."

"I only said that because I was upset. To hurt you." She cringed. "I'm sorry. I didn't mean it. Abram wanted to get back together, but I told him no."

Relief wafted over Jamie. He still had a chance to make things right with her! He took her hands in his.

"I know I hurt you, but I need you in my life. *Mei daed* made me realize I've been missing out on a lot because I've been too consumed with keeping the farm running, and I've been volunteering at the firehouse too much. I love my family, and I love being a firefighter. I have a high sense of responsibility toward both. But I've used that to bury my guilt and grief over *Mamm*'s death. That in turn kept me from finding a balance that would make it possible to be in a relationship with you. To put you first. But I have to find that balance, and I will figure it out. If you give me another chance, I promise you I *will* put you first. I will keep my promises."

He took a deep breath. "You're the most important person in my life, Kayla. And if you give me one more chance, I will show you just how much you mean to me. I'm not in love with the firehouse. I'm in love with you."

"I love you too," she whispered, her voice hoarse. "I can't imagine my life without you."

His heart felt as if it might explode in his chest. "I feel the same way."

"I'm so sorry for pushing you away." She squeezed his hand. "You were right when you said I hurt you in the same way Abram hurt me. I was selfish and insensitive, and I hope you can forgive me. No one is perfect all the time. I was much too hard on you, and I promise I will do better, too, if you give me another chance. I won't give up on you, Jamie."

She touched his cheek, and his heart felt as though it had turned over in his chest. "I was so determined to control every part of my life after Simeon died that I wasn't will-

490

ing to trust you or even trust God. I need to just open my heart and have faith in God and in you. I'm ready to do that now."

Her words were sweet music to his soul. He pulled her to him and brushed his lips over hers. The contact sent liquid heat shooting from his head to his toes.

When he broke the kiss, she leaned down and rested her head on his shoulder. "I'm so thankful you'll give us another chance. *Ich liebe dich,* Jamie."

"Ich liebe dich." He drew circles on her back with his fingertips. "I've never loved anyone as much as I love you."

Jamie wasn't sure how long he held Kayla, but every moment was a healing balm to his soul. They talked softly about plans for their immediate future, each proposal representing a promise to trust and love the other.

"Do you have any news on Amos?" he finally asked.

She sat back in the chair and held his hand. "He's going to be fine. *Mei daed* spoke to Amos's *sohn,* and he said he has some smoke inhalation like you, so they are going to keep him overnight too. He'll most likely go home tomorrow."

"Do they know what started the fire?"

"Amos thinks he forgot to blow out the

candles in his kitchen when he went to bed," she said. "His *sohn* said Amos has a bad habit of burning candles and then forgetting to extinguish them."

"That's a common cause for fires." He squeezed her hand. "I'm so thankful you're here. Your *daed* came too?"

"*Ya,* he stayed in the lobby so we could talk alone."

His smile faded. "I'm still so sorry for scaring you."

"Just don't do it ever again."

"I promise. I won't."

Kayla smiled as Mark, Vernon, and her *daed* crowded into Jamie's room. The men quickly fell into conversation, but her thoughts were her own. Her soul was overwhelmed with joy. Not only were Jamie and her neighbor going to be okay, but she also had Jamie back in her life.

And he loved her!

She imagined her heart might beat out of her chest with happiness.

After a few minutes, *Dat* said, "I think we need to get going. Our driver is going to be here soon." He shook Mark and Vernon's hands. "It was *gut* seeing you two."

Out of the corner of her eye, Kayla could see an unspoken conversation between

Jamie and his father.

"Willie," Vernon said, "why don't Mark and I walk you out to the lobby?"

"Oh, of course." *Dat* shook Jamie's hand. "Take care, Jamie. And no more responding to fires without your gear. It's bad for your health."

Jamie chuckled and then coughed. "I won't do it again. *Danki* for coming."

After the men left, Jamie took her hand again. "*Mei daed* is perceptive. He knew I wanted to say good-bye to you without an audience."

"That was kind of him." She frowned. "Our visit went by too quickly. Would you please call me after you get home tomorrow? I can come and see you if you feel up to it."

He cupped his hand to her cheek. "That would be perfect."

Jamie pulled her over and brushed his lips on hers, sending joy buzzing through her like a honeybee.

After breaking the kiss, he leaned his forehead against hers. "I'll call you after I'm settled at home tomorrow."

"I look forward to it."

"*Ich liebe dich,* Kayla."

"I love you too." She squeezed his hand and went into the hallway. As she walked toward the lobby, she silently thanked God for not only saving Jamie but for bringing him back into her life.

EPILOGUE

Happiness covered Kayla like a warm blanket as she rested her head on Jamie's shoulder. The glider moved back and forth in a slow, rhythmic motion, and Jamie looped his arm around her shoulders. She snuggled closer. Out beyond the pasture, the sun was setting in a deep azure sky, and a slight chill drifted through the air as fall teased the late summer evening.

She closed her eyes and listened to the murmur of voices inside the house. Jamie's father and siblings were eating the dessert she'd brought, and she was glad Jamie had suggested they come outside instead. They wanted some time alone before she had to head home for the night.

"I can't believe September is almost over." Jamie trailed his finger up and down her arm, sending shivers spiraling along her skin.

"*Ya*. Time is flying by."

They were silent for several moments, and she could hear the sound of his heartbeat.

"I've been doing some thinking," he suddenly said.

"Oh *ya*?" She sat up straight and angled her body toward him.

"You said something to me after I lost *mei mamm* that really helped me deal with her accident."

She searched his eyes. "What did I say?"

"You quoted a verse in Luke where Jesus says, 'Rise and go; your faith has made you well.' And you said my faith would heal my heart and make me well again. You were right. My faith did make me well. Once I started opening my heart to God, I realized what I had to do to mend my relationship with you. And also to forgive myself."

"I'm glad I could help," she said. "But I'm still so sorry I was hard on you when we broke up. I really expected too much from you. I thought having a *gut* relationship meant everything had to be perfect all the time. Eva helped me realize we're all human. We're going to disagree and argue. We just need to work through our problems together, and that's what will make us stronger as a couple. I'm sorry for hurting you when I pushed you away. I was wrong."

Kayla touched his cheek, and he grabbed

her hand and kissed its palm. "You don't need to apologize. I think we both were wrong. I was a wreck after I lost *mei mamm,* and I thought working all the time was the answer to my guilt and grief, the way to get through."

"That had to be such a painful time for you." She turned her hand and squeezed his.

"It all came crashing down the day I ran into the fire to try to save Amos Lapp without any gear. I had reached my breaking point, and I was on my way to see you. I needed you in my life. But when I saw that fire, I completely forgot to take the right precautions. It almost cost me my life."

Jamie paused and she could see he was gathering his thoughts. "I think somewhere inside I thought if I couldn't save *mei mamm,* I could at least save others, including Amos, as though that would make up for my mistake about the banister. When I was rushing off to help the man who had the heart attack that night, Mark told me saving everyone wouldn't bring *Mamm* back. I was angry when he said it, but he was right. I was trying to save everyone because I couldn't save her."

His expression brightened. "But I see things differently now. I've finally accepted that God forgives me for my mistake, and I have forgiven myself. *Mamm* died instantly when she fell, and there was nothing I could have done. God chose to take her."

"*Ach, mei liewe.*" Her chest constricted with grief for him. "I'm so glad you've forgiven yourself."

"I'm so thankful you're back in my life. You've been my rock with everything that happened this summer. And your whole family has been such a support to mine."

"I feel the same way about you and your family too. Standing beside you and your *daed* and siblings when your *mamm* died helped us as we continued to grieve for Simeon. We'll always have that bond."

Jamie leaned forward, and she braced herself for his kiss. Suddenly, his radio, sitting on the porch floor, went off. He stilled and listened.

"All available units respond to 1592 Gibbons Road, Bird-in-Hand, twenty-five-year-old man," the voice blared. "Serious lacerations from mechanical saw."

She braced herself as he leaned over and picked up the radio. To her surprise, he turned it off and set it back down on the floor. Then he turned toward her and grinned. "Where were we?"

He leaned down, and her breath hitched

in her lungs. He brushed his lips across hers, sending her stomach into a wild swirl. She closed her eyes and savored the sensation of his warm mouth against hers.

When they parted, she saw an intensity in his eyes. "You're my first and only love, Kayla. I love you with my whole heart."

She touched his chin. *"Ich liebe dich."*

As Jamie pulled her close for a hug, Kayla felt overwhelming gratitude — and silently thanked God for giving her and Jamie a second chance at love.

DISCUSSION QUESTIONS

1. Kayla is afraid to trust Jamie with her heart after losing her brother in a fire. She's also convinced Jamie won't keep his promises since he misses dates and fails to call her. By the end of the book, she realizes she's ready to love again. What do you think caused her to change her point of view on love throughout the story?

2. Jamie and his siblings are devastated when their mother dies unexpectedly. Have you faced a difficult loss? What Bible verses helped you? Share your response with the group.

3. Near the end of the story, Eva convinces Willie and Marilyn to allow Nathan to sign up for firefighter training. Why do you think she felt compelled to defend Nathan's desire to be a volunteer firefighter?

4. Jamie pours himself into volunteering at the fire station and doing chores on the farm as a way to deal with losing his

mother and having a falling out with his sister. Think of a time when you felt lost and alone. Where did you find your strength? What Bible verses helped you or would help someone in a similar situation?

5. Cindy is so devastated when her mother dies that she blames Jamie for her death. Toward the end of the book, she realizes her mistake. Why do you think she blamed Jamie? What do you think helped her change her mind about Jamie's involvement in their mother's accident?

6. Vernon is plagued with both grief and regret after he loses his wife. He tries to convince Jamie to slow down and enjoy life as a way to prevent Jamie from making the mistakes he feels he made. Could you relate to Vernon and his experience?

7. By the end of the book, Jamie is ready to find a balance between his work life and his romantic life. What do you think helped him realize that his father was right?

8. Which character do you identify with the most? Which character seemed to carry the most emotional stake in the story? Was it Jamie, Kayla, Eva, Cindy, or someone else?

9. What role did Nathan play in Kayla and Jamie's relationship? How did he help to

reconcile their relationship at the end of the book?

10. What did you know about the Amish before reading this book? What did you learn?

ACKNOWLEDGMENTS

As always, I'm grateful for my loving family, including my mother, Lola Goebelbecker; my husband, Joe; and my sons, Zac and Matt. I'm blessed to have such an awesome and amazing family that tolerates my moods when I'm stressed out on a book deadline.

Special thanks to my mother and my dear friend Becky Biddy, who endured my constant discussions (and whiny complaints) about this story and graciously proofread the draft and corrected my hilarious typos. Becky — thank you also for your daily notes of encouragement. Your friendship is a blessing!

Thank you to the awesome firefighters who generously (and patiently) answered my questions in person as well as via e-mail and text message. I'm beyond grateful to my supercool brother-in-law, Jason Clipston, who not only answered my questions but also read the book for accuracy. Thank you also to Chief Junior Honeycutt of Bakers Volunteer Fire & Rescue Department, Monroe, North Carolina; and also to Brooks Hasty, Jody Frazier, Graham McMancus, and Captain Nick Steffler of City of Monroe, North Carolina, Station 4. Thank you for all you do for our community!

I'm also grateful to my special Amish friend, who patiently answers my endless stream of questions. Your friendship is a special blessing in my life!

I'm always grateful to my wonderful church family at Morning Star Lutheran in Matthews, North Carolina, for your encouragement, prayers, love, and friendship. You all mean so much to my family and me.

Thank you to Zac Weikal and the fabulous members of my Bakery Bunch! I'm so grateful for your friendship and your excitement about my books. You all are amazing!

To my agent, Natasha Kern — I can't thank you enough for your guidance, advice, and friendship. You are a tremendous blessing in my life.

Thank you to my amazing editor, Becky Monds, for your friendship and guidance. I'm grateful to editor Jean Bloom, who helped me polish and refine the story. Jean, you are a master at connecting the dots and filling in the gaps. I'm so happy we can continue to work together!

I also would like to thank Kristen Golden for tirelessly working to promote my books. I'm grateful to each and every person at HarperCollins Christian Publishing who helped make this book a reality.

To my readers — thank you for choosing my novels. My books are a blessing in my life for many reasons, including the special friendships I've formed with my readers. I appreciate your kind and thoughtful e-mail messages, Facebook notes, and letters.

Thank you most of all to God — for giving me the inspiration and the words to glorify You. I'm grateful and humbled You've chosen this path for me.

Special thanks to Cathy and Dennis Zimmermann for their hospitality and research assistance in Lancaster County, Pennsylvania.

Cathy & Dennis Zimmermann, Innkeepers
The Creekside Inn
44 Leacock Road-PO Box 435
Paradise, PA 17562
Toll Free: (866) 604-2574
Local Phone: (717) 687-0333

The author and publisher gratefully acknowledge the following resource used to research information for this book:

C. Richard Beam, *Revised Pennsylvania German Dictionary* (Lancaster: Brookshire Publications, Inc., 1991).

ABOUT THE AUTHOR

Amy Clipston is the award-winning and bestselling author of the Amish Heirloom series and the Kauffman Amish Bakery series. She has sold more than one million books. Her novels have hit multiple bestseller lists including CBD, CBA, and ECPA. Amy holds a degree in communications from Virginia Wesleyan College and works full-time for the City of Charlotte, NC. Amy lives in North Carolina with her husband, two sons, mom, and three spoiled rotten cats.

Visit her online at amyclipston.com
Facebook: AmyClipstonBooks
Twitter: @AmyClipston
Instagram: @amy_clipston

The employees of Thorndike Press hope you have enjoyed this Large Print book. All our Thorndike, Wheeler, and Kennebec Large Print titles are designed for easy reading, and all our books are made to last. Other Thorndike Press Large Print books are available at your library, through selected bookstores, or directly from us.

For information about titles, please call:
(800) 223-1244

or visit our website at:
gale.com/thorndike

To share your comments, please write:
Publisher
Thorndike Press
10 Water St., Suite 310
Waterville, ME 04901